BROKEN STAR

A DARK ELF STORY

KIM KERR

BROKEN STAR
KIM KERR

Science Fiction and Fantasy Publications

HTTPS://SCIFIFANTASYPUBLICATIONS.CA
A division of DAOwen Publications

Broken Star / Kim Kerr
Edited by Douglas Owen and M. J. Moores

ISBN 978-1-928094-42-5
EISBN 978-1-928094-41-8

This is a work of fiction. Names, characters, places, and incidents either are the product of the author's imagination or are used fictitiously, and any resemblance to actual persons, living or dead, businesses, companies, events, or locales is entirely coincidental.

Jacket Art commissioned by MMT Productions

10 9 8 7 6 5 4 3 2 1

For my Father

1

GRANDFATHER

Murder is never a work of art. The victims are empty, the shine gone. This one looked sad, as though she'd been disappointed by something.

The walk through the gently falling snow to the old barn near Pier Six took only ten minutes from the Inn. Docks that ran along the wide river to the north of town were shut down for the night. Now, only the sound of lapping water from behind the buildings reached my ears.

The warm mug of mulled wine sat heavy in my stomach as I remembered what Wink had whispered when he appeared at my table.

"Grandfather says there has been another. This one's not his. Story is, she's a noble," the pink-eared boy said, a battered sheepskin wrapped around his skinny shoulders.

"He wants me to go out in this weather and investigate?" I asked.

"Ain't much snow comin' down and he said to tell you he was callin' in that favour."

"Ah, yes." Pushing my long hair into a tie, I rose to my feet.

Snowflakes drifted down, sometimes dancing in the gentle breeze before settling on a roof, a coat, or an eyelash. They caught the light of the lanterns held by the Men of the City Watch standing before the door, long blue capes brushing the ground, a single bronze button showing they held the rank of private. Both stared at me as I approached, my footfalls loud as I crunched the fresh snow.

"What do you want?" The taller of the two growled, dark eyes narrowed as he stepped toward me. I stopped and looked him up and down. His face was smooth and unlined, his jaw square. He hadn't yet made twenty summers.

"Grandfather sent me to see what I think about the victim. He's concerned it might be related to the death of one of his girls the other night."

"So, the guild sends its Dark Elf to snoop around," the shorter watchman sneered. This one held a club in his left hand and showed teeth. The weight of my black daggers pulled on my belt. I hoped this wouldn't get violent.

"Let him through, Private Crul," a deep voice from the shadows said.

A man in a long, black, fur-lined cape stepped from the open doorway.

"Investigator Benton – glad to see a friendly face."

"I'll never be that. Why Grandfather employs you Ash, is something I don't understand," the iron-haired man said.

"You can guess why."

"That seeing stuff we can't is bullshit."

"Then why do you call me Owl?"

"That's the name we use for all Dark Elves."

I rolled my eyes.

"Where's the girl, Benton?"

"This way."

I followed broad shoulders through dirty straw to a pool of light. A horse nickered and somewhere wood creaked.

"They found her when the last shift brought the animals in from the docks. It's a small barn and they only check on the horses twice a day," Benton said.

I looked at the girl and a small piece of me broke.

Her body hung from a chain wrapped around her wrists and thrown over a thick supporting beam. Strips of flesh peeled away from her body. Her legs were covered in shit, and three fingers were missing. The ground under the hanging body was dark with dried blood.

"Someone was angry," I muttered.

"The stableboy that called us saw nothing. He was shaken bad. Anyway, she's been here at least half a day."

"Nobody heard anything?"

"There was a gag. Part of her dress, we think."

The investigator reached into a pocket in his cape and pulled out a bloody strip of green material. I ran the fabric between my ebony fingers and it slide over my skin like cool water.

"Silk."

"That's why we think she's noble born. None of Grandfather's girls wear silk. Even the high-class ones aren't that rich – the stuff's worth a fortune."

I stared at the girl and noted the expression again. I'd seen that look on another body long ago, only the eyes were different.

"I wonder why he didn't touch the face?" I said.

"These crazies – who knows how they think? He doesn't touch the face but lets her bleed out. No throat cut like Grandfather's girl. She weren't chopped up nearly this bad."

"Perhaps that one was just the warm-up act. Anyway, why is she still hanging here?"

Benton scratched the stubble on his chin and pulled out a pipe, slowly packing it with leaf. "Waitin' for the sketch boys to come. You understand the captain's got his new ideas. Reckons it adds to the evidence."

"Still prefer the old ways, Benton? Get a couple of privates to beat a suspect until they confess?"

He stopped tapping the tobacco into his pipe. His eyes flicked up. "Got what you need, Owl?"

"Not yet, might just use these eyes to see things the Watch might have missed."

Benton lit a piece of dirty straw with one of the lanterns and used it to start his pipe, but his eyes never left me. I ignored him. He'd been at the rank of investigator for many years and, though he stayed clear of major corruption, he was not smart. I pulled a knife from my boot and started to dig around in the straw.

"Already done that."

I kept looking. Behind the girl's swinging body were a number of rough wooden boxes about half the height of a man. Some were stacked straight but a few stood askew. I pushed between the boxes. Deep shadows coated the area. I allowed time for my pupils to expand. Outlines became clear and objects appeared in different shades of grey.

A small glint at the back of the rear box looked out of place. I pushed one container aside and another crashed down, startling the horses.

"Careful what you're doing, Owl. Any damage and you'll pay."

I picked up the sharp metal and walked into the light. The razor sat in my hand like a dirty gem. Blood stained the handle.

"It's broken," Benton said.

I walked over to the corpse. She stared down at me as though trying to ask something.

"He broke the razor and then changed to a different blade. Some of these cuts are deeper. The second weapon must have been heavier, probably a dagger."

I thought for a moment and then gave the razor to Benton. He would have taken it anyway. "So, the privates have asked around but nobody saw anything?" I asked.

"Unless you count the horses, and they can't answer."

I smiled. "Some say the druids can speak to them."

Benton's eyebrows bent diagonal. "That magic is for elves and anyone else that likes to dance with butterflies."

I chuckled at the description of my distant forest cousins.

"They'll never say that about you Owls," Benton said.

I turned and shrugged. Benton had no idea about my people. I sometimes wondered if I did.

I walked back to my room on Lyre Street and opened the door to the shop with a heavy bronze key.

Rackhime worked late as usual, copying scrolls by the light of an oil lantern. Heavy tomes of leather and sheets of parchment lay scattered across a workbench the size of a wagon. A fire glowed dull red in a small hearth.

I unpinned the brooch and folded my woollen cape. Then pulled the throwing daggers from my boots and placed them on the bench.

"That surface is for parchment, not steel," Rackhime said.

He put down the quill and wiped his bald crown. I picked up the daggers.

"Messy business down at the docks, I hear."

The old man pulled out another quill and then searched through vials containing various pigments. I rolled up my sleeves and moved to a workbench. I dipped the swan feather quill into dark liquid and started to copy the letters onto a blank page.

"I don't understand how you can write if you can't read it," the old man said.

"It relaxes me. Anyway, how do you know about the latest murder?"

"Verelda was in just before I locked up. Everyone's talking about it."

"Gossiping about slaughter. They wouldn't if they had seen the girl."

Rackhime's quill stopped moving and he sighed. "Grandfather asked you to snoop around?"

"I owe him."

"You have no debt to that slime."

"I don't see it that way. Besides, someone is killing girls near the docks and I have to stop them."

Rackhime started writing again. "You don't seem like a white knight to me. If there is a noble family involved, it's better to stay clear."

I turned and observed as Rackhime's ink-stained hands danced across the paper.

"I can't do that. Besides, if I take this on my debt is paid."

"You think it will be that easy?"

I didn't want to write anymore. "It's never that easy."

Light streamed through the north-facing windows. I stood, wrapped the quilt around my shoulders, and walked to the light. The city below had been awake for hours.

Cogs and lanterns sailed toward the docks that lined the mouth of the Sigh River.

Only a few buildings obscured the view. Rackhime's Book & Scroll Preserving Store stood on a small hill between the docks and the Devil's Horns, large twin hills that towered over the city and guided the ships to the harbour. The peaks rose gradually to a height of roughly nine hundred paces and met at a narrow saddle at the top.

The falling snow had cleared but the buildings and streets were carpeted in a thick blanket of white that shone in the winter sunlight. A haze of smoke hung above the scene as a thousand fireplaces struggled to keep the people of Hope warm.

From below, the smell of cooking ham and mushrooms drifted through the cracks in the floorboards.

I splashed water on my face from a large bowl, and then pulled on a woollen shirt and pants before walking downstairs. The fire glowed the same leaden red, but now a blackened pan sat on it. The ham popped and hissed.

"Is there enough for me?" I already knew the answer but decided it would be polite to ask. Rackhime put down the scroll he was reading and reached for the pan with sheepskin mittens. He wore a black scarf high on his neck. The woollen hat he'd pulled over his bald head made his ears stick out sideways.

"I always make enough for my wandering apprentice. Seeing as he appears, without fail, just as the food is ready to eat." Rackhime scraped half the steaming food onto two trenches of hard dark bread. "Grandfather sent Wink around to say he wants to see you. It seems they found out who the noble girl was – Duke Vornhelm's eldest girl."

I whistled between my teeth.

"That'll stir the men of the Watch into action."

"It makes this business even more dangerous," Rackhime snapped. "I don't see why Grandfather needs to ask you for help."

"One of his girls got cut up first. He must think there's a connection."

"Isn't it likely to be some crazy? Someone who's lost his soul?"

I hunched my shoulders, hoping this wasn't about to become one of Rackhime's rants about the loss of spirituality by the races of the world.

"There are similarities in the two murders, but there are also things that don't make sense."

Rackhime grunted around his bacon. He didn't care for the details. He just didn't want me involved.

"You're going to go and see that repulsive old man aren't you?"

"As soon as I finish eating."

"The very thought should be enough to put you off your food," he said.

The snow melted. The streets to Grandfather's mansion were lined with dirty piles of slush mixed with rotting waste. I wrinkled my nose.

Grandfather's building sat behind a high stone wall at the end of Runner Street. Narrow two-storey buildings competed for space, but they had been pulled down in the area around the walled compound, creating the illusion that the mansion was an island. Marble lions guarded the entrance to the courtyard beyond a high fence. A small guardhouse built into the wall contained four men. As I approached the iron gate, one of them – who I recognised as Thelkar – left with a large set of keys. Another, Slan, wore chain mail and carried a loaded crossbow. He leaned against the doorframe peering at me.

"Grandfather sent for me."

Thelkar was easily as big as an ogre and just about as ugly. "I know," he grunted. "We been expectin' you all morning."

"I'm a late riser."

"Yeah, owls like the night." He barked with laughter at his own joke.

"You going to let me in, then?"

"Workin' on it."

He struggled to manipulate the keys with sausage-like fingers. Eventually the black metal gate swung open.

I did my best to ignore the sallow guard with the crossbow whose stare never left me, and followed Thelkar to the entrance of the mansion. The lower level of this solid building had been lined with arrow slits. A wide staircase led up to a solid bronze and wooden doorway on the first floor. Thelkar knocked twice before we entered a small room with a green tiled floor. Two more guards stood on either side of a second doorway while a man with a waxed moustache, wearing tight-fitting, black, leather armour approached me.

"You're late," Rantillious said.

"So I've been told."

"Put your weapons in the chest near the door."

I pulled my daggers and throwing knives from various hidden locations on my body and dropped them on the floor.

Rantillious frowned at me. "You didn't bring the Cold Blade?"

"This is all I'm carrying."

The small, sharp-faced man patted me down anyway before signalling one of the guards to pick up the weapons and put them in the chest.

"I'll take it from here," Rantillious said.

Thelkar grunted and left.

I followed through a large open room lit by lanterns. Men and women lounged around, sharpening weapons and playing dice. Two people sat at large desks reading different parchments and writing in massive books. The room smelt of sweat and leather.

As I walked I could sense his eyes on my back. The low buzz of conversation ebbed as I passed and then rose again as I moved on.

The stairs to the next level spiralled to the left. Another pair of guards waited at the top. I was patted down again.

I strode down a long corridor that ran though the centre of the building until I reached a final door made of steel. Rantillious knocked and a muffled voice answered. When the door opened, I walked into a well-lit room warmed by a log fire. Near the large window of clear glass stood a man of medium height, wearing a red jacket tied with a gold sash.

"More security than last time I visited, Grandfather," I said.

The man ignored me and continued to stare over the city. The heads of a tiger and boar mounted on the wall stared at me as I moved to a leather chair and sat down.

I put my feet up on his desk and leaned back. Let the old man play his games. He believed he needed me and would not dispense with my services easily. Part of me didn't care if he did.

"I understand you keep your own time, Ash, but for the sake of appearances could you not be late? I have a certain reputation to uphold."

Grandfather's clipped salt-and-pepper beard and perfect teeth sat above a thick neck of muscle. He sighed and glanced at my boots before frowning.

"I don't know why I keep you on."

"Is it because of the legendary skills of my people?"

"Those attributes are either myth or greatly exaggerated. I keep you on as you were one of the best Hunters in the Wild Lands and because Dark Elves can do a few things humans cannot. As for the increased security you observed, I take no chances when I sense a threat."

"That's what you think these murders represent?"

"I'm not sure what they mean, and that's why you're here. I want to see what you think."

I glanced across at Grandfather's desk with its neat row of ink bottles and the carefully rolled parchments. It looked like the desk of a banker.

"I haven't gathered enough information yet, but I believe the murders may have been committed by different people."

"That is not what the Chief Captain of the Watch thinks."

I shrugged. "I need to see the sketches of your girl's murder scene. I didn't view her body but I heard she had about twenty cuts, and then had her throat slashed. The bastard who killed the noble girl cut her to pieces and let her bleed out slowly. Perhaps it was the same person who was angrier the second time around, but it seems different."

"If you're correct, it's worrying for me. It could be the Dance Master trying to steal my business to undermine me."

I slipped my boots off his desk.

"And anyway, I don't like anyone hurting my girls. They are like daughters to me."

My fingers dug into the chair and I forced myself to relax. Trix, a good friend, had told me how Grandfather auditioned many of the women. He told them to call him Daddy as he took them on the bearskin in this very room. Trix often tried to distract him from the new girls. I remembered the tall half-elf twisting rings around her finger and looking at the floor as she spoke.

"Yes, your girls are really special to you."

Grandfather's head flicked around and his small eyes narrowed. Pink spots flared on his cheeks and then he spun back to stare over the city once more.

"You owe me, Owl. I killed for you. I cleaned up your mess."

"I haven't forgotten."

"I want this solved one way or the other. There are forty gold coins on the mantle – half for you, half for expenses."

"I don't need the coin. I just want to clear my debt."

"You fix this and we're done."

2

GOLDEN

The Watch building sat on the shoulder of one of the Devil's Horns. A cobbled-together affair constructed around a tower, it stood higher than any structure in the area. It sat on the shoulder of one of the Devil's Horns. These two peaks dominated the city and gave commanding views of the river and surrounding plains.

The law enforcement offices of Hope had grown since its humble beginnings more than three hundred years ago. The expansion of the city's Watch caused the tearing down of a number of single-storey houses, replacing them with squat, solid buildings made of granite and slate. Wooden steps led up to the Building of the Investigators. The structure itself used to be a merchant's residence but was now drab and patched up, with mismatched bricks plugging holes in the wall.

I needed to look at the sketches of the victims collected by the Watch, kept under lock and key by Captain Waldheigheim. After talking my way past a couple of privates and paying a bribe to a senior corporal, I found Waldheigheim's office on the first floor. Tall, with a long hooked nose, the man walked around and then sat behind a table stacked high with rolls of parchment. He then glanced up at me from under a single thick eyebrow and frowned.

"You would be Grandfather's pet Owl, I believe."

"I'm no one's pet. I came here to do a job, that's all."

"I apologise. A tame animal is an unfair comparison for a member of the Party of the Clenched Fist and one of the slayers of the Red Dragon Remalfex. With the gold you and your friend Golden pulled from that cave, I would have thought you'd retire to your own country villa."

"We didn't kill the dragon, but it killed most of the group I was with."

"Yet you survived."

For an instant I remembered Aldaha disappearing in a blast of flame and the smell of the elf's flesh as he vanished. I could see Tehana as the dragon tore her head off.

"Escaped would be a better description. You seem to know a lot about me. Am I a suspect in an unsolved case?"

"Not yet, should you be?"

Captain Waldheigheim obviously kept a file on me – the idea was uncomfortable. I wondered what other dark facts from my past he knew.

"I'm here to see the sketches of the murder victims."

"They're the property of the Watch and not for the public. I don't want any citizens of Hope getting in the way of my investigators. You should return to your people in their mountains and leave my boys to do their job."

Ignoring the insult, I dropped a pouch in front of him. It hit the table with a clank. Waldheigheim's face changed colour and he stood.

"I have a meeting to attend, and when I return, Owl, I expect you and your coins to be gone."

It was true what I had heard about this man, he wasn't a bribe-taker. I sighed and picked up the bag. Running fingers through my hair, I wondered what to do next. Bouncing the coin pouch in my palm, I left the office. I had only gone a few paces when a voice hissed at me.

"That you, Ash?"

I turned and peered into a small dark room. When my eyes adjusted, I noticed Investigator Benton leaning against the wall.

"Thought I recognised that black face. Might be, for a price, I can help you."

I thanked the Snow God there were still plenty of detectives open to bribery. The members of the Watch weren't paid much by the Council of Notable Elders and often sought to increase their pay in a variety of ways.

"I've got some Drams that used to belong to Grandfather. It's for expenses and I think that includes you."

"Come with me."

I followed the wide shoulders of Investigator Benton along passageways and through a variety of doors until we came to a long, narrow hall plastered with sketches of different people and crime scenes.

"I think what you want is down the other end of the room."

We walked past a little man writing notes with a feather quill on a parchment that showed an open window with a smashed shutter.

"The Owl shouldn't be here," he squeaked. "Waldheigheim wouldn't like it."

"The captain doesn't need to know, does he, Fentel. Give him something towards his retirement fund, Ash."

"It will come out of your coin."

Benton grimaced, then shrugged. I put three shiny gold Drams down in front of the man. He wrinkled his wizened face and bit down on the coin, then nodded.

"Just make it quick."

The drawings of the two women would never hang on the wall of a noble residence, but to me they conveyed the horror of their passing.

"Whoever did this really went to work on the rich girl. The job done on Grandfather's whore seems half-hearted by comparison," Benton muttered.

"Her name was Fendria, and she was from Two Bridges, a small town three day's ride inland," I said.

"I knew that, but it doesn't matter where she was from now."

"What was the name of Blue Eyes, the noble girl?" I asked.

"Duke Vornhelm's daughter was named after the Western Star."

"Elhnora?"

"That's right. The Duke sent one of his servants to identify the body. They are goin' to collected it later today."

"Any idea what she was doing at Dockside?"

"She was a bit wild, according to the accounts of some of her friends. Often went to the Dancing Mermaid and the Sprite to gamble. I don't think her father would have approved. The Duke has a reputation as no-nonsense man who stands high with the Notable Elders and wants to climb higher. The whole family have gone into mourning over the death."

"Wasn't the Duke the leader of the army that drove the Hobgoblins from their final stronghold this side of the mountains?"

"Vornhelm the Bloody was the general at the siege of Black Rock Fortress. He drove his men into the breach caused by magic and catapults until the bodies of his army filled the gap. Eventually the stronghold fell, but he lost half his force taking it. Still, he won, I suppose."

I looked at the sketch of Elhnora one last time, noting the artist hadn't captured the expression in her eyes. Then I saw a small tattoo of a heart on the upper area of her inner thigh. It was half ripped away by a dagger cut but I could make out two letters – Ak –drawn inside the heart. I couldn't read words but I could recognise some of the symbols.

"Is the tattoo correct?"

Benton nodded. "Yeah, I bet that wouldn't have pleased her old man. I wonder who Ak is. I don't suppose it matters now. Some crazy did her and past lovers aren't going to bring her back."

"Is that what the Watch thinks? There's a madman out there killing girls in the Docklands?"

"The captain says to keep an open mind. He believes it could be different killers and we need more evidence before we jump to any conclusions. But most of the investigators think there's a crazy doin' this and it just took him a while to warm to his task. What else makes sense?"

I massaged my brow with two fingers and looked again at the pictures, committing them to memory. Maybe Benton was right. What other reason could there be for the death of these girls?

Deciding to take my thoughts to Barnabus's Place after dinner, I worked on copying a manuscript. Then I ate a meal with Rackhime. He criticised my lettering and choice of pigments.

"Your people are supposed to be known for your eyesight and look what you produce."

"Our speciality is night vision, and besides, this is about the coordination of my fingers," I snapped.

I picked up the parchment and threw it onto the fire.

"They cost good money, you know."

"I'll buy more from my own coin."

"Yes, you will," Rackhime said.

"I'm doing my best."

"When I agreed to take you on it wasn't out of charity you know!"

"Why did you employ me again?"

"I'm sure I can't remember," the old man mumbled.

"It had something to do with your failing vision and needing a pair of sharp eyes as I remember."

"They're not as bad as I thought. Maybe it was charity after all."

I snorted and got my cape. The chill of the night air was seeping into the work room.

The snow returned as I tramped down Main Street before turning right onto Fishing Way. The building leaned in above me, reminding me of the caves of my youth.

Barnabus's Place glowed from the yellow lanterns swirled around by flurries of white flakes caught in the wind. The smell of turmeric and roast goat wafted up the road toward me and I wondered if I could eat another meal. I tried to shake the feeling that something was missing. If the Dance Master wanted to upset the trade of vice and gambling in Grandfather's area, then maybe he would use different killers to create fear and throw the Watch off his scent.

I opened the door to the inn and stepped into a wall of warmth and pleasant odours. I had only taken a few steps when I saw the Hunters gathered around the bar and one of the longer tables. They still wore most of their equipment, and looked as though they had just returned from the Wilds.

An elf wearing sat with an unloaded crossbow in front of him. His hair had been tied in a topknot, a tattoo of a crow inked onto his forehead.

The man next to him had shoulders as wide as a barn; a thick neck supported a ruddy unshaven face, and his nose looked as if hammers had squashed it.

At the bar stood a slender male dressed in faded red robes with gold trimmings. He held a carved staff, and carried a long sword strapped across his back. Besides him stood a tall man with a sharp black beard and pockmarked cheeks holding a mug of ale.

At the fireplace, a woman with short hair nursed a clay goblet. Around her neck hung the silver symbol of Tellonous, God of Justice and Truth, though whose truth often depended on your perspective.

They all stared at me with tight, grim mouths.

"We don't want your sort in here," the elf said.

I should have turned and walked out the door; I should have nodded and made my way to another inn. This was not the first time I had been on the receiving end of this type of hostility. But I was cold and hungry, and this was my favourite place to eat. I had never seen these Hunters before.

"Well, that's just too bad. This is my local and if you don't like me here, then go somewhere else."

The woman snorted and turned from the fire.

"Not smart," she muttered.

The tall man at the bar picked up his axe and stepped towards me.

"We don't like Black Owls. You're baby killers and eaters of their flesh."

I rolled my eyes. These stories about my people had been around for hundreds of years, despite there being no foundation to them. They just provided men with an excuse to try and take our lands.

"I haven't eaten a human child for at least a moon."

Thick Neck stood up. "You a smart mouth, are you? I think you better leave before we carve you into little pieces."

The elf reached for the short sword on his hip.

"Gentlefolk, there is no need for violence. I'm sure that Ash will leave and we can settle down," Barnabus said.

Thanks for the support, I thought. The short bartender and owner held out his hands as though he was trying to separate us. His moon-shaped face shone with sweat.

The few other patrons either left hurriedly or retreated to the corners of the room.

"Too late for that," the magician at the bar said, his voice calm and steady. "There's nothing like killing an Owl to give one a healthy appetite." He smiled at me but didn't show his teeth.

At this point I wished I was carrying my Cold Blade. Although, I should have bottled my pride and walked away when I had the chance.

The heavy door banged open and Golden crossed the threshold, his body filling the doorway. He stopped a pace into the room and took in the scene with his different coloured eyes. Smoothing his corn-coloured hair he stroked the stubble on his square chin. Above his shoulder, I could see the white hilt of his Cold Blade on his back.

Golden seemed almost as big as Thick Neck, but he carried himself with grace, wide shoulders and muscled torso narrowing toward the hips. He stood like a god in scale mail and a dark cloak, the wolf slightly behind him.

Spike growled softly and pushed into the room, his black fur seeming to swallow light. The wolf opened his mouth and bared teeth I knew from experience could take a man's arm off at the shoulder.

"Yalourn, please tell me that you aren't harassing a friend of mine," Golden said as he took two paces into the room.

He twisted around one of his many rings as if examining them. I remembered some had magical properties.

"I can't believe you would befriend an Owl," the magician answered, taking a step away from the bar.

Spike snarled and crouched low. Golden gestured with his hand and the animal dropped to the floor, but didn't take his eyes from the men in front of him.

"That's where you're wrong. Ash and I go way back. Standing before you is a Member of the Phoenix Band and the Clenched Fist, holder of one of the twelve Cold Blades and killer of the Red Dragon Remalfex."

"We didn't–" I began.

Golden cut me off. "Never interrupt a good introduction. You haven't brought your blade with you?"

I shook my head and wondered how he knew. I usually kept it hidden beneath my cloak. He raised a slender eyebrow and sighed.

"Ash was a Hunter for years. Explored the Barrow Lands and the East Forest. He's fought hobgoblins and ogres as well as all manner of monsters, both mundane and magical."

I wondered what else I had done in my career. It was true we had survived a close encounter with a dragon together, and plundered the old tombs at the edge of the East Forest, but Golden had a way of making a skirmish sound like a large battle.

"We don't care what he has done," Thick Neck said. "He's an Owl and all Owls should be killed."

Golden's eyes glinted and his hands dropped to his side. I prepared to draw one of my throwing daggers, deciding to hurl it at the magician first.

"Yalourn, you've seen me in action. Do you really think your band can take me?"

The magician hesitated and looked around. He glanced at the woman who turned and sat down in a tall chair.

"Don't look at me, I'm not going to be part of the dick-measuring contest," she said.

Thick Neck and the Man of Daggers stared at the magician. The elf stared at the wolf.

"We have been fighting his people for a season. Duke Coldborn employed us and others to help take back the Thumble Hills. The Owls have killed more than one of our group," Yalourn said.

"That is Dark Elf land, last I heard, foothills to their mountains. You try and take someone's country and they will fight back. That's war. Maybe the duke should be happy with what he's got. Anyway, Ash weren't there. He didn't kill any of your band," Golden said.

My friend slowly drew the Cold Blade from over his shoulder. It came clear of the scabbard in a shower of frost and gleamed with an inner silver glow.

"Enough talk. I've just got in from the Wilds and I'm hungry. So, leave or fight," Golden rumbled.

Barnabus sank slowly behind the bar as my tall friend held the gaze of the magician. Yalourn broke eye contact.

"Grab your stuff everyone, we're going."

"You have got to be joking!" Thick Neck roared.

"We can't win this one. You haven't seen Golden and Spike in action. I have. Now pick up your gear. We'll find somewhere else to stay."

The group slowly gathered up their possessions and made for the door.

Thick Neck stood before Golden. "This ain't over," he muttered.

"I see lips flappin' but all I hear is noise," my friend said.

Thick Neck bunched his fists and lurched forward, but the woman stepped in front of him. Spike stood and growled. The hackles went up on his back.

"You can't beat him, Greler. I haven't seen anyone in Hope who can," she said.

The big man shook off the restraining hands and strode out the door.

"Some things don't change, do they Golden?" the woman said.

"I didn't start this."

"But you could have handled it differently. Now you have four new enemies, maybe five."

My friend shrugged. "I'll add them to the list."

The elf glared at me as he left. Yalourn looked at his feet, face red, knuckles white on his staff.

When they had all gone, Golden grinned at me with those straight teeth.

"Nothing like a bit of chest-thumping to end a long day. Now what's on the menu? Spike and I could eat a bear."

3

ALL GODS DAY

Golden filled me in on the happenings of some of the Hunters I knew – a few dead and some retired, either scarred for life or rich enough to buy their own town.

"Threnweed lost an arm to a troll up on the Green Fens. He almost died but Sandral patched him up and prayed to his god, and the little thief lived. The bastard is rich, too. He got lucky with the old map that I laughed at. It showed him the way to the Giant's Burial Caves. Most of his group were killed by the tomb's guardians but Threnweed escaped, along with a couple of others."

Golden's stories made me feel nostalgic for the past, but then I remembered Milandy's brief shriek as the dragon's fiery breath turned her to cinders while she ran.

"Anyway, most of the bands have come in now. The weather's getting too cold for campaigning, though a few of the more desperate groups are going to the Stony Hills of the Ogres or are camping near the Southern Jungle." Golden tore at a steak the size of a small shield and threw every second piece to Spike.

"Are you going to be around long?"

"Only to the spring thaw then I'm up to the Aldersburg. I'm

meeting Garth and his band at the Red Crossing and then we're going to find the Golden Stairs. They're in those mountains somewhere."

"Those caves are a myth and so is the treasure they supposedly contain." I swallowed a spoonful of the goat curry and enjoyed feeling the water run from my eyes.

"I'll find them this time." He stopped chewing and glanced at me out of the corner of his green eye. "You should come with me."

I held up one hand. "I have seen too many friends die. My days as a Hunter are over."

He shrugged. "Well if you change your mind–"

"It isn't going to happen."

He shrugged and grinned, and I knew he wouldn't give up.

I filled him in on the death of the girls and Grandfather's insistence I help find the murderer or murderers.

"You owe that slimy old man nothing."

"So Rackhime keeps telling me."

"Those assassins were on his territory and he would have killed them anyway."

"But they were chasing me. After what happened with their first attempt, my options were limited. He did me a favour."

"We'll have to agree to differ," Golden mumbled.

He finished his dinner, sat back, and patted his stomach. "Barnabus still does the best steaks in Hope. Now, to finish off the night, we need some girls."

"Not for me."

"Oh, come on, Ash, the women love your exotic appearance and those oversized deer eyes."

I laughed. "My eyes are not oversized. It's just you humans have tiny piggy ones. And as for the girls, they come to you like bees to honey. When they stare at me they get a little nervous."

"Not all of them. What about Trix?"

I frowned and imagined the half-elf. She and I had been friends for years but I had never considered her erotic. Strange really, considering her job, or maybe it was why.

"Trix and I are just friends."

"Suit yourself, but could you do me a favour? I need someone to take care of Spike for a day or so. He sort of spoils the mood with the ladies."

I groaned. Rackhime would love having a dire wolf at the shop. Technically, my rooms were my own, but I would have to get to the wolf through his work area.

"All right, but just for a night."

I drank with Golden for a while longer and then he departed to clean up before he went to the Dockside area where the nightlife was.

Looking at Spike, I sighed. The northern wolf had known me since Golden found him wedged in the branches of a small tree many years before. His mother lay by a red bear she'd killed, slowly bleeding the last of her life onto the yellowing grass of the late summer's day. That happened four years ago.

"Come on boy, let's go and face the anger of Rackhime."

Spike thumped his tail on the floor a couple of times before he stood and stretched.

The old man remained surprisingly calm about the wolf.

"You clean up after him and he kills a few rats, I'll be happy."

"Golden house-trained him and he hates rats."

Rackhime reached forward and scratched Spike behind the ear. I froze for a moment, thinking Spike might take his hand off, but was pleasantly surprised when the wolf allowed himself to be touched.

"I think he likes you. He normally growls or bites if someone tries to pet him."

"I've always liked dogs. Maybe he picked that up."

Rackhime stood back and peered at Spike. "He is certainly big enough. Has he been fed?"

Spike's ears pricked up.

"Golden gave him some steak but I'm sure he'd be happy to have some of your chicken pie."

"Only got lamb," Rackhime said, as he made his way downstairs to the cold room.

He soon returned and gave the wolf a generous slice.

I settled down to copy a manuscript and felt a little jealous when I glanced across to see Spike curled up near the old man's feet. This reminded me of my own exhaustion and a trudged up to bed.

Waking late to the sound of bells, I noticed Spike was nowhere to be seen. I pulled on my trousers, shirt, boots, and cape, and made my way downstairs. The dire wolf lay in front of the fire snoring contentedly while Rackhime chatted to a customer.

"Five rats already. Worth all the pie I could feed him, Mr. Wornton. And gentle as a lamb. Mind you, he gets a bit touchy if strangers pet him."

I shook my head. It appeared as if Spike might not want to return to Golden's side in a hurry. "I've got to go and see Trix. Do you mind if Spike stays here?"

"No, and I don't know how Golden gets away with having him in town."

"He pays a lot of money for the privilege. He's supposed to have him on a leash, though he never does."

Mr. Wornton stared at me, his crinkled face frowning. I remembered the man as a book buyer for one of the dukes, though I couldn't think of which one.

I met his gaze with a blank stare. He turned away and muttered something about paying now.

Slipping past him and out onto the street, I walked north. It was already late in the afternoon and yet there were few people about. As I made my way onto Fish Street, a procession of white-robed men led by someone dressed in a purple and silver cape droned their way toward me. The man at the front held a board aloft on the end of a long pole with the symbol of Fenalias, God of Water and Storms.

Slapping my head in frustration, I realised it was All Gods Day.

Today, no one was to conduct business or work, though many such as Rackhime ignored the tradition. From early six bells until the fourth bell of the afternoon, people were to worship their chosen god. I wasn't religious, so had forgotten what day it was. People tended to consume alcohol in vast amounts after the fourth bell – it was also known as a day of release. This would make it hard to see Trix, as it was usually a very busy time for her. All Gods Day fell every tenth day; each one usually led to some sort of disturbance when people lost control drinking to excess.

Moving to the edge of the road under the eaves of a narrow building, I watched them. One of the clerics glanced at me as he passed; his face screwed up as though he'd stepped in filth. I ignored him and walked on toward the docks. The cobbles were clear of their usual filth. More snow wouldn't set in for a while yet but I could feel the chill in the air signalling it wasn't far away. I was glad most of the city was now paved – I had previously waded through mud up to my ankles at this time of year.

The road twisted around Old Hare Park and passed the Three Mansions. This area was under control of the Dance Master. These building were said to be his centre of operations, so I moved on quickly.

Three more blocks and I was through the warehouse district and at Dockside. This was not where ships loaded and unloaded, or where the river barges left from – that area was called The Port.

Dockside had always been a strip of inns, dance rooms, gambling halls, and brothels, all controlled by the Grandfather. It was said you had a river view from the upper balconies. You could certainly smell the water. Often the stench of fish, offal, and excrement which floated in the river was held at bay by the south-westerly winds, but they weren't blowing today. At every bell a street urchin on the upper balconies lit incense sticks or threw a different scent into the air to mask the odour, but it was only partially successful.

The Reclining Mermaid had been built as a dance hall but now had an attached brothel where Trix worked. Two storeys high, surrounded with wide verandas, it had a steep roof split by many chimneys which belched smoke in an attempt to keep its patrons warm. A sign out the front showed a buxom woman with a fish tail leaning over some rocks, her red lips revealing the tip of a pink tongue. The building stood out with its bright gaudy paint. It had been covered with different coloured lanterns that were waiting to be lit.

I hoped Trix hadn't started work yet as I wanted to find out what the girls may have heard, and if they had any ideas on the murders.

The large, bronze-plated door to the Reclining Mermaid opened without a sound.

I stepped across the threshold into a different world. Two big men stood near the door watching the room for trouble. They wore black leather jerkins and carried wooden clubs. A harp and lute played slow rhythmical music with a steady drumbeat. The room smelt of musk perfume and wood smoke from the open fire. Cotton curtains of various shades separated sections of the room where women in different stages of undress swayed on raised platforms. Lanterns with coloured glass created shadows in the corners. Through a second doorway, the noise of the gambling room drifted in with a tumble of voices.

A girl in a short toga, which left most of her shoulder bare, carried a tray with drinks across the room.

"Stella, has Trix started working yet?" I asked.

The woman turned and smiled. She touched the end of her button noise and pointed at one of the curtains. I peered and made out a female shape undulating on a surface at about waist height. A number of figures sat watching her.

Trix was already dancing and I would need to wait until she finished stirring the passions of the men. I hoped one of them wouldn't take her upstairs as I was in a hurry. Not minding being at the Mermaid, I relaxed. The only irritation was the price of a drink.

Folding the cloak over the back of a chair, the hilt of the Cold Blade touched my fingers. The chill on the hilt ran up to my elbow. It hung on a special scabbard built into the material. This short sword proved easier to hide than the larger Cold Blades carried by a small number of Hunters. After the confrontation at Barnabus's, Golden had advised me to carry it at all times. He wasn't sure if Yalourn's band would come looking for more trouble.

Touching the moonstone on the hilt allowed me to see through illusion, or notice hidden and even invisible, objects or people. The effect in the Reclining Mermaid as I stroked the stone made everything appear a little more washed out.

The show finished and I heard the clink of coins. Trix appeared, flushed, wrapping a short red toga around her slim body. She waved to me, went to one of the security men, and handed over four silver pieces – Grandfather's cut for her act. Turning around, she swayed across the room toward me, her silver earrings tinkling. She sat down, crossed her long legs, and ruffled the short hair which showed off her neck and the jasmine blossom tattoos on her shoulders.

"Haven't seen you here for a while, Ash. Where have you been?" Her blue eyes wandered across my face, trying to find something.

"I like to have as little to do with Grandfather as possible, so I tend to stay away from his establishments."

"I ain't Grandfather."

She sipped at a drink and then turned away. We fell into an uneasy silence.

"I'm sorry, Trix. You're right, and I've been a poor friend, as usual. How about I take you to dinner at Barnabus's? Golden's back in town and we could go out with him after we eat."

Trix smiled at the corners of her mouth and leaned forward. "We don't need to see Golden, but if it's what you want, when?"

"I've got a few loose ends to tie up at the moment, but soon."

She sat back again. I could see her disappointment. Trix was a beautiful woman and I knew she liked me, but I preferred to think of her as a confidante.

"I've got to get back to work, Ash. It's All Gods Day and we're going to get busy."

"Right. The reason I needed to see you is Grandfather asked me to investigate the killings Dockside."

"Well, I'm glad he's doing something about it, but I'm guessing he pulled the 'you owe me' line."

"Don't you start."

"No, this is one time I won't. I feel a little safer already, knowing you'll be handling this."

My ego swelled and chest puffed out.

"Can you tell me anything? I know the girls don't like talking to the Watch but they won't care what you tell me, will they?"

"You are a familiar face, and they trust you, despite your race. There's been this strange man around for the past ten days, maybe even longer. He comes in and pays for a dance, and sometimes takes the girl upstairs. Then he asks them to marry him and becomes angry when they laugh. He's been thrown out twice and security has banned him, but he still hangs around outside and asks the girls to go away with him as they head home."

"What does he look like?"

"Like a dwarf, but of human height. He is the hairiest man I've ever seen and has shoulders like a wagon wheel. I think he could walk through walls if he wanted to. He's got dark hair and wears forester's gear, like those mottled capes you had when you were a Hunter."

"Maybe he used to be with one of the bands. Does he have a weapon?"

"I saw an axe and a dagger which the boys always took off him."

"I'll see if I can find him, maybe Golden knows somebody who fits the description. Grandfather was concerned the Dance Master might be behind this to undermine his business."

Trix snorted. "That's why he really wants you to investigate this."

I shrugged. "Well, we know the young man is ruthless enough. He certainly rose up through the ranks in the thieves' guild, leaving a long trail of bodies. It's possible he's behind the killings, but there's been no pressure on Dockside from his crew of late."

Stella appeared and refilled my mug. She leaned over, showing her ample chest, and smiling at me.

"On the house, Ash," she whispered huskily.

Trix narrowed her lips and turned.

"He isn't here for a show," she growled.

"Pity, I'd give him one for free," Stella said, leaning in closer.

This was a game we played but it had been getting more serious of late.

"He is here about the murders."

Stella stood, looked around. "Finally, the old man's doing something."

"Have you seen or heard anything that could help me?"

"There's the crazy dwarf man."

"I've already told him about that." Trix's voice was clipped.

"And one of the Dance Master's pimps approached Miranda about going to work for him the other day. He wasn't very happy when she said no."

Trix sighed. "Yeah, I'd forgotten about that."

"Who's Miranda?"

"She's a new girl from down south. Absolutely stunning. Even the candles flare a little brighter when she walks past."

"You would probably dance for her too," Trix said.

Stella touched a finger to her lips and glanced up. "A pity, she's never asked."

I shook my head. It was this aspect of Stella that attracted me and frightened me at the same time.

"Where is she tonight?"

"Grandfather asked for her. Remember, she's new and young, and fresh."

"She won't be like that for long," Trix whispered.

"Did either of you know the Duke's daughter, Elhnora?" I asked.

"She was in here quite a bit. Used to come here with a friend. Another girl from the Peaks. They paid for me to dance more than once. Her friend gave me extra coin so she could touch me. Attractive girls," Stella said.

"I danced for them once, but then they stopped coming. I heard they started to go to the Red House instead," Trix said.

Raising an eyebrow, I nodded. The Red House had a reputation as the type of venue where anything could happen. Not the sort of place a duke's daughter was supposed to frequent.

I finished my second ale and decided to find the crazy dwarf man. Wandering up and down Dockside I asked girls who stood outside the inns and gambling dens, trying to entice customers inside, if they had seen him. No one had.

The street grew livelier as the sun went down. The temperature dropped fast so I bought some cooked goat on a skewer from a street vendor. Little eateries based around handcarts appeared every few paces, filling the air with spices and cooking meat. It was better than the scent from the river. I sat in the shadows and watched, but the individual the girls had described did not appear.

After a while, I had to move around to warm my limbs. This was a waste of time. I needed to talk to Golden and this Miranda for a trail to follow. It was also necessary to find out more about the wild life of the Duke's daughter, Elhnora.

4

DAGGER ALLEY

I gave up at twelve bells and started to walk home hoping to find Golden. My charismatic friend was probably tucked up in the bed of a young lady by now and wouldn't emerge until High Sun tomorrow. The stars glowed near the orange moon, Tantarless, only showed as a thin sickle in the night sky. There was virtually no light in the narrow streets that ran up the gentle rise towards Rackhime's shop.

The cobbled path tightened as I walked, becoming more like a tunnel. My eyes adjusted and I relaxed. Rats scuttled by in the boxes and refuse in a side alley. Waste in the gutters I stepped around easily, then I noted movement near the recessed doorway of an abandoned house.

Someone waited for me. I tensed. Quickly I tied back my hair so it wouldn't get in my eyes.

My ears picked up a noise from behind and I turned slightly. A figure in a cloak slunk from an alley to an empty cart that I passed before. I drew a dagger from my belt and pulled the Cold Blade from its hidden scabbard. Tucking it into the folds of my clothing I endeavoured to hide the blade's shine while crouching. The distance to Rackhime's shop was only five hundred paces, but I didn't know if I would be any safer there. At least Spike would be a potential ally as long as Golden hadn't collected him. I slid around the corner of a narrow laneway and waited.

A tall hulking figure appeared from the gloom, axe in hand. He peered into the shadows. Another figure moved from a doorway with a crossbow cradled in his arms.

"Where did he go?" the tall figure whispered.

The second shape put up one hand and gestured for silence. It appeared to be an elf – his hearing probably as good as mine, though thankfully his eyesight was no better than that of a human. A third figure filled the road behind me. He gripped a blade in two hands.

"Come out, little Owl. We know you're here," the large man said.

"So much for stealth," the elf muttered.

It seemed Yalourn's band of Hunters hadn't forgotten about me, and there was no Golden to help this time. I wondered where their leader was and hoped he had decided not to be a party to murder. It looked like the rest of his little troupe wasn't as concerned with the moral question of killing a defenceless citizen of Hope.

The elf with the crossbow had to go first. I stood and hurled the dagger. It spun thirty paces hitting my target in the neck. It struck with a thump, like a cleaver hitting a carcase at the butcher.

The elf turned at the sound of the dagger spinning through the air, but he wasn't fast enough. He fell, grabbing at the dagger, gurgling and spitting up mouthfuls of blood.

"There he is!" Thick Neck shouted.

He drew a glowing rock from beneath his cape and tossed it onto the street as I hurled another dagger at his tall companion. He saw it coming and swayed from its path.

The large man ran at me. He attacked with a blow from above, swing the sword around in an arc, aiming at my chest. I jumped aside and lunged, but he leapt back. He brought his weapon down at my head. I caught it on the Cold Blade. Our hilts came together and he tried to push me into the ground. My assailant was stronger and I could feel my shoulders straining. His tall companion came from the shadows, circling for a strike with his axe.

Drawing on the power of my sword, I focused my mind on an image of a frozen pool of water. I imagined a bitter wind and ice crystals forming in my hair before pushing the picture into the blade. Frost formed on its surface and ran down my opponent's weapon into his hands. He bellowed in pain and dropped the sword. The moonstone kept my hilt free of cold. Thick Neck held his fingers like claws and screamed. I rammed the Cold Blade into his lower chest, under the rib cage, and directed the ice I had conjured into his body. He slid from my sword to the ground with a moan and didn't move.

The swish of an axe sent me diving toward the cobble stones. I tucked in my shoulder and rolled away coming to my feet, facing my tall enemy.

A woman in chain mail carrying a mace strode down the alley. "You couldn't wait, could you?"

"We didn't think he would be that hard to kill."

"You should leave the thinking to Yalourn and me."

"I though you weren't part of, what did you call it? The dick-measuring contest," I growled at my new assailant.

"I didn't want this to happen, but they are my party so I abide by the group's decisions."

"Enough talk! Flank him, Kedra."

She slid to my left, swinging her mace at my face. I tried to catch it on my blade but she withdrew the weapon before I could create the surge of cold energy. The man slashed at me with the axe and I danced back toward the walls of the surrounding houses. I was running out of room.

"Don't take any risks. Just hold him here until Yalourn arrives and then he can fry him with a bolt of magic," Kedra said.

I flicked two blows at my tall opponent before slashing at the woman. My sword clipped the chain armour on her shoulder and the links split, sending fragments of metal falling to the cobbles.

"Watch his blade! It goes through iron like a knife through bread," Kedra said.

Unfortunately, my sword had not reached her skin.

A shadow leapt through the air. The tall man yelled as Spike's jaws closed around his neck and jaw. Both tumbled away. Hearing flesh tear and the noise of wailing, bubbling coughs, I was glad that I had no time to look at what Spike was doing to the figure beneath him.

Sliding forward, I stabbed at Kedra's face and neck. She batted my attacks away with her mace, but retreated. I stepped into her and caught her wrist, at the same time stabbing into her armpit with all my strength. The woman winced and her eyes grew wide. She made a circle with her mouth and sighed as if very tired.

I lowered her to the ground and looked around. Nobody had disturbed us. The sound of combat should have woken half the street but people would be too frightened to summon the Watch until the fighting stopped.

Spike padded toward me, his muzzle wet, steam forming from his breath like some dragon before a cave.

"Thanks, boy, but there's one more."

The bolt of blue energy crackled down the roadway and threw us into the air. Spike yelped. I screamed. We hit the ground hard. I tried to get up but only managed to lift my chin off the cobbles. Yalourn walked slowly toward me with sword in hand. He said nothing and raised the weapon above his head. I heard the thwack as the bolt took him in the chest. He spun slightly and fell on top of Kedra's body.

"Not a bad shot. It's a very good weapon but still, one hundred paces in the dark and my eyes aren't those of a Dark Elf."

Golden appeared with his crossbow on his shoulder in the pool of light left by the glowing gem. He wore only a woollen shirt, boots, and leather trousers.

"Get up, Ash, that bolt wasn't enough to hurt too much. Besides, he split it between you and Spike. I sent the wolf on ahead – I saw Yalourn and his little group leave the Red Raven equipped for battle, but lost them in the dark."

I groaned and rolled on my back. The scorch marks on my chest and throbbing ribs ached. Golden lifted my head and I felt a glass vial at my lips. He poured the contents down my throat. My eyes watered and I coughed loudly.

"That should steady you. Bloody expensive stuff, those healing draughts, so don't spit it out."

Golden crossed to Spike and checked the wolf's body. The animal slowly climbed to his feet, whimpering slightly, tail tucked between his legs.

"Spike's tougher than you, Ash."

"He's bigger than me."

"But he hasn't had any of the healing potion."

"That stuff doesn't heal you, it only dulls the pain."

"It speeds things up a bit! Anyway, you should be grateful."

"I would have been if you'd gotten here a little sooner." I pulled myself upright, wobbling for a few heartbeats. Then I sighed. "I am happy you made an appearance. Otherwise, I would be dead."

Golden glanced around at the carnage. "Well, you took out three yourself and that's not bad. Yalourn's team were experienced, though some of them weren't known for their brains. Anyway, we better get out of here before the Watch arrives." He dragged the bodies to the opening of the sewer and pulled a large metal grate aside. Then my friend removed their pouches and rolled each corpse in. "I left them enough for their spirits to pay for the journey across the Dark River. They're lucky I did that."

I nodded. When I was a Hunter, one of the main sources of income were the pockets of the dead. My body ached and I decided I needed to lie down.

The fire of Rackhime's shop welcomed me. Golden cleaned me up while the old man boiled water and fetched bandages for my burns. My wounds were dressed and ribs bound, before he checked Spike a second time.

"You're tough, aren't you boy," Golden said as he felt the animal's flanks and legs.

He glanced into the wolf's ears and eyes before giving Spike some meat dipped in the contents of another glass vial. "He'll sleep soon and will be fine in the morning." Golden turned and stared at me. "The Watch won't be happy when those bodies turn up."

I shrugged and immediately regretted the gesture as pain lanced through my ribs.

"They usually stay out of fights between different Hunter groups," I muttered.

"Maybe, but times are changing. I heard the new captain doesn't put up with what he calls unnecessary public disturbances."

"I'll fight that battle if it occurs."

The following day my wounds had stiffened and the bandages stuck to the burns. Rackhime peeled them away with the help of warm water and replaced them.

I limped out of the shop and hobbled down the street to the site of last night's fight. A few of the Watch stood around and eyed me suspiciously as I passed, but said nothing.

There were no signs of combat; early-morning sleet had washed any bloodstains from the road. I didn't feel any guilt about the death of Yalourn's group – they attacked me and brought about their own downfall. Precipitating the incident had cost them everything. That was what happened when you made poor tactical decisions.

Overhead the sky darkened and the wind picked up. The chill increased and reminded me of the pond I had envisaged last night when conjuring with my blade. I reached inside my cloak and ran fingers across the reassuring moonstone in the pommel. The sword pulsed back as though sensing my regard.

The first snow fell as I reached Dockland. They were not gentle flakes drifting down to settle on one's shoulder, but thick and wet and followed the north wind.

I decided to find out more about the noble girl's death because of the way she had been savagely cut. Trix and Stella had said she visited Dockland often with one of her friends. I knew the rich liked their little distractions, but the lady's choice of entertainment surprised me. Elhnora Vornhelm's father didn't seem to be the type of man to approve of his daughter's outings, though he probably turned a blind eye to her choice of entertainment. I hoped the women would be able to describe Elhnora's friend to me. I also needed to track down the new girl, Miranda, and speak to her.

Noise in the Mermaid hardly registered as there were few patrons, probably because of the weather or maybe because of All Gods Day. Hangovers tended keep all but the most desperate from the doors of Grandfather's establishments, for many, an extended length of time after half of the city had finished drinking. Trix wasn't around, but Stella was sitting wrapped in a fur-lined cape and little else near the fire.

"Come for your free dance?"

I smiled and thought about it before shaking my head.

"What a pity. I'm bored and need to do something to keep warm. Can you think of any way to help?" Stella raised a dark eyebrow and opened her red lips slightly.

Down boy. "Such a lovely invitation is hard to resist. However, I'm here on another matter. I was interested in what you said about the noble girl yesterday. I thought I might try and track down her friend. Maybe she can tell me if Elhnora was involved in any activity that put her under threat."

"You think she got involved in some dangerous business?"

"I don't know. It's just a starting point."

"What about the first girl?"

"I'm not really sure. Call it a hunch, a piece of the puzzle that doesn't seem to fit. If it goes nowhere then I'll have to find the Hairy Man."

"Well, sometimes we get lucky, though not me today." Stella pouted.

"The lady was here last night and asked me to dance for her.

Afterward she wanted a bit more and I obliged. I mean, she did pay and she is attractive in a skinny sort of way. We were getting intimate in one of the rooms when she started to cry. I tried to comfort her, but she apologised and left."

"What was she so upset about?"

"Her friend's death."

"So, they were close."

"It sounded like it. She cried as though her soul was broken."

I knew that feeling.

"Her name is Jalinta Vernheim and she lives up on the Horns."

My head snapped up. "Well done! How did you find that out?"

"She told me. That, and security had her family name from an expensive cloak she left one night. It had an inscribed pendant in the pocket. That was a while ago."

"Stella, you're amazing."

I reached in to kiss her on the cheek but she turned and caught me long and hard on the mouth. She pushed her chest toward me and her robe parted. I tore myself free and tried to steady my breathing.

I fled out the door into the snowstorm, as her laughter followed me. Stella captivated me with her well-rounded figure and there was something about the full shape of some human woman that attracted me. They were so different to the willowy females of my own race. Then Trix's face flashed before me. An instinct told me my friend wouldn't be very happy if I lay with Stella.

In my haste to leave, I had forgotten to ask about Miranda, but decided to find the young noblewoman first. See where that led me.

The snow swirled along the streets and the temperature dropped. My ribs hurt and I knew I wouldn't be able to make the long walk up to the noble district on the Devil's Horns. I hailed a cart pulled by a mule and told a man bundled in blankets where I wanted to go. He asked for two silver pennies, kind of expensive. Then I noted the old man's pinched face and the threadbare coat. The fact he worked in this weather smacked of desperation, so I kept my mouth shut.

The mule pulled us up the cobbled roads through the narrow

tenements house of the poor and onto the slopes where the merchants and lesser nobility lived. Here, the buildings were wider, but still competed for space in the constricted streets. There were few parks and no trees.

We passed through the old city wall and I looked downhill over the buildings. Most of it had been hidden from view by the falling snow but I could see the magical lights on the main roads and The Port shining through the gloom. As we trundled upwards, following the street as it wound along the slope, the dwellings changed. Individual manors, surrounded in some cases by walls of stone or hedges of prickle box, lined the street. Glow stones lit every corner and guards in the colours of the nobles who employed them stood behind metal gates.

The weather hid the citadel from view, yet I knew it sat on the taller of the two horns overlooking the city. Years ago, kings had ruled from behind its mighty walls. Now it was a prison and barracks, the Notable Elders choosing to meet at the Sanctuary of the Lake in High Park.

The cart made its way past the area of woods that surrounded the pond, crossing a bridge over the south-flowing Devil's Stream. The lake filled from underground springs, and the water that came from it was said to be sacred. It still became an open sewer before it reached the southern walls of Hope. We drove along a side street to a manor without a wall sitting amid overgrown grounds. Trees branches hung over the front entrance and branches lay in haphazard piles beside the short path to the door.

"We're here," the cart driver said.

His head disappeared inside the blankets, only puffs of steam escaped from beneath the folds. I had become chilled, even though I'm used to the cold. My thick cloak now covered in snow, I had to shake it loose as I climbed from the cart.

"Can you wait for me?"

For a while the man didn't answer. I wondered if he had heard me.

"It'll cost you two silver for the return and one for the waiting. I'll shelter around the back out of the wind. Maybe there'll be a stable I can pull into."

I had little choice. The weather had gotten worse and I didn't want to walk all the way back to the lower city. "Fair enough."

The home of Jalinta Vernheim sat in the snow, looking unusually bright in its yellow paint. The statues near the entrance were of musicians and dancers, with the only exception being a man holding a large scroll open. He looked as though he addressed a long-forgotten audience. The work was of high quality, but only made from limestone, not the more expensive marble. The pine door had been bound with tin and the balcony itself was small. I rang the bell and waited.

The door opened and a short, stooped man stared at me. He looked me up and down and then scratched his head. "And what would one of the dark ones be doing at my house in this weather, I wonder."

"I'm here to see Jalinta Vernheim, if I may."

"A very polite Dark Elf at that. Dressed well, obviously not a beggar. If he has money, he is probably a Hunter, yes that's what he is, or was."

"Is Jalinta here?"

"Should I let the stranger in? I am curious and would know more."

The short man's conversation with himself unnerved me. He stood back and I hesitantly crossed the threshold. I was ushered into a side chamber where rolls of parchment lay on the floor and table. Large books sat open on chairs and maps drawn on calfskin hung pinned to the wall. A small fire had almost gone out, but the room warmed me.

"This is quite a collection," I said.

"And educated too. I grow more interested."

He irritated me now. "Is any of Jalinta's family home?"

"Her father stands before you."

That made me blink a few times. This old man in the worn jacket who spoke his thoughts was the head of the house. I wondered where the servants were.

"I am guessing she will not be expecting you?"

I wasn't sure how to answer. If I said no then I might be asked to leave, yet the old man seemed friendly and I decided to take a chance.

"I want to talk to your daughter about the death her friend Elhnora Vornhelm. I'm looking into the murders of the girls at Dockside."

"Poor women. A lovely person. But will my daughter want to speak about this? She is in mourning for her friend. But the Dark Elf seeks to stop these killing. Yes, she needs to see to him."

The small man disappeared and left me with the chaotic jumble of parchment and vellum. Glancing around, I noticed that most of the drawings were about the other races, though I couldn't read the writings. The map on the wall showed the territory of the different groups a hundred years ago, before the pale humans crept inland and their cities grew along the great rivers. My own people were shown as occupying two separate mountain ranges and the high plateau. At least that hadn't changed.

The old man reappeared minutes later. "She will not see you. I am sorry. She is in pain and it may take some time for her to heal. I must encourage her to speak to you. You are trying to stop this, I'm guessing."

I nodded. "She can find me at Rackhime's store on Lyre Street."

The old man's face lit up. "I know that shop. Rackhime does good work and is talented. My respect for the Dark Elf grows. Yes, we will tell her to go and to help if she can."

I wondered if I could use my time on the Peaks to visit Elhnora's family. "Do you think you could write an introduction for me to have an interview with Duke Vornhelm? I know I won't get past the front gate without something formal."

The old man's face tightened. "The duke will not see you."

"I suppose he is in grief but it might help me to form a better picture of his daughter."

"To know pain, one must be able to understand pity. He hasn't any interest in individuals outside the great families. I think the Dark

Elf will need a more powerful introduction than any I could provide."

The cart driver had found an old barn at the rear of the house. He and a one-legged stable master sat by a small fire just inside a set of broken wooden doors. Only two horses stood in the stalls behind them. The men held their hands out to the blaze and passed a bottle back and forth. The driver looked at me and sighed. He didn't look pleased at the prospect of leaving the barn.

On the trip down the hill to Rackhime's the old man became more talkative. The wine probably loosened his tongue.

"The stable master said that Sir Vernheim is an unusual individual, but is generous with what he has. There are only a few other servants in the house, a cook and a cook's assistant. The old man employed my drinking companion when he returned without his leg from the Wars to the North. He says the family are looked down on by the other nobles, but Sir Vernheim is worth two of any of them, even though he's a bit crazy."

"What about his wife?"

"Died of the Flux years ago. Brings up his daughter alone."

"Does she help out, or is she betrothed to a richer noble?"

"The stable master said she is very wild and spent as much time as she could with Lord Vornhelm's girl. The Duke's daughter came to Jalinta's house. They never went to her residence."

I paid the cart driver an extra silver coin when I got off at Rackhime's and told him to get out of the storm. The old man said he thought he would. The snow now came down so heavily, it was difficult to see more than thirty paces. I was glad to shake off my cloak and sit in front of the fire. Spike had curled up asleep and Rackhime worked by candlelight at his workbench.

"Golden came through a while back. He says the Watch found the bodies of Yalourn's group near the sewer outlet to the river."

"Great, that's all I need."

"Story is that the captain isn't happy. Something about the lawlessness that Hunters bring to the city."

"I was just defending myself, not that it will make any difference."

"Well, if they ask me anything, I'm sure you were here all night."

"Thanks, but plenty of people would have seen me at Dockside. Don't worry – there's no evidence or witnesses, so I'll deny everything."

"One thing at a time, I suppose. Any luck with the inquiries?"

"Only more questions."

5

THE HAIRY MAN

The storm blew out in the early hours of the morning. Rackhime called me downstairs and I found two members of the Watch waiting for me at the door. Bundled in thick blue cloaks, their cheeks spotted pink, they moved from foot to foot trying to keep warm in the calf-deep snow. The wind dropped and the snow fell slowly, curling and floating before hitting the ground.

"The captain wants you at his office," the taller of the two men said.

Spike growled and I signalled the dire wolf to stay back.

"Keep your dog under control," the tall man said.

"He'll be fine as long as you don't come in," I said.

I grabbed my thickest cloak, pulled on heavy boots, and trudged out into the cold.

The city looked as if smothered in a white blanket. In the main thoroughfare, men shovelled in order to allow wagons to pass, but in the smaller streets, movement became difficult. People waded through snow up to their waist, often falling and coming up spluttering and covered in powder. Coal sellers moved from door to door unloading bags of black rocks. Wood merchants sold bundles of split timber in the main streets. Winter dropped early. I heard my two escorts discussing how the river had frozen over, shutting down the port area and putting the workers out of employment until the water thawed, probably not until the end of the season.

The two members of the Watch didn't converse. When I asked what the captain wanted me for, they stared ahead, as though I wasn't there. It was a fair guess he would be asking about the dead Hunters in the sewers. I was worried about the interview, but if I held my nerve he'd have to release me. Unless he handed me over to a couple of privates and let them pound me until I confessed. I counted on Waldheigheim's belief in evidence and justice to get me through. My other concern was the behaviour of my irascible friend.

Golden perched on a stool, against the wall, and Waldheigheim sat frowning behind his desk. My friend had his eyes closed as if dozing.

"Now, perhaps you can add to the tale your companion has told me about the previous evening," Waldheigheim said. The tall man's single eyebrow arched down his nose, making it seem even longer.

"Always happy to help," I answered.

"Where were you the night before last?" Waldheigheim asked.

"Down at Dockside until late, and then back at Rackhime's."

"Did you notice any disturbances around two bells?"

"No."

"Fighting was reported by residents only five hundred paces from your shop. There was a small battle that night. Swords clashing, screams of pain, flashes of bright light. And you heard or saw nothing?"

"Not a thing."

"We pulled five bodies from the grate at Outlet seven of the sewers yesterday. Three had puncture or stab marks, but one looked as though he'd been savaged by a bear, or maybe a dire wolf. The other, a big man, had a strange wound. There was a stab wound below the ribs that lanced up into the heart. Nothing unusual about that except that it was surrounded by what looked like frostbite."

"It's been cold," Golden said.

"You are not to speak," the captain snapped.

He turned back to me while my friend shut his eyes and stretched out again. "The frostbite was only located at the point of the wound. It was the sort of thing I would expect from a Cold Blade."

I scratched the back of my neck. "Well, Cold Blades have different properties, so it's hard to know."

"That's right," Golden said.

Waldheigheim's eyes blazed. "If you speak again, I'll throw you in the cells."

My friend sat forward. He was unarmed but twisting one of his rings. The magic stored in them could be released with a phrase or gesture. He was also deadly with his bare hands. I hoped he wouldn't do anything stupid.

"Yalourn's band was known to the Watch. They had a record for violent and threatening behaviour. Maybe they bit off more than they could chew this time. I don't care why they died. They might have had it coming, but I will not have battles on the streets of the city I protect. The day of the Hunter is going to end and there are signs it isn't too far off. The Watch is going to lock up anyone who disturbs the peace of Hope and I won't listen to excuses. You and your arrogant friend are on notice. If there is any more trouble that can be traced to you, I'll throw you in the bottom-most cell of the Citadel and forget about you."

This was one of those times it was best to stay quiet. Of course, Golden didn't see it that way.

"Well, we sure hope you catch the scallywags who disturbed the fair citizens' rest."

The captain's face reddened and his fists balled. I cringed.

"Go!"

I took off out of the door and didn't look back. My friend came at a more leisurely pace.

"Are you trying to get us locked up?"

Golden put a hand on his chest and looked surprised. "He said I was arrogant."

"And that's why you decided to push it? You idiot. The captain is not a man to mess with. He's one of those rare individuals who believe implicitly in what they do. That makes him very dangerous."

"But I'm not arrogant!"

"I would also add that Captain Waldheigheim is an extremely good judge of character."

"A little harsh," Golden mumbled.

I grunted and started to walk away but changed my mind. "Come on, it's late enough for a drink. Let's get some mulled wine. The Lazy Dog isn't far and they should have some warmed in this weather."

Golden grinned and fell into step next to me.

We sat in a dim corner of the inn away from the fire. A number of the Watch drank at the bar as it was close to their headquarters. I wanted to maintain a low profile, always difficult with Golden next to you, and it wasn't as though I didn't stand out. But it was the closest place to get a drink.

"I wanted to ask you about a man that Trix and Stella mentioned. It seems there's this hairy individual that's been hanging around Dockside making trouble for the girls. He's described as looking like a dwarf, but being as tall and broad as a port worker. He carried a couple of war axes and flashed about a bit of gold. It's all very similar to what a Hunter would do. Is there anyone you can think of who fits the description?"

Golden scratched at the perfectly trimmed stubble on his chin. "Not that I know of. There are a dozen Hunter groups which operate from Hope, now down to eleven, and I've met them all. Perhaps he's from Thantis. Bands often winter there, as it's closer to the frontier. Or he could be from a border town. A number of the less experienced teams stay in them during the colder weather so they can get back into the action earlier come spring. I'll ask around though. Maybe one of the other groups will remember someone like that."

I nodded and wondered what to do next. Grandfather would want a report and I had little to tell him. I needed to either confirm or disprove his suspicions about the Dance Master. My best lead remained the Hairy Man.

After a few drinks, I returned to Rackhime's and wrote a note for Grandfather in my own language. I knew he had people with him who could translate. It didn't tell him much other than I was still working on various leads.

I then left for Dockside to find the elusive Miranda.

The front doors of the Reclining Mermaid were bolted. I hammered on the woodwork until security opened up and told me Grandfather had told his workers to take the day off. The clients were staying home due to the depth of snow.

Beggars and other down-and-outs had been thrown some silver to shovel the area clear and I could see them toiling at the end of the street under the gaze of two of Grandfather's toughs.

Most of the women had gone to the Pig and Whistle for a meal. I thanked the guard and walked through the snow to a small inn at the edge of the merchant district. The girls liked to go here because of the cosy atmosphere, good music and the distance from any possible clientele.

Lively fiddle playing and the buzz of conversation filled the warm air. A drum tapped and a woman sang "The March of the Brave Company" from a stool near the fire. The smell of lamb pies and hot chips made my stomach growl. I spotted Trix in a woollen shirt and long skirt seated at the back table with five other women. It was rare to find her with so much clothing on, but I was pleased.

Next to her sat a woman who took my breath away. Her eyes were almost as large as mine, her nose small. Her face reminded me of those carved on the walls of the temples of Palos, God of Dance and Music – young and full of wonder. She had a rounded figure, like Stella's, but dressed in a tight outfit that buttoned up to the throat. The woman's honey-coloured hair had been pulled up in a rough bun on top of her head, exposing a swanlike neck.

I saw her smile at some comment Trix made, and then our eyes met. She stared and Trix turned to look. My friend's face lit up and she gestured for me to come over. I weaved about the tables and stood before the group of women, feeling self-conscious, although I knew them all. They looked at me with friendly expressions.

"Miranda, this is Ash. He's looking into the death of Fendria and the noble girl."

"I've heard a lot about you. Trix often sings your praise."

Who says the dark-skinned races can't blush? Miranda's voice was low and throaty, like a cat purring.

"She exaggerates."

"The way the girls tell it, you and Golden killed a dragon together."

"We escaped from one. Those beasts are impossible to kill."

"Sit and give us a tale about it," Teel said. "I'm in the mood for a good story."

"That's why you love all bards," Genna teased.

Teel's smile made her freckles dance. "The stories and songs of the past are full of magic."

"Yes, they cast a spell which puts you flat on your back with legs in the air," Aneeta said.

The women burst out laughing and I felt myself lifted by their good humour.

"Are you hungry?" Trix asked.

"The moment I walked in my stomach rumbled."

Miranda chuckled and it sounded like small bells. "The Pig and Whistle has that effect on people. I can never get enough of the potato wedges."

"I'll order you something," Trix said.

The slender half-elf pressed close to me as she made her way to the bar and I could smell rosewater in her hair. Miranda patted the seat next to her and I obediently sat. Her leg rubbed against mine. She caught my eye and glanced away. I felt unsure and awkward.

"So, what have you found out about the murder?" Teel asked, her face serious.

I shook my head. "Not as much as I would like. I'm trying to track down the Hairy Man at the moment, as he seems to be the best lead."

"You saw him last night didn't you, Miranda?" Aneeta said.

"I was harassed by him on the way home. He wanted to marry me and take me away to a place of beauty and comfort. Kept trying to push some gold coins in my hands. I would have taken the money but I didn't want to encourage him."

"Can you describe him?"

"He's as tall as a doorway and as broad as a dwarf. He has dark hair and a beard that climbs up his cheeks almost to his eyes which are brown. And he carries a double-bladed battle axe. He looks wild but doesn't smell."

It was a good description. "What did the coins look like?"

"I only got to see one. It was old with a crown on it. The others were of different shapes and sizes. He had a handful of them. I haven't seen that much gold in a long time."

I thought for a moment. "The more I hear about this man the more convinced I am that he is, or was, a Hunter. He must have had some success to be carrying so much gold, but somehow he's become unhinged."

"Do you think he might be the killer?" Teel asked.

"I'm not sure. I have to find him first, and then I'll know more."

Trix returned with some roasted potato wedges and lamb pies. When she saw Miranda and me pressed together on the narrow bench she frowned and pulled up a chair on my right, pushing the pie toward me without a word. I mumbled my thanks as I bit into the crust and then blew through my teeth – it was too hot to swallow.

"The hairy man said he would seek me out again, soon," Miranda whispered.

I looked at her sideways. "Tonight?"

"I don't know for certain, but if I make myself visible then he might show up."

"I'm not in favour of the idea. It's too dangerous," Trix said.

"He's going to come after me anyway."

"Unless he fixes on another girl in the meantime," Genna said.

"I'll bring Golden and Spike to make it even safer," I said.

Trix turned away from me slightly and mumbled something under her breath.

———

That evening, Golden and I watched from the shadows in Dockland as Miranda appeared at the doorway of the Reclining Mermaid, and walked out on to the front veranda occasionally. There were few people about with the area still closed down, and I realised the Hairy Man was unlikely to show up. At twelve bells I approached Miranda as she stepped out onto the street.

"We'll try again tomorrow night. He probably wouldn't expect you to be around as everything is shut down. If Grandfather reopens we might have more luck."

Miranda nodded. "All right, but you will escort me back to my rooms, won't you?"

"Of course."

I signalled Golden to approach and he glided from the shadows with Spike in his wake. He had the hand-and-a-half Cold Blade strapped across his back and wore his bearskin cloak. Grinning at Miranda, he bowed slightly at the waist before standing tall.

"I don't think we've met."

Grimacing, I made the introductions. Golden grasped Miranda's hand and kissed her fingers, which caused her to raise an eyebrow. He looked at me and then, noting my twisted face and blazing eyes, stepped backward.

"I'm taking Miranda home." I didn't mean to place all the emphasis on the first word, but that's the way it came out.

Golden glanced back and forth between the two of us and then nodded. He scratched Spike's ears and backed away.

"Right, well, I'll try and find what I can from Grondar's group about the Hairy Man. He has brought his Hunters into the city and is staying up at the Eagle's Look Out."

"They must have done well this season. That's an expensive inn," I said. I started to feel guilty about my possessive attitude toward Miranda.

"They found the death mound of some Hobgoblin chief, and after driving away the local tribe, tore it open and took out a lot of burial goods – silver cups, swords with gems in the hilt, those sorts of things."

"Well they had to get lucky sometime."

The silence stretched before Golden said his goodbyes and disappeared.

As I strolled next to Miranda she slipped her arm through mine. In these streets the snow had been shovelled into dirty piles, making walking easier.

"We have something in common," she said suddenly.

"And what is that?"

"I'm from the south too. The fishing village where I was born lies near the mountain range of the Dark Elves, just before it runs into the Western Sea."

I didn't want to remember home. The memories of disgrace and the anger of the Tribunal of Elders remained fresh.

"And what did your family think of their near neighbours?" I asked.

"They had no opinion. The local knights and men-at-arms hated your people, but the common folk didn't really care. Some feared the stories about you, but when things were calm, Dark Elves would sometimes trade with the fishermen, swapping snapper and shark for goatskins and rugs made from your shaggy cattle."

Memories flooded back. "I haven't been home for a long time."

Miranda hesitated, then pulled me closer with a gentle tug. "I sense there's a reason."

"It is all so long ago, though it always seems fresh. I trusted someone who disappointed me. I let emotion become entangled with duty, and when disaster occurred, the responsibility lay at my feet."

"I ran from home too, but for different reasons. I know I'm attractive to the eye and sometimes that brings the wrong sort of attention. Nobody is interested in who I am. They just want to bed me. Now, I use that fact to keep me alive."

"I don't care what you, Trix, Stella, or any of the girls do."

"Maybe that's because you're an outcast, too."

We arrived at the door to a narrow building set on a street running up one of the twin hills of the city. Miranda took both my hands in hers and kissed me softly on the lips. An emotion that I hadn't felt for a long time surged though me. I was in trouble.

"I'll see you tomorrow then, Ash," Miranda whispered as she slipped behind the door.

I stood there for a moment, trying to collect my thoughts. These feeling scared me. The last time I felt them, death, misjudgement, and betrayal had almost destroyed my life. I fled my home and became a Hunter, using the skills I had learnt in the service of the Dark Elf nation to plunder ancient tombs and chase down marauding ogre tribes. But this human woman had a quality to her that was captivating. I realised, also, that she was in danger. The killer with the broken razor could strike again and she might easily be the next victim. My determination to catch the murderer intensified.

The following morning, a freezing blanket of fog mixed with wood smoke hid Hope from view. Golden waited for me downstairs, eating my bacon and mushrooms.

"You were too slow," Rackhime said from his workbench.

"I don't suppose you left me any?"

Golden held up one small piece and grinned. He wiped grease from his stubble and pushed the almost-empty plate toward me.

"Didn't want it to go to waste."

I finished off the remaining piece and went to the kitchen to cut off a slice of bread.

Golden called after me. "I found out who the Hairy Man is, or was."

I came out with my bread and ran it round the edge of the pan to soak up all the fat before stuffing it in my mouth. "Who?" I said while chewing.

"Tearwyn the Axeman. He worked with a team called the Red Dawn out of Vellron, one of the border towns. The Hunters of his group are scattered or dead now, but for a while they operated in the Great Woods. Anyway, Tearwyn fell for a beautiful magician named Araine, Arriana, something like that. She didn't return his affections but tolerated them. Last summer they were tracking some ogres when their band was ambushed. Tearwyn's fantasy girl was turned to jam by a club before she had enough time to gather any power. He was distraught and killed the creature by himself."

"No easy feat to beat one of those brutes."

"Soon after, our hairy friend leaves the group and disappears. Now he turns up in Hope wanting to marry every attractive girl in Docklands. Speaking of beautiful girls, how did things go with the lovely Miranda?"

"We're just friends."

"You never shoot daggers from your eyes at me when I flirt with Trix."

"Has Ash got himself a lady love?" Rackhime asked.

"No, I haven't," I snapped.

I saw Golden nod at the older man and decided it was time to leave.

"Meet me at the Mermaid tonight," I said to my friend. "I have to report to Grandfather before he sends someone looking for me."

Security was tight at the mansion when I arrived just before the midday meal. I walked through to where Grandfather sat behind his desk with a steaming trencher of roast beef covered in gravy. He tore a piece from the bone and then cleaned his beard with a cloth. Teel sat waiting in a flimsy toga near the fire, her face a mask. I tried to keep the pity from my eyes – Teel was a proud girl and she wouldn't want that.

Grandfather saw me glance in her direction. "You can speak in front of her. I trust all my girls as a father trusts his daughters."

Something blazed inside me but I pushed it down. "I want to try and catch the Hairy Man tonight. Golden is helping me and one of the girls has volunteered to be the bait."

"Which of my women?"

"Miranda."

He smiled, white teeth even and sharp. "That is a lure that is hard to resist. You take good care of her. She is one of my prizes."

I didn't answer, but turned away and clenched my fist. I was happy that all my weapons had been taken from me as I might have used it.

"Is he the killer?" Grandfather asked.

"I'll be able to tell you soon enough."

I was glad to get out of Grandfather's fortress and back to Rackhime's shop. Golden had gone, taking Spike with him. I settled at a workbench and started copying old parchment covered in dwarf runes onto sheets of vellum. It was one of the short people's never-ending histories and, as usual, I couldn't read it. But the process eased my mind.

Rackhime left me alone except to look over my shoulder and grunt at my work. I liked writing in the dwarf tongue – the straight lines and angles led to me making fewer mistakes. Before I knew it, the light faded and I needed to go.

The dancing and drinking businesses were back in full swing, with some patrons behaving as though they had to catch up on the day they'd missed. Groups of drunken port workers clashed with young nobles, both being separated by Grandfather's army of toughs that patrolled the area. There was no sign of the Watch. The lanterns, ablaze with colour, music, and laughter drifted from the various inns and gambling dens along the road. Men in red jackets wearing tall, gaily coloured hats tried to entice more people inside, singing the delights to be had within their establishments. I waited with Golden in a side alley and watched the front of the Mermaid, hoping to find the Hairy Man.

"If he's going to come, it will be tonight. The weather gives him cover and if he is as good a Hunter as rumoured, he'll use every advantage to get close to Miranda," Golden said.

"Well, at least he doesn't know there will be people waiting for him, and the gloom gives me a certain edge."

We had to keep our position for most of the night. Miranda knew we were in the alley and wandered out onto the street occasionally. She didn't stay long as her lightweight dress gave little protection from the weather. I struggled to keep warm and had to rub my hands together to restore their circulation.

Eventually, in the small hours of the morning, Miranda, wrapped in a fur-lined cloak, left the Mermaid. She turned onto Hose Street, and started to climb the hill. Golden and I trailed behind in the shadows.

As Miranda passed a narrow alley a bear-like figure stepped in front of her. She stopped. I could hear conversation. Then the man took her by the arm and started speaking to her in urgent tones. When he pulled her toward him I broke into a run. The man wrenched her hard and she fell. Then the Hairy Man turned and saw me. Letting go of Miranda, he spun, then ran. I was surprised at how quickly he moved. He disappeared back into the darkness as I drew the Cold Blade from inside my cloak.

"We want him alive, Ash!" Golden yelled.

Spike bounded past me as I halted next to Miranda. She looked up from the cobbles and gestured at me.

"I'm fine, go."

Running into the alley, the shadows melted before my night vision. I noted the deep tracks the Hairy Man had made as he pushed his way to intercept Miranda and could see the trail he ploughed as he ran. The area had not been cleared of snow and it was hard for me to chase him. Spike had no difficulty. I heard a thump and then a growl before turning the next corner. The dire wolf had knocked Tearwyn to the ground but he scrambled up and stood with his back to the wall, battle axe in hand. The wolf backed away but continued to snarl.

"Heel, boy. We don't want to hurt him, yet," I said.

The dire wolf dropped to his haunches.

"Why do you chase me, Owl? I ain't done nothin'."

"You have been making trouble for a friend of mine."

"The lady Miranda should come away with me. I can make her happy. I just need to be given a chance."

Golden glided in next to me, Cold Blade glowing in his hands.

"I know you two. You're Hunters."

"As are you, Tearwyn. What are you doing in Hope?" I asked.

"Tryin' to make a lady safe and happy and to get another chance."

"And what happens if they say no?" I said.

"What business is it of yours, Owl? You got no right to threaten me."

Tearwyn stepped towards us, raising the axe high. Golden held his fist out and whispered a word. From a silver ring shaped like a ram's head, a bubble of force shot forward and slammed into the big man's stomach, making him double over. He fell hard on a pile of broken crates and gasped in pain.

"What did I ever do to you? The girls need me to help them and you got no right to stop me."

Miranda touched me gently on the shoulder. Her hair remained hidden in the hood of her cloak but her eyes shone with the soft light of the Cold Blade.

"Let me talk to him," she said.

I gestured for her to do so.

"We don't want to go with you. Why do you need us to?"

"To keep you safe. To give me a chance to show you that I can love."

"But I don't want you to feel that way about me."

Tearwyn sobbed and pounded his fists into the snow. "I know. I have to get my chance. I just need to make you safe."

"These girls are not your magician," I said.

"You don't know what happened, Owl. You weren't there."

Miranda held her hand up to me. "No, we were here, but that doesn't matter. We can't love you because we have only recently met you. When we say no does that make you angry?"

Tearwyn shook his head and put a hand to his shoulder where Spike's teeth had pierced his skin. "Just unhappy."

"Why does it make you sad?" Miranda asked gently.

"Because it means I'll always be alone and never get to prove myself."

"Tearwyn, do you have a razor or dagger?" I said.

"I'm an axe man. Don't carry that type of blade. Why?"

"Girls have been dying and people think you are responsible," Miranda said.

The big man's mouth fell open and he stood up. "I would never. couldn't – I mean I wouldn't do anything like that!"

Horror contorted his face. He twisted his hands together and tears filled his eyes.

"I want to save the girls! I would never hurt them, you have to believe me."

He took a step toward Miranda. Spike growled and I thrust my sword forward. Tearwyn stopped and turned to Golden. "I have never hurt a girl in my life."

"Then you won't mind if we search you for razors or daggers, just to make sure."

The big man dropped his axe and stood with his arms outstretched. I searched him carefully, trying to avoid his wounded shoulder. He'd spoken the truth.

"I don't think it's him," I whispered.

"I agree," Miranda said.

"The dagger or razor could be wherever he drags his victims to," Golden muttered.

"That's unlikely. All the girls have been killed in different places, and my gut tells me he's not the one."

I turned to the bear-like man and saw the lines of anguish in his face.

"You better get out of town, Tearwyn. The Watch may not be so believing."

We left him there in the alley, crying onto the snow.

"He is either the best actor in the world or innocent," Miranda said.

"The life of a Hunter can inflict many different types of wounds," I mused.

"Come on, Ash, he probably always had the potential to go mad," Golden said.

"But it was the death of a woman he loved that drove him over the edge."

Miranda's hand reached for mine in the darkness and our fingers linked.

6

JALINTA VERNHEIM

I walked slowly down into the workroom well before lunchtime the following day. Rackhime, sat in a large chair covered in sheepskins feeding the wolf some trenchers of bread drenched in fat.

"You're lucky he doesn't take your hand off," I said.

"Me and Spike have an understanding. He catches the odd rat and I keep him well fed. If he nips a finger the supply dries up. He's a smart dog, he knows that."

"It's going to be shock for him when Golden takes him back into the Wild Lands."

"I'm sure he'll do just fine."

"Has my wandering friend been in?"

"Not yet. You're up unusually early, and with a smile. That wouldn't have something to do with Miranda, would it?"

"I will not rise to the bait." I threw some salted fish into a pan.

Rackhime grunted and wiped his fingers before crossing to the workbench. "This came by cart at first light. It looks like one of the nobles wants to see you."

He held a scroll tied in string and sealed with red wax.

"You read it. You know I can only speak your tongue," I said.

Rackhime broke the seal and took the parchment toward the burning candles.

"It's from Jalinta Vernheim. To Ash the Dark Elf. My father has convinced me of the importance of seeing you as soon as possible. I will visit the Reclining Mermaid at eight bells after night fall and wait for you in one of the curtained alcoves."

Rackhime passed me the scroll. To me it was a series of meaningless lines and scribble.

"You be careful dealing with these nobles," he said.

"Jalinta's family is harmless. Her father is a crazy historian. He knew your shop."

Rackhime scratched at his bald head for a second before realisation hit him.

"Not Old Petar. That man is not as insane as people like to think. He knows more about the history of these lands since us pale humans crossed the seas than anyone in Hope. Some of his scrolls are priceless."

"Well, it's his daughter that wants to meet me."

Rackhime shook his head. "It feels like a small city sometimes."

As I made my way down to Barnabus's Place. The freezing fog that had settled over Hope had yet to lift, forcing many people indoors. Two men in brown capes tried unsuccessfully to blend in with the sparse crowd. The taller of them was armed with a long sword and I thought I caught a glimpse of a chain vest when he passed under one of the glow lights near the street corner. The other man seemed to waddle as he walked, as though he was more accustomed to riding. Both failed at staying hidden, and I decided to find out what they were up to at the next alleyway.

I had secreted the Cold Blade beneath my cloak and pulled it clear while stepping into the gloom. Slipping behind a broken stairwell I let my eyes adjust. The humans would struggle to see me before I was on them.

The tall man came first. He advanced within reach. I struck him.

When the sword hilt hit, his head rang like a bell and he toppled without a sound.

His broad companion filled the alley as he came at me with a yell. He pulled a dagger from his belt and jabbed at my stomach. I swayed aside and hit him across the neck with the flat of my sword. The man dropped to his knees in the dirty snow, and I touched the blade to his throat.

"Don't move," I said.

"No need to be like that, young Ash," a voice behind me said.

If I thought the broad man had filled the alley, then I had been mistaken. The dwarf may have only reached my chest, but his shoulders nearly touched either wall. His red-gold beard tucked into a leather belt and a war hammer hung at his hip. He held a throwing axe.

"Tickles, I should have recognised the Dance Master's men."

"We only want to have a talk, there's no need for violence," the dwarf said.

"Why didn't you just approach me at the inn, or at Rackhime's?"

"I wanted to make sure Golden wasn't with you. There's bad blood between me and him, and that bloody wolf makes me nervous."

When Tickles and my friend had belonged to the same hunting group, they had never agreed on anything, and it nearly got them both killed. To hear Golden speak about it, you'd believe the dwarf was stupid, stubborn and greedy. The dwarf had a reputation as one of the most experienced Hunters in the north and a fierce warrior. His standing and Golden's competed for attention and both of them had egos to match the stories told about them.

"I don't mind talking but I'd prefer to do it somewhere more comfortable."

I let the man at my feet rise and move away. He rubbed at his neck while backing toward the alley's entrance.

"On your way to Barnubus's? I'll leave these two and have a drink with you if that's okay."

The walk to the inn didn't take long and we filled the distance with talk of the different Hunter groups and where they were operating. Tickles was better informed than Golden. Through force of habit, we sat at the rear of the room with our backs to the wall.

"The Dance Master wants to know the state of your inquiries into the death of the two girls," Tickles said. He stroked his beard, smoothing and teasing out knots.

"Why should he care?"

"It was noted that Grandfather called you in to look into the murders, and the growth in security at the mansion has also drawn a certain amount of attention. The old man's paranoia is well known but what my employer wants to know is what he's scared of."

"Murder and torture down in Docklands is bad for business. Young nobles stay away from the fleshpots if they think they might not make it home again."

"That makes sense, except for the increased security at the mansion. There are enough toughs hanging around the place to form a small army."

I shrugged. "Nothing to do with me."

The dwarf grunted and eased a hammer from his belt. He placed it on the table next to his ale and stared at me for a moment.

"You know, you could work for the Dance Master. He'd pay well and keep you safe."

I was never going to be employed by anyone again. My responsibilities were to myself and no one else.

"Can't do that. Grandfather helped me out once and I've got a debt to repay. But he doesn't own me." That was true, but it wasn't the whole story.

"That old man won't be around forever. The Dance Master's influence is growing, and one day, he'll run the underworld in this city."

"I can't say as I care."

The dwarf grunted. "Tell the Old Man that his little army better stay within the walls of the mansion. We are recruiting as well, and won't be taken by surprise."

"Sounds like paranoia is catching."

"We're just being cautious. The Dance Master likes to be prepared."

The day lost its shine. The thought of gangs of armed men killing each other in an undeclared war that raged through the city's alleys and streets was disturbing. The Watch would not stand by idly and their involvement would only make any conflict worse. I had to warn Grandfather about my conversation with Tickles, but I couldn't go straight there.

I wondered if Golden could see the old man for me but dismissed that as a bad idea. My tall friend wasn't to be trusted to deliver the warning from the Dance Master with the diplomacy that was needed. Eventually, I decided to write everything down and send the information with Wink to be translated later. I pushed away my half-eaten curry and returned to Rackhime's shop.

Night crept over the walled city of Hope. I sat by the bar at the Mermaid and tried to ignore the patrons who stumbled in from the cold streets. Trix came over and offered me a drink.

"Thanks," I said.

"Just doing my job. Anyway, Miranda's not here," she growled.

"I haven't come to visit Miranda."

"Someone else caught your eye then?" She almost snarled the question.

"What's your problem? I'm here to see Jalinta Vernheim."

Trix turned away in a swirl of flimsy material and the scent of rosewater washed over me. She returned with a pint of ale and slammed it down in front of me.

"Why is it that whenever I introduce you to one of my friends you forget about me?"

"What are you talking about?" I didn't know how to respond to the anger. Trix stared at me as though willing me to understand something, but all I could see was a furrowed brow and blazing eyes.

"I've got work to do," she finally said, before stalking off to the gambling room.

All I could think about was the fact that Miranda wasn't here. I could still feel her small hand in mine.

A thin young woman with a pointed chin appeared a little later. On her hip she carried a scimitar similar to those becoming popular with noblemen from the Peaks. She glanced in my direction and nodded before disappearing into an empty booth.

I picked up my ale and crossed the room. The woman sat in the corner of the curtained area. A small stage dominated the middle of the space. The gloom made it hard to see but I noted the woman's eyes flitting from side to side.

"Jalinta?" I asked.

"You must be Ash. My father said he liked the honesty in your face. He often says strange things like that." Jalinta's eyes brushed over me before settling on the stage.

"One of the last times I was here with Elhnora, we sat in this very booth and watched one of the girls dance. The one with the freckles."

"Teel," I said.

"You know her?"

"I know most of the girls here."

"They are all so beautiful."

"I started coming here as a Hunter, then some of them became friends. Now I'm looking in to the death of one of the girls and of your friend. I'm sure there is a link, I just don't know what it is."

Jalinta looked away. "I'm not sure if I can help you."

"You came here often with Elhnora and you've gone upstairs with some of the girls. It's my belief that you prefer the company of women to men."

"That would be frowned upon by the high society of the nobles." Jalinta turned up the corner of her lip as though she shared a secret memory.

"You've never really been part of high society. My guess is the closest you came was when you were in Elhnora's company."

"My father's behaviour and our lack of a fortune has precluded me from the guest list of the rich and famous."

"But Elhnora's friendship changed that?"

Jalinta laughed softly. "You've got it so wrong. The friendship with me led to her being excluded from many of the most prestigious gatherings, much to her father's fury. But she didn't care. She said the world of balls and sewing circles was boring. Elhnora appreciated the female form as much as I do."

"So, you became lovers?"

"For a while, yes. But then our relationship became more open. Sometimes Elhnora came to the Mermaid alone, sometimes I did. She had her favourites – the half-elf, Stella. And she was very taken with the new girl, Miranda."

"I can understand that," I muttered.

"Her father wasn't happy with her trips to Docklands but that was all about to end. He was arranging a marriage to the Delrin family. Elhnora was furious but there was little she could do."

Aneeta stuck her head in past the curtain. "I don't suppose you two are interested in me dancing for you?"

I shook my head but Jalinta smiled. "Maybe later. At the moment it's all business." Her eyes followed Aneeta until she disappeared. "I have never had Aneeta dance for me."

"She has had other female clients before."

Jalinta snorted. "Noble girls who come here with their boyfriends to keep them happy don't count. I've seen those girls coming through the door on the arm of some rich young knight and then help him paw one of the girls to fulfil some fantasy."

"Did Elhnora make any enemies that you know of?"

"No, she angered her father and many of the richest families sneered at her behaviour, but she was about to be tamed." Jalinta played with the hilt of the sword and her eyes became distant. "We often fantasised about running away together and becoming Hunters.

She taught me how to use the bow and this weapon. It was one of the useful skills she learnt at finishing school. Singing and sewing were never going to help her kill an ogre."

"No offence, but neither is that blade or a thirty-pound bow. You need something with grunt to bring down one of those monsters. I'm glad you didn't become Hunters, because if you had you'd both be dead."

"I can handle a sword."

"I believe you. It's just you need something heavy when you're in the wilderness. I carry a dagger and short sword in town. Out there"–I gestured with my hand–"I carry a long sword or an axe."

Jalinta shook her head. "None of that matters now. Elhnora's dead at the hands of some madman and I'm alone."

"You still have your father, and I've heard that he's a good man."

"Yes, there is Dad." She smiled.

"I hope you don't take offence, but I need to ask where you were the night Elhnora died?"

"I was at home with my father. We had agreed not to go out that night. I still don't know why she did. And why she didn't pick me up on the way."

A tear formed at the corner of Jalinta's eye before running across her cheek. "If she'd stayed home or got me she'd still be alive."

"Did she usually take her sword with her when she went out?"

"Nearly always."

"It wasn't with her on the night she was killed."

"That's unusual."

A thought occurred to me and I stuck my head out of the curtain and looked for one of the girls. The first face I saw was Miranda's, as she hung her cloak on a hook near the bar. My heart skipped a beat but I forced control into my voice.

"Can we ask you a question, Miranda?"

The beautiful woman swayed across the room and pulled aside the curtain. She smiled and ran her fingers along the other woman's arm. I saw a shiver pass through Jalinta and felt the stirring of both passion and jealousy.

"What can I do for the two of you?" She emphasised "two" as though suggesting she was open to an encounter.

Jalinta sat forward on her chair but I frowned. "We are talking about Elhnora and need a little information. Did anyone see her at the Mermaid the night she died?"

"I was working that evening and I didn't. The Watch asked around and from what I heard, no one had."

"Would she have gone somewhere else?" I asked Jalinta.

"It's possible, but this is our favourite place."

"I'll ask around. Can I come to your house if I have any more questions?"

"Yes."

I moved towards the curtain and saw Miranda's eyes follow me. "I'm going," I said.

"Well, I've got some time. Stay and dance for me," Jalinta whispered.

Miranda smiled and slid toward the small stage.

"I thought you were going to see Aneeta?" I almost snapped it out.

They both stared at me, then Jalinta's eyes flicked between the two of us.

"I'm sorry," she blurted.

I threw back the curtain and stalked toward the bar to collect the Cold Blade. Miranda followed me.

"Ash, this is work. I thought if you stayed it would be more enjoyable."

I sighed. "If we are to be together, I don't want it to be like this."

"This is my job. I just wanted to make it a little more fun."

"I know. It's all a bit confusing. Look, I'll see you soon and take you out for some food."

"Do you want to court me?" The smile lit up her face and my heart lurched.

"Something like that," I mumbled. It is what I would have done among my own people, but I'd been away from them so long the old customs sat uneasily.

"I look forward to it." With that she turned and walked back toward the screen.

The following morning, Rackhime yelled for me to come downstairs. From the window, I could see the fog hadn't lifted. I pulled on some clothes and stumbled to the work room. I'd spent the rest of last evening trying to find someone who'd seen Elhnora in Docklands, without luck. It started to look like she'd been snatched on the way down the hill.

"Ash, Noble Vernheim is here and he wants to know where his daughter is," Rackhime said.

The old man stood by the door with a fur-lined hat in his hand. He ran fingers along the rim and shuffled his feet.

I stopped near the fire to gather my thoughts. "I left her at the Mermaid last night. She had told me about Elhnora and was going to have a few drinks before leaving."

"The Dark Elf is kind, but I'm aware of her proclivities. She would stay for a dance and maybe to spend some time in the arms of a woman. This I know. Do not try and shield me."

"But she didn't come home?" I asked.

"No, I hoped she would be here."

"I will find her." I started pulling on heavy clothing. "Where's Spike and Golden?" I asked Rackhime.

"Down at the ports. He thinks the wolf is getting fat and needs some exercise. Eating too much pie, he believes."

"I'll get them and begin searching. Miranda saw her last, so that's where we'll start."

I found Golden and Spike on the ice of the river.

When we reached Miranda's lodging. She came stumbling downstairs, half-asleep to a small landing just inside the front door.

Miranda remained the only woman I'd ever known who continued to be as beautiful in the morning as she was the night before.

"I danced for her and then she wanted to go upstairs. Jalinta had the gold but because of you I couldn't do it," Miranda said.

She looked annoyed at the idea of turning down an attractive young client but I couldn't get distracted.

"Where did Jalinta go after that?"

"She didn't say. I thought she might ask for Aneeta, but she just sighed and left."

"Did you see anyone around, someone you hadn't seen before?"

"There was this big guy, he had a small scar on his chin and he watched Jalinta as she left. Do you think—"

"I don't know what to believe."

I took her hand and kissed her on the lips. "Stay safe," I whispered.

Golden was waiting outside, stamping his feet to keep warm.

"We need to try the other dance clubs. Someone must have seen her," I said.

He nodded and fell into step next to me.

We hadn't walked far when Wink appeared from a side alley and stopped in front of me.

"Me mate Tracker just found another girl. A noble up in the warehouse behind the woolsheds. I ain't told the Watch yet, thought you might want to look first."

A sense of dread crept over me. "Show me," I whispered.

7

THE WRONG MAN

B lood coated everything. I hadn't seen damage this severe on a corpse in all my days as a Hunter.

Jalinta's eyes were glassy and her body stiff. She hung from a crossbeam of dark oak. The thick rope was frayed and rough. Her feet didn't touch the ground. Hair covered her face. Most of the left side of her torso had been hacked away and chunks of flesh lay on the earthen floor.

"By the Gods, whoever did this was in a frenzy," Golden said.

Jalinta's stab wounds covered her lower torso and slash marks crossed her chest. Her right shoulder hung by a strip of flesh.

"A long sword, I'd say. She has puncture marks in the stomach which exit near her spine," Golden said, bending a little closer to the corpse.

"He started on her with a razor first." I pointed to long shallow slice marks on Jalinta's left side. "Then he lost control and hacked into her with a heavy weapon."

I had talked to this woman last evening and it was hard to come to terms with what happened to her. Thinking of her gentle father and how distressed he'd be, my anger rose. Jalinta and Elhnora's deaths could not be a coincidence, but the link between them and the working girl eluded me. I caught a glint of steel near one of the wool bales and walked in that direction. A long, thin sword lay broken near a pile of sheepskins. Blood covered the blade.

Golden came and stood next to me. "She fought back. Whoever did this is wounded."

I nodded. "She told me she knew how to handle a rapier."

"There's another thing. She has marks on both arms where somebody held her, but there are four sets of bruises," Golden muttered.

"So, there is more than one killer."

"It certainly looks like it."

Wink called suddenly from the doorway. "The Watch is on the way. We need to go."

On the walk to Rackhime's, I thought of Jalinta's terror as she hung from that beam. She'd shown courage in fighting back, but in the end, was defenceless, hanging from a rope waiting for death to come. In some ways she'd been luckier than Elhnora – when Jalinta's attackers lost control, death would have been swift.

Whoever killed her would be covered in blood. I remembered red footsteps leading to the street and then stopping, so the killers left by horse or cart. It was unlikely they stopped to clean their feet before continuing. I asked Wink to tell Grandfather everything and to ask his contacts if they'd seen anything.

Noble Vernheim broke down when I told him we found his daughter's body. I didn't go into the details but he probably filled in the blanks. The old man curled up into a ball on the floor of Rackhime's shop and wailed. He beat his head on the rough boards until the skin split and blood seeped into his short beard. I held him to prevent further injury while Rackhime patted his shoulder and made soothing noises. The old man's pain washed over the room drenching us in his anguish. Part of me wanted him to stop as I didn't know how to respond. Golden stood looking uncomfortable until I told him to make some tea.

"I told her to be careful! Why wouldn't she listen to me?" the old man screamed, over and over.

There was nothing I could say that would make it any better and I didn't try. Noble Vernheim had one love left in this world and the young girl now hung like a side of beef in a butcher shop.

Eventually, Rackhime took the old man home on a cart and gave him into the care of his cook. Wink arrived just as I finished eating and told me Grandfather wanted to see me now. I was ushered through to his private chamber with haste and found the crime lord striding back and forth in front of a smouldering fire.

"It must be the Dance Master!" he yelled as soon as the door closed.

"I don't know if we can say that."

"You eliminated the Hairy Man, and now you believe there are two killers. At least that is what you told Wink."

I nodded. There was no point in lying, even though I hadn't considered Grandfather would reach the conclusion the Dance Master was behind the killings.

"Two men mean a conspiracy, not a lone crazy, and it all points to my competitors. The most threatening of those is the Dance Master. I know he's wanted to expand out of smuggling and theft for some time. He was never going to be satisfied with a small operation and a couple of hidden gambling dens. I must stop him."

"Slow down." I made myself comfortable in the large leather chair. Grandfather ceased pacing but his face remained red and puffy.

"The two noble girls who knew each other were lovers. I'm sure there's a connection between their deaths, but I haven't found it yet."

"What about Fendria's death?"

I shrugged. There should be a link between the first killing and the others but I couldn't find a single thread that would join them. "Something in this doesn't fit. I'm not sure what it is yet, but I advise you against rash actions. You don't want to start a war with your main rival over nothing."

"Maybe I don't need a reason," Grandfather growled.

"That is up to you. I'm just saying I don't know if the Dance Master is orchestrating these attacks."

He sighed and sat behind his desk. "Up to now, you've been a disappointment, Owl. All you managed to do is tell me that the ex-Hunter is not the killer. I suppose that is one step up on the Watch."

"What do you mean?" I asked.

"Your friend Benton arrested the Hairy Man just before you arrived."

I couldn't believe the stupidity of the City Watch. I thought Captain Waldheigheim was smarter than that. I was going to collect Golden and visit the cells – make my feelings known, but decided my tall friend's presence might not be helpful considering our last encounter with the Watch. Bribing the private on the front desk to let me pass, I barged into the captain's office.

"You seem to have your own key to this building," the captain said without looking up from the scroll he read. His gaze skimmed over the page until he stopped to make a mark with a large quill under some of the words.

"Tearwyn is not the killer."

Captain Waldheigheim put down the parchment and looked up at me. One side of his single eyebrow raised toward his brow and he stood.

"You may leave now. This is not your business."

"You're performing an injustice if you lock up this man."

There was probably nothing else I could say that would have made him listen. He stopped and frowned. "Benton believes he has the killer."

"There are two killers and Tearwyn isn't one of them."

"How do you know there's more than one murderer?"

"I examined the body of Jalinta Vernheim and found an extra pair of finger and thumb bruises on both of her arms. As though a couple strong people had been dragging her at the same time."

The captain's frown deepened. "I'm getting a little tired of your interference, Owl."

"Be that as it may, this shows that it couldn't have been the Hairy Man."

"He might have an accomplice, but that doesn't rule him out. Benton tells me he has a wound that could come from a blade."

I knew how that mark had occurred but hesitated before saying anything, knowing the captain was unhappy with how much interest I had taken in these murders. But the captain noticed my pause.

"What do you know?" he asked.

"Spike put that wound in Tearwyn. We trapped him in an alley just after the heavy snowfall. We were asking him a few questions about the murders."

I told Waldheigheim the conversation that had followed but I left Miranda's name out of the incident, referring to her as "the girl". The captain sat down heavily. "I should throw you in the cells right next to Tearwyn and then get your friend Golden and put him down there as well."

The way he said it I knew he wasn't going to do any such thing.

"But as you know more about this case than my own investigators, that would seem churlish. Do you have any idea who's behind these killings?"

"Not yet, but I think it's connected to the death of the two noble girls. I don't believe in coincidences."

The captain nodded. "Neither do I." He pulled out a fresh parchment and started writing on it. "I'm setting Tearwyn free. You can take this down and release him. I don't know what condition he will be in – Benton is of the old school and was trying to get a confession out of him."

The captain finished writing and stamped the paper with a seal of ink. He handed it to me and looked into my eyes. "If I find you anywhere near this case again. I'll hand you over to Benton myself."

I took the scroll and nodded. He would have to catch me first.

The way to the cells led me down a steep spiral staircase of dark stone into a basement of dripping walls and smoky torches. My eyes adjusted easily and I caught a glimpse of a rat scampering along the wall. I handed my parchment to yet another private. The young man with curly blond hair looked out of place in these stinking tunnels.

"Letting him go, are we? Well, I suppose the captain knows best."

He picked up a huge bunch of keys and led me down another set of stairs to a cell at the end of a corridor. On the way we passed a number of iron doors. Behind me I could hear sobbing or pleading. Waldheigheim's threat began to take on more meaning.

"I don't know if he'll be able to walk," the curly-haired guard said. "The boys were down there with Benton encouraging him to talk. He's tough though. Refused to admit to the killings. I suppose the captain lettin' him go shows why he stayed tight-lipped."

Tearwyn could just walk. I had to keep his arm over my shoulder to support him. One eye had become swollen shut and his lip was split. All of his fingers were bloody and he had bruises over his chest and shoulders. He kept thanking me for freeing him. I told him to save his strength, but then he started to cry. Taking him back to the shop – I didn't know where else to go.

"This isn't a home for strays," Rackhime said as I dragged Tearwyn inside.

"He'll be in my room and I will care for him until he can walk. Then we can put him on a wagon train south."

"Don't know who you'll be bringing in next."

"This is first time you've objected."

"I would just like to be asked once in a while."

"Three or four days and he'll be gone, I promise."

Rackhime muttered something under his breath and went back to copying a manuscript at his workbench. First, I fed the Hairy Man and then washed away some of the blood. Later I gave him some tringal root for the pain and left him to sleep in my bed. Wondering where to lay my head tonight, I decided the floor would be fine. I had slept in a lot worse places when I was a Hunter.

Dinner that night was with Golden at Barnabus's Inn. We sat near the fire and warmed our feet while drinking mulled wine. Spike lay under the table snoring like a troll.

"What am I missing? The two noble girls were lovers and they're dead. That's the connection. But we had Fendra's murder as well – that seems to have no link at all to the other deaths. Each killing is different yet certain facts are consistent. I have no suspects except for the possible involvement of the Dance Master."

"Could Grandfather be caught up in this some way we have yet to discover?" Golden asked.

"I don't think so. He is absolutely convinced that his rival is behind these deaths. If he wanted to start a war with a competing crime lord he wouldn't go to such elaborate lengths to set the stage. He would just launch a surprise attack in the middle of the night."

"Could it be another crazy, or group of crazies, someone we haven't come across yet?"

"Possible but unlikely."

"Well if you think it's linked to the noble girls we better find out more about them," Golden said.

I sipped my drink and mulled over what Jalinta had said to me. She wanted to run away with her lover but Elhnora had recognised that to be impractical. She was about to become betrothed and her world would change forever. I had no idea how she felt about her impending marriage. There was a need to find out more about Elhnora and her place in the society of nobles of Hope. Perhaps, Miranda would know more.

"She laughed a lot and drank heavily though she held her alcohol well." Miranda sat cross-legged on the stool. She'd wrapped a shawl across her shoulders as the chill of the fog crept inside the Mermaid.

"I want to build a picture of her because I'm starting think she is the key to all this," I said.

"Why?" Miranda played with her hair and leaned a little closer.

The smell of her filled my nostrils. I wanted to kiss her, but forced myself to concentrate.

"Jalinta was her lover but she is from an unimportant noble family. Fendra was an out-of-town girl just trying to make her way in the world but Elhnora, like her name, is the star at the centre of this."

"You could be wrong."

I smiled. "That's highly likely."

Miranda's eyes sparked and she reached across and touched my hand. My head spun and wondered what I had gotten myself into.

"You promised me dinner," Miranda said.

"That I did."

"I'm free tomorrow."

"Then I'll take you to Barnabus's for the best curry you can find."

Her hand had not left mine. I felt a shadow and saw Trix out of the corner of my eye. Her face was twisted and eyes red. She didn't stop but walked straight into the gambling room.

"Now I'm in trouble," Miranda whispered.

"No, Trix and I are just friends."

She patted my hand and smiled. "Males are such fools."

I spent the following morning trying to find a way to see Lord Vornhelm. First, I went to his mansion up on the peaks. From his front entrance I had a perfect view of the Devil's Lake and the park that surrounded it. All of the dwellings in this part of Hope stood behind walls. Hedges or wrought-iron fences marked the boundaries of most houses, but Lord Vornhelm's sat behind a stone wall thicker and higher than Grandfather's. I could only make out part of the house through some bare trees inside the compound. The guards at the gate didn't even pretend they were going to deliver my interview request to their employer, merely laughing and waving me away.

After returning to the store, I asked Rackhime if he ever conducted any business with the Vornhelm family. He hadn't. I tried to think of an alternative approach when Trix entered. She looked around nervously before taking a small step toward me.

"Is there somewhere we can talk?"

"I'd say my room, but the Hairy Man is up there."

"You can use the preparation area if the smell doesn't bother you," Rackhime offered.

I took Trix through to a small room out the back of the store where we kept the calfskins. The area stank of the urine used to cure them, but it was warmer than outside.

Trix had bundled up in a scarf and thick cloak. She looked at me with red-rimmed eyes from between a gap in the wool, then entwined her fingers together and stared for a moment. "I am going to give you and Miranda my blessing. I can see the two of you have feelings for each other and I won't interfere. When the fog lifts, I'm traveling south."

I was stunned. "You shouldn't leave. What would I do without you?"

"You seem to be doing just fine."

"But we've shared so many good times. You are always here. Stay!"

"Why?"

What did she mean? The question was ridiculous. Trix was one of my oldest friends in Hope. She didn't judge me and never saw my skin colour. I had confided many of my deepest secrets to her. "That doesn't need answering," I snapped.

The frustration of the day boiled over and my anger focused on Trix.

Her eyes filled with tears. "I didn't come here to argue. Just to take my leave. I'm going to work for a few more days then that's it."

"I won't say goodbye. You should stay. My relationship with Miranda has nothing to do with you. You're being stupid."

She just looked at me, shook her head, and walked away.

"I'll see you tonight and we'll talk about this!" I yelled.

Later I found Tearwyn downstairs eating eggs. Rackhime glared at him and then switched the look to me as soon as I walked into the room.

"Back up to bed, big guy," I said.

"I want to thank you for what you did for me," Tearwyn muttered.

"It was nothing."

"No, it was everything. I would have died in that cell without realising what I was doing. I've had time to think and take a step back from the madness. I owe you my life, Owl."

"Well, you can repay your debt by calling me Ash. The name *Owl* tends to annoy my people."

"My life is yours, Ash, until I even the score. As yet I don't know how I can do that, but I'll find a way."

I had a thought. Tearwyn had been around Docklands at many different times of day.

"Did you seen anything that would help me solve these murders? It might not be something that you considered important at the time, but if you can assist in any way–"

"I told the Watch that I saw a big man follow the second noble girl on the night of her death, but they didn't believe me."

"That confirms what Miranda told me."

"And there's been a different man, one wrapped in black, that I noticed watching the Mermaid. He's hard to see. Excellent at blending with the shadows, but I was a Hunter and I know what to look for. I saw this individual twice."

This was news. I stepped forward and took Tearwyn by both shoulders and looked up into his brown eyes.

"What was his height, eye colour, weapons? Can you describe him? Are you sure it was a man?"

"Yes, I believe the figure was male and probably human. He was of medium height but that is all I could tell. He hid himself well, which is why I noticed him. I think I saw a sword."

I let him go and gestured for him to leave. I barely heard his feet tramp up the stairs as I considered his words. There was another player in this, one who had yet to reveal himself.

My dinner with Miranda was relaxed. We held hands and laughed at our stories. I told her some from my youth, the happier ones, and she told me of her life by the sea. We didn't speak of the murders and I left Trix out of the conversation. I remembered my promise to catch up with her tonight, but convinced myself it could wait until tomorrow. Taking Miranda home dominated my thoughts, but Tearwyn was still in my bed. I kissed her as we walked through the fog until we arrived at her lodgings. We stopped at her door.

"I'd invite you in but I share a room with two other girls," Miranda said.

"And my bed is filled by the Hairy Man."

She smiled. "We can wait. Our time is coming."

I told Golden of the Man of Shadows the next day.

"Should you tell Grandfather?"

"No, he would take it as a sign that the Dance Master has sent spies into the Docklands."

"Maybe he has."

I scratched Spike behind the ears and the dire wolf curled around my thigh.

"He could have, but I'm not saying anything until I know more. I don't want to start a war between the most powerful crime lords in Hope."

"What next, then?"

"I'll go and visit Jalinta's father. See if he can get me an interview with Lord Vornhelm, or if he knows someone who might be able to help."

The weather broke as the cart took me up the peaks into the Noble district. The tunnel-like roads of the lower city gave way to wide boulevards lined by bare trees. The driveway to Sir Vernheim's was more cluttered with debris than on my last visit. An old wagon sat by the entrance, its tray piled high with firewood. Cut branches lay in heaps by the path waiting to be cleared. The kitchen chimney puffed smoke into the air but the others were all unused. I walked to the front door and knocked. After some time, a round-faced lady with red cheeks appeared. She looked me up and down and her eyes grew hard. "We don't want your lot here."

I ignored the insult. "I've come to visit Sir Vernheim."

"He ain't takin' visitors."

"He'll see me."

I pushed past the woman; her face puffed up like the chest of a rooster. "You can't just barge in – I'll call the Watch! Fredrick!"

A one-legged man hobbled from a side doorway. "I've got this Martha, you can go."

The woman stood with hands on hips for a moment before stamping her foot and heading for the kitchen.

"You come at a bad time, Owl. The master isn't doing well, what with the death of his daughter and all."

"That's why I'm here. I want to find this killer and he may be able to help."

Fredrick scratched at his grey stubble, then nodded.

"He's in the study. I was tryin' to breathe some life back into the fire. He just sits in the cold and stares. Hardly eats or drinks. I'm worried for him."

"I'll do what I can." I didn't really know what I could do. Slowly, I walked to the study.

Sir Vernheim sat wrapped in a blanket on an old leather chair. In front of him the fire smoked around some kindling that leaned against a blackened log. Scrolls lay scattered across the floor and maps and books buried the desk. A plate of cold sausages and potatoes lay untouched on the desk.

The old man's eyes flicked up briefly before returning to the fireplace. "If he comes for answers I have none."

"I need to find out if there was a connection between Jalinta, Elhnora, and the first girl that died."

"Does he not think that I thought of this possibility? I searched for meaning and looked for a link."

"Petar, your daughter and Elhnora had been lovers and remained friends. I don't believe their deaths to be a coincidence."

The old man's eyes moved and settled on me, red and raw. "I knew my daughter, and loved her. Her choice of partners never concerned me."

Sighing, I tried to bring the fire to life. I had underestimated the old man. He was more aware of what was going on than I'd thought.

"I have looked for a connection between the different murders without luck."

"Perhaps the Dark Elf seeks for something that doesn't exist."

I straightened. This had not occurred to me. Maybe there was a connection between the deaths of the noblewomen but the first murder wasn't related; perhaps it was almost accidental. "You think that the dancing girl was not supposed to become a victim?"

"There is no link so it would be logical."

I blew on the kindling and a small flame appeared. It grew and I fed larger sticks into the fire.

"I need to see Lord Vornhelm, now more than ever. Perhaps he will tell me more about his daughter. Maybe he even knows what the tattoo on her thigh is about. Can you get me an introduction?"

"The Dark Elf thinks I have influence, but he is mistaken. Great lords see the world as a place filled with bugs which they either crush, or ignore."

I looked at the fire with satisfaction and thought about who could get me an audience with Lord Vornhelm. It would need to be somebody important, and the only two people I knew who fitted that description were in charge of the largest criminal groups in Hope.

Telling Petar to eat and drink, I informed him he was worrying Fredrick. The old man ate one of the sausages and I left him sipping on some warmed milk.

The stable hand smiled at me and handed over my cloak. "It's a start. Now we just need to bring some life to this house," he said.

I nodded and promised I would check in soon.

The fog cleared as I travelled down the hill on a hired cart. A bitter wind picked up from the north and chased the clouds out to sea. In the distance I could see a line of dark thunder heads rolling from the horizon. The weather was about to change and I would need shelter so I moved quickly.

I stepped into Rackhime's shop and found Wink warming himself by the fire. Rackhime sat at his workbench, his face blank.

"There's been another one," the young man said.

8

DESCENT INTO DARKNESS

My heart lurched. I imagined Miranda hanging from a wooden beam with her flesh cut into strips.

"Who?" I asked.

Wink turned away and spat into the fire. "Grandfather's girls don't even give me a look, so how would I recognize one of them? The old man said for you to take a peek, as we ain't told the Watch yet. Grandfather says he wants you to look around. The Watch is useless except the captain, he seems to be good at his job."

"I'll come with you, Ash." Tearwyn stood at the top of the stairs. He had a thick bearskin around his shoulders and boots in hand.

"I think he should," Rackhime said.

I didn't like the sound of that and had the feeling I wasn't being told the full story.

"Take me there."

The tumbledown windmill had been used to grind the city's flour in earlier times. The sails had disappeared and the wooden support on one of the blades broken off. The door was missing and some of the stonework from the top wall removed. The old mill sat away from other buildings on a spit of land that stuck out into the river. Bits of broken barrels and other pieces of refuse floated in the water, near the brick embankment.

I hurried my companions to the building, urging them to greater haste every time they slowed. Wink wouldn't tell me who the latest victim was – anxiety ate at my mind until I could hardly think. Pools of blood and sliced flesh fuelled my fear until I broke into a run. The bitter wind from the north slowed me but I pushed on.

"She ain't going nowhere, and you don't know the way, so slow down," Wink growled.

I yelled at him but he stopped and caught his breath, ignoring me. Two of Grandfather's men stood in the shadows nearby, watching.

"Clear your mind, Owl! You can't help catch her killer when you're like this," Wink said.

Stumbling through the broken doorway was like stepping into a gaping mouth. The light dimmed and it took a second for my eyes to adjust. Trix hung on a rope fixed to a hook in the stones. Her throat was cut and her arms and legs sliced in a dozen places.

The floor seemed to drop from under me. I fell to the ground, wailed, and beat my hands on the ground. My beautiful friend, the first welcoming face I'd seen in Hope, swung in the wind, her eyes lifeless. She stared in shock at a hole in the wall through which the wind blew. I failed again, and this time the price was too high.

Large hands took me by the shoulders and gently pulled me to my feet.

"I remember her," Tearwyn said.

"She was my friend, but we argued. She was going to leave town and travel south."

"That would have been news to Grandfather. He wouldn't 'ave liked that," Wink said.

"Well it don't matter now," Tearwyn said.

I gazed up at her face and felt guilt as bitter as the time I had held

Zenta when her life slipped away outside the Imprisonment cave all those years ago. I had failed two females, and I didn't think there was any way back.

"Do your job, Owl. What killed her?" Wink asked.

I turned and snarled. "A knife, you idiot."

I flew at Wink, fingers outstretched like claws. The young man recoiled in fright and threw both hands in front of his face.

Strong arms grabbed me and hauled backward. "It's not the lad's fault. He doesn't understand. Tearwyn spun me around. "But I do." Tearwyn held me but addressed Wink over his shoulder. "He can't help, not at the moment. I'll take him back to Rackhime's and then I'll get Golden. Why don't you have a look around and I'll meet you outside the Mermaid and you tell me what you've noticed."

Wink's eyes were round and white. He nodded, and then disappeared from my vision as Tearwyn dragged me from that slaughterhouse.

I sobbed as I staggered back to the shop, barely aware of Tearwyn's supporting shoulder. Trix's swinging body burnt into my eyes and her look of surprise and pain crushed me.

Rackhime gave me something to drink. My eyelids grew heavy. Tearwyn lifted me in his arms as I went limp. Some of the tension drained from my limbs.

I woke in the dark, but my pupils expanded quickly.

Outside, the wind howled a lament as it raged between the buildings. Golden slept on the rug by the stairs with Spike curled up at his side. Tearwyn slept in a chair near the window with an old blanket pulled over his lap. His head thrown backward, he snored loudly. I wondered at the presence of my old and new friends and then it all came flooding back. Trix was dead, and I would never see her smiling face again.

I remember the first time we met. Summer. I was so drunk I could hardly walk. Golden had left with a different group of Hunters to explore the Northern Mountains and I refused to go. The death of my companions at the hands of the dragon was still fresh in my mind, and I decided to settle down. Trix had smiled at me and taken me back to Rackhime's. Later I'd bumped into her in the street at Docklands and she'd asked how my head was feeling. She'd always done that, asked about how others were feeling. Sobbing quietly, I pictured her smile. I didn't want to remember her as a swinging corpse hanging from a length of hemp.

"She was a great lady," Golden said.

"I didn't mean to wake you," I muttered.

"That's all right. Between the Hairy Man's snoring and these floor boards I wasn't getting much sleep. On the road, I have slept in the rain or on hard cavern floors. A few days in a city and I get soft."

"Maybe I should take to the roads again. I'm certainly making a mess of it here."

The extended silence made me think Golden wouldn't answer.

"This isn't about you. Nobody could have put this together yet, so stop being so hard on yourself. You do it all the time and it never helps. Anyway, I wouldn't take you on as a Hunter in your present state. You're too messed up. You need to put a stop to these murders and fast. If you can't then we need to find a way to keep Grandfather's girls safe."

I lay back and stared at the thatch roof above my head. My friend was right; the women who worked Dockside needed protection.

"Thanks for coming, Golden."

"You should thank Tearwyn. He brought you back here and sent for me. Says he owes you. I thought he was mad but it's amazing what a spell in the deep cells can do for a man's sanity, though I suppose attaching himself to you means he's not completely cured."

I smiled in the darkness and set my mind to work on finding a way to protect the girls of Dockside.

The following day I gathered as many of the women who worked for Grandfather as I could to Rackhime's shop. The storm had stopped, but it still snowed gently. It was early and most of them wouldn't be due at the Mermaid or other establishments at Dockside until five bells. Many of the women stumbled out of the snow wrapped in expensive cloaks lined with rabbit fur, their cheeks pink. Miranda fell into my arms and we sobbed together.

"I thought it was going to be you," I whispered into her hair.

"And now you feel guilty that I was your first concern," Miranda said.

"Yes, that's one of the things I'm struggling with."

Golden cleared his throat. "The place is filling up," he said. "And Rackhime is running out of tea."

I would have to discuss this with Miranda at another time. The shop was full of some of the most beautiful young women in Hope, except one was missing. My eyes filled and I felt my arm squeezed. Miranda smiled and I nodded back.

I called out to get everyone quiet and then waited.

"I want to take this moment to remember the women who are no longer with us, whether noble or working girl. They didn't deserve this and we honour them."

"We honour them," the crowd chanted.

Everyone bowed their heads.

After some time, I looked up. "The Docklands are not safe so Golden, Tearwyn, and I have come up with an idea that should help. We are inviting all of the girls to stay at a location up on the Devil's Peaks. It is a noble house with plenty of room, and it's very comfortable."

A few of the women looked sideways at Tearwyn, who stood by the fireplace trying to look small, and failing.

"Miranda and I can vouch for the Big Man. Now what I propose is that at the end of each working day everyone meets on the front porch of the Mermaid or just inside its doors. We will take you by cart to the noble's residence and guard you and then bring you back in the morning."

There was muttering among the different groups of women but the tone was pleasant.

"What does Grandfather think of this?" Aneeta asked.

"I'll handle the old man," I said.

"He should be happy that we are safe and guarded. After all, we bring in the customers," Miranda said.

"How will you keep us safe in Docklands?" a dark-skinned girl with short hair asked.

"The Strip where you work is well lit and patrolled by Grandfather's men. As far as we can work out, girls are being snatched when they move outside this area. Don't be tempted into alleys or away from Docklands. There is more than one killer. One suspect goes around garbed in black and is of average height and build, the other is a bigger man with a scar on his chin."

"When does this start?" Stella asked.

"Tonight."

"And where are we staying?" Teel asked.

"At Sir Vernheim's residence."

Old Petar had agreed readily to the idea and set to clearing his house for the new arrivals with renewed energy. When Ash left, Fredrick was lighting fires in all of the rooms and Martha cooked up an enormous pot of stew.

The round-faced lady didn't look pleased when I made my way into the kitchen late that night, but Fredrick's eyes were wide.

The women gathered late in the foyer of the Mermaid and all sixteen who worked for Grandfather took up the offer of protection. It had been difficult to find the necessary beds, but in the end, Tearwyn found them at a number of inns along Martyr's Street, near the City Watch House. The women slept four to a room, with Petar sleeping on a bed in his study. The old man fussed around the women, taking them tea and making sure they had enough to eat and that they were warm.

I patrolled the perimeter of the mansion first with Spike, while Tearwyn sat inside by the wide stairwell that led to the bedrooms of the girls. Golden slept but said he would relieve me at three bells.

Taking watch turned out to be the hardest part. It had been a long day and it was bitterly cold outside. The snow finally stopped, but it was at least as deep as my knees. I understood what Golden meant about city living making you weak. I staggered 'round the house in near-exhaustion, peering into the bushes for any sign of intruders. The cold seeped into my legs and I jumped around to warm them. Golden approached just after the distant chime of the third bell.

"This must be one of the reasons we never went on the hunt in winter," I said.

"That and the fact you're soft," Golden said.

I slumped down on the couch in the study. The sound of Petar's breathing came from the bed and I thought sleep would soon take me. I was wrong. As soon as I closed my eyes, Trix's swinging body jumped into my thoughts. I tried to push it away, but the image refused to go. As light crept back into the sky, Miranda found me sitting in a leather chair in the drawing room staring at the coals of a dying fire. She didn't say anything as she curled up in my lap and held me.

My eyes felt as though someone had filled them with soot and my mood was best described as surly as I decided to go looking for Grandfather the following afternoon. When the women had all been safely delivered to Docklands, I spent the early part of the day organising more food and firewood for Petar. The old man made sure everyone ate as much lunch as they liked, for most slept late. At one point I found Petar showing Miranda his old books.

"We wonder if the Dark Elf knew that the lady can read," he said looking up as I entered his study.

"She will have to teach me as I never learnt."

"But you speak our tongue easily," Miranda said.

"I can read my own language but that is all."

"We could teach him, fair lady. Then I could instruct you in dwarven," Petar said.

Miranda laughed and threw back her head. "I do love it when he calls me my Lady."

The sight jabbed me in a way I didn't expect. I saw Trix's throat and the red line that marred the white skin. I turned away.

"We're leaving soon," I said as I left the room.

"You never do well when you've missed out on sleep," Golden said.

I grunted at him as I scanned the road. Grandfather wasn't at his fortress and had taken a large group of his followers toward Red Market Square. This was the Dance Master's territory. The guards at the Mermaid told me something was afoot – Grandfather told his men to make sure they were fully armed today. I regretted not going to see him earlier, but there were only so many bells in a day. Maybe Golden was right and I was too hard on myself.

I caught up to the old man at the corner of Fish Street and Temple's Way. He brought sixty or more hard men and women with him, all armed with weapons of different varieties. As I approached him, at least four crossbows levelled at me. Golden's blade slid from its scabbard with a metallic scrape and saw Tearwyn take his new axe from the strap on his back. Spike growled deep in his throat but Grandfather held up his hand and the crossbows lowered.

"You took your time finding me. I suppose you realise that Trix's death points in one direction," Grandfather said.

I shook my head. "I don't understand what it means, but if you want to start a war, I can't stop you."

Part of me didn't care anymore. If Grandfather was cut down or the Dance Master caught a stray bolt in his throat it wouldn't really matter. The thugs and thieves who surrounded both men could slaughter each other. It was only the girls I worried about, and they were safe now.

"Then you've come to join us, to avenge the death of Trix. I thought the two of you were close," Grandfather said.

He kept walking as he spoke. I had to fall in next to him to continue the conversation.

"I'm here to tell you that I've made arrangements to keep the girls safe from these killers until I find out who they are."

"You're lucky that your plans help me. I want to make sure the girls are safe as well, but you should have checked this out with me first. Where are they staying?"

I hesitated and realised I didn't want the Old Man to have that information. There wasn't a reason he shouldn't, but I wanted to irritate him, to nibble at his sense of power and entitlement.

"It is best if I don't tell you. That way it can't leak out."

"You go too far, Owl. What's to stop me or the Dance Master following you?"

"If you think your men can outfox three of the best Hunters that the Eastern Wilds have ever seen, then you're welcome to try."

The Grandfather grunted. "It won't matter after today. We'll storm the Dance Master's quarters and put him to the sword."

"Do you think it'll be that easy? He's been gathering men too. Your approach will have been noted and preparations made. What about the Watch and the Knights of the Citadel?"

"I'm not a fool, Owl. This is not the only force that approaches the Dance Master's territory. As for the Dogs of the Watch, they've been paid to take their time, and the knights will not find their way to the fray until the deed is done."

Our discussion took us along Fish Street and into the Red Market. The area was empty. Grandfather stopped and waved some men armed with bows forward.

They hadn't gone far when the shutters on the northern side of the square opened and a rain of bolts hit the advancing group. Men screamed and fell onto the snow, splattering it with their blood. Others drew bowstrings to ears and returned fire. A man lurched forward and hung from a window like an old sheet.

Golden whispered a word and an area in front of us swirled with sudden wind, scattering a number of bolts that had been sent in our direction. Men holding weapons appeared from alleyways on the other side of the square and charged forward, screaming. Grandfather yelled a command and his followers answered the challenge with a roar of their own. Soon the area was full of figures cutting and striking at each other.

It was impossible not to become involved. I saw Golden catch a descending mace on his blade and flick it away. He continued the stroke, reversing it upwards and hitting the man on the bottom of the chin. The stroke continued through the face exiting at the top of the skull. Tearwyn battered aside the buckler of a tall thin man and then chopped him to the ground in a flurry of blows. A sword lanced toward Golden's back but Spike grabbed the offending arm and tore it off the man in a spray of blood.

I stared at Grandfather. His face blanched. Close Combat was not what he expected. There was obviously more blood than he thought, at least near him. He backed away from the combat signalling two of his largest guards to cover his retreat.

A screaming man stabbed at me with a short spear but I stepped aside. He over committed and I grabbed the shaft of the weapon and pulled him close. The Cold Blade was in my hand and I thrust it into the man's chest. It slid through his chain vest as though it were paper and plunged into his heart. He fell, blood pouring from his mouth.

The scene became one of heaving bodies locked in combat. A fresh group erupted from a side street and joined the battle. Grandfather's back-up force had arrived. A ball of fire erupted among them, turning three into pillars of flame. The Dance Master must have a magician on the payroll. He or she wouldn't be able to cast again for a while, until they gathered the necessary power. Men and women fell quickly and a number of them lay piled around Tearwyn and Golden.

Over on the far side of the square, a heavily muscled dwarf chopped down a number of Grandfather's thugs with his axe. Tickles surrounded himself with three other dwarves and they cut their way across the square.

"This is not our battle. We need to get out of here!" I yelled at Golden.

He glanced at me, but I could see the battle lust had taken him.

"Tearwyn, grab Golden. It's time to leave."

The Hairy Man didn't even look at me as he cut down a short man wearing a leather apron. I rolled my eyes. I'd have better luck getting through to Spike.

Then Tickles stood in front of Golden.

"I have dreamed about this day," the dwarf said.

He raised his axe, but my tall friend sidestepped and brought his blade around in an arc. Tickles caught it on the shaft of his weapon and then jumped backward. Both antagonists eyed each other, readying themselves for the next attack.

We heard the knights just before they burst into the square. Their huge mounts knocked over men and women. Hooves thudded into soft flesh. Swords rose and fell and both the forces of Grandfather and the Dance Master ran.

The knights didn't discriminate. Their blades cut people as they pushed into alleyways or crouched in doorways. Some of the thieves fought back. A crossbow fired from an upper window and an armoured man tumbled to the ground clutching at his shoulder. He stood and clawed at the bolt that had found a gap between two pieces of metal plating and then punched through the links of his chain mail. Another man, dressed in furs and leather, hit him from behind with a large mallet and the knight fell. I lost sight of him as he disappeared among the swirling bodies.

Tickles tumbled away from Golden as the horses came between them. A knight slashed at the dwarf with a long sword but it caught on the blade of the axe and rebounded. Tickles chopped into the man's thigh, splitting the chain links protecting the knight's leg and cut deeply into flesh. The man howled. His mount spun, kicking the air with its hooves. Golden backed away from the thrashing horse and glanced around.

"Time to go," I snarled.

I whistled for Spike, who bounded through the swirling mass. Tearwyn appeared covered in blood and panting.

"The Watch has arrived," he wheezed.

"This way," I said.

We ran. Snow made the street slick. We skidded and fell but regained our feet and fled once more. Only the wolf seemed to say on his feet. Once we were out of the square and in a side alley, the noise of the battle died away. I urged everyone to keep moving. The Knights of the Citadel would kill anyone who crossed their path. The nobles who kept order would think nothing of killing the unwashed swill of the lower city. They wanted to maintain control and the cost in blood was immaterial to them.

The shop was a welcome sight. I had to hammer on the door to get Rackhime to let us in. He closed the business when he heard the horns calling the Knights to make ready for battle, and cranked and loaded an old crossbow.

As he dropped the bar into the brackets to relock the door, he looked us over.

"Golden and Tearwyn, go and wash off the blood, and make sure you clean the wolf's muzzle as well. If the Watch turn up we want to look as though no one has been in a fight. Hide your weapons, too!"

We all rushed to obey, and soon hot water was available and clothes were being scrubbed. Rackhime watched the streets from a small hole in the wall near the front door. A little later, cavalry came cantering down the street. A loud voice yelled that the city would be placed under curfew at dark and that it would remain that way for the following day.

"We need to get the girls up onto the Peaks before the city is shut down," I said.

Golden pulled a clean shirt over his head and picked up his Cold Blade.

"No weapons. We have to do this unarmed. The Watch will have set up roadblocks and we can't draw any attention to ourselves. Spike will have to stay under cover in the wagon or not come," I said.

"We can't go out unable to defend ourselves," Golden said.

"We can fight unarmed if we need to. I'm trained and you have your rings. I'm sure Tearwyn is handy with his fists. Take some daggers but keep them hidden."

"I can handle myself," the big man said.

"I'd wait to three bells before you go. Just to give people's blood a little time to settle. Those knights are probably still riled up and ready for a fight," Rackhime said.

The advice made sense. We dressed in fresh clothes, hid a number of knives and daggers around our bodies, and then we waited.

The sound of the bells took forever. As soon as we heard the first chime we were on the move.

The women waited in the front room of the Mermaid. Miranda and Teel had gathered them all as soon as the battle at Red Market Square became common knowledge.

"I thought you'd come," Miranda said. She sprang down onto the road as Tearwyn pulled the wagon to a halt.

"We need to go now." I motioned for the girls. "Before they close down the city. We can't protect you if you scatter back to your old accommodation."

"That's what Teel and I told everyone. They are ready. A few of us have collected some extra food and clothes as we might not be able to move around much for the next few days."

I smiled at her. She and Teel had done well – gathering all the women in one place was going to save a lot of time. They had even managed to talk the security at the Mermaid into giving them a few weapons. I was going to leave the extra equipment behind when Stella suggested they hide it under the women's spare clothes.

"There were no roadblocks on the way here, but our luck can't last," Golden said.

As the women scrambled into the wagon, one of them squealed and jumped back. The head of a large wolf appeared from the tray. It regarded everyone with calm yellow eyes and then yawned.

"Spike needs to ride under cover with you. That way he's less likely to spook the Knights or the Watch," I said.

"He is just a big dog, girls. Pay him no mind," Miranda said.

She climbed in first and gave Spike a scratch behind the ears, which he tolerated. Slowly the horses started to clop along the cobble stones.

The wagon creaked as Tearwyn urged the two horses up the snowy incline. We'd just passed the end of Fish Street when we saw a roadblock set between a wine merchant's house and a bakery. Members of the Watch regarded us from behind an overturned wagon. Barrels and crates blocked the other half of the road.

"Nobody is to be outdoors," a young man with a thick beard said. His blue cloak was wet with snow where it dragged on the ground. He looked cold and on edge.

"The knights said the city wasn't closing until nightfall," I said pleasantly.

The Watchman squinted at the sun as it hovered just above the horizon.

"I just need to keep you here a little longer and it'll be time for you to be off the road."

His eyes were hard and his hand strayed to his sword hilt. Behind the barrels crouched men with heavy crossbows aimed in our direction.

"Is there a problem?" Miranda jumped down from the wagon. Teel and Stella followed her onto the road. I noticed Stella had thrown her cloak back, exposing cleavage and neckline. The Watchman relaxed and his hand moved away from his blade. Behind the barricade the crossbows dropped.

"I'm sorry, but the road is closed until further notice. Those are our orders. There has been much blood spilt today in Hope by criminal gangs. It's not safe to be on the street."

"But we need to get to our lodgings on the Peaks." Stella leaned forward.

An older man carrying a mace wandered forward.

"And what would a bunch of whores be doing staying among the good folk of the Peaks?" he growled.

Stella took a step backward, as did the first guard. I felt a surge of anger at the man's choice of words.

"We have lodging up there provided by Sir Vernheim. He will vouch for us," Miranda said.

I wished she hadn't told the Sergeant where we were staying, but I understood her reasoning. We needed to establish why we were travelling up into the area.

"Never heard of him. Now turn this wagon around and get off the roads before I lock you up."

Golden moved up next to me and I saw those different-coloured eyes staring at the Sergeant. "You've got no reason to turn us around. Curfew doesn't start until the sun disappears. You're just being a bastard."

My friend was right, but sometimes I wish he would keep his mouth shut.

"And what if I am, pretty boy? What are you going to do about it?"

I saw a dangerous smile touch Golden's lips. The Watchman had underestimated him. I had no doubt that even without the Cold Blade he and Spike would carve the twelve men guarding the roadblock into little pieces. The three rings on his left hand contained enough power to blow the barricade into matchsticks. They would then be useless, not that it would matter to those who'd been killed by their magic. But what then? With the city on high alert, every member of the Watch and the Knights would be looking for us.

I was just about to step between the two men and suggest that we turn the wagon around when a clear voice rang out.

"Is there a problem, Sergeant?" Captain Waldheigheim sat on a bay mare a little off to the right of the wagon. He'd approached unheard with the snow and conversations.

"Just telling these whores and their pimps to turn around and go home."

"Pimps!" Golden's frown deepened.

"I prefer to call them working girls, Sergeant. And as to the males, they may be many things but they are certainly not pimps."

The captain sat on his horse with a straight back. His dark-blue cloak hung over its rump as though he attempted to share some of its warmth with the animal. Waldheigheim's dark eyes regarded me from under his single eyebrow and he eased his mount toward me. "What brings you out on such a dangerous evening, Owl?"

"My name is Ash, Captain."

He inclined his head slightly and nodded. "Indeed, it is. I have been told that your people don't like the name Owl, though some people consider the bird an animal of wisdom."

"You gave us the name because of our eyes, and they're not that big."

"It is all a matter of perspective I suppose. However, you have a name and courtesy dictates I should use it."

I decided to take a chance. Of all the members of the Watch in Hope, Captain Waldheigheim was the most honourable, though that came off a low base.

"Sir, with the deaths of a number of working girls near the Docklands, one who was a dear friend, I thought it a good idea to gather them together in one place and find somewhere safe for them to stay."

I explained my plan to the captain and even trusted him with the location of the safe house.

He bent forward and patted his horse's neck. It snorted, blowing out a cloud of steam. "A prudent precaution. One I would have thought the Grandfather would have taken some time back."

"He has had other matters on his mind," I muttered.

"Speaking of which you weren't at–"

He stopped. I believed he was going to ask if I had any involvement in the violence that had occurred earlier in the day, but like any good officer of the law, he didn't ask a question he didn't want to identify the answer to.

"Never mind. I will grant you passage and escort you to the lodgings of the women."

I breathed out slowly and felt the tension drain away. Then I thought of something.

"The sergeant and the other trooper will know where the girls are staying. If anyone comes a-calling, I'll know who to blame."

The captain stiffened. "There is no need for threats, Ashley."

Then he sighed and looked away. "Though I do take your point. I will warn both men and put them on notice that their discretion is expected."

I nodded, then smiled. "It's just Ash, by the way."

"I rather like the sound of Ashley. I think it will stick."

I always hated that name and hoped the captain would revert to calling me Owl again.

The sergeant frowned when ordered to move the barrels and crates aside. Captain Waldheigheim was as good as his word and got us through another roadblock before delivering us to Sir Vernheim's residence.

He pulled me aside as the women gathered their possessions and disappeared into the house. "So, Grandfather thinks that the Dance Master is behind these deaths."

"I thought you didn't want me interfere in this matter anymore?"

The beginnings of smile touched the captain's lips. "Just don't get caught doing it." Waldheigheim laughed with surprise. I didn't think this man was capable of having a sense of humour.

"He thinks that, yes."

"But you don't."

"Something doesn't fit. Each death is different. The two noble girls were butchered, though there are even some differences there – both Trix and Fendria were only cut up a little bit."

"First names, hmm – you were obviously close to these girls."

"Especially the last one."

"Then I hate to bring it up, but why do you think the working girls were less-cut up? Maybe this will help your distress. We understand the last girl was already dead when her assailant started to cut her. There was very little blood you see."

Trix was dead before her murder started to carve into her; strangely, it did help.

"We are missing something, Captain. The two noble girls were lovers and I don't believe in coincidences, yet how that fits with the less-brutal deaths of the others, I can't tell."

"I didn't know they were lying together. Did the tattoo on Lord Vornhelm's girl match her dead girlfriend's name?"

"I asked Jalinta's father for possible pet names and nothing matched. Who Ak is remains a mystery to me."

The captain stared off into the darkness. "And we can't even tell if it's important."

"Every piece of the puzzle is important, Captain."

He smiled. "I wish you would speak to some of my investigators – they don't see it that way."

The compliment warmed me on that cold winter's night and gave renewed hope.

"We will find these killers, Ashley, and when we do, they will see the end of a noose." With that he turned his horse and cantered along the snow-covered road into the night. I turned and headed for my own bed.

Weak sunshine woke me late the following day. After finishing my stint on guard duty, I collapsed into an exhausted sleep. The laughter of women pulled me from the couch into the dining room. Stella and

Teel sat on a low bench while Golden played a lute. At every note, Spike would start to howl and the girls would laugh.

"No wonder I woke up."

"It is past eleven bells," Miranda said.

"He always likes to sleep late when he can," Golden said.

Miranda sat by the window and the sunlight streamed in around her. My breath caught in my throat and I thought for a heartbeat that one of the fairy queens had found her way from the realm of the fey into our world. She smiled at me and stood.

"Would you like some food?"

Realising how hungry I was, I nodded.

"There's some bacon, and if I ask Martha nicely, she may cook you some eggs. She is really not too ferocious if you handle her carefully."

The day was one of the most carefree I'd experienced in many years. The city was on lockdown, so we couldn't go anywhere and none of us really wanted to. Petar read to some of the women in his study while Golden and Spike played run ball outside with Stella, Teel and a thin, petite girl named Cassie. From what I could tell, Golden allowed himself to be tackled a lot more often than he would have in a real game. I sat and watched while Miranda combed my long white hair.

"When your people came to my fishing village to trade I would dream of going with them," she said.

"Why?"

"They were so exotic and proud. They seemed to be free compared to my life of drudgery."

"The society of my people is not as free as you would imagine. We are forever bound by our families and our every action is measured. If you are seen as failing your family, you are cast out."

"Is that what happened to you?"

I could visualise the hard faces of the tribunal staring down at me. I sighed. My sister and brother turned away and my father ripped the snow leopard badge from my cloak.

"It's too nice a day to speak of dark memories. What I've always wanted to understand is where you learnt to read and why you don't speak like the other girls."

"Well, since you seek to change the subject, your people are part of the answer. I wanted to find out more about the world and you can't do that if you don't read. As soon as I started to work in Southran I saved some coin to pay for lessons. The old cleric who taught me said he wouldn't help me unless I focused on speaking properly and learnt some manners. Now, I could pass for a noblewoman at the tables of the rich if I wanted to. Later, I moved north."

"And met me."

"The most important day of my life."

I could hear the laughter in her tone and turned and kissed her. She slid into my arms and we remained locked together for what seemed like a day.

"When you two come up for air, Tearwyn is back. He has news," Golden said.

The big man had sneaked through town to Rackhime's shop to check that the old man was safe. It been a dangerous undertaking, but Tearwyn was happy to do it. He also brought back a side of lamb and a bag of carrots. Spike followed him into the kitchen before being chased away by Martha. Even the wolf was in awe of her.

"The roads are opening tomorrow," he said. "Word is that Grandfather and the Dance Master's people both took heavy casualties. They're lickin' their wounds. The streets are full of knights and the Watch but the armoured men will return to the Citadel at dawn."

The big man stopped and stared at me. He looked away nervously. "Grandfather has arranged for Trix's funeral. It will be on the river just before dark, out on the ice. Wink said that Ash is welcome and whoever else can come."

"Let him try and stop us," Golden said.

"He also said that the girls are all expected back at work by four bells after high sun, otherwise he'll come looking for them."

9

THE FUNERAL

The boat sat on the ice a hundred paces from shore. Underneath my feet, the surface of the river occasionally flexed. I knew from experience the ice was thick enough to take the weight of a warhorse.

Trix lay in the boat covered in dried flowers mixed with incense. Grandfather had spared no expense for the funeral, and I heard later he wanted to make a gesture "to his girls". Oil-soaked wood rested around her body, clothed in a high-necked green dress – her favourite colour. All of the women were there, as was Grandfather and a retinue of guards. Golden and Tearwyn stood with me near the women. We left Spike back with Rackhime as he had tried to bite the crime boss the one and only time they'd met. An act which raised my estimation of the wolf's intelligence considerably.

Everyone bundled themselves in thick cloaks of wool, though many of the mourners had capes made from rabbit or fox furs. Tearwyn wrapped his body in the pelt of a brown bear. It looked warm. I envied him. Grandfather wore a leather cloak lined with wolverine fur, and sheepskin boots. He smiled at the girls, pretending he was some benign benefactor.

The Cleric of Narkull, the Black God, led a procession of four grey-robed figures onto the ice. They chanted their prayers in an unknown language while pounding small drums made from the skin of jackals. Eventually, the men gathered around the boat surrounding Trix in her bed of tinder and flowers. The Cleric stood at the bow with a burning torch in his hands. He placed a coin in Trix's hand and wished her swift passage through the Never Ending Realms to the Fields of Eternal Rest. With a final yell, he threw his brand into the boat and stepped back. The fire took on the oil-soaked wood, spreading fast. Trix disappeared into the flames.

The smell of sandalwood and incense filled my nose, bringing to mind Trix's rosewater perfume. I could see her smiling at me across the bar and pulling my boots off after she'd brought my drunken form back to Rackhime's. Tears overflowed and I wished she'd rise from the fire. A surge of guilt hit me and I sobbed. "I should have saved you," I whispered.

Miranda stood next to me and squeezed my hand.

I felt angry but wasn't sure with who or why. Pulling away I scowled.

"Is she always going to come between us?" Miranda asked.

I should have said nothing, I should have reassured her, but instead, I drove a sword through our relationship.

"Yes," I answered.

Then, like most males, I compounded the problem. I strode away from her. If I could take back that moment I would, but not even the gods can reverse the flow of time. I left her standing by herself, pale and alone, while I went towards the fire. The heat melted the ice and pools of water lay around the vessel. Soon the stern disappeared into the river with a hiss and sank, taking Trix away in a cloud of steam.

When I turned, Teel and Aneeta held Miranda. I couldn't see her face – it was hidden in the hood of her cloak – but Aneeta gave me a stare that furrowed her brow. I moved over to Grandfather and his men.

"A good send-off," the old man said.

I ignored the self-congratulations and looked at his bodyguards, some of whom carried minor wounds.

"What's next?" I asked.

"We have a wake. I've organised a gathering at the Black Duck near the East Gate."

"I know the place, but that's not what I meant."

Grandfather frowned. "That is none of your business. As far as I'm concerned, the matter is closed. I have no doubt that the Dance Master is behind the deaths and have responded accordingly. We're at war, and the conflict will continue until one of us is dead. And I can tell you, it won't be me."

"Two things, Grandfather. I'm not sure the Dance Master is behind these murders, and I wouldn't underestimate him if I were you. He climbed to the top of the smugglers at a very young age."

"He's inexperienced and doesn't have the contacts I've cultivated among the nobility. As for the deaths of my girls, that no longer concerns you."

"I hope you don't mind if I keep protecting them?"

Grandfather scratched at his beard. "That suits me, for now. The Battle at the Red Market has left me a little short on muscle, so you can continue to hide them. They are valuable to me."

"Like your coat and your gems," I said.

Grandfather's face flushed and one of his thugs stepped forward. My hand slipped under my cloak and felt for the hilt of my Cold Blade.

The old man's arm shot out and blocked his bodyguard's approach. The big man froze but didn't take his eyes off me.

"Ash has lost a dear friend and is upset. This is a funeral and we all need to respect the dead. We wouldn't want a restless spirit trapped in the Grey Realms because we interrupted the death rites, would we?"

Turning away, I felt my pulse quicken and tightness in my throat. Inwardly cursing at my lack of self-control, I noticed Tearwyn and Golden looking over at me. My tall friend raised an inquiring eyebrow but I shook my head. I'd let my emotions rule me. Had damaged my relationship with Miranda and almost come to blows with the Grandfather's hired help.

Golden wandered over and put his hand on my shoulder. "Let's get a drink."

I nodded and followed him away from the ragged wound in the ice.

The Black Duck didn't dominate the street, but its taproom always drew me in. Oil lanterns and beeswax candles gave the room a cheery glow. The fireplace added to the light as coal burned slowly in its depths. The smell of spices and cooking fish made my mouth water as I moved to the bar.

At the far end of the long room, the women gathered on a low couch. Some had pulled over a chair. I kept my distance. I felt Miranda's eyes searching for me but I didn't trust myself to approach her. The bar had been emptied for the wake and Grandfather allowed his thugs to drink, though he warned them to take it easy.

A couple of the men wandered down to the women and tried to engage them in conversation, but only Stella seemed willing to talk. Before long, three bodyguards had clustered around her and she smiled at each in turn as they bought her drinks. I shook my head and got warm cider for my friends.

"Did you get anything for Miranda?" Golden asked.

"I think it would be wise if I kept my distance."

My friend fixed me with his blue and green eyes as his mouth became a thin line. "What did you do?"

"Told her that Trix would always be between us," I sighed.

"You're an idiot," Golden said flatly.

"I know."

"That girl wants to be with you. Don't throw that away. As one who has loved and not seen it returned, it's not something that you should do lightly," Tearwyn said.

"She's the best thing that's happened to you in years. Fix it," Golden added.

"Thanks for all the advice, but I'd appreciate it if you both dropped the matter."

There was a moment of awkward silence but I knew they wouldn't speak of it again unless I brought it up.

Golden changed the subject. "So where are we at with the investigation?"

"Well, Grandfather has decided the matter is over and the Dance Master is behind everything."

"And what do you think?" Tearwyn said.

"It could be another crime lord – I mean, the murders certainly have led to a drop-off in business at Dockside – but I'm not convinced. I've even started to wonder about the Old Man." I dropped my voice to a whisper. "These deaths have given him the perfect excuse to attack the Dance Master. At first, I thought it unlikely one crime lord would need an excuse to attack the other, but when Grandfather reminded me of his contacts in the nobility, I became suspicious. If he needs outside help in this, then maybe he would have to convince his backers he was attacked."

"Then there's the death of the two noble girls, and the differences in the killings," Golden said.

"I need to know more about the second victim. Elhnora Vornhelm is still a mystery."

"I'll talk to some of the bodyguards and see what I can turn up," Tearwyn said.

"Keep it subtle," I muttered.

He rolled his eyes. "I might be big and hairy and slightly insane, but I'm not stupid."

I watched as my new friend wandered toward a group of bodyguards with a smile.

"I think I might go and spoil Stella's fun. She's got those men on a string. I wonder if I can turn the game around," Golden said.

"That would appeal to your warped sense of humour, wouldn't it?"

He smiled and glided across the room.

I decided to push Grandfather a bit further. Naming him as a suspect in the death of his own girls, I needed to confirm my suspicions or eliminate him as the possible murderer. Thelkar and Rantillious stood near him, both nursing ales. The bigger man squeezed his meaty fingers inside a dirty bandage around his hand. The other man was immaculate in his black leather and high boots.

Grandfather's eyes narrowed as I approached and I knew I hadn't been forgiven.

"You are certain the Dance Master is behind all this then?"

Grandfather nodded slowly, never taking his eyes off me. "He has motive, and the presence of two killers points the finger of blame firmly in his direction. I always thought it was him, but the death of the second girl threw me off for a while."

"The fact that the two noble girls used to be lovers doesn't bother you?"

"An irrelevant coincidence. They were just in the wrong place and the murderer took advantage of the confusion their deaths would create."

Rantillious signalled he was going to check the guards outside. Grandfather nodded.

"So, you're sure that your friends in the nobility will back you, seeing that the Dance Master started this?"

"I'm positive, but I own my contacts, they're not friends. They usually follow my lead, if they know what's good for them."

The door burst open and four men dressed in tight-fitting black-and-grey outfits charged into the room. Each man's face was covered by scarves. They carried short blades.

The first of Grandfather's bodyguards died as a dagger slashed across his throat. The dead man spun into the bar, knocking over drinks and spraying blood in all directions. The women screamed. Golden drew his Cold Blade, held it in two hands, and stood before them.

A second man died as a short sword thrust into his lower chest.

Tearwyn grabbed one of the masked men by both wrists. They tumbled to the floor in a tangle of furniture. Two of the assassins dispatched the guards. Telkar charged forward but a crossbow bolt flew from the shadows and hit him between the eyes.

The men moved toward Grandfather. I should have moved out of the way and given encouragement, but reflexes took over. My Cold Blade sung as I pulled it out. I parried a number of thrusts while imagining a dark winter's night. I caught the final feint on my sword and sent a pulse of freezing energy down the man's weapon. His fingers frosted and blackened but he continued to hold the short sword. The pain must have been unbelievable. He jabbed at my throat. I rolled aside but felt the blade slice my flesh. Golden sprang away from the girls, severing my assailant's arm with a single blow. The assassin's blood pumped from the stump and sprayed me in the face. I finished him with a quick thrust into his neck.

"Vultures! Watch their daggers, they'll be poisoned." Golden yelled.

The two bodyguards who'd been talking to Stella attacked one man and chopped him to the floor with their long swords. The second assassin confronted the guards whose longer weapons got tangled in the combined space. The attacker jabbed his dagger into the forearm of the tallest guard and looked over his shoulder. The bodyguard clutched at the wound and then his eyes rolled back as the poison flowed.

"Take the shot," the assassin yelled into the shadows.

Golden had switched to a pair of daggers and helped the surviving bodyguard. Tearwyn still rolled around on the floorboards with the other assassin. I saw clearly through the darkness. Rantillious raised a crossbow and aimed it straight at Grandfather. I threw my weapon at him. Watched it spin across the room. It wasn't accurate – short swords are not made to be thrown. The Cold Blade hit him in the wrist, almost cutting it from his arm, just as he pulled the trigger. The shaft flew sideways toward the crowd of women. Rantillious turned and fled. Golden killed the last of the Grey Vultures with a swift thrust to the chest as Tearwyn snapped the neck of the man on the floor.

"Ash, help!" Teel yelled.

I turned and saw Miranda. She sat with a crossbow bolt pinning her arm to the wall, her face pale. I looked on with horror, glued to the floor. Then my time treating wounded Hunters in the forests and hills of the east flooded back to me. I was at her side with Golden and we gently prised the shaft from the wood panelling. My blond friend then pushed the bolt through the flesh before sniffing the point.

"Cobra venom. The tip is poisoned."

"We need an antidote," I said.

I turned and stared at Grandfather. He looked at the carnage around him without moving. I knew he'd have the cures to most poisons back at his mansion. The women sobbed softly. Teel hushed them and told them to stay where they were.

"Do you have a cure?" I yelled.

The man looked at me for a moment and then his eyes narrowed.

"Rantillious betrayed me. I will kill him and his family. I bet the guards I left outside are dead, too."

"Forget about that. Miranda is poisoned and will die without a cure."

Grandfather's eyes clouded. "Those antidotes are expensive."

I crossed the room and snatched up my Cold Blade, then turned and held it at the old man's throat.

"I saved your life, though I don't know why. You will get me the cure or this blade is going through your throat."

To his credit, he didn't flinch. "If you kill me then she will die, too."

"Then you'll join her, but I'll make sure it is slower for you."

The remaining bodyguard stepped toward us.

"I wouldn't if I was you," Tearwyn growled.

The man froze and then retreated toward the wall.

Grandfather sighed. "You're right. I owe you a life and I pay my debts. I'm fairly sure I have a cure for cobra venom." He crossed to the bar and tore some parchment from a notice on the wall and then got some charcoal from the edge of the fire. He wrote a quick note, poured some beeswax on the material, pressed his ring into the liquid, and handed it to his guard.

"Take this to Simon and ask that he is quick. The poison's fast-acting."

Golden wrapped a scarf tightly around the wound and laid Miranda on the couch. She moaned softly. The sound pulled at me. Tearwyn dragged all of the bodies into the back alley, helped by the barman. He confirmed the guards stationed outside were dead.

"The Watch will be here soon, and I'd prefer not to be around when they arrive," Grandfather said.

I gave him a single nod, my eyes never leaving Miranda. He slipped from the room and disappeared without another word.

The Watch arrived before the antidote. I had to pay a number of bribes in order to stop Benson and his squad taking everyone into custody. As he questioned the girls, the tall bodyguard burst through the door with a small vial of clear liquid. Benson intercepted the man and snatched the antidote from him. I crossed the room and twisted it from his grasp. The other members of the Watch moved toward me but Tearwyn and Golden blocked their path.

I tipped the liquid down Miranda's throat while snarling, "It's the cure, you idiot. Sent by Grandfather."

"Why should I believe you?" Benson held his wrist.

"Why would we lie? You know the funeral took place and the crime lords are at war. The Dance Master must have decided this was the perfect chance to strike at his enemy."

"And why are you here?"

"Ask the captain, and if you have any other questions, he knows where to find me."

The Watch trooped out a little later after helping themselves to a few drinks, leaving the innkeeper to organise the disposal of the bodies.

Miranda's breath became shallow, but at least colour returned to her cheeks.

"You're wounded?" she asked.

I felt at my neck and my fingers came away covered in blood. "It's not mine – well, most of it's not."

She nodded, her eyes half-closed. "I know you're a little confused and angry right now, but you didn't have to get someone to shoot me." She smiled to take the sting out of the words.

"I don't know what got into me. I should have let Rantillious kill the old man."

"I forgive you. The question is, will you ever forgive yourself."

I stood and walked to the bar. I faced away from her and pressed my hands into the woodwork until my knuckles turned grey. Why did I keep making these mistakes?

We moved Miranda and all the girls back up to Petar's residence on the Peaks before dark. Grandfather wasn't insisting they all turned up to work at four bells anymore, though I knew he'd want them there tomorrow. Golden put a bandage around my neck after rubbing greasy ointment on the wound.

"It wasn't a poisoned blade but the cut may need stitches."

"I'll recover."

"Maybe, but keep an eye on it."

"Do you think Miranda will be all right?"

Golden shrugged. "I think so, but it's hard to tell. She should rest for a Ten Day. We got the antidote into her quickly."

"I should have let Rantillious shoot the old man."

"In the heat of battle, our reflexes take over. It's what keeps us alive in the wilderness."

"But the shot hit Miranda."

"What? Can you see the future now? How could you know that the bolt would fly in that direction? It could have just as easily gone into the roof."

I knew Golden was right, but I couldn't get the sight of Miranda with her arm pinned to the wall out of my head.

We loaded her and the other women gently onto the wagon and took them up the hill to Petar's house. Golden and Tearwyn carried Miranda on a makeshift stretcher to a bed in the front study. Petar stoked the fire and fussed around her until my friend chased everyone from the room. He then left the two of us alone.

"I heard Golden at the inn and he's right. That bolt could have gone anywhere," she said.

"But it didn't. It hit you instead of Grandfather. This is not the first time in my life a snap decision has almost killed someone I…"

Miranda smiled and her eyes fluttered as she fought off sleep. "Can't you say it, Ash? That you love me. I think I knew how I felt from the moment I first saw you."

I looked at the floor, unwilling to meet her eyes. It didn't matter if I loved her, because Trix's ghost cast a shadow over us. My past also paralysed me, as did my ability to hurt those close to me.

"Will you put your fears aside and just be with me, Ash?"

Tears filled my eyes as I strode from the room.

———

Golden found me later sitting in the cold, dark barn. Snow fell lightly, carpeting the branches of the trees and covering the cut timber that lay in piles on the ground. He put a steaming bowl of lamb stew next to me and then started to eat his own. "That old cook might be a dragon, but she certainly knows how to make an excellent meal."

I looked at the bowl and picked it up. It smelled good, but I didn't feel like eating. I pushed the chunks of meat around with a knife and ate a potato.

"If you're not going to have it, I'll eat it," Golden said.

Shoving the plate toward him, I stared out at the trees. The snow seemed to be getting heavier. A horse snorted in one of the stalls behind me.

"The old man dug out these books full of pictures of human bodies. Gruesome-looking things with the skin pulled away showin' all the muscles. Then he found another book and started saying how he could do this. He got me and Tearwyn to hold Miranda steady while he restitched the arm. One of the best jobs I've ever seen, too."

"I suppose that made him feel useful."

"It has probably saved her getting a nasty scar and lessened the chance of infection. You should have a look."

I had no intention of viewing the wound and felt an irrational surge of jealousy.

"Come inside, Ash. It's cold out here and you'll freeze. The drawing room is empty and warm. Everybody is listening to Old Petar read one of the tales from the Book of Heroes. Miranda is asleep and Tearwyn and Spike are guarding outside."

The offer tempted me, but I was digging myself a hole filled with self-pity and I hadn't finished yet. Golden ate all of the food in both bowls and then stood.

"Well, I'm not staying out here to freeze. I'll see you when common sense reasserts itself."

Watching my friend depart I wondered why he put up with me. His loyalty to our friendship was something I had always taken for granted. That I would need to rectify.

I remembered the first time he'd come striding out of the mist in the East Forest and attacked the hobgoblins that had ambushed my group. He'd cut them down as they turned to face him, and then chased them into a wall of green and grey. Later he eased an arrow from my calf and teased me when I moaned in pain. From that day onward, we had been friends.

And he was right about one thing – it was cold. I stood, stretched, and followed him inside.

Life settled into a routine for the next few days as we took the girls to and from Docklands. I spent the time away from the mansion either copying manuscripts at Rackhime's shop or questioning guards and patrons about what they may have noticed around the area in the last Ten Day. Though some had seen the mysterious Man of Shadows, nobody could describe him. The individual with the scar on his chin had only been spotted once.

I was getting nowhere, and attempts to get further information from Grandfather were met with outright refusal. Visiting Captain

Waldheigheim crossed my mind, but I decided against it as there was no new information to offer him.

Miranda's condition slowly improved but I visited her infrequently. When I did, old Petar was usually there reading, bringing her hot drinks and food. Once, I heard Miranda laughing and stuck my head in to find her with him. His face was red and he grinned happily. She saw me in the doorway and beckoned me in.

"Ash, Petar is reading to me from Justinian's Book of Comedy. You should stay and listen."

"I am just passing through and wanted to see if you were all right, but I can't stay."

Her smile fled.

"Maybe the Dark Elf thinks he has important tasks, but nothing should be more pressing than bringing joy to Lady Miranda," Petar said.

I hated the old man at that point. He sat in a high-backed chair in a dark shirt and hose and looked over the top of the book at me. That stare reminded me of my father.

"I'll be back later," I mumbled.

I ran away like a coward.

10

THE DANCE MASTER

The city settled into an uneasy calm after the Battle of the Red Market. The weather improved and the ice on the river grew thin. Some thought maybe winter would end early, but I doubted it. The next storm was always just around the corner.

Grandfather's and the Dance Master's men gave each other plenty of space, but occasionally a small ambush would take place in the darkness of the winter's night. In the morning, the cobbles, and snow of the streets of Hope would be splashed with blood, and the Watch would be called. Usually, the combatants would be long gone with only bodies remaining. The City Watch roamed in greater numbers but it didn't seem to help, and rumours circulated that the Council of Notable Elders was not happy with the captain, and considered putting the Knights of the Citadel on patrol.

A black mood followed me like my own personal cloud. Miranda thought of returning to work and had asked that I visit her, but I stayed away. I wouldn't allow my failures to put her at risk. Golden had stopped helping with the investigations and fell back into the habits of previous winters. He moved from inn to inn, either picking fights or chasing women. My tall friend still helped out guarding the girls, but even this was half-hearted. On a cold, clear evening I waited for him to relieve me from outside watch in vain. Eventually, I went into the mansion and found him in one of the upstairs rooms. Slender Cassie was asleep across his chest, head resting on his shoulder while Stella lay curled at his side.

I smacked him on the foot with my frosty woollen hat. "You were supposed to take my place half a bell ago," I growled.

He blinked a couple of times but hardly moved. "I was busy."

"I can see that. You're supposed to be *guarding* the girls, not bedding them."

"It was Stella's idea, and a very good one I must say."

"Why am I not surprised?"

His blue eye opened and focused. "I don't know why we're guarding them anyway. There hasn't been a murder in a Ten Day."

"That doesn't mean it's safe. The Dance Master is still at war with Grandfather and the girls might be on his list."

"You worry too much." Stella curled into Golden. "Why don't you come and join us? It would help with your stress. I bet Golden's ready to go again."

She stretched like a cat, letting the covers fall away from her shoulders. I tore my eyes from her half-naked form and walked to the door.

"Just be outside as soon as you can." I stepped into the hallway.

Two days later, Golden moved back down to his inn near the river, and the girls started to discuss the possibility of returning to their old rooms.

When I could, I stalked Dockside like a panther, but failed to find my prey. The Man of Shadows didn't appear.

The evening before All Gods Day, I thought I'd spotted him. A figure briefly appeared in a side alley and I was after it. The man moved fast, and soon I was out of Docklands and in the area of warehouses near the ports. I'd brought my hand crossbow with me and tried to get to a position where I could shoot at the fleeing man, but every time I stopped and steadied my arm, the target disappeared around a corner. I had to be careful – I didn't want to kill him, just slow him.

As I entered the long alley between two buildings, I noted other men hidden among crates and in alcoves. They probably believed they couldn't be seen, but my eyes pierced all but the darkest recesses. I slowed and waited. The running figure had been bait to pull me into an ambush. I almost fell for it.

A pipe flared at the end of the narrow street and a slender figure of medium height stepped out.

"I said he'd notice your men, Tickles. Dwarves and you fair-skinned humans always underestimate the eyes of the Dark Elves. My people were dealing with them before the invaders arrived from across the sea."

I realised at once this must be the Dance Master, and he had just let me know he was one of the race of original humans who lived here in peace with my people for thousands of years. He was trying to put me at my ease, but I knew how ruthless this man could be.

A short, broad-shouldered figure stepped to his side. "You're right as usual, boss."

I kept my distance, but didn't lift my crossbow into firing position.

"I'd like to talk, Ash. Is it all right I call you that? It seems less rude than Owl or baby-killer." The thin man stepped toward me, puffing on a long-stemmed pipe. Tickles followed a pace behind.

"I don't mind having a chat but the dwarf will need to stay where he is."

The Dance Master put up his hand and gestured for Tickles to remain behind. He made his way to within four paces of me and stopped. All I could see were eyes under his hood as they caught the light of his glowing pipe.

"It's rare that somebody uses my real name, but I appreciate the courtesy. What should I call you? The Dance Master seems a little formal and dramatic."

For a moment there was no answer, and I felt as though I he studied me. Dark eyes weighed me and I didn't enjoy the experience.

"You may call me Sundeep."

"A name of the first people, but is it your real one?"

"It belonged to a friend."

"Then it will suffice, though I thought there were no friends in your profession?"

"It was a long time ago, when I was much younger."

I nodded and a scanned to see if any of his men were trying to get closer. None had moved.

"You brought me here for a reason. It must be important."

"I didn't kill those girls, and want to find out who did."

"Why should I believe you? And if you aren't the killer, why would you care who was?"

"I can't prove my innocence. But I tell you now, I have never killed a woman, or ordered one murdered. That day might come, but I intend to keep it at bay for as long as possible."

"A thief with honour."

"Hardly – you know my people, that we revere women. It cuts against the grain for me to kill them."

"I have heard of these beliefs, but you must have lived in Hope for some time. I'm guessing you haven't had a lot to do with your tribe for many years."

The thin man sighed and tapped out the pipe on his shoe. I looked for movement, in case this was a signal. Again, nothing happened.

"You're right, but I still try and respect my people. I thought if anyone would understand this, you would. Both of us are outsiders in Hope."

"But you have done more than survive, Sundeep. You control most of the smuggling in and out of the city, and have now branched out into gambling and dance halls."

"It is true I'm ambitious, but that doesn't mean I killed those girls."

"Even if I believed you, what can I do about it? Grandfather believes you're the murderer and he won't listen to me."

"If you find the killer, then this war will end and I will get back to expanding slowly and carefully. One day, Grandfather and I might come to blows over territory, but next time I want to be ready."

The wind picked up and Sundeep's cape fluttered around him. The cold caused me to shiver.

"I've struck a dead end. I don't know if I can help you. There's been no progress for over a Ten Day."

Sundeep said nothing for a few heartbeats. "The Man of Shadows, who you seek, has been seen in the Devil's Horns. What he is doing in the noble district, I don't know. My people tell me he moves and acts like an assassin but he is not one of the Grey Vultures. I sent a tracker to follow him but my man was found with a bolt in his eye, in the Lake Park that sits in the saddle between those peaks."

This was news. I'd been looking in the wrong place. The Man of Shadows had moved on and may now even be watching Petar's mansion.

Sundeep read my mind. "The girls are safe. The house where you keep the women is not at risk."

"You know where the women are?"

"Of course."

"But we were sure we had not been followed."

"You haven't been."

There was another way that he could have found out. It was either a member of the Watch the captain had said he would speak to, or he had someone on the inside, possibly one of the girls. I nodded and decided that I'd talk to Waldheigheim soon.

"The information you've given me will be helpful, but why don't you look into it yourself?"

"I need someone outside my organisation to find the truth or it won't be believed. You're my best hope to ending this war."

"The fact that the Man of Shadows is now stalking the Peaks opens a new range of questions. Why would he have moved his centre of operation, and what does he plan to do up there?"

"I hope you'll find out." With that, Sundeep turned and strode into the shadows.

I searched for Golden and found him at the Mermaid playing dice against the house and losing. When I pulled him from the table he frowned at me. "I was close to turning the tide."

"You were about to blow a season's worth of adventuring gold, but forget about that. I just met the Dance Master."

Golden's eyes widened. "What did he say?"

I looked around quickly. "Not here – I'll tell you at Rackhime's. Where's Tearwyn?"

"Already there."

I thought of finding Trix and telling her, then I remembered she was gone. The memory stabbed but I pushed on. "Let's go."

I filled both my friends in on what had happened while we hitched up the wagons.

Tearwyn whistled between his teeth. "Do you believe him? I mean, I know the old race can be funny about their women, but do the same feelings carry over to ours?"

He made a good point. "He told me they do, but I have no way of knowing."

"How does this help us? I mean, we don't know who this mysterious assassin is," Golden said.

"I'm not sure yet, but I'm going to move my focus from Docklands. I want to find out about Elhnora. It's time to go to some of the inns on the Peaks and see if any of the servants from Lord

Vornhelm's household drink at them. The servants of the rich may be able to help me build a picture of that young woman."

Only ten of the girls turned up that evening for the trip to Petar's. Aneeta was among those who had chosen to return to their own rooms. Teel, Cassie, and Stella stood inside the front of the Mermaid waiting for the wagon.

"I'm sorry, Ash. They decided that it's probably safe enough down here. Nobody's been attacked for fourteen days so they believe they're going to be okay," Teel said.

"Did they think that maybe there hasn't been an attack because of the steps we had taken?" I growled.

Teel looked away and took a step back.

"It's not your fault. I'm sorry. Your strength and leadership helped get most of the girls here in the first place."

Teel turned and smiled. I marvelled how somebody who looked so young could provide that level of guidance to the women.

We arrived late at Petar's, and after a quick snack, I left to look for the Man of Shadows. I searched the park and the area around the lake, then patrolled the street where a small strip of inns near the roads to the Citadel stood. They had all closed, a stray dog the only sign of life.

The area around the mansions of the nobles stretched wider than those of the lower town, so I often had to cross areas of open ground. I did this carefully. The Watch and some of the guards from various houses patrolled the streets and would not take kindly to finding a Dark Elf prowling the neighbourhoods of the rich.

Just before dawn, I found myself alongside the high walls of the Vornhelm manor. I was about to head home when I spotted a figure go over the wall near one of the high trees. Running to the spot, I found it empty. I had no way of knowing whether it was the Man of Shadows or someone else. The idea of going to the guard box and warning them they had an intruder crossed my mind, but realised at this time of night they would be likely to arrest me. Using the last of the darkness, I headed back to Petar's house.

The following day, I got up late and made my way to the kitchen prepared to brave the wrath of the cook in order to fill my grumbling stomach. Miranda sat at a long bench eating bread and reading a large, leather bound book. Her hair had been tied up on the top of her head, exposing her smooth neck. She looked tired but radiant. I stared at her, not knowing what to say.

"If you are hungry you can have some of the bread."

It did smell good, but the urge to flee was stronger. "I'll come back later."

Miranda's voice pulled me up short. "What is wrong with you? I know you want to be with me."

I stopped. Her face was imploring, eyes moist.

"I can't put you at risk."

"Life is dangerous and the decision is mine."

"No, it is also mine."

"You're leaving me with little choice, Ash."

I didn't know what she meant but her statement sounded like a threat.

"What do you mean?" I asked.

Her eyes filled with tears now, she looked away, and refused to answer.

"Don't do anything hasty."

Her head snapped back. "I'm not a silly girl. I don't make foolish decisions."

Well at least one of us didn't. Nodding, I backed out of the room. I heard a sob and a growl of frustration as I walked away.

The Whistling Kite was a well-appointed inn with polished floorboards and a massive fireplace. The windowpanes held expensive frosted glass and the candles were all beeswax.

Every head turned and stared as I shook off my cloak and stepped inside. I had come here to find a serving woman, or maybe a guard from Lord Vornhelm's residence. The barman put down a large ale in front of a man dressed in leather armour, carrying a long sword. Near the fireplace, two young men in fine robes sat and held me with their eyes. A woman with a white apron and dark hair stopped wiping tables and looked at me. I ignored them all and made my way to the bar.

"Any mulled wine?" I asked the bald barman.

He didn't answer but his mouth twisted. He turned his back on me and walked toward a set of stairs that went down into the cellar.

"Not very friendly," I muttered.

"He probably doesn't want to serve a Dark Elf," the man in leather armour said.

I turned and looked at him. His shield leaned against the wall. It bore the device of a red griffon on a black background.

"You're one of Lord Darnor's men," I said.

"What if I am?"

"Do you know if any of Lord Vornhelm's soldiers drink here?"

"I'd say that's none of your business, Owl."

One of the nobles near the fireplace wandered across the room. He wore a thin sword the rich used to duel with.

"Why don't you leave, Owl. This is a respectable establishment," Lord Darnor's man said.

"I didn't realise I was lowering the tone."

"You and your whores are not welcome up here."

I grabbed my Cold Blade and took a step toward him. "What do you know about the women?" I hissed.

He stepped back and almost tripped over a stool in his haste to put space between us.

"We heard yesterday about the whores and we want you off the Peaks," he said.

I grunted and eased my hand away from the weapon's hilt. So, our secret was out. Well, I didn't suppose that our hiding place could remain unknown forever.

The barman returned with a big bearded man who held a crossbow in his hand and pointed it in my direction.

"You need to leave my inn," he said.

"So, I guess that means you haven't warmed the mead," I muttered.

He brought the crossbow up to his eye and took aim. I left quickly thinking my idea to visit the inns on the Peaks was a poor one. Down by the river the sight of other races, such as dwarves or elves, was more commonplace. Up here, it was a humans-only zone. I'd have to ask Golden to undertake the task in the noble district and see what he could find out.

The Watch House hummed with activity and looked more like the control centre for a small army. Men gathered in groups of eight to ten before going to patrol the city, all of them heavily armed. Officers stood on the steps of the main building or in front of the gates to the inner courtyard directing each group or getting reports from the senior man in each returning patrol.

I found Captain Waldheigheim at his desk, talking to a number of investigators. Each man had a long sword strapped to his side, some carried crossbows. I waited for the meeting to conclude, then stuck my head around the door. A flicker of a smile appeared on the captain's face.

"Ah, Ashley, I hope you've brought me some good news. I haven't had much of that of late. This little war between Grandfather and the Dance Master is keeping me busy."

"I have news, though I don't know if it's good. And I also have a question."

"The question first then, if you please."

"I don't want to strain the improved relationship between us, but I need to ask what you did about the two Watchmen who knew about the girls' location."

"I take it then that your little hideaway is compromised."

I didn't answer but nodded briefly.

"I sent the sergeant to a country posting as I didn't like his attitude and I put the younger man on my personal staff where I could keep an eye on him. I told both of them that if they gave away the secret of the working girls' location they'd find themselves at a Watch House in the Far East."

"Okay, then I can probably eliminate them as the source of the leak, which means my problem is internal. One of the girls must have given away our location, though I think the locals could have worked it out for themselves."

I told the captain of my meeting with the Dance Master, leaving out the man's ethnic origins and any information that might have compromised the smuggler's operations.

"This Man of Shadows, as you dramatically call him, why is he important?"

"Because he was seen in Dockland around the time of the first and last deaths, and he has kept himself hidden."

"The Dance Master described him as an assassin. The fact that one in the profession is killing girls is strange. And what of the evidence of two assailants?"

"There is still the man with the scar, but no sign that he's ever met or worked with the assassin. So, there are a lot of unanswered questions," I said.

"Well I have now established that the working girls were both killed with long-bladed daggers. We tested a number of weapons on a pig carcase and the marks are identical. The two noble girls received the blows of different swords and daggers."

I was impressed. It must have shown on my face. The captain looked away and reddened around the ears.

"It was just a thought of mine. Most of my men believed it insane."

"I think it's a very clever idea."

"But what does it show us?" the captain asked.

"That there is a possibility that different killers have murdered some of the women."

Why would an assassin kill Trix and Fendria? It made no sense. The noble girls were killed by someone in a deranged fury and my friend had been murdered almost clinically. A surge of anger for the killer overtook me and I balled both hands into fists. All along I'd thought one group had been responsible for all of the deaths. Now, I was starting to think this was a mistake. Could Grandfather be behind this, using the assassin to kill his own girls and paying some crazies to kill the noblewomen? It seemed unlikely. The relationship between the two women was supposed to be irrelevant but I wasn't so sure. Maybe a meal and a warm fire would help me think.

I walked down the driveway to Petar's small mansion, kicking snow in frustration. Tearwyn waited for me on the balcony and the look on his bearded face told me he wasn't happy.

"The girls have decided they aren't comin' anymore, well except for Teel, Stella, Cassie, and Miranda, that is. The rest say that the killer has moved on."

In a way, they were right, but I still liked having the women in one place. Tearwyn took guarding the residence seriously. He often pulled double shifts at night while I was out scouting and tried to catch up on his sleep during the day. Golden came and went as he pleased, taking Spike with him. The loss of the big wolf put extra strain on our efforts to protect Petar's house. Spike's senses had given us an increased chance of intercepting any intruders.

"I can't say as I blame them. To start with, they looked upon their stay here as a novelty, but now it's an inconvenience."

"The killers are still around, they're just layin' low," the big man said.

Walking past him, I patted his arm. I'd told him all I knew, and he was as committed to the cause of finding the killers as I.

Sending Golden out early that evening dressed in his best outfit, I gave him instructions not to start any fights. I even made him leave the Cold Blade behind – it didn't seem appropriate to take a hand-and-a-half sword into an inn frequented by nobles. He insisted I lend him my short sword.

Waiting for his return and the arrival of the women on the wagon back from Docklands, I sat in the front study. The room had been returned to its original condition by the removal of the bed. Scrolls and books were again strewn around with what seemed to be no particular purpose.

Petar wandered in soon after the last dong of the mountain bell. The night lengthened and I was surprised the old man was still up.

"The Dark Elf doesn't realise I worry for them, too. He thinks he is the only one that cares," Petar said.

"I have a name, and I would prefer you use it."

"Ash can't see. He has remarkable eyes but he is occasionally blind."

Now the old man annoyed me. Since Miranda had been brought up the hill with a large hole in her arm, he'd been rude to me more than once.

"What do you mean? If you have some amazing insight about how I can solve the mystery of your daughter's murder, then tell me."

For a moment, Petar looked distressed. The reminder of Jalinta's death struck home, but he composed himself.

"It's not the murders. Lady Miranda is the blind spot."

I turned away and fought to control my anger. My relationship with Miranda was an open wound and he stuck his finger in it.

"He cannot see the window is closing and soon the lady will be forced to make a choice."

"You need to mind your business, old man. I know you're close to Miranda but your daughter is dead and none of these women can replace her. Just accept that you will be alone and move on."

It was cruelly done, and Petar turned white. He bowed his head. "Nobody takes the place of my girl. Ash doesn't understand that every relationship is different, each filled with new, exciting possibilities and dangers. Maybe one day he will learn and start to take risks again."

He walked from the room, leaving me in turmoil. Anger became the prevailing emotion, but something about what the old man said struck home.

The women arrived with Tearwyn and Spike. They smiled at me as they passed into the kitchen for their evening snack. Only Miranda didn't meet my eyes. I followed them into an area rich with herbs and pastry and soaked in the sounds of soft conversation and occasional laugh. The warmth and atmosphere soothed me. Looking across the room, I saw Cassie smiling at me, her brown face glowing from the heat of the open fire, before looking down at a piece of lamb pie. I realised her curly hair and fine build, as well as the colour of her skin, marked her as one of the first people.

"What is your real name, Cassie?" I asked.

She regarded me steadily, though I saw her fingers tighten on the tabletop.

"I was once known as Shafali, but that was a long time ago."

I nodded and picked up a trencher of thick dark bread. The pie that sat on it ran with gravy and my mouth watered.

"Then we are both of this land," I said.

"We are all of this country now." Stella patted a spot on the bench beside her.

I saw Miranda watching and sat.

"Cassie is of the first race, the Original Men. The human tribes that lived here are all gone but she's one of them. Now they only live in the far south. She doesn't talk about it much." Stella pressed into my side.

I nodded and changed the subject – I could see the slender woman sat as tense as a bowstring. "I thought Golden would be back by now," I said.

"You sent him to visit a number of inns with a bag of gold. Do you really think you'll see him before dawn?" Teel asked.

She munched on a piece of bread dripping with butter and wiped the oil from her lips as she spoke. Teel had a point. Golden could consume enormous amounts of alcohol and liked telling stories to any who'd listen. On the Peaks he would have a new audience.

I sighed and enjoyed the pie and the sensation of Stella squeezing my thigh under the table. Miranda left after finishing only a small portion of her meal.

Guilt surge and when Stella's hand crept higher I made my excuses, pulled on a thick cloak and left. The cold air hit me as I went out onto the snow. The look of disappointment on Miranda's face burned into my memory. I decided that very soon we would have to talk.

It wasn't until the ninth bell the following morning that Golden returned. His eyes were red-rimmed, tunic crumpled, and cloak torn. His usually perfect stubble looked a little grey.

"Water," he croaked.

Falling onto one of the larger couches in the drawing room he kicked off his snow-covered boots and pointed his feet at the fireplace. Teel brought him a clay jug and a cup. He picked up the container and drank it all. I watched the water pulsing down his throat and wondered if it was possible for a man to suffocate in the act of drinking. Finally, when it was drained, he stopped and drew breath.

"I feel better," he said, wiping his mouth with the back of his sleeve.

"Big night?" Tearwyn asked.

"That's putting it mildly. Those noble girls sure know how to show someone a good time."

"You were supposed to be questioning staff from Lord Vornhelm's mansion!" I snapped.

His bleary eyes held me and his mouth twitched. "Just wait for the whole story, Mr Grumpy. I did question a serving girl from Vornhelm's place and it was a most entertaining and enjoyable interrogation, but that was at the start of the evening. The noble girls also had plenty to add in the way of rumour and gossip about the Vornhelm household and I remember most of it. Anything that I was told after four bells is probably lost."

He saw my expression and hurried on. "But I still have a wealth of new information."

11

GOLDEN'S BIG NIGHT OUT

W e sat around the fire in Petar's sitting room as Golden started on his second jug of water. Spike pushed into the room and got a scratch behind the ears from his master.

"Where to begin? I think it's best to start at the beginning. I returned to the inn where you received such a cold reception, Ash, and found the place a little dull. What was its name?"

"The Whistling Kite," I answered.

"Ah yes, well I had an ale there and talked to a guardsman who said the young folk liked to go to an establishment called the Corner Inn. So, I left and found that establishment. It was a bigger inn with music and dancing. There were women everywhere, but I stayed on task, Ash, truly I did."

I thought that unlikely but kept my mouth shut.

"Anyway, I stopped this young woman who looked a bit lost and offered to help her carry her drinks to her table. And guess what, when I get there I find all her friends are other women and they work for noble households. I thought I'd found a mystical genie, and he'd granted my first wish."

"Can you move the tale along to the part where you actually gather some information," I said.

"Ash, you know a good story should never be rushed. Anyway, I found a young red-haired lady with eyes of the darkest green," Golden said.

I growled in the back of my throat.

He hurried on. "Her name was Sophia, and she worked for Lord Vornhelm as a housemaid. She was sweet and soft and made me tickle the information out of her, can you imagine!"

I could, and that was the problem. In the corner of the room I caught Stella and Teel grinning at each other.

"And what did she tell you?" I asked.

"Well, Sophia was employed as a housemaid when she was fifteen and has worked for the Vornhelm estate for the last five years. She had many stories about Lord Vornhelm and saw *a lot* of him to start with, and he was very nice to her but his wife moved her into the kitchen. She saw Elhnora only a few times, but heard that she and her father were very close when she was younger. That changed as she got older and became wild. Now he dotes on her little sister. Sophie told me the household is run to very strict rules and if anyone breaks them they are either dismissed on the spot or flogged."

"I though flogging without legal authority is against the law," Stella whispered.

"The nobles do what they like," Teel said.

Golden arched an eyebrow. "If I may?" He took another mouthful of water and swallowed before continuing. "Anyway, the Vornhelm place sounds like it's run similar to a military camp. Sophia doesn't get far from the kitchen but she hears plenty from the other maids, who are all older than her. Elhnora and her father had some huge fights, especially over the marriage. But then he threatened to cut her off without a penny and she gave in. She was to be married to Lord Carsterl's oldest son and seemed calm about the engagement."

"I know him! I danced for him once. He's a good-looking man," Teel said.

"He's also fought a number of duels, both to first blood and to the death. Lord Carsterl's son has never lost. He has a reputation of being arrogant and bad-tempered, according to the ladies I spoke to," Golden said.

"Did Sophie know of Elhnora's relationship with Jalinta?" I asked.

"No, she didn't, but she does now."

"That will spread like wildfire among the staff," Teel said.

"Let's hope they don't trace the source of the story to us," I muttered.

"What do we care if they do?" Golden said.

"Slurring the character of his dead fiancé might not go down well with Lord Carsterl's oldest. What's his name, anyway?"

"Alder, and I'm not worried about duelling with a noble with his skinny sword."

Maybe, I thought. But I knew there was always somebody better with a blade out in the world and it was best not to get too confident.

"The Carsterl family are even richer than the Vornhelms and they are related directly to Duke Ern who sits on the Council of Notable Elders. Sophia said the match would have strengthened the Vornhelm family's position in Hope immeasurably. The Carsterls were happy gaining a connection to a house with strong military connections. It was a winning deal for both families."

"I wonder how Alder would have felt if he knew his future wife was having an affair with a woman, and one from a low-ranking family?" I asked.

"Is there any sign that Alder realised?" Teel said.

"Sophia mentioned the Carsterls were very unhappy at first about the death but then the younger daughter was promised to Alder instead and they were pleased."

"I think I want to meet this Lord," I said.

"I know where he likes to drink," Golden said.

Miranda found me in the study looking at maps of the interior. I traced some of my journeys into the East. My finger travelled along rivers and through forests I remembered.

I looked up and noticed her standing there. My heart leapt as it did whenever I saw her.

"I heard you were going to see Lord Alder," Miranda said.

"That's right."

"I've met him at the Mermaid. He's a dangerous man."

"Why do you say that?"

"He held an air of menace and his friends were scared of him. I could tell. They fawned over him like he was ancient royalty."

"Did he threaten you?"

"No, he was charming and very complimentary with me and the other ladies, but when another noble group came in, the tension rose. A lot of alcohol had been consumed that night and when the other nobles tried to get me to come to their table, Lord Alder told them not to try and poach his 'little swan'. They didn't understand the warning, probably too drunk. Alder's face changed, and he called the leader of the other group out. I noticed everyone visibly shrink away from him. Unfortunately, one of the security men saw the exchange as well and decided it was time for Lord Alder to leave. The guard grabbed his arm and was warned to let go, but he refused to. The guard died quickly. I didn't even see Lord Alder's blade move. There was a bit of a fuss over the death, but the Carsterl family paid some money to Grandfather and it was all hushed up."

"He sounds like a typical spoiled noble, but one who's good with a blade."

"I think he is more than that. Don't underestimate him."

I nodded and turned back to the map. Miranda came and stood next to me. My pulse quickened.

"You and Golden have seen parts of this land that most of us only read about."

"Those that can. There is so much out there. Even the Great Moors beyond the East Forest have a beauty all of their own. There's a waterfall that drops into a plunge pool at the edge of the woods where the moors begin. I watched a silver bear fishing where the river ran from the small lake. Golden and I had just escaped from the tower of some long-forgotten dwarf lord. We were tired but relieved. I remember the sun was high, and I was warm and had eaten well on a deer we had shot. I felt relaxed and almost happy."

"Almost happy? Do you think you'll ever move beyond that?"

I looked at her and my resolve cracked. Taking her head in my hands I caressed her cheeks. Kissing her, I pulled her to me. She melted into my body; her hand curled around my neck. The kisses were frantic, and she started to moan into my mouth. I pulled at her clothing, all my restraint gone. She pushed me away.

"Why now, Ash? Don't you understand? It's too late. You ignored me and told me to go, saying it was dangerous for me to be with you."

"That's still all true. But every time I see you I fight an internal battle. I can't keep doing this."

"You decided that you needed to protect me by denying what you feel, but the truth is you are protecting yourself! I have other opportunities now, and in light of your rejection I have grabbed them."

"What are you talking about? You have gone back to dancing. Where is this opportunity coming from?"

Miranda's eyes narrowed. "You are as arrogant as Golden sometimes. Do you think you are the only one who is interested in me?"

Jealousy surged and my voice rose, "Who else is there?"

"If you're so smart, you work it out." She spun around and disappeared through the door, slamming it behind her.

Golden and I dressed in our finest clothes. We had bathed. Teel cut my friend's hair and Stella trimmed mine. Golden's chin was shaved, and he looked like a rich nobleman's son. I took the Cold Blade but he took an ornate long sword.

"It's dwarven made and holds a razor-sharp edge. I thought taking anything larger would stand out."

"It would be a little conspicuous."

"I don't even know what that means."

I smiled.

Golden grunted and then arranged his cloak on his shoulder.

The White Horse was an inn with position. It sat on a small spur of rock that protruded from one of the two peaks like a pimple. The view over the low town made me gasp. The weather remained clear so we could see the lights of the city below as well as the shining ribbon of ice that marked the course of the river. A pall of smoke and fog obscured the waterfront and mist formed in the dips and shallow valley to the north.

The inn itself stood two storeys high, built from redbrick. Its steep roof held no snow, but long icicles hung like spears. Inside, the tables were all oak, and the chairs padded with leather. An enormous stuffed brown bear reared up in the corner and the head of a red deer was mounted above the bar. Near the windows, a group of men played javelins with small darts they threw at a square target. The room smelt of pipe smoke and hot chips. One older man sat on a stool near the door, a wooden club hanging from his waist. He supervised the other staff from this position.

I received some hostile stares as I ordered a drink from a tall woman dressed in a red-and-white uniform. She smiled at my friend before retreating with our silver. The man at the stool came over and stood before our table. He addressed Golden. "The Owl with you?"

"He is my comrade and I'll vouch for him."

"Problem is, I've never seen you before either, pretty boy."

"I'm Golden."

"Yes, I bet you are."

"We just want to have a few drinks."

"Your silver's fine and we have had Hunters here before."

So much for our disguise. The older man looked around the room, then back at us.

"We have a minstrel playing a little later and we serve venison, chips, trout and pheasant, but the food's expensive. You can stay, but don't make any trouble."

"We have plenty of silver and just want a quiet evening," Golden said.

The man grunted and glanced at me. His face wrinkled, and he shook his head before moving back to his stool.

"We're in, but how do we find Lord Alder?" Golden muttered.

"Well, we know he is handsome, tall and has dark hair. Miranda said he was surrounded by other young men who fawn over him."

"I don't like the sound of him already."

"We need information, not a brawl."

"And how are we going to get that? We can't walk up to him and ask if he killed his fiancée, can we?"

"Of course not. Leave the questions to me, but if I raise my eyebrows, that is the signal for you to needle him."

"So, you want me to have a duel with him?"

"Maybe, but even if you do, we mustn't kill him. We need to find out if he knows anything and he can't tell us dead, though he may talk if he has been humiliated."

Golden sat back and ran fingers through his hair. Our drinks arrived, and he offered to buy the waitress a drink. She smiled and said she couldn't until after she finished at ten bells. The two of them flirted until she caught the frown of the man near the door. She excused herself and then disappeared with a swirl of her skirt.

"Don't get distracted," I growled.

"I'm just fitting in. Besides, she has exceptional legs and the prettiest dimple."

I shook my head. There didn't seem to be a feature of the female species Golden wasn't attracted to.

The noise in the hallway at the front entrance grew, and a group of men dressed in expensive cloaks, wearing slim sabres at their waists pushed into the room. The man by the door stood and bowed deeply.

"Lord Alder, welcome. Your table by the fire is empty, and I presume you would like the usual fare sent?"

A tall man with long dark hair and grey eyes smiled. White teeth flashed against olive skin and he placed his hand on the older man's shoulder.

"I feel like beef tonight. Is there any chance you can find me a thick steak? Throw some chips in with it and I'll be happy."

"My lord, I have one or two steaks left, but not enough for you and your friends."

"They can have the pheasant as they usually do. That's all right, isn't it, boys?"

The group nodded their assent and then they all made their way to a long table near the fire.

"He didn't offer us beef," Golden grumbled.

"Probably keeps a few of the best cuts for his richest customers."

"I like steak."

"I know, but I'm sure the venison will be fine."

"It's just another reason to dislike Lord Alder."

I rolled my eyes. "He didn't deliberately steal your steak."

The tall woman brought us drinks and took orders. I settled back to watch the group of noblemen. The action swirled around Lord Alder. His friends tried to engage him in conversation or sought to please him with a joke. They shouted over each other and called to the waitresses to serve them. The women were sucked toward the table and flirted with the men as they plied them with beverages. Soon, the meals arrived and the noise level dropped. Golden eyed the enormous steak as it went past. His disappointment with not getting beef didn't seem to slow his consumption of the venison when it turned up.

"How do we approach him?" Golden sucked the gravy from his fingers.

"We'll warm ourselves and see what transpires."

I waited until Lord Alder had finished eating, just in case my friend pounced on his steak, and then crossed to the fire and started to warm my hands. Putting my drink on the mantle I kept my back to the group. Golden stood next to me but faced the other way.

"I think we have heard of you," a reedy voice said.

I turned. All of the nobles had stopped talking and looked in our direction. A man with a narrow chin and small blue eyes spoke, "You are the Owl staying at the Vernheim dump."

I smiled and leaned against the fireplace. "I find it comfortable and Old Petar is a very good host."

"He has a noble title which you should use," Lord Alder said.

I ignored the comment and waited. They had opened the conversation and I would run with whatever came my way.

"You brought a group of whores up onto the Peaks. We heard about it just the other day," Little Eyes said.

"We did. It was for their protection. Someone was killing women down at Dockside. Some of them were my friends, and I didn't want any more of them to die."

"I'm not surprised an Owl would call whores friends."

"So, you've never been to any of Grandfather's establishments?" Golden asked.

I thought I saw a shadow of a smile play across Lord Alder's face.

"That's different," the noble snapped.

"So, you use these women and then don't care if some madman carves them up like a butcher," I clarified.

Alder's fists clenched and his gaze fell to the table.

Small Eyes glanced at his lord before looking back at me. "We all grieve for those killed at Docklands, but that doesn't mean you needed to bring them up here."

"I protect those I care for and I'm not worried who it offends."

"Well spoken, Owl," Lord Alder said.

"My name is Ash."

He nodded but didn't introduce himself.

"Anyway, your sensibilities need no longer be injured. Most of the working women have returned to Dockside. Since the murders have stopped, they feel safer and have gone back to their old lodgings," I said.

"This murderer hasn't been captured, though," Lord Alder murmured.

"That's what I tell the girls, but it is more convenient to live near where they work, so they take the chance."

I hesitated, knowing it was a risk to introduce Elhnora to the conversation.

"A couple of noble girls got killed as well, I hear."

Everyone in the group looked at Lord Alder, and I saw the man tense. The hand that had been tracing patterns on the table clenched into a fist. "This is true," he whispered.

"Did you know them?"

His eyes bored into me but I didn't flinch. The stare remained, but he continued his silence.

"We take that as a yes, then," Golden said.

Lord Alder's gaze flicked to my friend and then back to me. "Your question is impertinent, but I can tell from your stance and attitude that you are both Hunters and are probably unaware of how to behave around your betters."

"It is true we didn't see many of the nobility in the Stony Hills as the ogres charged towards us," Golden said, only just managing to keep the sneer out of his voice.

Lord Alder ignored the implied insult, but I saw his brow furrow. "We both lost those who were close to us in those murders, so I forgive you, this time."

"I believe the noble girls knew each other," I said.

"That is true," Lord Alder said.

"That's some coincidence. It's amazing two women who were lovers both got murdered by the same man." I watched him closely as I muttered the words.

His eyes narrowed, but I saw no surprise or confusion. I heard Golden gasp and noted the wide-eyed looks of the other nobles.

"I will kill you for that, Owl," Lord Alder said.

The dagger appeared in his hand and he sprang over the table in a single move. I was ready and caught the thrusting arm just below the wrist with my palm. The chopping motion jarred the weapon from Lord Alder's grip. He recovered quickly. His other fist lashed at my head. I went under the blow and snapped a punch into his stomach. He fell back into his friends who all rose to assist him. Golden added to the chaos with a kick to the chin of Small Eyes.

I threw another punch at Lord Alder but he blocked it and hit me with a short jab that clipped my cheek. He followed with an attack that would have knocked me down had it connected. I swayed aside and chopped at his throat with my hand, but he was fast and twisted clear. My tall friend had a noble by the neck and used him like a shield to keep the others at bay.

The waitresses scream and the man who sat by the door yelled. Somehow the two groups came apart and stood eying each other.

The older man jumped in the middle and brandished his club at Golden and me. "I knew I shouldn't have let an Owl in here!" He turned to the nobles. "I'm sorry. I take full responsibility."

Lord Alder ignored the older man. "We will duel to the death, Owl. Tomorrow at dusk we shall meet by the Sacred Lake and I will kill you."

"You'll try, but others have made similar promises and they are no longer here."

I could see the fury barely contained within the man's stance. "Bring your second and the choice of weapons is yours as the challenge is mine."

"Then it will be short swords and no armour."

Lord Alder blinked with surprise but nodded once.

Outside, Golden punched me on the arm. "I thought I was to do the duel, if there was going to be one. Lord Alder is a champion of single combat and I'm a better fighter than you."

"Normally, I would agree, but I knew if he challenged, I would get to choose the weapon. If it had been you, then you would have chosen the hand and a half, but they're not allowed in duels. Then the choice would pass to him."

"They're all using skinny needle swords these days."

"Yes, and we have never even picked one up."

Golden grunted his agreement but I could tell he wasn't happy. "You think you can take him with the short sword?"

"Using the Cold Blade, I'm very confident."

My friend nodded and fell into step beside me.

"What I found interesting about our little confrontation is that he already knew," I said.

"Knew what?"

"That Elhnora and Jalinta were lovers."

"That means he might be the killer then?"

"He could be behind the murders, or at least have some idea of who is. When I hold my blade at his throat tomorrow, we will find out."

12

THE DUEL

I trained in front of Petar's manor the following day, spending the time between the first bell of the afternoon and the second, sparring with Golden. He found a short sword from somewhere in his mountain of equipment and made sure it was blunt by chopping it into a small log.

Later I did a series of stretches and then went through a number of different moves with the Cold Blade as my instructors had taught me on the high plateau of the Dark Elves many years before. I swept through the heron and leopard, following on with the kingfisher and then the eagle. It took me back to my examination for entrance into the Companions of the Snowcat. I had remembered the one hundred attacks, and in the correct order. My family had been proud of me that day.

"You move as though you are a dancer," Miranda said. She stood wrapped in a thick cape that swept the snowy ground. "Not like I dance, I mean similar to the classical dances you see at the Festival of Death or at the River Celebration."

"Thank you," I said.

"You're not going to die tomorrow, are you?"

"I don't think so. Lord Alder issued the challenge, so I got to choose the weapon. He didn't expect me to go with the short sword."

"If you kill him, what will you learn?"

"I don't plan on that. I want to get my blade at his throat. He needs to be defenceless, but that does make the duel difficult. I won't be able to grab any advantage and plunge a sword through him at the first opportunity."

Miranda nodded. I stopped my moves and wrapped myself in an old bearskin. I needed to keep the chill at bay.

"Will Tearwyn or Golden be your second?"

"Golden, though Tearwyn is going to come along in case the nobles try to cheat."

"From what I hear, that's not Lord Alder's style. What did you think of him?"

I scratched my chin and pulled the bearskin tighter around my shoulder. "He wasn't what I expected. He seemed to show remorse for the loss of life at Docklands. But he believed he was entitled to a certain level of subservience. He was arrogant, and in some ways he reminded me of Golden."

"Except that your tall friend would never slaughter women."

"We don't know if that's what Alder has done."

I accompanied her back to the house in silence, our shoulders almost touching, but we separated at the front entrance. She made her way to Petar's study.

I continued to train, and then waited for Golden and Tearwyn to arrive. Time moved slowly and my thoughts chased each other in circles. I tried to find a fact that I had missed and re-examined all of the information gleaned from my various sources. No new revelation came to light. There were still too many holes.

Then Miranda's face floated to the front of my consciousness. I wondered if I should put aside my fears and try and salvage our relationship, but remembered another suitor appeared and I had no idea who. Her feelings for me were still obvious and mine hadn't changed. Every time I was near her I wanted to hold her. Yet the mistakes I'd made with Trix and Zenta haunted me.

My Dark Elf lover had bled to death in my arms. I had led her and my company into a cave that plunged into the depts of a mountain, against explicit orders from my superiors. Everyone died. It left me unworthy of being with anyone.

When dusk approached, I dressed in a thick black leather jacket and pants. They were as close to armour as possible without being so, and had served me well in the wilds of the East. I usually would have worn a chain vest over them, but I had outlawed this for the duel. I strapped the Cold Blade to my waist after checking the edge, though the magical sword never seemed to dull. Golden wore most of his adventuring gear except for his pack, as did Tearwyn. Spike bounded around in the thinning cover of snow as if sensing the tension.

We strode through the shadows in the park to the frozen lake near the bridge across the Devil's Flow. Ahead, a small group of well-dressed nobles waited. A tall man wearing a fur-lined hat broke from the group and made his way toward us.

"I'm Sir Larnerd, and have been asked to oversee today's duel. I have no connections to Lord Alder's family and obviously no connection to you. Does this meet with your approval?"

I nodded briefly and ran my gaze over my opponent. He wore tight-fitting brown leather with a chain coif covering his head and shoulders.

"No armour was what stipulated when challenged," I said.

"The coif is accepted under the rules of noble challenge as laid out in the Charter of the Citadel. I take it that you are familiar with it?"

Of course, I wasn't, but I didn't want to let this peacock in on that. I only had a passing knowledge of the rules. Eying him coldly, I walked toward Lord Alder and his preening followers.

"Did you tell him he wasn't to use his Cold Blade?" Lord Alder said as I drew near.

I stopped in my tracks and felt for the hilt of my weapon.

"I've done some research on you, Owl, and have been informed about what you carry. I didn't think you would understand the Charter. Magic isn't allowed in a duel – no rings, armour, and especially blades."

Sir Larnerd bobbed his head like a nodding vulture. "Your challenger is correct. You may use a short sword as you requested for the duel, but it must not be magical."

"But I didn't bring another blade."

"In that case, you have until sundown to get one, or the choice of weapons reverts to the challenger."

I should have investigated the rules thoroughly. If I didn't find a short blade quickly, I was as good as dead. I was sure Lord Alder would choose either the long sword or the rapier. If it was the rapier, then I would be bleeding from a dozen wounds in less than a heartbeat. If it was the former weapon I would have slightly longer.

"Golden, have you got a short sword on you?"

"There's that one I sparred with but it's back at the house. I started to sharpen it again but I didn't finish the job.

"What about you, Tearwyn?"

"I just brought my axe and a long knife."

I looked at the pale disc of the winter's sun hanging above the horizon.

"Can you run and get it, Golden?"

"Your second is not allowed to leave the area of the duel once the parties have met," Sir Larnerd said.

I looked at Tearwyn, my eyes pleading.

"I'll sprint," he muttered.

As he started to run back toward Petar's house, Golden called after him, "It's under the desk in the front study, along with the sharpening stone."

I watched the sun slowly drop. Beads of sweat moistened my forehead.

"What a mess. If Tearwyn doesn't make it back, he'll choose the rapier. I've used it before and there are some similarities between it and the short sword. You can thrust and slash, but you need to lean into the attacks to drive the point home. Your footwork is more important than ever with the rapier, so that will help you," Golden said.

"If he chooses that ridiculous skinny sword, then I'm dead."

"Don't give in. There's always hope. I've watched nobles use their different blades, and a gifted amateur could do well with them."

I didn't believe him, but was grateful for his attempt to build my confidence. My best chance lay in how fast Tearwyn could run.

The sun had touched the ground when Sir Larnerd approached us again.

"Time is almost up. Lord Alder wishes to choose the rapier and also has said that he wants to fight in white shirts."

This was getting worse. Now I couldn't even hope that my leather would give me some protection.

Puffing and the steady thump of feet came from nearby. I turned to see Tearwyn approach out of the gathering darkness.

"I've got it," he wheezed.

Sir Larnerd's lip lifted at the corner and he eyed my big friend. "Very well then, you have the correct weapon so we will proceed with the original challenge. Be ready. The area for the contest is between the large trees at the edge of the lake."

Nearly free of snow, the space looked a little slippery. I was glad I wore boots with good grip.

"The blade isn't sharp," Tearwyn said. "Stall as long as you can, Golden, while I fix it."

My tall friend nodded and then moved over to Sir Larnerd. "We have some questions regarding the area of the duel. Are there any penalties if you go beyond the space that you have indicated?"

"No, you can move as far as you like, though if you run then you may be followed. Or the duel could be started again whenever your opponent sees fit with his choice of weapon, or the second could be attacked."

"I see. And what about the throwing of dirt or snow into your enemy's face?"

"Though such moves are legal, no true gentleman would use them."

"I shall tell my friend this. We will be with you presently."

"The duel should have started by now. You need to be quick or it will start whether you are ready or not."

Tearwyn worked quickly, running the stone up and down the blade of the short sword. He tried to smooth out a small dent but returned to the main edge as the sun sank below the horizon. Some of the servants brought by the nobles lit torches and tied them to long poles, thrusting these into the ground at various points to create a patchwork of light and shadow.

"Where did you get this sword from, Golden? It's not going to snap on me with the first block, is it?"

"The weapon is dwarven. It's strong and its balance is good, but I haven't used it much."

"Except for chopping wood, by the look of the dents," Tearwyn growled. "You said you'd started to sharpen it and yet I don't think it would slice through a block of cheese."

"I have used it to cut up the ribs of deer. It was good for getting into those difficult spots inside the carcase. I started to sharpen it and then Cassie distracted me. She said she had an itch that needed scratching."

I rolled my eyes. It was lucky he had a short sword, but a blunt one was not very helpful.

"I'm making progress, but see if you can buy me a little more time," the big man murmured.

"We are ready to start, Owl. It's not my fault that you don't understand the rules," Lord Alder yelled.

"Do you really want to fight me with a blunt sword? Would that be the act of a gentleman?" I answered.

"It wasn't a very noble to think you could use one of the legendary Cold Blades to defeat me. Why should I show a level of regard for fairness that you were obviously not prepared to give me?"

"He makes a solid point," Golden said.

"Shut up," I whispered.

"I will start the duel presently," Sir Larnerd called.

We got another sixty heartbeats until the tall man summoned the duellists to their positions.

"The point and the top section are all right but the closer to the hilt you get the blunter the edge becomes. The tip is very sharp," Tearwyn said. He had worked a miracle in the short time he toiled on the blade.

The wait had given me another advantage I hadn't foreseen. The light faded and it was now dark except for the pools of illumination near the lanterns. My eyes had no difficulty with this, but I knew my opponent's would.

I took up my position on the other side of the open area as Sir Larnerd dropped his arm. Lord Alder came at me quickly with a series of thrusts. I only just turned them away. Each jab aimed at my throat and neck so I was wary he would try and get me to focus my defence on my upper body then attack low. Instead, he spun his sword into a chop at my thigh. I blocked again and was forced backward. Kicking at one of the poles holding the torches, I caused it to fall near him. Lord Alder retreated. I followed with a lightning-fast thrust at his neck, but the chain coif defeated my point. Lord Alder swung his free fist at my face, connecting with my chin. I reeled in the direction of the icy lake. Backing away, I knocked over another pole. He didn't give me any respite and slashed at my waist. His blade cut through the thick leather of my jacket and opened a shallow wound below my ribs.

Lord Alder was good. He fought with speed and economy of movement, his blows delivered from the wrist and not the shoulder.

I batted another pole onto the ice, sending the torch skidding into the darkness. The first light I knocked over had gone out. Moving into the shadows under the canopy of bare trees, I waited. He hesitated. He squinted. Lord Alder moved forward and then slashed at my neck, but I caught the blow easily and forced his arm down. I drew my blade back and thrust as quickly as I could and was rewarded with a grunt of pain. A finger's length at the end of my sword was red with blood. He withdrew and put his hand to his side. It came away wet and I could see the look of surprise on his face. A gasp came from the onlookers and Lord Alder's eyes narrowed.

He attacked hard, slashing at my head and neck before thrusting at my chest. His stamina was admirable, but I knew the wound near his stomach would be flowing. It wouldn't kill him, but eventually it would slow him down.

In the meantime, I needed to stay alive.

In the near darkness I saw piles of branches covered by a thin layer of snow. I retreated behind them and Lord Alder followed. He stepped forward and thrust at my neck, but his foot became tangled in a hidden obstruction. I came in hard with a slash at his head. He twisted to block and lost his balance. I swung at his shoulder just below his mail coif and felt resistance. Lord Alder staggered backward and fell heavily. Jumping over the branches, I stabbed at his leg as he rolled away. The blade bit, but not as deeply as it might have had it been sharp. Lord Alder yelled in pain and sprang up. He was now near one of the torches and the crowd could see the blood. They muttered to each other and shuffled their feet. I didn't look, keeping my eyes firmly on my opponent. Crimson liquid ran from his calf muscle and shoulder. I circled like a hunting cat, letting the wounds weaken him.

"Finish me, Owl, and be done with it."

I kept my distance, waiting. The muttering grew, but I ignored it. I saw the attack coming long before Lord Alder's sword descended. It had taken all his strength to move toward me. I caught the blade and stepped into him, hammering my fist into the wound in his stomach. He screamed with pain and fell to his knees, his sword spinning from his hand. I put my foot on his chest and pushed him into the snow. Bringing my blade to his neck, I pressed the blunt portion of the weapon against his windpipe.

"This is for Elhnora and the other girls you murdered," I whispered.

He looked at me in shock. "What are you talking about?"

"You killed her because she had a female lover."

"I spoke about this with her. She said that it was over and that she liked men and women."

"You couldn't live with the shame."

"No, nobody in the nobility knew about her affair until you spoke out. She told me herself when we first met." His breathing was shallow, skin white.

I realised he would soon pass out from loss of blood. "She told you herself?"

"Yes, it wasn't a love match but I liked her spirit and we connected. The relationship held promise. Why would I have killed her?"

"Then who did?" I pushed a little harder with the blade.

"I don't know. I told her I wouldn't hold old lovers against her. That would have been hypercritical of me."

"How forward-thinking of you. Not all nobles would agree with such a sentiment."

"I have a different perspective. I'm my own man. Now, are you going to finish me or not?"

I stood back and lifted my blade. "I never wanted to kill you, Alder. I just want to find the murderer of your fiancée."

He put has hand to his throat and rubbed it carefully. "I thought that was the job of the Watch."

"I lost a friend to the killer, or killers. I want justice."

He pushed himself up on to his elbows and stared at me. "As do I."

"Do you have any idea who would murder Elhnora and her old lover?"

"I've been over it and all I could come up with is a rival family who'd be against the alliance of our two houses, or someone jealous of our marriage. I suspected Jalinta at first, but her death ended that thought," he said.

"Do you know who AK is?"

"The tattoo on her thigh? I asked her about it once but she wouldn't tell me. She said that was from a time past, too dark to remember."

The group of nobles led by Sir Larnerd made their way toward us.

"I gather that the duel is over and you are not going to kill his lordship?" the thin man asked.

"No, there is no reason to execute the innocent. Our misunderstanding is at an end."

Lord Alder's eyes held me as I stepped away. "Now that I understand what you are doing, Owl, I'll send word if I hear anything."

"My name's Ash, and I'd appreciate that."

They placed Lord Alder on a stretcher and carried him away into the darkness.

I wondered about my judgement of the man. He was obviously proud, but his engagement with Elhnora wasn't what I'd expected. Lord Alder seemed to have accepted her affair with Jalinta and appreciated the honesty of his fiancée. He'd spoken of not having double standards and he'd believed Elhnora's assurances that the relationship was at an end. Yet, he had said that there were other families in the nobility who were not happy about the match. He hadn't mentioned names, but Captain Waldheigheim would know.

Petar stitched up the wound below my ribs with the same small curved needle he had used to repair Miranda's, except he wasn't as gentle with me. He seemed to pull a little too hard every time the needle passed through my skin. I bit my bottom lip, determined not to moan with pain.

"That was well fought, Ash. I didn't know what your chances were when they insisted you use a normal blade," Golden said.

"Lord Alder was good, but he couldn't see in the dark. I can."

"But he ain't the killer," Tearwyn said.

I winced as Petar pulled another loop of twine tight on the tear in my skin. "No, he didn't have anything to do with the deaths. He believes it might be one of the families that was against his marriage."

"So, we are back to where we were before," Golden said.

"I don't think so. I'm starting to build a picture of Elhnora and now I've got another strand of this web to follow. Whether it leads to the centre of these murders or not, we will see."

The captain sat on his bay mare at the entrance to Fish Street. Two men lay in a doorway, both transfixed with crossbow bolts.

"Grandfather's or the Dance Master's?" I asked.

"I don't know yet."

He frowned deeply. "If this little undeclared war doesn't end soon I'm going to be out of a job."

"Why not arrest both crime lords? Throw them into the dungeons until they come to their senses."

"I would if I could," growled the captain. "The Grandfather has a number of the highest-ranking nobles as allies and nobody can tell me where the Dance Master is."

"So, you have to work at the problem with one hand tied."

He turned on his horse and looked down at me. "Well put, Ashley."

I winced at the use of the name and watched the sketch artist set up his easel and start drawing.

"I hear you defeated a certain young noble up at the Sacred Lake last night. I will take a guess that it had something to do with the case?"

"It was the only way I could think of to extract some information and to eliminate him as a suspect."

"Well, I'm glad you didn't kill him, because his father would have thrown you in the dungeons. Did you find what you needed?"

I told the captain of my conversation with the wounded lord and of the man's suspicions.

"The Snowfelds are the family that had most to lose from the alliance between Lord Vornhelm and Lord Alder. When Lord Ern dies, the Snowfelds are in line to take his seat on the Council of Notable

Elders. Widow Snowfeld has the necessary votes and connections to make sure it goes to her eldest son, Lord Taren. I believe that would have changed if the marriage had gone ahead. I don't understand the ins and outs of the politics – I try to stay clear of such machinations. There is one interesting connection in all of this. Grandfather has links to the Snowfelds."

"That needs investigation."

"Furthermore, I believe Lord Ern is extremely ill. He's old but had been healthy until the first storms of winter."

I thanked the captain and walked back to Rackhime's – I hadn't seen much of the irascible scribe of late. We spent the night copying maps and scrolls together.

In the morning I made my way up the slope to Petar's, just as the worst of the winter storms hit Hope.

13

ANOTHER THREAD

The snow blew at an angle across the open area in front of Petar's small mansion. The temperature dropped and forced us to close the shutters on the windows. Roaring log fires kept the cold at bay, and it was a desperate individual who crossed the courtyard to the stables for more wood. I made the journey more than once and noticed the horses wrapped in thick blankets and the doors firmly shut.

We had plenty of supplies, now the number of women staying at the house had dropped to four. Cassie, Teel, Miranda, and Stella still made the journey to Docklands by cart every afternoon and returned in the early hours of the morning; at least they had before the storm hit. Tearwyn had been caught down at the bookstore and had taken shelter with Rackhime, but Golden, Spike, and I were under Petar's roof.

The city had shut itself up as the storm howled down from the north. Gusts of wind rattled windows and blew snow down the chimneys. A tree fell near the stable, but didn't do any damage.

Golden disappeared upstairs for most of the day with Cassie, only showing himself when hunger forced an appearance. Stella resumed her favourite game of trying to seduce me, but I remained strong.

Miranda and I had reached some sort of understanding – we were civil at all times. She even started to teach me how to read the human tongue, with Petar's help. I had copied many scrolls and books in the language so I was familiar with the symbols and learned fast. After three days of fury the storm blew itself out to sea, and the sun made an appearance. It was little more than a weak, hazy blur, but it was there.

Outside the snow lay as deep as a man's thigh, drifting to greater depths in the lee of buildings. Everything sat covered in a white blanket, unbroken and pure. It didn't stay that way for long. Soon people ventured around Hope in search of fuel for their fires or food for their stomachs. News reached us that over two hundred souls had frozen to death, all of them in the poorer areas near the river or in the Run Down, an area of the southern walls of the city. Golden and I took to the fallen tree with axes. It wasn't long before we'd accumulated a large pile of branches and carried them back to the stables.

"I'm going to scout near the Snowfelds' mansion tonight, and I was wondering if you would ask around at the inns about the family, as you did last time," I said.

"I don't know if Cassie would like that."

I stopped pulling the branches and looked at him. "Are you two together?"

"Well no, but she might have the idea that we are."

"And how does that work?"

"You know when someone starts talking about how they see the future to be and you don't say that you agree with them but–"

"So, you didn't do anything to discourage her vision splendid."

My tall friend shrugged. "I didn't want to spoil the moment."

"It seems there have been lots of them lately. You need to tell her the truth."

"I don't know what that is. I really do like her but I'll be heading east as soon as the weather breaks and I've never stayed with any girl for very long. There are so many of them."

"You're a coward."

"You can talk," he mumbled.

I nodded. "Fair point, but I do need to gather information about the Snowfelds."

Suddenly Golden brightened. "I could take Cassie with me!"

The mansion sat behind a high wrought-iron fence. A snow-covered hedge obscured a view of the main building. I could see part of the second storey and the round towers that rose above the roof at the corners. The large windows were shuttered, but there was light between the slats of wood. Ivy climbed the walls, covering some of the carvings of gargoyles and dragons that arched outward from grey stone. Four men bundled in thick cloaks stood guard at the main gate; another two protected a smaller rear entrance.

The weather chilled me as I hunched near the trunk of a bare oak and watched until I heard the twelfth bells start a new day. I had to stay still or anyone trying to leave the mansion of the Snowfelds surreptitiously would spot me. My extremities numbed. I was about to give the idea away when I saw movement. A figure slipped over the fence next to a group of rowan trees. It crouched low to the ground before moving toward the park surrounding the Sacred Lake.

Following carefully, I stayed on the path ploughed through the snow by others earlier in the day. At first I moved quickly, excited by my discovery of the strange manner of the individual's departure from the mansion, but then I slowed. If I got too close and gave my surveillance away, then I would have wasted my time. The person made their way through the park and headed up a broad street to Lord Vornhelm's wall.

I got a little closer as they readied themselves to climb. Now I could see it was a woman dressed in tight-fitting leather. She'd hidden her cape in the bushes at the wall's base. A metal hook curled through the air and caught on top of the wall, and then the figure climbed. She carried a scimitar on her hip and a crossbow on her back. I wondered if she planned on using them. The visitor disappeared before I had a chance to think of what to do next. I decided not to risk going to the guards to tell them —it was too dangerous to approach them at that time of night.

It wasn't far to Petar's so I decided to get Spike and Golden to help me capture this mysterious female. I wanted to ask her what she was up to and I'd need assistance. Running, I slid on patches of ice, falling frequently, until I burst into the house. My tall friend sat in front of the fire with an expression like a thundercloud, smelling mildly of wine. I had forgotten that he had also been out that night gathering information with Cassie, but I had no time to enquire about that now.

"Sober up fast, Golden. I need your help to capture a spy working for the Snowfelds. She went over the wall into Lord Vornhelm's not long ago and I want to catch her as she leaves."

He stood quickly and reached for his sword and then gave Spike a shove. The dire wolf opened one eye and closed it again. "Get up, you fleabag, we've got work to do."

The animal stretched and yawned and then padded toward the door.

"So, you think a spy working for the Snowfelds might be able to tell us something useful?"

I watched as he pulled the bearskin cape around his shoulder and picked up a short bow.

"There's a chance."

Grabbing my hand crossbow, I quickly loaded it. It was a small but powerful weapon I had specially commissioned years ago. Two bolts sat one above the other, both fired with separate triggers. The problem with the crossbow being, once it had been used, it took a long time to reload. Opening the front door the cold hit me and I suppressed the urge to go back inside.

We crouched just inside the park where we could see the place the spy had left her cape. I didn't think we'd have long to wait. The intruder had limited time before the cold seeped through leather armour. The night was freezing and the tree branches were now outlined in frost.

I started to wonder at the wisdom of fetching my friend. He stumbled in the snow, his movements slowed by alcohol. I knew Spike would be an asset. The big wolf seemed to sense we were hunting and crouched low, watching the area I stared at.

"We will let her come over the wall and then head her off just past the footbridge," I whispered.

Golden grunted and strung his bow. I wasn't sure how he would fire it accurately while wearing his thick cloak, but it was too late to worry now. I reminded him that we wanted the woman alive.

She came over the wall gracefully and retrieved her rope. After throwing the cape around her shoulders, she slid across the road and entered the park. I signalled Golden to advance and made my way to the oak trees that stood near the footbridge. My friend stumbled, fell, and I cursed him under my breath for the noise. Spike glided through the snow like a shadow. I worked to slow the beating of my heart and waited. The woman didn't cross the bridge or take the track at the edge of the lake as I expected her to.

I heard a curse and then a thump on the other side of some snow-covered foliage and realised the spy must have flanked us and attacked Golden. Hurdling the bush, I landed in a small drift.

Extending my arm, I aimed at the two struggling figures. A small hand chopped sideways and Golden dropped to his knees. The female pulled back his neck and held a long dagger to his throat.

"Stop!" I yelled.

The female's hood fell away and I got a clear view of her face. The pointed ears and high cheekbones gave away her elf race in an instant.

"Well met, cousin," she purred.

Her knife pressed a little closer to Golden's neck and a thin line of blood appeared.

"I'm not your cousin and my race and yours, though related, hardly get on."

"Be that as it may, we seem to be at an impasse. If I slit your friend's throat you will shoot me before I take to two steps. And yet I don't think I should let him go."

"Sorry Ash, she got the jump on me."

"Shut up, human. Your clumsiness was ridiculous and you are no longer part of this discussion."

I thought that little barb would hurt my big friend's pride, but if all he received was a wound then he would get off easy. "I just wanted to ask you a few questions."

She seemed to consider my request. "I don't think so. I've got a report to give, but not to you – unless you want to pay me?"

I could tell she was being flippant. She would never trust a deal forged in these circumstances. Yet I found her demeanour interesting. The elf seemed prepared to engage in banter while her life hung in the balance.

"I'm investigating the death of Elhnora Vornhelm and the murder of three other women around Docklands a while back." I thought I saw a glimmer of understanding in the female's eyes.

"Hence your presence near his lordship's walls at this early hour. Well, I don't know anything about those murders."

I had no way of telling whether she was lying, so I decided to press a little harder. "Then what were you doing in Lord Vornhelm's grounds?"

"I can't tell you that."

"I need to know if it has any bearing on the murders."

"Too bad. Now how are we going to solve this stand-off? I don't really fancy dragging your tall friend all the way back to my lair as a human shield."

"I'm prepared to let you walk if you tell us what you are doing for the Snowfelds."

The elf's face hardened and I realised I had made a mistake. She now knew that I had been following her for longer than she thought.

Lifting her hand to point the dagger at me, she had just opened her mouth to speak when Spike sprang from the darkness without a sound and caught her wrist in his jaws. He hauled her backward as the weapon flew into the snow

"No, Spike!" I yelled. I didn't want the elf to lose her arm, but I had heard a snap. The spy screamed in pain and turned to run, her right wrist dangling by her side. The wolf was on her again before she took more than a few steps. He hit the elf in the shoulder and knocked her down onto the ground. I waded through the snow and yelled at her to stay still. She froze and I went to her, keeping the crossbow aimed at her legs.

"You all right Golden?" I asked.

"Just a shaving cut, I'll live."

"Can you tie her? We need to take her back to question."

"Why bother? Maybe we should stand on her wound until she talks,' Golden answered.

"That's just your pride talking because she took you down."

"I'm not at my best tonight, all right."

"I think you owe Spike an extra-large steak."

Golden didn't say anything, but I could hear him muttering to himself as he tied her arms. She grimaced in pain but tried to hide her discomfort. I admired her toughness.

We took the spy to Petar's and tied her to a chair. I put her arm in a splint and made sure she was comfortable but secure, then bandaged the teeth marks on her wrist. No one woke up, despite the noise. The fact that I had left the house so vulnerable disturbed me – a mistake I would not make again.

"What are we going to do with her?" Golden asked.

His expression had changed and I could see him eye the female with interest. She was certainly a striking individual with more curves than most elves, who usually struck me as an androgynous race. Her corn-blonde hair had been tied back in a plait and deep-blue eyes sat above high cheekbones. The elf's nose resembled a small pink button and the upswept ears were almost concealed.

"We keep her until she talks," I said

"But then she will return to the Snowfelds and tell them what we are up to," Golden said.

"So? If they have nothing to do with the murders that won't matter."

"But if they do?"

"We will deal with that if it happens. Do you have a name?" I asked the elf.

She continued to stare at the floor, her expression frozen.

"I could get Spike to bite her again."

That caused a flicker of movement on the elf's face. The wolf, however, didn't move from his place in front of the fire.

"I don't think he likes the taste of elf," I said.

The thought of hurting this female made me ill. Golden, despite his tough talk, wouldn't touch her either. I thought time and care might work better.

"We need to call you something," I said to her.

"Why? I'm content to use Owl when addressing you."

"My name's Ash."

"I know who you are, and who your big dumb companion is. It's amazing how disappointed I am now that I've met you. You really didn't measure up."

"There's always the chance of a rematch," my friend growled.

"No there isn't. Look, I just want a name," I said.

The elf stared at the floor, then mumbled, "Kat".

"Your name is Kat?" I asked.

"Yes, short for Katina."

"And are you a paid spy, or an assassin?"

She remained silent. In the end, Golden went upstairs to rest and I fell asleep on the chair across from our reluctant guest.

Sometime later I was awoken by voices.

"You can't keep her here," Cassie said.

"Why not?" Golden answered.

"Because, she might be dangerous. Perhaps she's the killer."

The elf snorted and turned away from the arguing pair.

"Where else can we take her? I mean, we can't carry her around town like a sack of potatoes."

"She may have information we need to find Trix's killer," I added.

Petar and Miranda entered the room, followed by Stella.

"Are we playing bondage games now?" Stella said.

Her comment was answered by a number of frosty stares and she shrugged her shoulders and drifted toward the fireplace.

"The Dark Elf really thinks his captive may know something important?" Petar said.

I explained the connection between the Snowfelds and the Vornhelms, and how we had caught Kat going over the wall into the manor. "I want to find out why," I finished.

"Then keep her here if you must," Petar said, "but do her no harm."

"I didn't plan to."

Cassie stomped out of the room, followed by Golden's perplexed stare. Miranda offered to bring everyone food, and Petar left for his study.

Stella walked over, lifted the elf's chin, and looked straight into Kat's eyes. "You're certainly pretty enough." It was the first time I'd seen the elf unnerved.

Stella kissed Kat on the mouth quickly before stepping away. "She smells of lavender," she said.

"Is sex all you think about?" I asked.

"Mostly, yes. It goes with the job. But don't you two boys pretend to me that you hadn't noticed."

I had, but the elf wasn't my type. Though I did see my tall friend staring at her again.

Stella saw the look and laughed. "I think she might be too hot for you to handle, Golden. Bested you in single combat and immune to your charms." She giggled as she left the room.

I shook my head. Stella certainly knew what buttons to push with men.

Golden's stare fixed on the elf and she held it.

"What happened between you and Cassie last night?" I hoped the question would distract him.

He looked at me as though coming out of a trance. Shaking his head, he tried to focus. "We met the redhead, Sophia, that I mentioned last time, the woman I had to tickle the information out of. We were all getting on really well, but I suppose Cassie was a little quiet, when I suggested that the three of us retire to one of the rooms at the inn. I mean, Cassie had done that kind of thing before with me and Stella, and Sophia was very interested. This time Cassie exploded in anger and slapped me and yelled about my stupidity before leaving."

"So, you didn't get any information about the Snowfelds?"

"Only that the old mother rules the house with an iron fist."

"We already knew that."

"Then I suppose the answer is no."

Kat clicked her tongue. We had both forgotten she was there. "Your stupidity is truly astounding, Long Shanks. The girl obviously feels differently about you than in the past. The casual aspect of your relationship is over and you can't expect her to share you around like she once did."

"My mother used to call me Long Shanks," Golden said.

My tall friend became even more captivated by our prisoner.

"Oh, I'm not your mother," Kat whispered. She gave my friend a look that smouldered.

I could see her game immediately and started to push him from the room. "Don't even think it. Go and find Cassie and sort out your problems with her one way or the other, but stay clear of the spy."

Golden blustered objections, but he went. I saw his broad back ascend the stairs and heard him mumbling.

I tuned to the elf. "You are too clever for your own good."

She smiled at me and licked her lips.

"And that won't work on me."

"No, your eyes are fixed on the quiet woman, the one with the long hair."

I didn't deny it, though I wondered how she knew. Kat was obviously extremely observant.

"You can't keep me here forever."

"Can't I? You were spying on Lord Vornhelm. I could take you there and hand you to his guards."

"You wouldn't do that."

"Why not?"

"Because you have an unfortunate streak of morality that prevents you from putting people in harm's way. You have a code."

"And you don't?"

She broke eye contact and her face tightened. I guessed Kat used to follow her moral inclinations but something had driven it from her.

"I still need to know what you were doing there."

"It doesn't have anything to do with the deaths of those girls."

"You may really believe that, but I want information. If the Snowfelds want to stop the alliance between Elhnora's house and Lord Alders, then they might be prepared to do anything to prevent it."

"I've heard nothing that would help you."

"Then just tell me what you were doing there."

Kat didn't answer and closed her eyes. A short while later she started to breathe deeply. I marvelled at her self-control.

Calling Spike, I put him in the room with her as an extra guard

I decided to let Kat sweat for a bit and told Miranda to watch her. She smiled and said she would.

The weather remained cold – ice crystals blew off the road and into my eyes as I caught a cart down to Rackhime's shop. He copied a large tome about the history of the Original Men and didn't stop his work as I entered the room.

"Wink came through before. Says Grandfather wants to see you. I thought he had dispensed with your services," Rackhime said.

"I believed he had."

"Well, the kid wants you to hurry. The old man lost something and had decided you're the best one to find it."

I would let him wait and started to copy a manuscript while talking with Rackhime about the gossip of Hope.

"Things have settled down since the last storm. No killings, but it feels like the tension is still around. People aren't relaxed. They walk with their heads on a swivel, always looking in case trouble is about to pounce."

"The war between the Dance Master and Grandfather isn't over yet. Both sides are just building their strength," I said.

"When will it stop?" Rackhime asked.

"Not until one of them is dead."

Grandfather sat having his beard trimmed and his nails done by a couple of attractive young women I hadn't seen before. Both had honey-coloured skin and long straight hair.

"You've been recruiting?"

"Yes. Some of my older girls are getting tired and some are just wilful. Yishna and Jamillar are from the south and are very obedient."

And both look very young, but I kept my mouth shut. Grandfather looked relaxed and pleased with himself. I tried to think of a way to spoil his day, but none came to mind.

"Ash, I leant out one of my best operatives to a noble household on the Peaks. They seem to have misplaced her and I want her back. She is freelance, but it looks bad to lose employees."

Kat was Grandfather's spy! I kept my face carefully neutral. This could be my chance to shake the old man up. "Not a dancing girl then?"

"No, no, this female is very different. She is an expert at finding hidden secrets, and I like secrets."

This information was useful. The question was, how I could best use it? I realised Grandfather would be annoyed when he found out that I had his spy and I didn't tell him, but I wanted to see what he knew about the Snowfelds. "Who did you lend her to?"

He hesitated for a heartbeat and then shrugged. "Matron Snowfeld."

"What did they want her for?"

"I don't know. They are one of the families that I have some connection with. When they need a favour, I oblige, no questions asked."

I didn't believe that. Grandfather just told me information was power. He wouldn't have released his favourite spy without finding out some details. One of the girls glanced up at me briefly before returning to her work. I thought I saw a spark of fear.

"It's not much to go on. I'll have to ask the Snowfelds some questions."

He nodded. "I have written you a letter of introduction but I doubt they'll tell you what she was doing for them."

The Snowfelds' front entrance impressed me. The double doors made of sandalwood and the floors of polished teak spoke of wealth. The servant who had brought me in led me down a corridor that ran down the middle of the mansion. Large doorways on either side went to dining and drawing rooms. One held a huge table covered in green felt. Round balls of different colours sat on it and I remembered the nobles liked to play a game called pool. The smell of different herbs drifted along the corridors and filled my nose. Light conversation came from a room in which four women perched on chairs embroidering. Two children played with wooden toy animals at their feet. The boy looked at me curiously until the servant pulled me by the cuff of my cloak.

"Come along please, we shouldn't keep the master waiting."

I followed him to a massive study complete with an archaic suit of armour standing in a corner. Shields and spears hung on the wall, as did a number of other weapons. A massive stone axe sat mounted above a fireplace at the far end of the room. I wandered down to look at it as the servant left. It was definitely made by a giant. I had seen axes like this before. One narrowly missed taking Golden's head off when we tried to find a way to the old burial grounds in the Flint Hills. A local patrol of the creatures intercepted us. I remembered my friend running for his life when Michal's bolt of power threw the giant to the ground.

"It was retrieved from the field of battle near the edge of the Old Woods by my grandfather."

I turned and found a short, slim man standing before me. He wore a black shirt and pants with high boots and carried a riding crop.

"I've seen a few up close," I remarked.

He ignored me. "You have a letter, I believe."

I handed him the parchment from Grandfather. He stood by the large windows to read it. "My name is Lord Rygon Snowfeld."

"Mine is Ash."

"The elf was looking into a personal matter for us when she disappeared."

"Can you give me some indication regarding what this problem was, Lord?"

"Is it really important?"

"I need a place to begin looking."

He waited, staring at me.

"Sir," I finished. By the gods, I hated the nobility.

"She was to investigate the area near the road to the Citadel."

I didn't really care where she was sent – I had only come here to find out why she had been asked to break into Lord Vornhelm's.

"With respect, Sir, that gives me little to go on."

"Well, isn't that why you've been brought into this, to sniff around and see what you can discover?"

"He isn't going to find much on that snippet of information."

An old woman hobbled into the room. Leaning on an ivory cane topped with silver, she stood a head shorter than I, and her hands were set like claws. Large, dark eyes examined me carefully.

"Mother, I was just talking to the Owl about the missing elf. He seems to think why we employed her is important."

"Of course, it's important, boy. It gives him a place to start. But that doesn't mean we should tell him."

Her eyes never left me, but I held her gaze with a steady one of my own.

"You got a name, Owl?"

"Ash is what I'm called, Matron."

"Well-spoken and handsome and exotic, if you like that sort of thing, and I do." She cackled at her own comment before making her way to a small couch and sitting down.

"Mother, please."

"Please what, please stay? I do believe I will. I have never met a Dark Elf. You are much like your fair brethren in looks."

"But less asexual I would hope, Matron."

The old lady laughed. "A cheeky one. I do believe I like you. But I must say that the spy appeared desirable to me."

"Well, now I know which elves to cross off my list."

"And they would be?"

"Nearly all of them, Matron."

The old lady laughed again. It was a deep-throated laugh, almost like a man's. "We sent the elf to spy on the Vornhelms."

"Mother!"

"How is else will he find her?"

The old lady turned to me. "Lord Vornhelm is our enemy, both in life and in politics. He is a brutal dictator who would squash the energy out of this city with draconian policies designed to further his own power. Of course, I would be very disappointed if word of our little spying mission got out. Everyone does it, just no one talks about it."

"I understand. I know something of the politics on the Peaks."

"Do you? Educated as well as handsome. You don't really recognize what's at stake, is my guess. It's not just a seat on the Board of Notable Elders. It's the chance to affect policy in the city. My family doesn't seek power for power's sake – we want to change the course of this city, free it up to outside influences."

Lord Snowfeld looked extremely uncomfortable with his mother's revelations, but I knew what she was doing. The old lady had drawn me in, shown me trust and then gained some in return. At least, that was her aim, but I was here for a different reason. I wanted to know if her family was behind the killing of four innocent women.

"I will be the soul of discretion, and relay any information on the elf's disappearance as quickly as it is discovered."

14

ESCAPE

"Teel is staying at Docklands and Tearwyn is down at Rackhime's shop," Golden said.

We were down to three women at Petar's. I didn't blame Teel as there hadn't been a killing for many a Ten Day. We were now approaching the end of winter and I worried I would never find Trix's killers. "How is our guest?"

"She's okay." Golden wouldn't meet my eye as he spoke and I wondered what he had been up to.

"Don't get attached to her. She would slit your throat as soon as your attention wandered."

"You needn't worry."

"Last time you said that, we found ourselves faced with an angry dragon."

Kat was still tied to the chair but I could tell by the knots that they had been redone. Miranda gestured for me to follow and I went with her to the kitchen. The strong smell of roasting chicken made my mouth water.

"I supervised the elf going to the toilet and washing but you need to keep an eye on her," Miranda said. "Golden is totally smitten by her and Cassie is extremely jealous."

"I'm not going to hang on to her much longer. She is one of Grandfather's spies out on loan to the Snowfelds."

Miranda went pale. "He doesn't know you have her, does he?"

"Not yet. When he finds out he won't be happy, but I don't care."

"He's a dangerous enemy."

"I'm not worried. I was wondering when Cassie, Teel, and you were moving out? We aren't really protecting this place anymore and it looks like the killings have stopped."

Miranda stared at me and then she took a step backward.

"I will probably be here for a long time – it's hard to explain. The other girls I haven't been told about it."

"What are you talking about?"

Miranda hopped from one foot to the other and wrung her hands. She looked as though she wanted to flee. "Petar and I are getting married." She turned and disappeared out of the kitchen, leaving me with my mouth hanging open.

I couldn't believe her. It had to be a joke. I steadied myself to confront Kat.

Golden fed her and then they laughed as bits of food fell from her mouth onto her chest.

"You could get that with your teeth if you wanted to," the elf said.

My friend turned and saw me in the doorway. His face fell and he shuffled away from her bound form.

"You can go," I said.

He pushed past me and disappeared.

"So, you're one of Grandfather's murderers," I began.

Kat's playful expression fled. Her eyes became narrow and brow furrowed. "I'm no murderer!"

"You spy for him. You kill for him, don't you?"

"You're only half-right."

"I'm trying to find a killer, or killers. Do you understand what they did to these girls? They sliced them up while they were hanging by ropes. I saw the bodies and it wasn't pretty. You seem to think this is a game. And I can see you attempting to seduce my friend so you can cut his throat and escape."

"I'm the prisoner here, don't forget. I didn't ask to be tied up and brought to this house."

"Who are you protecting?" I was yelling at her now, my fists clenched and I moved close to her.

"Me! I'm looking after myself. If I talk about what I'm doing, then Grandfather will drop me through a hole in the ice. So, you can yell at me but there is nothing that will make me open up."

I took a step backward and ran fingers through my hair. "You really don't care about what happened to those girls, do you?"

"Of course, I do, but I learnt long ago to look after myself first."

"Ah, the lack of a code, or the loss of it. Don't you want it back? Didn't it give you a compass bearing that you now miss?"

That struck home. I thought I saw her eyes mist over for a moment. Then she shook her head.

"You don't know anything about me."

"I understand enough."

I left her there and walked out onto the veranda. The sun cast its weak light on the twin horns towering over Hope. The long icicles that hung from the eaves dripped as the sun's rays turned solid into liquid.

Banging my head against one of the uprights, I wondered what to do next.

"Why are you doing that?" Stella sat on a bench farther along the veranda in the shadows.

"Because it feels so good when I stop."

She laughed loudly, stood, and stretched like a panther. I pulled my eyes away from her curves.

"What's the problem?"

"Just that I'm at another dead end trying to find the killer of one of my closest friends. And the woman I love is going to marry someone old enough to be her father."

"She told you, finally?"

"I thought you didn't know?"

"Of course, I knew. You can't blame her. You rejected her and Petar is kind. She will get security and a title and he won't be lonely. As for the other issue, I think you need to take some big risks."

Stella flowed to my side and rested her head on my shoulder. I could feel her hair on my neck.

"I've kidnapped Grandfather's spy," I said. "That's a risk."

"She seems to be a bit player in all this. You need to jump to the heart of the matter."

"The Vornhelms and the Snowfelds?"

"Elhnora is at the centre of everything," Stella said, nuzzling my ear.

I knew she was right.

Later I collapsed into bed as soon as I had eaten. The roast meat and mead sat comfortably in my stomach for a change.

I woke as the first rays of light filtered through the shutters. Thinking about Stella, I was glad that she hadn't pushed the seduction game yesterday, or I might have given in.

What she said played over in my mind. If Kat was not important, then why wouldn't she talk? Was it as simple as fear of Grandfather? What was she doing for the Snowfelds at Lord Vornhelm's mansion? I couldn't decide what to do next.

There was a loud knock at the door and then, without waiting for an answer, Miranda burst in. "The elf has escaped and Cassie and Golden are unconscious! Petar is trying to revive them."

I jumped to my feet, glad I was wearing trousers. Stumbling down the stairs, I pulled my shirt over my head. "How long ago did she escape?"

"I have no idea."

When I reached the drawing room, Cassie stood glaring at Golden and while my tall friend rubbed a huge lump on his head.

"What happened?" I asked.

"I really don't want to talk about it," he mumbled.

"Yes, how did your head end up between her thighs?" Cassie snarled. Her eyes bored into him and she clenched her fists as though ready to strike. "She was almost untied when I entered. He was crouched down in front of her when the elf snapped her legs around his neck and slammed his face into the floor. When I turned to run, something hit me in the back of the head. Petar said that there was a wooden mug near where I lay."

My tall friend sat rubbing his forehead. Cassie stormed from the room and slammed the door behind her, rattling it on its hinges.

"I don't know how you've stayed alive as long as you have," I said.

"I'm different out there." He gestured toward the east. "It's confusing in the city."

It was true, Golden's attitude was sharper away from Hope. He was focused and tactical. He didn't seem to understand the city could be just as dangerous as the wilderness.

"She could have killed you."

"I don't think that was part of her plan," Golden whispered.

"Well, you're lucky you have a thick skull. That makes the score two-zero."

"I know."

"The question is, what will happen once she reaches Grandfather's."

"Perhaps she won't go there," Miranda said. "Maybe she'll make her way back to the Snowfelds."

I nodded and thought that was more likely. Kat hadn't mentioned anything about Grandfather that sounded particularly affectionate – the only emotion she had expressed toward him was fear.

For two days it remained quiet.

I sent Golden to the inns that the nobles or their staff frequented, but he came back with little information. The Snowfelds seemed to be respected and liked by their employees. Lord Rygon was said to be fair, though cold and distant, but he didn't control the family. His mother ran the household and often made the important decisions. Everyone spoke of her with respect.

"She doesn't sound like a killer," Golden said.

"You don't know what people are capable of until they are desperate."

He grunted, shoulders slumped as he tried to pull his hair over the lump on the forehead. "I've had enough of playing spy. Use Tearwyn next time. I want some downtime before I head out east again."

I nodded, life was becoming a little too complicated for my friend. Cassie wouldn't speak to him and his attitude toward Kat was confused.

"He's happy down at Rackhime's and he'd struggle to fit in at the establishments on the Peaks. No, we won't get any more information by sniffing around the edge of things. Stella said I need to jump to the heart of the issue – maybe she's right. It's time to take a risk."

"What will you do?"

"What I do best –scout ahead in places where you don't want to get caught."

The following day, a carriage drove up Petar's driveway. They had only recently been invented and I had never seen one before. Light grey in colour and pulled by a pair of horses. It was a tall vehicle and rode on slender wheels. The interior was enclosed with a roof and the glass panels in the doors were an unheard-of luxury. The coachman directed the horse from an elevated perch and next to him sat a man-at-arms clad in mail and wearing a fur coat. Sitting on at the rear of the cab were two more soldiers wearing the surcoat of Snowfeld: a blue mantle with a snow-capped mountain in its centre.

The carriage stopped in front of the house. A man-at-arms opened the door and assisted Matron Snowfeld down the step onto the gravel driveway. Lord Petar rushed out to meet her.

"The Great Lady didn't warn me of her arrival. A house lies unprepared, but this unimportant man is humbled by the visit."

"Sir Petar, I should have come earlier. When word leaked out about your choice in house guests your residence suddenly became the most interesting on the Peaks."

"The Matron must understand that after the loss of my daughter I just wanted to protect others from the same fate."

"Of course, and how rude of me not to immediately extend my commiserations at her passing."

"It is beneath the importance of the great houses, something that this individual understands."

"It is not below the notice of my house. That is not the way I want us to be thought of."

"This old man means no disrespect."

"It is I who should beg your forgiveness."

Petar stood as though frozen.

"May I come in? You have a house guest I wish to speak to. It is cold out here and this cloak doesn't keep the chill from my bones."

He shook himself and gestured at the door. Watching the exchange from the front veranda, I quickly went inside as Matron Snowfeld shuffled forward with her white cane in hand. I was impressed with the respect she had shown Petar and the grace she had exhibited, but I had an idea of why she was here. Miranda's hunch looked like it panned out and Kat had returned to the Snowfeld manor.

The old lady made her way into the house and settled in a chair in the drawing room. Everyone gathered there to meet her. She ran her eye over the assemblage and then back to Petar.

"You have filled your house with beautiful women, Sir. I can see the attraction and it gives me an idea to do the same thing at my home, though of course I'll have to seek out the most handsome of males."

The old man blushed and mumbled something about that not being his intention.

"I tease, that is all." Matron Snowfeld's gaze turned to me. "And you, Ash, would once have been on that list, but I'm afraid you have let me down."

"That was never my intent, Madam."

"Leave us," the old lady snapped. Her voice changed and now there was iron where there had been silk.

Everyone left quickly and I found myself standing before this tiny woman feeling like a child who'd been caught stealing apples.

"You could not seriously believe that my family had something to do with the death of those girls." Her voice cut like a stiletto and she peered at me from over the top of her cane. Its silver head had been carved to represent a snow hawk. It stared at me.

"Your house would gain much from stopping the alliance between Lord Alder's family and the Vornhelms."

"We would never stoop to the murder of innocents to achieve such a goal! I know those who are not of noble birth tend to view all of us on the Peaks in the same way, but to think I would sanction the killing of young women to reach my goals! It is beyond belief!"

Matron Snowfeld was either the best actor I had ever met or told the truth. I suspected it was the latter. I sighed and sat next to her. "I didn't know you or your family, and I suspect everyone. I lost a dear friend to these killers."

"You look in the wrong place, and grief is not an excuse for foolishness."

"I didn't believe I was being foolish. I saw Kat go over the wall into the Vornhelm manor and pieces of a puzzle seemed to be coming together. If you are sending a spy against that household, then I would like to know why."

Matron Snowfeld's grip on the head of her cane tightened, the lines around her mouth hardened, then she sighed. "I can tell you because nobody will listen to a Dark Elf. I do not mean that as an insult but as a truth, and though I'm not used to explaining my actions, I see I need to put your mind at rest about my family's intentions. Lord Vornhelm started employing a number of unscrupulous characters at the start of winter and I want to find out why. Grandfather warned me of the arrival of these men in Hope and of their contracts. Kat was trying to discover what he means to do with them."

"You are telling me this is simply part of the game of politics that the nobility play?"

"I thought it was a small ploy to frighten me, but Kat wasn't sure. She told me last night she didn't think the out-of-town mercenaries were at his manor to interfere in the affairs of the Council of Notable Elders, or to attack my house directly. I wonder if they are here to strike at my ally, Grandfather, and thus weaken my family indirectly."

"Do you think that the Vornhelms are allied with the Dance Master?"

"It is possible," the old lady said.

"And why does Grandfather support you?"

"That is none of your business! Suffice to say he is a necessary evil at this point in time."

I nodded, remembering Matron Snowfeld's comment about wanting to open up Hope to outside influence, and wondered if such a policy would suit Grandfather. He was involved in many reputable trading enterprises and the repeal of tariffs and taxes would certainly improve the profits of those businesses. Maybe their alliance was based around mutual profit, but perhaps there was more to it than that. "I apologise Matron. I just want to solve these murders."

"Well, I'm hoping there hasn't been another one."

"What do you mean?"

"Kat went over the wall into the Vornhelm manor again last night, and she's disappeared."

Matron Snowfeld explained that some of the statements I had made to Kat while she was our prisoner had left her wanting to further investigate the Vornhelm manor. The old lady had pressed her for more information, but the elf wasn't prepared to elaborate until she returned to the house.

The Snowfeld carriage left a short while later. I called Golden to me and repeated what I'd been told.

"We need to assault the place and rescue her."

"That would be suicide. The mansion is heavily guarded and I have no doubt that the Watch and the Guards on the Citadel would take a very dim view of us attacking a noble household. Besides, she might already be dead."

My friend's face went white. He clenched and unclenched his right fist.

"You've really fallen for this elf, haven't you?" I asked.

He looked away and nodded.

"How long do you think you'll be in love for, this time?"

"It's not like that." My friend's different-coloured eyes were flat and cold and his voice broke on the words.

I wondered how Cassie would feel if she could hear this, but then it was not really Golden's fault.

I made a decision then. "We go over the wall tonight, but you need to keep your emotions in check. Gather all your best equipment and remember that I will be giving the orders. This type of operation is my speciality, so what I say goes."

He stood tall and held my gaze. "I'll go to the mage in Fish Street and get him to cast some extra tricks on one of my rings."

"That'll cost some gold."

"It's time I spent my money on something worthwhile."

Usually my friend made the quick decisions. In combat he was a master tactician. When we were on the road I dithered over what choices we should make, he was the one who cut through my second-guessing and got us moving. Most of the time he chooses the correct course of action. On this occasion, I had jumped. What Stella had said about getting to the heart of the matter still resonated and I didn't like the thought of Kat being held in a noble's dungeon. Enough women had died and the thought of the elf being tortured was enough to spur me into action. The thought that Trix would have approved of my plans added an extra level of motivation.

15

THE CELLAR

Golden moved around the city with energy and vigour. He hired a horse and galloped down to the mage at Fish Street before making his way back to Petar's, where he sorted through his equipment and sharpened weapons. Golden then had a long talk to Cassie – it left her in tears, but at least she now knew where she stood with him. He carefully selected his clothing for the night, choosing a tight-fitting but warm outfit.

Following his lead, I oiled my double-stringed crossbow as well as checking my leather armour. I coiled some silk rope and wrapped a small grappling hook in cloth so that it would make little noise as it caught the wall.

We summoned Tearwyn from Rackhime's. His job would be to watch with Spike from outside the mansion and cover us if we needed to flee. He readily agreed.

It was dusk before we knew it. Golden returned to the mage, retrieved his ring, and died his blond hair with dark henna before blackening his face. He was smart enough to not make any poor-taste jokes about looking like I did. We collected some meat laced with sleep poison to knock out any dogs we might meet. We also took other precautions in case the animals were trained not to take treats from strangers.

Soon, after a small dinner, Miranda approached me as I strapped on various weapons.

"Do you think she's still alive?"

"I don't know. The one thing in her favour is Lord Vornhelm is away at a small estate he owns just south of the city. He is due back tonight, according to Matron Snowfeld. They might not kill her until after he has questioned her."

"Then it's a race against time."

"It may be."

"I liked her. She had the spirit of a lioness."

"I agree."

Miranda raised one eyebrow and a smile crept across her face.

"Not like that!"

"I know. I was just teasing. You don't look at her as you do with Stella."

"I'm not in love with Stella."

Miranda blushed and she stepped toward the door.

"Are you in love with Petar?"

She frowned but didn't look away. "In a way I am. He is a very kind man."

"So, you're a replacement daughter?" That was cruel, but I wanted to hurt.

"If I am, what's wrong with that? It's what he needs and I get my freedom."

"Do you think Grandfather will let you go that easily? When I told him Trix was going to leave Hope, he wasn't happy. He indicated he would have brought her back. Grandfather is not likely to allow you to wallow in marital bliss."

She slapped me hard. I saw it coming. I didn't flinch or move aside. My head snapped sideways with the force of the blow.

"I hoped we could at least stay friends, but now I realise that is impossible. When winter officially ends, I'll ask Petar to tell you to go.

After that day, I will do my best to never see you again." She turned and strode from the room.

I almost ran after her, but instead, I just watched her go.

The wall looked higher than I remembered, but that wasn't my main concern. The moon was full and clouds flew across the sky with the speed of charging horsemen. When they parted, the street bathed in a soft light; when they returned, all was darkness. It didn't matter to me as I could see equally well in both, but I knew it would help any guards who were on duty.

The grapple caught on the second throw and bit in the stone with hardly a sound. I climbed over the wall and dropped into a small drift of snow. Golden followed, bringing the rope with him. We crouched behind a row of low bushes. Four guards stood near the front gate and two at the entrance to the main house.

After a while, I noticed another pair who made a circuit of the building and stables. They moved at a steady pace and conversed softly as they walked.

A small stone building had been built into the compound near the front gate. Reasoning that they wouldn't keep a prisoner in the main house, Kat would be in the stables or this building. I signalled to Golden we would move along the wall and around the rear of the mansion. We crept slowly and kept low until we reached the end of the row of trees. I waited until the moon disappeared before we crossed an open area to the greenhouse. We were forced to tuck ourselves between the glass panels and the high wall as the moon appeared and cast its pale-orange light across the snow.

The guards who circled the house returned. We hugged the ground. The best way to hide in winter is in the snow, so both our cloaks were light grey.

A long roof lined part of the rear fence of the compound and stuck out at the height of a very tall man. Wood lay piled under its shelter, and saws and axes hung from various hooks. In the corner was an open shelter with two walls, stacked with a number of barrels. We used the elongated shed as cover to move along the back wall until we reached an area of garden. Low hedges were shaped into sweeping walls in front of dormant rose bushes. It was a difficult expanse to cross – unusual shapes stood out against the angles of the plants and shrubs.

A line of rowan trees ran along the walls. It would be possible to follow them until we reached the other side of the compound. The only problem was an open area covered with pristine deep snow which would make our tracks easy to find. In front of us was the side of the stables. Hay bales were stacked and a cloth figure had been pinned to a wall. It looked as if the men-at-arms used the space for archery practice – A long clear yard ran from the end of the rowan trees. We had to be careful as the windows of the mansion overlooked it, some of which were lit.

Waiting until the guards had gone, I led Golden in a crouch close to the house. At the archery target I noticed a small metal bolt buried in its head. Removing the strange arrow, I saw it had a bent tip – I placed it in a pocket in my cloak. It intrigued me. The space in front of the stables remained empty. We slipped quickly inside. My friend stumbled and I grabbed his arm.

Darkness swallowed us, and even my eyes needed to adjust. The large room had a loft and twelve stalls for horses. I could smell manure and smoke. At the end of the area sat a small chicken coop with a stove built into it. It must continually burn to keep the birds alive through the bitter winter. Saddles and tack were neatly put away and the cobblestones swept clean. At the far side of the building near the chickens, a light shone under a door. I crept forward and, as I got closer, heard soft snoring. The stable master slept with an oil lantern on in case he had to check his animals in the middle of the night.

The growl of the dog took me by surprise. The animal rested on the straw in an empty stall. I reached for some meat and threw onto the straw; the noise stopped. The dog stood and stretched before sniffing the treat. It seemed to be as big as Spike but it had a broad head and small ears. The body reminded me of a barrel and its legs were short sticks in comparison with the wolf. It urinated on the meat and growled low in its throat. I pointed my crossbow at it and aimed but then it whimpered softly and collapsed, its chest rising and falling. It looked like it was sleeping.

"That spell cost me a small fortune," Golden whispered. He twisted a ring on his pointer finger a few paces away.

I signalled my thanks. There was no guarantee my bolt would have killed the dog quietly, and if it failed, we would have needed to run. I checked the barn for hidden cellars or other rooms and, finding none, decided Kat wasn't being kept here. Then we heard voices.

Making our way to the door of the stables, we saw two figures crossing the courtyard. A large man with shoulders the width of a long sword stood near a tall thin individual. Both were wrapped against the chill of the night.

"She told us something, Lord," the large man said.

"Enough to work with, yes," the other replied.

"Should I kill her, Lord?"

"No, I want Vultar to do that. Spies cannot be tolerated. We will go and plan a little visit of our own, I think."

They walked over to the front door of the mansion and disappeared inside.

Kat must be alive. Golden griped my arm. His eyes glow. I'd have to warn Matron Snowfeld – it sounded like Vornhelm planned to either attack or infiltrate her household. Judging by the direction the two men had been walking, the only place left Kat could be was the stone building near the front gate.

We checked the area and moved carefully to the wooden door. There was no light, so I started to open the latch. It creaked slightly. I stopped and greased the catch with some lard and tried again. My ears picked up no sound. We slid inside.

Crates of dried foodstuffs and sacks of grain and flour were stacked around the room. A cat sat on a barrel with a mouse in its mouth. It took one look at us and hid, taking its prey. A trapdoor lay in the middle of the floor boards, covered in a thin layer of rushes. Light leaked between the seams.

I knew as soon as we lifted the hatch that we be spotted by Kat's guard. We couldn't put them to sleep as Golden had already used that spell, and I doubted they'd eat the poisoned meat. This needed to be done the old-fashioned way.

Cupping my hands, I leaned close to Golden's ear and spoke softly, "Try not to kill anyone."

He frowned but inclined his head in what I took to be a nod.

My friend lifted the door. I dropped down into the room below. He followed and the portal fell with a soft bang.

Kat dangled, naked and unconscious from a wagon wheel that hung from a hook on the wall. Her body looked a tapestry of pain, with red welts, some bleeding, and dark bruises. I couldn't see her face as blonde hair covered it, hanging as though a shroud. Her fingernails were missing, as were her toenails. My fists clenched and I fought to control my fury. An image of Trix hanging from thick ropes flashed through my mind and I had to force it away.

Three men jumped to their feet and drew steel. I took in the room with a glance, racks of wine bottles and barrels lined the walls; a couple of oil lanterns hung from posts created bright pools of light but left the corners of the cellar in shadow.

One look at Golden's face said my request not to kill would not be followed.

The first man tried to block my friend's huge sword and then screamed as his weapon went white with frost. The Cold Blade froze the man's hands. He dropped his sword and fell to his knees. His head flew from the torso in a spray of blood. My friend stepped over the body and thrust the tip of his weapon at another guard's chest. The man fled deeper into the room. His companion moved forward to attack Golden's open flank. I caught the blow on his downstroke and my friend twisted and hammered his sword into the guard's stomach. The chain mail split with a metallic ping and he dropped sideways. I stabbed my sword into his throat to stop the gurgling. Our third opponent threw a sword at Golden's feet.

"Don't kill me. The duke told us what to do. I didn't want to hurt the elf," he pleaded.

I took in the blood running across the floor and the smell of urine. Looking at Golden I saw the muscles around his eyes tense. The Cold Blade split the guard's head like a melon.

We cut Kat down from the wheel and wrapped her in a spare cloak. Golden gently carried her to the ladder and put her over his shoulder before he climbed the rungs.

Leading the way, I checked for other guards. I worried the sound of combat had made it to the guardhouse at the front gate, but the cellar seemed well-insulated. Deciding we should go through the roof of the building, I stacked boxes and crates until I reached the higher beams where I removed the slate tiles.

The outer fortifications had been built as an extension of the room where we could lower ourselves to the ground using the rope. The hardest task was lifting Kat up through the hole in the roof and getting her safely outside. Golden managed most of it, though I could see the strain on his face as he climbed down into the street with her on his back.

We made our way to Tearwyn who took Kat from an exhausted Golden with little comment. Spike sniffed my friend and received a scratch in return.

"It's okay, boy," he muttered.

"We need to get her warm and take her to Petar. He knows his way around wounds," Tearwyn said. I nodded and led the way back through the park, scouting ahead so as not to run into the Watch.

The old man was rapidly becoming our group's field surgeon. We got Petar out of bed and he came to the room where we had laid Kat on one of the single beds. All of the women gasped when they saw the wounds on the spy's body.

"I tell you, they are not as bad as they look. The scars will fade on the flesh, yes, yes, but perhaps not on the mind."

"Did they…did they, touch her?" Golden stammered.

"Looking quickly, I can tell that the elf has not been raped. Whipped, beaten, and wounded, yes. Now go, so that I can stitch, bathe and clean. Only Miranda is to stay."

We left the room and made our way to the kitchen where Cassie put some water on for tea.

"What now?" Tearwyn asked.

"In the morning I'll warn Matron Snowfeld about what we overheard. We'll wait until Kat wakes up. Maybe she'll be able to tell us something."

Golden said nothing and stared at the stove.

"Tearwyn, can you stay here with him? Make sure he doesn't do anything stupid."

"I should go and kill them all," Golden muttered.

"I'll keep him here."

I thanked Tearwyn and went to the drawing room.

Stella brought me hot tea and bread. "So, you took that risk."

"Something is going on at that house – from what Matron Snowfeld thinks, it started before Elhnora's death. It is possible whatever Lord Vornhelm has planned caused his oldest daughter to be killed by enemies unknown."

"You don't believe the old lady is involved?"

"In the deaths, no. She was angry with me for making the accusation. Either that or she's missed her calling and should be on the stage."

"I don't know about that. Some women are very good actors. I can be, to keep the customers happy."

I smiled at her and she came and sat next to me. Her hair matted and tousled, she wore a cloak over her bed dress to stay warm.

"So, if it's not the old lady, then who?" Stella asked.

"Both families have connections in the crime world so I might return to that theme. If I had a better idea of what Lord Vornhelm is up to, I would know what questions to ask."

"I think you're getting closer."

Glancing at Stella, I gave a grim smile. She just might be right. Trix's killer was almost within my grasp.

I went straight to Matron Snowfeld. A servant led me up the stairs of her mansion past a guard. She sat by the fire in the drawing room and listened as her daughter read from a leather-bound book. The young blonde woman had a sharp, upturned nose. She smiled shyly at me before retreating. I could see shades of her mother in her eyes.

"I had Miriam when I was forty years of age. Some thought I was too old to have another child, but I proved them wrong."

"She has your eyes," I said.

"I wish she had my strength. Anyway, you are not here to discuss my youngest daughter."

"No, we have taken the spy from the cellars in the Vornhelm mansion and Petar cares for her."

"Old Petar is called Sir to those not of noble blood."

I shrugged. I was here to deliver a message and then go. "While we were there, I overheard Lord Vornhelm say he planned to return the favour with a visit of his own. I think he means to attack this household in some way."

The old lady's brow wrinkled. "I don't know why he would. The use of spies is accepted practice by all the great houses. It's his hiring of large numbers of ruffians which is unusual. But I'll put the guards on alert."

I waited for a question on Kat, but Matron Snowfeld sat and stared at me.

"Is that all?"

"Your spy was tortured and may have given away information to Lord Vornhelm. She is recovering and will be fully healed from her physical wounds in a matter of days."

"She would have told him nothing important. Her capture would indicate we were interested in what he was up to. As for her treatment in captivity, that is to be expected."

"Then you would do the same to any spy you captured?"

"Of course, and they know the risks, though I wouldn't sit in on the process."

I shook my head. "Now it is my turn to be disappointed in you, lady."

Matron Snowfeld's mouth fixed in a straight line and her eyes darkened. "It is my role to protect my family from anything that could damage it. Be that scandal, shame, physical attack, or loss of power. I will do whatever needs to be done, and if that means sacrificing a playing piece, then that is what I shall do."

Finally I understood her motives.

The nobility were all the same. They would burn the rest of us just so they could stay warm. We were nothing to them. Among my own people there were important families, but essentially all Dark Elves were seen as equal under our law. The humans had two sets of rules and they differed depending on whether you were born with a coat of arms or not.

I walked out of the Snowfeld mansion convinced they weren't the killers, not because of the matron's declaration, but because to do so wouldn't have served the purpose of her family. On the walk back to Petar's mansion I tried to work out where next to direct my effoerts.

Standing on the balcony of Petar's mansion, I watched as the snow melted off the tree branches. Occasionally a sheet of ice slid from the roof and landed with a crunch on the ground. I fingered the point of the bolt I took from the target dummy in the Vornhelm gardens.

Golden walked out and stood next to me in the sunlight. He chewed on a chicken leg before throwing the bones out onto the snow. His hair had been brushed and he looked well rested.

"You've slept?"

"From soon after you left until High Sun," Golden answered.

"Lucky you," I muttered.

He took the bolt from me and turned it over in his hand. The bent point would need to be fixed by a blacksmith. "Never seen anything like this before. Most bolts are wooden with iron tips. I've heard you can find some men out to the east who use steel crossbow bolts, but I haven't come across any myself."

"Maybe Petar has something in his books that might help. I'll give him the bolt later. It indicates someone in Lord Vornhelm's mansion is using unusual weaponry. It's unlikely this was fired by a man-at-arms."

"Could be the big individual we saw?"

"I'm thinking the shadowy figure we spotted going over the wall on my first visit to Vornhelm's house. It makes you wonder what he's up to and if Elhnora got caught up in it."

"Perhaps Grandfather could identify it."

"I'm going to let the old man sweat. If I go to see him I'll have to tell him we have Kat. He may want to look after her himself, or interview her. I'll get to Grandfather eventually, but when I'm ready."

16

UNEXPECTED VISITORS

The river ice cracked and ground as it shattered and reformed. The grinding made me jump and got on my nerves. I walked down to Docklands with Tearwyn to speak with Captain Waldheigheim.

We found him in one of the back alleys pacing through the slush in knee-high boots.

"There was another victim of the Crime War last night. The shot that killed this man was over fifty paces in the dark and hit him between the eyes," the captain said.

"Whose man was it?" I asked.

"One of Grandfather's. It's been quiet for a while but this death might liven things up. It seems the individual killed had a reputation for being able to source all sorts of illicit substances, from drugs to poisons. He was shot with this."

The captain held up a small steel bolt with metal fletching. It caught the rays of the sun and glinted in his hand.

"Now there's a coincidence," Tearwyn said.

I wish my big friend hadn't spoken, but it was out. The captain looked at me with his eyebrow raised.

"I went over the fence into Lord Vornhelm's the other night and found one of these in a target dummy," I said.

"That is interesting on so many different levels," the captain muttered. "Why did you feel the need to break into a noble residence?"

"We were retrieving something for Matron Snowfeld."

"Ashley, Ashley, you are not getting caught up in the affairs of the nobility, are you?"

I grimaced knowing the captain was from the merchant class and didn't think highly of our lords and masters.

"The fact that you found a metal bolt there similar to this one is fascinating, but I'm not sure what to do about it. I may pay the lord a visit to update him on the status of our investigation into his daughter's death and then ask a few questions, but I'll need to be careful."

"Has his lordship inquired into the investigation?"

"No, he has left me to it, and for that I'm grateful."

"I've heard that he has hired a number of ruffians as described by a certain matron."

"Well, the great houses always employ a spy or two."

"No, this was more than that. Have you heard of any movements by the Vornhelm house recently?"

"Nothing that I haven't already discussed with you, but as I said, I'll visit and we can share again in the future."

I nodded and walked to the end of the alley with Tearwyn.

The captain called to me, "It seems some of Lord Vornhelm's desires are coming to fruition. Lord Ern died late last night – his mystery winter illness finally finished him. It looks as though there is a position vacant on the Council of Notable Elders."

Kat woke up when I returned to the Peaks. She sat propped up in bed with a tray of freshly baked bread, cold meat, and cheese. The smell made me hungry, and I eyed the food with longing.

"Golden has already had some and I can't eat it all," Kat said around a mouthful.

"You sure?"

She gestured again at the meal so I cut myself a thick slice and put some cheese on it.

We ate in silence, then Golden entered the room with three mugs of ale. He gave me the smallest one, but I understood his priorities.

"I've said it to my indulgent friend here, but I'll say it to you. I cannot thank you enough for rescuing me. The best I was hoping for was a quick death and I don't think that was planned. Lord Vornhelm seemed very angry at my presence within his walls."

"You should save it all for Golden."

"No, I don't think it is as simple as that. He couldn't have saved me alone."

"You led the attempt Ash," Golden said.

"Anyway, we're glad we got you out."

"And I need to apologise," the elf whispered.

"What for?" Golden said.

"I held firm through the whipping, but when my toenails and fingernails started to come out, I broke. I told them everything including your investigation of his daughter's murder. Lord Vornhelm seemed very interested in what you were up to. I tried to be vague and misleading, but no one can last against experienced torturers."

"What type of questions were they asking?" I said.

"At first it was about why I was there and who I was working for. Then when I mentioned the murder and how you suspected the Snowfelds he became very interested. He had been informed about you, Ash, and about who originally employed you. He even knew you weren't employed by Grandfather anymore and asked who was employing you now."

"What did you tell him?"

"That it was a matter of justice for a good friend. Then he said that made you a dangerous individual."

The mention of Trix caused my heart to clench, but I also wondered what he meant.

"I picked up enough of the side conversation to understand he loathes old Petar and his daughter and they planned to make their move soon, but I don't know what he was talking about."

"Well you have no need to worry about that now," Golden said softly.

"Lord Vornhelm is up to something, and whatever he plans is drawing to some sort of conclusion," Kat muttered. "I need to warn Matron Snowfeld."

"You don't owe that family any loyalty," Golden growled.

Kat's eyes widened at his change in tone.

"The Snowfelds were prepared to sacrifice you," I said. "They did tell me of your likely whereabouts, but the matron was resigned to your fate and wouldn't have lifted a finger to help you."

Kat sipped on her ale and her eyes clouded. "Damn, I liked that old lady. She had a certain ferocious charm."

"Family first is her position, and you're not part of her clan," Golden said.

"You need to let Grandfather know I'm safe. Otherwise he might make life difficult for us if he finds out I'm here and you haven't told him," Kat said.

She was right. I had her location from him for long enough.

"I'll send him a note," I said.

Tearwyn brought the four girls back up the hill and we invited him to stay the night. I hadn't seen much of my hairy friend of late and we sat down and shared ale. He told me of the small comings and goings at Rackhime's shop and of the conflict between Grandfather and the Dance Master.

"I can't pick a winner at this stage. The Old Man seems to have more resources but his opponent is a clever operator. He strikes and slips away before anyone can respond. Most of his business has gone underground, making it hard for the Grandfather to strike back. But occasionally someone makes a mistake or is bribed and then Old Man attacks with deadly force."

"Grandfather is not an idiot. He must know that the Dance Master wouldn't deliberately have provoked a war with him."

"But that takes us back to Grandfather being behind all this," Tearwyn said.

"Well, now I know he's allied to the Snowfeld family, which does put him in the picture. Striking at Lord Vornhelm's daughter would help his noble allies, even if he wasn't asked to."

"So, he kills her as a favour and does his own girls as a pretext for starting the war?" Tearwyn said.

"It's possible, but it doesn't explain why the murder of the noble women was so vicious."

"Maybe Grandfather isn't behind the deaths but is just taking advantage of them."

"That, Tearwyn, is distinctly probable."

"Then he has no idea who the murderer is either."

A cold clear night made sure that all the fires had been stoked before everyone retired to bed. Shingles creaked as the frost hardened the moisture between them. Spike slept before the coals and snored softly. Warmth in the room made me drowsy, and I dropped into a heavy sleep on the couch.

I woke suddenly. Spike growled and I heard a yell upstairs. Pulling on a shirt, I grabbed the Cold Blade before opening the door to the passage. Two men stood on the stairway to the second floor. Both held crossbows in one hand and steel in the other. I glimpsed a large man near the front entrance pointing a bow at me before he was hauled backward. Tearwyn must have been sleeping in the study and attacked him. That left the two on the stairs.

I threw myself back into the sitting room and twisted around. One bolt struck the door and the other the floor. I got up and ran toward the stairs. Spike turned and went the other way. That's when I realised someone must be in the kitchen. The first man leapt at me with his arm extended. I blocked his attack and tried to send a surge of frost into my opponent's weapon but he withdrew his sword too fast. Parrying, he forced me backwards. The narrowness of the passageway gave me some advantage, but these men fought like professionals and worked as a team.

From the cursing and screaming upstairs and furniture breaking in the study, I knew a group attacked the house. I moved quickly, blocking one sword before snapping a blow at the arm of the second man. He yelped and jumped backward as the Cold Blade bit into him. His partner lunged for my face. I swayed aside but felt the skin split next to my ear.

Spike flew from the darkness in a blur of dark fur and slammed into the man with the wounded arm. I saw the wolf's bloody muzzle drawn in a snarl just before the teeth sank into the man's shoulder. He shook his head from side to side, ripping into bone and muscle. My opponent hesitated, shocked by the furious attack on his partner and fell back up the stairs. I followed, hoping to slash his legs from behind, but he turned and faced me halfway up. He had a height advantage, but the stairwell was dark compared to the lantern-lit hallway. Catching his sword, I flicked it toward the wall then struck with my left fist, knuckles crashing into his face. I knocked him off his feet and my blade sliced through his throat before he could regain balance.

I ran up the remaining stairs three at a time and turned to find a semi-naked Kat fighting with her fists and feet against a man cloaked in grey. Golden crawled on the ground in a pool of blood near the wall, a dagger in his shoulder. Cassie stood in the hallway with a loaded crossbow in both hands, but she couldn't get a clear shot. The hooded individual glanced at me and then sprang toward the window.

He went through the shutters, wood and glass shattering. I ran across the room with Cassie and watched a figure roll to upright and hobble away.

"Give me the crossbow," I snapped.

She glared at me and I had to wrench it from her hands.

"I can see in the dark," I said.

I tried to aim at the running figure through the branches of oaks and maples but the bolt clipped a limb, diverting it from its course.

"Bloody trees," I muttered.

By the time I had turned, Kat was leaning over Golden. My big friend smiled at her. "You should put some clothes on," he slurred.

"I thought you preferred me like this."

Cassie wrapped a blanket around the elf, covering her stitched and bruised body. I marvelled at her strength. She had fought off an armed assassin with her bare hands while recovering from her wounds. Miranda appeared with a bandage and peered at the dagger embedded in Golden's shoulder. Stella looked around the door. They had stayed hidden in their room until the fighting stopped. Then I remembered Tearwyn and Spike. I made it to the stairwell when I saw my hairy friend slowly moving toward me.

"My attacker escaped, but I left him with a set of teeth marks as a memento of his visit."

"You bit him?" I asked.

"It was good enough for Spike," Tearwyn mumbled.

"Where is the wolf?"

"He went after the man who attacked me but I called him back. If the attackers turned on him out in the gardens there would have been no one to support him."

"Are you injured?"

"My knees hurt and I've got a new collection of bruises, but I'll be all right."

"Could you move the bodies to the stables? I don't want the women to see them, especially the man Spike killed."

Tearwyn grunted his acquiescence, and I hobbled back to the

bedroom, exhausted. Petar had appeared along with a panel I had never noticed revealing an area of wall and boards.

"I heard noise outside so I slipped into a secret door built by the old owners of the house. Nobody knew, and I didn't tell but I always remembered it was there. Yes, yes, and it kept me safe."

"They weren't after you," I said.

"Sorry, Ash, but they were," Golden whispered.

He was pale and his lips barely moved. Petar prodded carefully around the dagger and checked the vein on the neck.

"They were at our host's door trying to unlock it when I walked out to go for a leak. The man in the cloak came at me and I rolled back into the room but the dagger flew so fast. If it hadn't been for Kat, I would have been killed."

"Now we're even," the elf grinned.

"It is safe to remove the weapon, but bones in the shoulder have been broken. Golden cannot use the arm for some time. There will be more blood but not for long."

Spike pushed his way into the room and rubbed his nose on Golden's leg while whimpering softly.

"It's all right, boy," my wounded friend muttered.

Petar removed the dagger slowly and stitched the hole closed as Miranda mopped the area, trying to staunch the flow of blood and allow the old man to see the tear in the skin. Golden groaned and clenched his fist. Kat took his hand and gazed into his eyes.

"Come on Cassie, let's boil some water and make some bandages," Stella said.

She led the curly-haired woman from the room, giving me a small smile as she left.

"Why would anyone want to kill you?" Miranda asked.

"I have no enemies. I have never made any," Petar said.

"You sure they weren't after Kat? If they were Vornhelm's men they could have been trying to finish what they started," I answered.

"They seemed determined to pick the lock to Petar's door," Golden said through gritted teeth.

I watched as the curved needled pierced the skin and the thread pulled the flaps together. I remembered my own wounds from the duel, now long healed.

"But that makes no sense," I muttered. "Maybe they weren't Vornhelm's men. We can check the bodies but the cloaked man and one other got away."

"It's no longer safe here," Golden murmured.

"I will not leave my house," Petar replied.

"Then I'll be staying," Miranda said.

"They won't be back," Kat stated. "At least not for a while. You killed two of their men and probably injured the others. If we had more numbers I'd watch all possible suspects for the next few days and see if there was any change in behaviour. But as we don't, all we can do is wait."

"No, I will be more proactive than that," I said. "It's time I visited Grandfather again."

———

We looked at the bodies of our attackers the following morning. There were three of them, not two – Spike had killed another in the kitchen. It was a source of some embarrassment that the wolf had been more effective than the rest of us put together. The throats of men were ripped and torn as were their chests and shoulders. The final man had a single puncture wound in the throat.

Each of the corpses carried purses containing three small diamonds and a little gold and silver. They had been well paid. A careful search didn't shed any clue on who they were. One of them had a fair complexion, appearing thin with the build and looks typical of the men from the West. The other two were shorter and had dark hair. They were from the South; men who'd probably come from families that had lived in our great continent of Theros for hundreds of years. As to whom they worked for, I had some suspicions, but no proof.

The mansion remained shut down tight, making it hard to see Grandfather. The walls bristled with warriors armed with crossbows. I didn't know any of the men on the front gate and had to wait while they asked for instructions. It was not certain that I would leave Grandfather's abode alive after this visit, and I was sure I would never be allowed past the entrance again. Golden had sworn to kill the old man if I didn't come out and I was confident that he would succeed. I hoped it that need wouldn't arise. If it came to a confrontation, then I still had a few tricks of my own.

My weapons were taken and I was ushered into Grandfather's presence on the roof of the main building. He stood wrapped in a coat made from wolverine fur. Three men flanked him, each armed with bows and swords. The wind blew from the south, ruffling his beard and playing with his hair. "Spring is here. I soon won't need a coat like this when I'm in the open."

"The river will be navigable again in a Ten Day," I said.

Grandfather grunted and continued to stare. I noticed the dark circles below his eyes and how stooped over he stood. "What do you want, Ash? I have meetings soon."

"I need to know how long ago you realised the Dance Master wasn't behind the killings of your girls."

He sighed and turned to face me. "I always knew."

"So, you decided the deaths were an opportunity to go to war with an up-and-coming rival."

"Yes. I had to convince my backers I hadn't started the confrontation and the murders gave me the chance to do that."

"Is that why you made no attempt to protect them, did nothing except hire me to investigate what was going on?"

He turned to look at the river. His eyes watered from the wind and he leaned on the railing. "The Dance Master is a threat and I need to defeat him. I didn't kill the girls, I don't know who did, but I grabbed the opportunity it gave me."

"Why are you telling me this now?"

"Because it doesn't matter anymore. The war has started and my backers are with me. Nothing you say or do is going to change that."

Anger seized me. These women were my friends, and he sacrificed them, just as Matron Snowfeld had been prepared to sacrifice Kat. "Didn't you think some of your favourite sex toys might get damaged in your little game?"

"Spare me your melodrama. I live a dangerous life and have many responsibilities. I will use whatever comes to hand to fulfil my ambitions. As for the women, there are always more."

"You are the same as the killer – no, you're worse. You are a perverted old man who throws lives away on a whim. What you don't realise is you're on borrowed time and soon everything you have built will be gone."

I knew Grandfather had a strong streak of paranoia and I wanted to feed it.

He turned and signalled his guards. "What do you know, Ash? Who's coming for me?"

"Well, Golden and Tearwyn will if you kill me."

His eyes flicked away from me and he hesitated. Then he laughed. "The gorilla and the pretty boy won't get past the front gate. I'll hunt them down and kill them first."

I knew he didn't believe it would be that easy. "Give me the killer or killers and I won't bother you again," I said.

"You are in no position to threaten me," he snarled.

"Actually, I am."

I pulled a small ring from where I had kept it under my tongue and pointed at him. Behind me a hiss broke the silence and I saw at least one bow aimed in my direction. "I will trigger the magic before an arrow hits me."

Grandfather glared at me but put up a hand. The guards relaxed their bows.

"I don't know who killed the girls."

"But you must have a possible suspect, or a suspicion," I said.

"I have no doubt it is linked to the plans of Lord Vornhelm."

"Why?"

"Because Lord Ern's death was not caused by his illness."

I must have looked away or blinked because Grandfather nodded at his guards. Spinning, I triggered the ring. A blast of energy surged forward in a wave and threw two of the men off their feet. The third man came at me with his sword, but I had one more trick. I banged the heel of my boot on the ground and a blade appeared from just below the toes. Twisting past the downstroke of the weapon, I kicked hard into the man's hip. He screamed and dropped his sword as the blade snapped in his flesh. I pounced on the weapon and turned to Grandfather. His face went white and his mouth opened as I put the point of the long sword on his throat. Behind me the wounded guard moaned.

"I must tell them to search more carefully," he muttered.

"I would like to kill you, but now is not the time. Just leave me to find the killer."

"Why should I?"

"Because if you do, I'll discover what is going on at Vornhelm's manor and probably knock one of the Dance Master's allies out of the way. If I'm right, he's working with Elhnora's father and that's why you are allied with the Snowfelds."

"If you swear you will stop him from taking a position on the Council of Notable Elders, you can walk away and feel secure in the knowledge I won't touch you or your friends, for now."

Nodding, I wondered how I would keep my bargain. Realising my bonds to this ruthless old man had become tighter, I cursed softly.

17

THE SPY

I had to see Lord Vornhelm so I could make some judgement of his character and get a better feel for his household. I knew he was aware of my investigations, but all attempts at gaining an interview had been rebuffed. Not being sure if it was his men who had attacked Petar, I could only suspect he was behind the attempt to kill the old man. I didn't understand why, but it might have something to do with Petar's daughter's relationship with Elhnora. Grandfather wouldn't help me and even though Captain Waldheigheim was going to visit Lord Vornhelm at some stage, I couldn't rely on his judgment.

"The bolt is from the east and used by the Hunters of Men. The books told me and now I tell the Dark Elf," Petar said.

"I've heard of those killers," Golden said. "I thought they were no longer around. The League of Eastern Towns banned them after many of their members became kidnappers." My friend eased his arm off the table and readjusted the sling before reaching for a mug of ale with his good hand.

"The books say they were once numerous, but how they stand now I cannot tell," Petar added. "The writing is old."

"Well it's the best we have to go on," I said. "Though I don't know how it helps us."

"The contract of the Hunters of Men is for life or until released by his employer. That is how it was," Petar muttered.

"Which means our man will not be leaving, unless Lord Vornhelm sends him on his way," I said.

"That seems unlikely. I would put money on this individual being the one who threw the dagger into my shoulder."

"I agree, but I wonder if he is also the mysterious Man of Shadows," I said.

"This individual works for Lord Vornhelm?" Petar asked.

"Yes, and is the same person seen around Docklands," I answered.

"Then the Great Lord wants to kill me?"

"Without a doubt."

The old man fell silent and stared at the fire that smouldered in the hearth. "He must blame my family in some way for his daughter's death."

"I no longer try to work out the motivation of the families. All I can say is he doesn't like you."

Chewing on the problem of seeing Lord Vornhelm brought me no closer to a solution. Cassie carried in a bowl of stew and mug of ale from the kitchen. She sat across from me and ate bread and mutton, carving off small pieces of meat with a sharp knife. I thought of how she looked like the Dance Master in terms of build and colouring. Knowing they were both from the race of Original Men, I could see the similarities clearly now. Then it clicked into place.

"Shafali, how long have you been working for the Dance Master?"

She gripped her knife, knuckles turning white. Maybe I should have broached this topic when she didn't have a weapon in her hand.

"I'm called Cassie," she whispered.

"But you said it used to be Shafali. That is a name for one of the

Original Men, the people who were here before the fair-skinned humans crossed the sea and started to take the land."

"I left that name behind."

"Ah, but you didn't really because you owe your allegiance to one of your people, someone who helped you long ago, maybe when you were a child."

Cassie looked around as if she might run and then slumped back on her stool.

"How did you find out?"

"It took me a long time to realise it and the pieces only just fell into place. When I met the Dance Master he said to call him Sundeep, the name of an old friend."

Cassie sat a little straighter and her eyes grew round.

"I'm guessing you knew Sundeep. Anyway, this told me he was of the race of Original Men. Then he mentioned he had the location of all of the working women. I said he couldn't have followed us and he informed me he hadn't. Which meant someone told him. That person was you."

She looked down at the table and her eyes grew moist. For a moment I thought she wouldn't speak. "I didn't want to tell him, as I wasn't sure if he was behind the killings. I kept hearing the Grandfather believed he had committed such horrible acts in order to destroy his business at Docklands, but the Dance Master assured me he didn't have anything to do with the murders."

"He didn't, and Grandfather knows it. He always knew but used the deaths as a pretext to start the war."

"So, I told him everything, about your suspicions, about the duel, about the capture of Kat, I didn't hold back."

I nodded. "Well, now I need his help. I know he has some influence with Lord Vornhelm and I want an interview. Every attempt I have made so far has been rebuffed. There are clues in that house to the identity of those behind these killings. If I can expose the murders then Grandfather's reasons for starting the war will collapse."

Cassie nodded. "I can pass along your message."

Now I needed to wait. I decided to try and visit Lord Alder and see if he had any information that would help. Not being sure what reception I would receive after almost killing him in the duel made me hesitate, but I also wanted to shake him up with what I knew about Lord Ern's death.

When I presented myself at his mansion I was let in almost immediately. I followed a servant through the guardhouse and along a long driveway. The hedges on either side of the path were shaped like men-at-arms or knights on horseback. All the trees were in rows and the garden beds laid out with military precision.

The house at the end of the road loomed three storeys high with towers at all four corners. A large stable with a steep roof decorated with stone dragons sat to the side of the structure. All of the buildings were made of marble and many of the upper windows glistened with stained glass. The sound of men-at-arms drilling behind the house to the sound of drums rang clear and loud.

I was taken along polished teak boards to stairs that wound up through small towers to the upper floors. Lord Alder sat on a balcony facing north. He held a cane in one hand and looked tired. The view of the river and the lower city spread before me.

"Impressive, is it not? I like to come here and think sometimes."

"And what do you contemplate today, Lord?" I asked.

"I often go over our duel in my mind's eye trying to find a way I could have defeated you."

"I just got lucky, Lord."

"No, you were better, and stop calling me Lord, my name is Alder."

This man had changed. Gone was the insistence on protocol and formality.

"You haven't come here to gloat, so why the visit? Ash isn't it?"

"Yes, it is, Lord, I mean Alder. I came to ask if you knew anything of the plans of Lord Vornhelm."

"He is very ambitious for his family, which is only right and proper, but he is also a ruthless man."

"Why do you say that?"

"Because of his military reputation. Any stories you may have heard about his conduct of the assault on the Great Hobgoblin fortress are correct. He spent men's lives like copper coins. My father told me, as he was there."

"Your father admires him?"

"He did before he became ill. He is an old man now and recently had a fit. He can no longer walk or talk."

"I'm sorry."

"I head the family and until our duel I must say I didn't take the responsibility seriously. I thought I was indestructible. Now I know better."

"You will recover in time though, won't you?"

"My wounds became infected, and I lay with fever for a while. I'm weakened but I will recover fully, eventually."

I was embarrassed at how I had brought this great man low. Having pushed him into the duel as a way of gaining information with little thought of the repercussions I now felt a slither of guilt.

He must have read my face. "You did me a favour. I was arrogant and stupid."

"I pushed you into the duel because I wanted to find out who killed Elhnora."

"I know, and you suspected me."

"I suspect everyone."

"And now you seek information on her father?"

"The Vornhelm schemes are at the centre of everything. I'm sure. Somehow Elhnora got caught up in the family arrangements and his enemies killed her, or she was sacrificed. I don't know really what led to her death as I have no idea what her father plans."

"That's easy. He wants a seat on the Council of Notable Elders when there's a vacancy."

"And now there is a position."

"Indeed."

"One brought about through murder."

Lord Alder's brow furrowed, and he looked at me. "What do you mean? Lord Ern died because his lungs filled with fluid. He was old and sick."

"I have it on the best authority that he was poisoned, and I believe Lord Vornhelm is behind the death." I explained my reasoning leaving out Grandfather's name but mentioning the Hunter of Men employed by Lord Vornhelm.

Alder nodded. "But you have no absolute proof."

"Not yet."

"If you get it, I want to know immediately. I will not be party to such actions and my house resolves to no longer support his."

"You would cancel your marriage to his second daughter?"

"I would do so without delay, if you find proof."

My estimation of Lord Alder improved by the heartbeat.

My next visit let me to Captain Waldheigheim and for once I found him in his office. He closed the door as I entered and gestured at a chair. I wondered at the improvement of our relationship since the start of winter and sat down smiling.

"It's not often I see you happy, Ashley."

I ignored the name. "Just a memory."

"Well your recollections aside, I'm glad you're here. This time I have some information for you. The man killed in the alley was dealing in poisons. He had a large quantity of white spider venom at his abode. I believe whoever assassinated Lord Ern had been purchasing the toxin from our poison merchant and then murdered him to cover his tracks."

"And that man is employed by Lord Vornhelm," I said.

"Exactly!"

"And the poison was used to kill Lord Ern."

The captain looked confused, sat back in his chair, and drummed his fingers on the table. "Lord Ern was supposed to have died of natural causes."

"Not according to Grandfather."

"Oh, Ashley, I thought I would be surprising you with news but you have trumped me again."

I spread my hands and smiled.

"So, is Grandfather behind the killings?" the captain asked.

"No, I don't think he would have told me what he knew if he was."

"Well, this apothecary was a freelance agent as it turned out, who worked for Grandfather occasionally. So he could have been working for someone else."

"And now we know who. Did you find out anything when you visited Lord Vornhelm?"

Captain Waldheigheim looked at his shoes. "He wouldn't see me. He said he was far too busy and to come back when I had caught the killer of his daughter."

"Well, I'm going to visit him, one way or the other."

It was raining when I got outside making the cobblestone road slick. Walking quickly I pulled the hood of my cape over my long hair.

I passed the information onto Lord Alder as quickly as I could. Stopping at Rackhime's shop, I got him to write it on a parchment and send it by messenger. "That's a powerful accusation, Ash."

Glancing at my old friend, I noticed the extra lines on his face. With a start, I realised he would be sixty-eight cycles in a few days' time.

"I'll be back for your birthday," I said.

"If you're alive."

There was nothing flippant in his comment. His face set in a look of concern. I went to him and slapped him gently on the back.

"I'm not that easy to kill. You won't get rid of me."

"I want you to outlive me, Ash."

I had no answer to that and smiled weakly before leaving.

When I returned to Petar's house I found Golden and Kat in the drawing room. They were laughing together, and I realised I hadn't seen my friend this happy in a long time. He grinned at me as I sat down.

"How are the wounds?" I asked Kat.

"Toes still hurt, but I'm a big girl. I'll be okay, but this sook keeps whingeing about his shoulder."

"It hurts!" Golden said.

I chuckled and then launched into the tale of all I learnt. At the end of it my friend whistled.

"It's all coming together, Ash. If you can push Lord Vornhelm then he might tell you who he believes killed his daughter."

Kat shook her head. "He is a very dangerous man."

"I have to try. So much of this doesn't make any sense to me. If Elhnora was at the centre of this, why where the other girls killed? I can even understand Jalinta's murder but Trix's–" my voice broke slightly as the pain surged. "I just can't connect the facts."

"Maybe you never will. Sometimes life doesn't tie up very neatly," Kat said gently.

"No, that's not good enough. Not this time. Somebody knows why this happened and when I find that person I will make them talk. Trix's death is not going to go unpunished."

"And I'll give you whatever help you need," Golden said.

Smiling, I tapped him on his good shoulder before making my way out to the kitchen.

I found Miranda stirring a pot of soup. Her hair hung tied at the back, her skin flushed from the heat, and she wore a large leather apron that almost brushed the ground. I moved toward her instinctively. Our lips met, and we kissed long and hard. She sighed into my mouth and pushed against me. I didn't care anymore. I just wanted to be with her. Then there was a cough behind us.

Turning, I saw Petar looking at the floor. Miranda pushed away from me.

"I'm sorry, it was a rush of blood. Nothing has changed."

For an instant I couldn't understand why she was apologising to the old man, but then the reality of their engagement hit me.

"It is understandable. The Dark Elf is here, and he tempts. You are right, he must go."

"My name is Ash and the reason I'm here, old man, is that I search for your daughter's killer."

He spun on me and pointed at the door. "You can do that from somewhere else. But now leave!"

Petar's shouting attracted Golden and Kat from the drawing room and Stella from upstairs.

"You all must go. I want my house back so I can share it with my wife-to-be. You must be gone by morning."

He stalked off toward his study with Miranda following closely.

"What did you do?" Golden asked.

Walking slowly up the stairs, I went to pack my things.

I found an inn to stay at on the Peaks, paying the owner extra so as to grease the wheels of commerce, and told my friends they could have my room at Rackhime's. Tearwyn could sleep in the workroom. I needed to be close to the source of the action, and that was all up in the noble district. Stella sighed and returned to Docklands, as did Cassie.

Cassie tracked me down in the Mermaid the following day. She pushed a slip of parchment across to me.

"The Dance Master has set up a meeting for you tomorrow. You have to go by yourself and all your weapons will be taken," she said.

"That's to be expected," I answered.

"The Master also would appreciate it if you didn't tell anyone else about my role in his organisation."

"I would never do anything to put your life in danger, Cassie."

She sighed and took my hand. "We have something in common now. The person we love has chosen another."

I smiled. "Yes, but in my case, I brought fate down upon myself."

Cassie looked at the wall and hesitated. "I like you, Ash, and want you to be happy. It's not too late for you and Miranda. I see the way she stares into the distance sometimes – what happened in the kitchen would not have been possible if she didn't still feel deeply for you."

"But she is to marry Petar."

Cassie squeezed my hand and looked into my eyes. "If you made a really strong effort to change her mind I think you would succeed."

I left the Mermaid confused. At Barnabus's, the goat curry was delicious, but I struggled to enjoy it.

Too many of my thoughts had Miranda attached to them. She had stopped working in Docklands and the only place I could see her was at Petar's. Her marriage date had been announced, and it coincided with the spring equinox. I wanted to follow up on Cassie's advice about her, but I knew my focus needed to be on the investigation.

Finishing my meal, I noticed a large dwarf at the other table eating a leg of lamb. "Tickles, I thought my date with your master wasn't until tomorrow," I called.

"We moved it forward, just to keep you on your toes. When I finish this snack we'll trot over to the safe house. Of course, we'll have to follow a few simple precautions on the way."

I followed Tickles to a side alley where two men appeared and blindfolded me. They took me along cobblestoned surfaces and through tunnels where I was told to duck. At times I felt wooden boards under my feet before they led me out onto a rocky surface again. It was designed to confuse my senses, and it worked – not that I tried very hard to follow where I was, as I had no intention of betraying the Dance Master. If I didn't know his location, then Grandfather couldn't torture it out of me. I just hoped the old crime lord wouldn't find out about the visit.

Finally, the rag disappeared, and I found myself in a small room lit by a pair of beeswax candles. Warming his hands in front of an old iron stove in the middle of the floor was a slim man with dark curly hair, his face mostly hidden under a scarf. He turned and glanced at me before turning back to the heat. Near the door a woman with short hair sat on a stool, a loaded crossbow on her lap.

I felt Tickles nudge me forward.

"Sorry for all the precautions, Ash, but I am at war," Sundeep said.

"Perfectly understandable," I answered.

"I was foolish to let you know I knew the location of Grandfather's girls. It led you to Cassie. I underestimated you – that is an error I won't make again."

"There had to be a spy, but it took me a while to figure out it was her."

Sundeep signalled, and a blade prick me between the shoulder blades. Tickles held a short dagger against my spine.

I stayed still.

"Cassie is special to me and I would hate for anyone to put her in harm's way."

"I wouldn't do that. She is someone I count as a friend – I will protect her, if I can."

Another nod and the pressure on my spine disappeared, though I still felt tingling between my shoulder blades.

"She speaks highly of you and that is one of the reasons I'm not going to kill you…today."

I heard the emphasis on the last word.

"I can get you your interview with Lord Vornhelm, though it won't be easy. My alliance with him is only one of convenience. He is a man who doesn't take orders and he will need to be persuaded. I'm not sure what you hope to gain from your visit, but that is not my business. Cassie explained the benefit to me if you succeed in your investigation, so that is another reason to support you. If you can prove Grandfather to be a liar, then I will be in your debt. However, our mutual friend must not be involved in any way. She is to be protected."

"If you get me this interview, I'll be very happy. As for Cassie, I have found that she makes her own decisions, but I will shield her where I can."

"That is all I can ask for the time being. Also, keep this Golden from my sight or I might be forced to kill him. His rejection wounded her."

The regard that Sundeep held for Cassie interested me. She was obviously much more than just somebody in his employ.

I decided prying further might not be good for my health. "Understood."

"My sources inform me that you are no longer in the service of Grandfather."

"I don't work for him directly, but he still expects a certain level of loyalty."

Sundeep put a pot of water on the stove and then lit his pipe, both without taking his eyes off me.

"I would be interested in your services, Ash, and I would repay it with more respect than you receive presently. I know you are independently wealthy and do not respond to greed. But I would always listen to your advice and I'd allow you to run relatively free, if you worked for me."

"It's nice to be appreciated for a change, but at the moment I would prefer to concentrate on the task at hand," I said.

"Be that as it may, just remember I can help you. Perhaps I could even clear the way for you with the woman you love."

That got my attention. If he was offering to kill Petar it was something that I would have to put out of his mind immediately. As much as the old man irritated me I didn't want to see him murdered. Or did I?

After a second of fantasising I shook my head. "That bird has flown, though I thank you for your offer. I will complete the task of finding these killers and then consider your proposal."

The Dance Master nodded. "If I get the interview I'll let you know."

"Thank you."

"Don't thank me yet. And Ash, be very careful."

Later in the day a note arrived at my lodgings. The interview was set for High Sun tomorrow.

18

THE INTERVIEW

The bathwater caused me to flinch. I decided to look and smell my best for tomorrow's appointment with Lord Vornhelm. So, I made certain my clothes were washed by the ladies of the Fish Street laundry. The red-faced woman said they would be ready by late morning. That was not long before the interview, but I thought I'd have time to change into the clean outfit before I rode back to the Peaks on one of the hire carts.

Scrubbing myself, I enjoying the sensations of the water and of dirty skin becoming clean. The soap I had gotten from Stella before walking back to the inn – a mistake, as she did everything she could to get herself invited into the tub. I argued that it was not practical – the distance from her rooms to my new residence was a long way. She pointed out there were plenty of tubs at her inn, or she could stay the night at mine. For the second time that day I was tempted by an offer that probably wasn't in my best interests. In the end, I fled. Sometimes Stella's raw sexuality drew me in, but it also frightened me. I found her intoxicating and yet overpowering. I knew her avert sexuality never worried my tall friend and wondered why it affected me. Perhaps I'd ask him.

Drinking cider with Golden and Kat at Rackhime's shop, I relaxed. Tearwyn joined us a little later. We talked about our plans and city gossip. I felt warm and happy for the first time in what seemed like a season, but then I remembered Trix's presence on past occasions similar to these. Biting my lip, I tried to force away the tears.

Golden caught my change of expression and raised his cup. "To friends who are no longer with us."

I returned his smile and lifted my mug, marvelling at the invisible connection that can sometimes exist between close companions.

Kat looked back and forth between the two of us. She frowned and rose to heat more milk, before sighing and returning to her stool. "I wish I had a friend like you, Ash," she said.

"You do," Golden said, putting his hand on her knee. "You just haven't realised it yet."

I slept well that night. Maybe it was the bath or the warm companionship which had reassured me, but I felt everything would work itself out. And I would bring justice to those who had murdered Trix. The answer was inside Lord Vornhelm's house

The mansion could have held back an army with its fortification. I hadn't appreciated its construction during my nocturnal visit. The lower-floor windows were arrow slits and the upper ones stood covered by iron bars. The roof contained areas where ballista could be positioned. I saw workmen cementing broken glass along the top of the thick walls surrounding the house. Lord Vornhelm made it hard for visitors to scale them during the hours of darkness.

Soldiers drilled in the open area before the stables with halberds and spears. There were a lot more men-at-arms present than at Lord Alder's mansion.

I had been met not by a servant, but by a sergeant dressed in chain mail with a long sword strapped to his waist. Two other men carrying crossbows flanked him. I was expertly searched and my daggers placed on a wooden bench near the main door. Lord Vornhelm was making it clear my visit was not going to be a friendly one.

Following my escort, we walked up a huge central staircase to a wide balcony. In a side room sat a young woman dressed in silks of pink and red, her hair tied in ribbons, playing a harp. Glancing at me briefly, she sniffing before turning away. The girl looked like one of the princess dolls you could buy from the toyshops where nobles bought presents for their children.

A woman walked from the shadows and stood before me dressed in a grey high-buttoned gown and gloves made of calfskin, her hair hidden under a small hat. She started at my presence before stepping back into the dim light of the corridor.

"Sorry, my lady, just taking the Owl to his Lordship," the Sergeant said.

"Then do not let me delay you," the woman whispered.

Mother and daughter couldn't have been more different. I passed up a small set of stairs to the next floor. Lord Vornhelm's young son wasn't around.

The Sergeant took me into a large room in which weapons of all varieties hung on the wall. The centrepiece was the stuffed head of a small dragon above the fireplace. The red and black scales were old and worn, but the teeth still looked sharp. Before the glowing coals stood a tall, thin man with the nose of an eagle and the eyes of a tiger. I could see a glow that seemed to suggest a smouldering, barely repressed anger. He positioned himself near the fireplace with his hands behind his back, unarmed except for a dagger on his hip. The doors closed behind me with a soft click.

Lord Vornhelm regarded me. His lip curled slightly before he turned and prodded the coals with a metal poker. "You wanted this interview so start, Owl. My time is precious."

The soldiers didn't intimidate me and I wasn't concerned by the disdain. I had held my ground before raging giants and contempt from different groups of humans was something I dealt with routinely. "Do you know who killed your daughter, Lord Vornhelm?"

He hesitated, and then turned slightly. "The question is, do you? I have waited for someone in authority to find my daughter's killer, but there seems to have been little progress. Then I hear that a Dark Elf from the south is involved. I believe you lost a friend, and seek justice, but I cannot help you."

The answer was evasive. He attacked the Watch for being unable to discover the murderer, but gave me assistance.

"You have many enemies, Lord. Do you think one of them might have killed your daughter?"

"Who knows? Though why then kill the other girls? I suppose these are all questions you have considered."

"All my investigations have led me to believe that Elhnora's murder is at the centre of this."

"You should address my daughter as Lady Vornhelm, even in death, Owl," the lord growled.

Funny, I thought, I had a name too. "Did your daughter know of your ambitions to take a seat on the Council of Notable Elders?"

"I do not discuss the business of my house with women or outsiders."

"Yet, I believe a position has become available in the Council, one that all my contacts suggest will fall to you. The alliance between your family and Lord Alder's, through marriage, having sealed the deal."

Lord Vornhelm strode over to his desk and sat. He linked his fingers together in a bridge and stared at the wood grain. The lines above his impressive nose deepened and the fire in his eyes glittered.

"You know much of the politics of the great houses, yet you do not understand everything. There is no alliance between my house and Lord Alder's. There will not be a marriage. And I don't cut deals like some petty merchant haggling over the price of a pig. My little girl is to remain in my household."

My information on the death of Lord Ern had severed the connection between these two great families. Lord Alder had kept his word and I fought to keep the smile off my face.

"Lady Elhnora was engaged to Lord Alder, and her death may have been seen by others as a way of breaking the growing link between your families," I said.

"I always had a second child."

My eyes widened. Even the children of these great families were only playing tokens in their game of state. The death of his daughter seemed to bother this man in terms of the slight to his family and nothing more. "Do you suspect the Snowfelds?"

"That is a question you should ask yourself. I believe you have had some contact with the old lady and I'm sure you have gained an idea of where our two families stand. She spies on me whenever she can, though her attempts are clumsy. When I catch her people, I kill them."

He was trying to unnerve me, but it wasn't working. His hostility only made me more determined. "I suppose the loss of the seat in the Council of Elders is a blow to your family."

"I never held the position to start with, and the fight to take the vacant one is wide open. I still have a good claim. It is not just a matter of taking a seat for the glory of my family – it is also about creating a strong city that can enforce its will on the wider world. The Snowfelds would open up Hope to the influences of the outside, diluting our strength and resolve. I would close the city like a fist so as to smash our enemies and to expand our reach. There are threats to our growth in the south and the east. Your people are an example. Now that a Dark Elf has taken the Snow Leopard Cloak and the Mantle of the Eagle, the Owls are united under a war leader. This individual has already defeated the Southern Dukes in battle. I predict that in the not too distant future, Hope will be at war with your race."

My mouth fell open. I didn't know about the recent history of my people. For a Dark Elf to unite the two ancient posts of the Snow Leopard and the Eagle was unprecedented. It would only occur if our land were under extreme pressure. Part of me celebrated at the news of a victory over the Southern Dukes but I wasn't happy my home city might go to war with the Dark Elves. That would place me in a difficult position.

"I suppose when that happens I will arrest you as a spy," Lord Vornhelm said.

Now I was unnerved but refused to be thrown from my task. "The death of Lord Ern was expected, but I have it on good authority he was poisoned."

Lord Vornhelm's head snapped up, eyes becoming pits. "Be very careful, Owl. I know what you are suggesting with such an accusation. Lord Ern was old and he became ill. Our winters often do that to the aged. I do not take slights against my family lightly."

"Then you would have been furious with those individuals that spread the scurrilous rumours about the Lady Elhnora and the Lady Jalinta."

"I heard those stories but could never find their source. If I had, there would have been a reckoning."

"Sir Petar's house was attacked recently and the nobleman was definitely the target."

"Obviously you are drawing some sort of connection, but I would point out that most of the families on the Peaks were disgusted at the presence at his house of the whores of Docklands and now we hear he is to marry some slut. I would suggest there would be a long list of nobles who would like to remove that old man from the Ranks of the Worthy."

I felt my anger surge at the reference to Miranda, but I forced the feelings deep. Again, Lord Vornhelm had not answered my question. "You have employed a member of the Hunters of Men recently. I have been wondering why?"

The lord's nails dug briefly into his desk before he sat back. He looked at me before clapping his hands twice. The sergeant appeared immediately.

"The interview is over, Owl, and there will not be another one. I doubt you have the talent to find my daughter's murderer."

"I will discover the killers of all four women and I'll bring them to some sort of justice."

"Words are easy. I find actions harder." He nodded at the sergeant and I heard the heavy footfall behind me.

I followed the armoured man downstairs to the second floor but then sensed eyes on me. The woman in grey watched, twisting her hands together. Tears lined her face. The grip on my arm tightened and I moved on.

When I was back on the street standing under the limbs of a bare oak tree, I stopped. The gate behind me clanged shut and the tension drained from my body.

Lord Vornhelm had not answered any of my questions, but he had shown me he was not concerned about the death of his daughter. His demeanour indicated that if his enemies had killed her to interfere with his plans, they had failed. I had been more successful in that regard with the information I had given Lord Alder. It was imperative Lord Vornhelm didn't know of my part in the cancellation of the engagement to his youngest child. If he found out, I would need to watch the shadows.

Kat and Golden were at Rackhime's shop. They sat in front of the fire sorting through their equipment. The old man had gone out to buy parchment and took Spike with him.

"Are you going somewhere?" I asked.

"Just getting ready," Golden said. "Tearwyn's out looking for new boots to travel in. We won't leave until after Miranda's wedding. Tearwyn is going to come with us and then we'll join with an adventuring group at Waddington out on the East River. Joppo and Tonk were there last I heard and they plan to explore the Tombs and Caves of the Green Moor."

"That's ogre country," I said.

"There are a few tribes there," Kat said. "But they are not the greatest concern. The Order of the Black Mage used to experiment in the area before they were destroyed."

"And you have agreed to go there?"

"For glory and gold, as they say, and somebody has to keep this idiot out of trouble," she said.

I shook my head and then told them of my interview with Lord Vornhelm.

"He sounds like a power-mad killer," Golden muttered.

"Don't underestimate him. He isn't crazy, though he does enjoy inflicting pain," Kat said.

"What do you mean?"

"He was the one who pulled out my nails while the big man held me still. The guards laughed but they didn't participate, and our shadowy friend wasn't present. Lord Vornhelm explained his disdain for all other races. Indeed, his feelings for anyone not from the nobility were decidedly unfriendly. Then he spent some time describing how he was going to kill me. The rest of the time he was shouting and seemed to be in a rage. I can honestly say that the man terrifies me."

"I will destroy him for you," Golden said.

Kat patted my tall friend on the shoulder. "You're sweet and I have no doubt you could, but I don't want to see you hung and drawn. So please leave him alone, for now."

Golden muttered under his breath but didn't pursue the topic.

"He mentioned my people and the wars," I said. "I'm ashamed to say I had no idea of what is happening to the south."

"I have heard a little of the Mountain Wolf, as some of the Dukes are calling him. He has brought about some military innovations and is allied with the tribes of Original Men from the southern jungles. His army came into the Golden hills as the weather broke and took the Dukes by surprise. Then they thrashed them in a battle by some river. Matron Snowfeld was talking about it and the need to keep Hope from getting involved."

"Lord Vornhelm has a different opinion. He can't wait to send some of the army south."

"Maybe you should come with us, Ash. It might not be safe for you here if Hope goes to war," Golden said.

"And it will be safer in the Green Moors?"

"No, but at least the danger should be manageable."

I knew what he meant. Fighting ogres and avoiding creatures from the Pit was preferable to rotting in a dungeon or being lynched by a mob.

"I will think about it. If Lord Vornhelm gets his way, then my choices may be limited."

"Do you believe you're any closer to finding out who killed the girls?" Golden asked.

"Yes, but I don't want to say anything at this time as there are a few more parts of the puzzle to put together. For one thing, I would still like to know whom the tattoo on Elhnora's thigh referred to."

"You mean the mysterious AK," Golden said.

"Yes. Lord Alder said she mentioned the tattoo was a connection to a dark period of her life."

Kat's brow furrowed and she looked as if she were puzzled.

"What is it?" I asked.

"Those letters are trying to trigger a memory. But I can't quiet grasp it."

"Maybe you are trying to remember something you saw?" Golden said.

"Heard, I think, but whatever it is it escapes me at the moment."

"If you remember, please let me know," I said.

My friend adjusted his sling and started to pack some of his possessions away. Tearwyn came through the door and threw a large sack onto the workbench.

"The captain wants to see you. He says he found the man with the scar."

The Watch house appeared quieter than it had during the recent troubles. Captain Waldheigheim met me on the roof looking out over the lower city through a spyglass. I had seen one of these devices only once before, as they were new. The captain saw the direction of my stare and held the metal tube out to me.

"A remarkable device. It makes the faraway appear close. It cost me a fortune to purchase but the spyglass fascinates me."

I held it to my eye and pointed it at Docklands. Everything appeared blurred and out of focus.

"You turn the end and the details come together, Ashley. It reminds me of a well-conducted investigation. Of course, with crime it is not so easy to bring everything into sharp relief."

I did as he instructed and gasped. The tops of distant buildings appeared as though they were a stone's throw away. It felt like I could reach out and touch them.

"It helps me keep an eye on things, but really it is not much more than a hobby. At night, I like to look through it at the stars and the moon."

I gave the device back to him and marvelled at the creations of men.

"Tearwyn said you found the man with the scar on his chin."

"Indeed, I have, and it was quite by accident. I was trying to visit Lord Vornhelm once more and was in the process of being turned away from the gates when a large individual was let through in front of me. I only caught a glimpse of him but I saw the scar and, like you, I don't believe in coincidences. I'm sure it's the individual you are looking for."

"Then both the Man of Shadows and the Scarred Man work for Lord Vornhelm – the same two men who attacked Sir Petar and who were seen around Dockside at the time of the murders."

"Of course, this proves nothing, Ashley, except that they were at Sir Petar's mansion. They could both claim they were not at Docklands."

"Miranda could identify the Scarred Man. She saw him in the Mermaid the night Jalinta disappeared."

"The testimony of a working girl would never be taken seriously in the courts. Remember, a roster of nobles chairs them and they always take the side of those who live on the Peaks over the common folk. If

Lord Vornhelm says they weren't in Docklands, then that will be the end of the matter.

I told him of the interview and he whistled between his teeth. "You are collecting enemies like a squirrel collects nuts."

"And I do it so effortlessly."

"If he is behind the death of Lord Ern and finds out about your visits with Lord Alder then he will try to have you killed."

"I know. Is there anything you can do to help me?"

The captain stroked his bottom lip and looked into space. "If I come across either the Scarred Man or the Man of Shadows, I'll bring them in for questioning. That might shake something loose."

It was all I could hope for. To do even that would bring the anger of Lord Vornhelm down on the captain. I thanked him and made my way back to the inn where I had based myself on the Peaks

———

After eating a small meal of bread and cheese, I sat in front of the fire and sipped warm mead. I was marked for death, but the question was who would try and kill me first? Grandfather might, for both my insolence and for becoming too involved in his plans. The Dance Master may if he believed I would betray Cassie's true role in Docklands, and Lord Vornhelm would if he discovered I'd been instrumental in ending the engagement between his daughter and Lord Alder.

I sighed and finished my drink. Being too wound up to sleep, I decided to take the battle to my enemies. Gathering my crossbow, daggers, and Cold Blade, I dressed in my grey cloak and leathers, and left the inn through the window of my room. I was going to watch the Vornhelm manor until I discovered something that would prove my suspicions.

Surveillance is a tedious process but it can also be dangerous. For me, the task focused my mind and gave me something to do. And there was enough activity at the Vornhelm manor to keep me entertained. Representatives from at least two different noble families visited his lordship that evening. They rode in with a small group of retainers and clattered noisily through the gates before dismounting inside the courtyard. I couldn't see what happened after that but I found it interesting the second assemblage didn't arrive until the first had departed. Lord Vornhelm was trying to keep his allies apart.

Watching until my eyes started to close, I decided I needed to sleep and made my way back to the inn. I checked the hair and the crumbs I had placed at various points within the room and found they hadn't been disturbed. They were still there, just in different positions, so my visitor was not a mouse. Already my enemies were on the move.

I grabbed my gear and made my way to Petar's stables where I climbed into the loft and curled up in the hay.

As the sun rose, I fell asleep to the sounds of the horses moving in their stalls and the chirping of swallows in the rafters.

19

DEATH IN THE PARK

I woke late as Bryson, the one-legged stable master, hitched a horse to the small cart. Lifting from the straw, I peered down. My head pounded. Lack of sleep was catching up with me.

"What are you doing up there?" Miranda stood framed by the light coming in from the doorway. She put her hair up and wore a blue cloak and high boots. "Petar wouldn't be happy if he knew you were here."

"I needed somewhere safe to sleep."

"Is Rackhime's dangerous?"

"The Peaks are where it's all happening."

"What is wrong with your inn?"

"I had uninvited visitors last night and I'm fairly sure that they wanted to end my investigations permanently."

"I see. Then, you may sleep in the barn when you need to. Just don't bring trouble back here with you."

"I'll do my best. I can generally tell when I'm being followed."

She nodded and made her way to the cart where Bryson sat watching.

"Where are you going?" I asked.

She turned, her brow furrowed. "Not that it's your business, but I'm off to choose a wedding dress. The date of the ceremony fast approaches. Of course, you are invited and I expect you to be there."

I wished I hadn't asked the question. Pulling straw from my hair, I sat up. By that time the cart was on the move and Miranda had disappeared.

Making my way to the inn, I ate a large breakfast before walking back to Lord Vornhelm's residence, where I stood in plain sight near the front gate for some time.

Later that morning I caught a cart to Rackhime's shop. Only the old man was there. Everybody else was out enjoying the sunshine. I sat at a workbench and copied a faded manuscript onto fresh parchment. I could read some of the words now, and decided learning more of the human script would be beneficial.

Rackhime came over and glanced at my work. "Your time away seems to have improved your style. It's flowing, for once, and not stilted like a spider walking on the paper."

I looked at Rackhime and took his words as praise. His wrinkled face frowned as he lifted the pot from the fire with a curved poker. I could see him straining with the weight of the iron kettle. "Do you want me to get it?"

"I'm not so old that I can't make us both a mug of hot chocolate."

I shrugged and went back to work. Rackhime wasn't getting any younger.

He placed the clay mug next to me before shuffling to his bench. Picking up a quill, he said, "You better enjoy it as that's the last of it. Golden bought the chocolate and I certainly can't afford any more."

"I'll get some if you like."

"No, too much of a good thing makes you soft."

Nodding, I let my quill flow across the fresh parchment. I always loved the sensation of words appearing in blank space. Even if the writing wasn't mine, I was a party to the creation of something important, a story or document which would remain long after my death.

"The crime war took another turn last night," Rackhime said. "Four of the Dance Master's best were caught in an ambush."

"How do you know they were his best?"

"That's the rumour, though of course I'm just repeating a rumour. Both sides spread lies and misinformation about each other. One thing's for certain, there are four bodies and they are riddled with crossbow bolts."

"Was Tickles among the dead – the big dwarf?"

"I know who Tickles is. No, there was no dwarf. But there was a tall redhead and some say it was Larkin, the Dance Master's head of smuggling."

Grandfather must have gotten someone inside Sundeep's organisation to set up an ambush that was so effective. Unless Sundeep found the informant, he was in danger of losing the war.

Not returning to the inn until after dark, I again pulled together my equipment and splashed cold water into my eyes before making my way back to the trees that lined the edge of Lake Park. From there I had a clear view of the front entrance to the Vornhelm manor. This time, there was only one family who visited, but they proclaimed their allegiance to his lordship with flourish.

The MacRobs rode in wearing their surcoats and flying their banner – the black boar on a yellow background. Six knights escorted a small man on a warhorse through the front gates. The two families who'd made their way to Lord Vornhelm's residence last night were the Rolims and the Frauldwrens, both houses holding extensive lands to the south and both standing to lose everything if the Dark Elves continued to advance. The MacRobs, however, were from the north, clear of the attacking army.

Later, I watched as a large individual led a group of mounted men toward the citadel. I guessed this was the Scarred Man, but there was no way of being certain in the dark. Chewing on some dried fruit, I thought of following them, but decided they were moving too fast for me to catch up.

I waited for a while longer until the MacRobs left. It was cold, but I forced myself to scan my surroundings every sixty heartbeats.

Knowing the watcher could always become a target, I remained wary. In the wilderness I often observed camps or villages of ogres and hobgoblins. One evening, the task almost saw me dead. Three scouts sneaked up on me as I watched a campsite by a river, saved only by Spike's warning growl. The arrow hissed by my face sent me diving into the water. By the time I'd surfaced, my unseen enemy disappeared, leaving my band of adventurers stumbling around in the dark trying to find them.

My vigilance protected me. A shape slipped silently between the trunks of two trees and approached my position from the depths of the park. Dark Elf eyes pierced the gloom and I saw movement again. Whoever attempted to stalk me was experienced and quiet.

I removed my small crossbow from under my cloak and checked the bolts. The threat made me wide awake and ready to hunt. Dropping low, I slithered to a new location behind some shrubs. The bushes were sparse but they broke up my outline. I knew whoever stalked me was unlikely to see in the dark. I waited and didn't notice any further movement. Not sure if I missed any change of position, I decided to be patient. Years of hunting in the mountains as a young adult taught me Hunters often moved too soon and frightened away their game. The only difference, my prey was now probably intent on killing me.

When the move came, it was small. The shape advanced quickly between two trees before dropping into a crouch. I couldn't see any weapons but suspected a poisoned metal bolt sat on a powerful crossbow ready to reach out and take my life.

My parading before the gates of the mansion during the day

provoked the response I'd hoped for. Lord Vornhelm must be annoyed at my presence. You could always count on the arrogance of the nobility. I slid to a young oak tree and then slowly stood, using the trunk to screen me. There was a V in the branches at chest height and I intended to use it as a firing position.

A man broke cover and crossed a small patch of open ground to a group of birch trees clustered by the path. Nearby, a low evergreen hedge ran along the walkway toward the bridge by the lake. I guessed my assailant would follow the hedge until it ended at the road. He probably believed I was still watching the manor and would use the bushes and scrub to get as close as possible to what he thought was my position. I wouldn't be able to shoot at him from here. Deciding to move to an ancient oak near the start of the path, I approached my Hunter from behind. The foliage blocked both our views, so I crossed to the tree.

When I reached the oak, I saw an unusual shape lying near a small mound of snow that had been shovelled from the path. I dived as the figure burst into movement and rolled behind the tree.

A bolt flashed past my shoulder. I landed hard. My small crossbow flew from my hand. Pressing myself against the cold bark, I cursed my overconfidence. He must have seen me move at some stage, probably when the thin moon peeked out from behind the clouds.

I scrambled for my weapon, but by now there was no sign of my Hunter. He knew my position but I didn't know his. I crawled to a park bench before sprinting to a statue of Duke Hellan, the founder of Hope.

Hearing a soft click off to my left, I tensed, expecting a bolt to slam into my side. When nothing happened, I realised the sound was of a crossbow being reloaded. His weapon was therefore only capable of a single shot, but it outranged mine. Not that it would give him an advantage in the dark. I slipped away from the regular shape of the plinth at the base of the statues and into the pine needles under two small trees.

Movement came from my left as a figure dashed behind an

evergreen bush cut to the shape of a rearing dragon. Throwing a pebble, I hoped it would tempt my Hunter into a sudden move but he was too experienced to fall for this ploy.

And so, we waited. The moon disappeared once more and I wiggled backward out from under the limbs of the pines, following a low stone wall. He must have done the same, for suddenly we were only thirty paces apart behind the barrier. Firing simultaneously, we dived for cover. You cannot shoot accurately when moving through the air – both bolts missed by a wide margin. My advantage was I had a second shot, and he knew it.

My assailant turned to flee. Now the only Hunter, I ran after him. We jumped through bushes and over low walls as the Man of Shadows tried to circle 'round me to get to the Vornhelm manor. I was determined to cut him off. All attempts at stealth were abandoned as we skidded on frost-covered grass and sprinted along gravel paths. I crossed my assailant's path, crouched and took careful aim with both hands. He sprinted toward the lanterns that lit the main road, only a dozen paces away.

I squeezed the trigger gently and heard the soft thud as it hit. He twisted and staggered from the path into a group of high bushes. I pulled a dagger and ran forward, forgetting a wounded animal can be the most dangerous of prey. He stood and threw his knife in one motion. It was only my eyesight that saved me – I swayed aside. My dagger flew before I had time to think. My shot hit him in the shoulder. I need him capable of answering some questions before I handed him over to Captain Waldheigheim. The man was hurt and couldn't see in the dark. The blade hit him on the right side of his chest. He slumped sideways to the ground and rolled onto his back.

Running over, I kicked his crossbow away before crouching over his form. My dagger had sunk in his chest to the hilt. Dark liquid already stained his teeth and lips.

"I told Vornhelm I couldn't take you at night," the man said.

He was plain, with grey eyes and a square chin. A bent nose looked as though it had been broken long ago. His hair was cut short and a tattoo of a small bow could just be seen near the collar of his vest.

"Why does he want me dead?"

The man laughed and coughed up a mouthful of blood. "I don't think he likes you much. My lord doesn't need any other reason."

"Did you kill the girls?"

"You figure it out, Owl."

I put my foot on his shoulder and pushed. He screamed in pain and rolled on the ground. I wasn't proud of myself, but I was running out of time. The Man of Shadows didn't have long for this world.

"Torture won't do it, Owl. I serve until realised or dead. Looks like death it is."

"Why did you want the poison? Did you kill Lord Ern?"

"I can't do everything. Sometimes I clean up the loose ends. Now, why don't you let me die in peace?"

Pushing my heel into his shoulder again, this time I ground down hard. Bones ground beneath my foot. "Sorry, I can't do that, I need answers."

The man screamed again. Then he rolled on his side and spat out more blood. He lay there panting and the pulled himself into a ball. "His lordship said you were dangerous. Something about this seeking of vengeance. Was it the half elf who made you so angry?"

He gurgled. Blood poured from his mouth before slowing to a trickle. His foot kicked feebly a few times before his body stilled.

It had to be him! The direct reference to Trix screamed at me. I wished my dagger hadn't been so accurate. I could have gotten the Man of Shadows to talk about the other deaths, but it was too late for that. Leaving the body in the slush, I walked for ten minutes back to the stables at Petar's house, and burrowed into the straw. Thinking Vornhelm's men would come looking for their missing assassin toward dawn, I hadn't hidden the corpse, though I took the weapons and poured a vial of poison I found in one of his pockets over the body. Throwing the steel bolts into the lake with all the daggers, I then smashed the crossbow on the path and left it near the statue.

It rained the following day. Black clouds flew in from the south and cleansed the city with a downpour that lasted most of the morning. The last of the ice broke up on the river and swept out to sea.

I found a trencher of black bread covered with dried apples, cheese and a slice of cold pie. Nearby sat a pitcher of ale. Miranda had visited while I slept and I imagined I could still catch a hint of her scent in the air.

Trix's killer was now dead. He spoke of revenge and I thought I understood. Why he killed her – and if it was Lord Vornhelm's orders that drove his blade – I didn't know. He was probably the same man who murdered Fendria. I wasn't sure who hacked apart the two noble girls, but believed I was getting closer to solving the mystery. The final piece of the puzzle lay in the tattoo on Elhnora's thigh.

Stepping from the barn, I felt tired but refreshed. The cobblestones gleamed in the sun and I could see the first tinges of green in the trees and lawn. Walking to the inn down the road, I collected my belongings.

When night arrived on All God's Day the Docklands were full of men and women who had either drunk too much alcohol or were about to. The southwest wind blew the stink of the river inland, away from Hope.

I stepped into the Mermaid through the press of bodies. The noise slapped me when I broke through. Someone played the lute and people crowed at the bar. Dancing had been dispensed with and the working women either flirted with the patrons or helped serve drinks. Stella sat on the knee of a rich merchant. She winked at me and kissed the man's wife. The crowd roared with approval as the drunken woman kissed her back.

Smiling, I shook my head. A message needed to be delivered.

Cassie carried a tray of drinks to a table of young men. They called her and threw some coins, begging her to stay. Cassie smiled and shook her head. I caught her eye and signalled her in my direction. She raised an eyebrow and weaved her way across the room.

When she was close, I pulled her into my arms and kissed her quickly on the lips. She stepped back, her mouth becoming a small circle of surprise. I held her shoulders and smiled at her. "Trix's and Fendria's murderer is dead."

Cassie shook her head. "What?" She couldn't hear me over the noise. I pulled her into a side alcove where the volume of conversation was lower and repeated myself.

Her eyes brightened and she put down her tray. She then pulled me close and hugged me. "You're sure?"

"I'm certain. I have one more piece of the puzzle to find and then I'll have the reasons behind her death."

"What about the murderer of the noble girls?"

"That is a different killer, or should I say killers."

Cassie hugged me again and her smile split her face from ear to ear. "We should tell Stella and the others."

"I'll do that. I want you to inform our mutual friend, and ask him if I can see him. He may be able to help with the final piece or point me in the right direction."

"You want me to go to him now?"

"Tonight, or tomorrow would be good. I'm so close, Cassie, I can almost taste it."

She nodded and disappeared.

It was a lot harder to get Stella alone. She was always popular on nights like these. Stella burned like a beacon that men and women approached as moths did a flame and she shone on all of them. When she saw me, I could read the hunger in her eyes. I thanked all the gods the place was crowded and I would be able to slip away from her without incident. At first, I thought it might be best not revealing my news, but Stella deserved to know. She had stood next to me through the entire journey and her help was pivotal to the investigation.

When Stella finally stood but a pace from me, I held out my hand.

She stopped and frowned. I leaned in and whispered in her ear and she screamed with delight. "Did you do it? Did you kill him?"

I nodded and she kissed me. It wasn't like the way Cassie kissed me; this was the embrace of a lover and I melted into her. It was some time before I pulled myself away, gasping for air. Now wasn't the time to be overwhelmed.

"Come upstairs with me now and celebrate," she said.

I took another step backward and she pouted. My escape wasn't going to be as easy as I thought. One of the young men who'd tempted Cassie grabbed Stella around the waist and pulled her to his table of friends. I heard her shriek in frustration and I moved as fast as I could to the doorway. Outside, I gulped in a lungful of fresh air before walking back to Rackhime's house to share the news with Golden and the others.

The story of the fight with the Man of Shadows echoed in Rackhime's rafters many times before Teel, Anita, and Cassie arrived. The women brought bottles of wine sealed with cork and wax, and we all toasted Trix and drank to my success.

As I drank depression consumed me. Soon I was crying in my wine and the girls were trying to console me. Golden laughed and Kat rolled her eyes. Tearwyn kept filling my cup and Rackhime tried to ignore everyone. The night became a blur.

I woke the following morning in the large chair near the workbench. My head pounded and my mouth tasted like I had been licking a fur coat.

Questions danced around in my mind. I was certain I'd killed Trix's murderer. The man said I was partway along my quest for justice. The two working girls had been murdered quickly with precise cuts to the throat. The slices on their bodies occurred after death and the weapon used was a dagger or heavy knife, not a razor. It seemed to me as if they had been killed and cut up in order to convince the

Watch there was a mad man at work in the Docklands. The murderer of Trix and Fendria had not been enthusiastic about his task. He killed as fast as he could without passion or anger. The Man of Shadows took their young lives for money. On the other hand, the two noble girls were butchered. They had not been assassinated. Yet, I could be wrong.

Perhaps it was the hangover. The story that Dark Elves didn't get sick after drinking large amounts of wine was a myth. My fairer cousins were said to be able to drink all night with little sign of inebriation. I also knew that to be a lie, one that I was certain Kat would agree with when she awoke.

When Golden appeared looking not much better than myself, I realised everybody who made it to Rackhime's last night was likely suffering.

"What time did we finish?" I asked.

"About dawn," Golden said.

"Was anybody sober?"

"Maybe Rackhime, but he told us he was going home soon after you passed out. He is coming in late, but expects the shop to be clean when he gets here."

"I passed out?"

"And just in time, too. Stella turned up and she was determined to take you upstairs, but you were too far gone."

I grunted at having been saved again, but on this occasion only by crawling into a bottle. My fear of that young woman was weakening. Looking around the room, I noticed the tipped-over furniture and empty wine containers lying everywhere. "We better get to it, then."

While we cleaned, I voiced my concerns to Golden. Had I really killed the girl's murderer?

"Your logic is sound, so stop tying yourself in knots. Everything you said makes sense. The only question is why he murdered them. It seems likely Lord Vornhelm ordered their deaths and that means he either knows who killed his daughter and Jalinta, or he did it himself."

"That's what I've been thinking. Though why he would protect his daughter's killer or have her murdered is beyond me. I was wondering if someone else killed Elhnora and then he had Petar's daughter murdered in revenge. But again, the link eludes me."

"I can't help you there. Are you any closer to finding out whose name starts with AK?"

"No, but I want to ask the Dance Master if he does, or if he can make inquiries. When I find that piece, the puzzle will be almost complete."

It was late in the afternoon when Cassie arrived, appearing grey and tired. She told me Tearwyn was at Docklands and looking very different than when I had last seen him.

"Why?"

"You don't remember? Teel said she would take him home if she could shave him from head to toe and the big man agreed. I thought at the time he was likely to bleed to death during the process, considering the state Teel was in, but I believe he's remarkably cut-free and smiling from ear to ear today."

"Then she kept her side of the bargain?" Golden asked.

"Apparently," Cassie said. "But I'm not here to discuss our wild evening. Ash, I've got a meeting time and place for you to see the Dance Master but it can't be until tonight. He wants to be very cautious as he knows someone is leaking information to Grandfather."

Golden looked shocked. "You work for the Dance Master?"

Cassie turned and smiled at me. "You didn't tell him? I thought you two shared everything."

"About each other, yes, but this wasn't my secret."

Golden's eyes narrowed and he stared at me. "How long have you known?"

"Only a short time."

"Don't worry, Golden. Ash didn't realise until after you moved on to a new female."

My tall friend looked at his feet and mumbled what sounded like an apology under his breath before retreating upstairs.

"My estimation of you grows by the day, Ash. You are worthy of trust and I will make sure the Dance Master knows."

I glowed in the praise of an attractive woman and felt the effects of my hangover fade into the background.

20

A DEBT OF GRATITUDE

By the time Rackhime arrived the shop glistened. He inspected the workbenches and the storerooms and returned satisfied.

"I would prefer parties to remain a rare event, please, Ash," he said, readying his ink and quill.

"They will. My body can't take too many nights like that." My head started pounding again soon after Cassie left. It seemed the stroked male ego could only drive away the effects of wine for a limited time.

"I was surprised by your revelations about Trix's killer, but then I realised the nobles, particularly the great families, are capable of anything."

"Yet, some of them are your best clients," I said.

"I take their money but I never socialise with them. They usually send a representative of their house to deal with me – they don't want to have to associate with tradesmen like myself."

This wasn't strictly true as a number of the lesser families did visit Rackhime's store, but I was too tired to argue.

"What will you do next? You could walk away now, happy you

have avenged the deaths of Trix and Fendria. That would be the sensible course of action."

It wasn't that easy. I had made promises both to the Dance Master and Grandfather I hadn't fulfilled. And I didn't know who had killed the two noble girls, though I was close. Having met Jalinta, I wanted justice for her father, despite the fact he was marrying the woman I loved. I needed to solve this mystery for Elhnora. Never having met her was irrelevant. I believe I would have liked the wild noble girl. The picture I had built of her had come from others. But these people, with the exception of her father, had spoken highly of her. I wasn't going to walk away from this. "I will bring Elhnora's killer to account, one way or another."

Rackhime rubbed his forehead. "I thought you would say something like that."

The market thrummed with noise and movement. I had promised the old man I'd get him some fresh bread, cheese and dried meat. Our impromptu celebration had exhausted all the food supplies at the shop, so it was my responsibility to restock the larder.

I decided I'd go to the small market on the Devil's Peaks – I had seen sheep cheese there and knew Rackhime had a taste for it. Missing his birthday, I thought I'd purchase other delicacies he liked, too, such as coco beans and tea from the far south. The only place you would find them was where the rich people shopped.

An area near the park between the two peaks, just before the land dropped away toward the slums of Southern Hope, was set aside for the merchants who sold items that appealed to the nobility.

I collected some of my gold pieces and chopped silver from a chest hidden behind the cesspit in the rear of the shop. Holding my nose, I whispered the command word to disable the magic that would scorch anyone who tried to steal my savings. Then I used a large bronze key and retrieved what I needed.

I could see that there was a lot more space in the chest than in the past, but the bag of diamonds and other gems was still intact, ready to be traded for more silver.

At the market I purchased a large sack of coco beans and a wheel of sheep cheese. Glancing around, looking for the tea stall, I spotted a lady veiled in grey. Behind her two men-at-arms argued with a stallholder about the price of dried apples. They both wore the surcoats of Lord Vornhelm – a mailed fist on a black background.

I remembered Lady Vornhelm's face running with tears as I left the interview with her husband, and wanted to find out if the grief was for her daughter. She moved further away from the men-at-arms and I circled behind her, using some stalls holding livestock for cover. Moving slowly, I pretended to look at the animals as I approached her. I got distracted at one point and decided I would get a turkey to roast for Rackhime later.

When I looked up again, Lady Vornhelm was only a few paces away, appraising strawberries packed on ice that had been shipped from the south.

I stepped into her path and she jumped. "Lady Vornhelm, I'm sorry to disturb you on such a fine day, but I was wondering if you could answer a few questions?"

Her daughter's large blue eyes started back at me, and her face showed the same lines. She stood slowly and her mouth fell open. For an instant, I thought she would faint.

"I shouldn't be talking to you," she whispered.

"I'm sorry, I didn't mean to scare you."

"My life is filled with fear and you are the least of it, Owl."

"My name is Ash, and I don't wish to cause you any pain."

"It is a little late for that."

"Lady Vornhelm," I said with more power. "I seek the killer of your daughter. I want to bring her murderer to justice."

She sighed and looked away. "I wish it were that easy, Ash."

I was surprised she had used my name, but pushed on. "Do you know who killed her?"

She stepped toward me and grabbed my hand. The strength of her grip startled me.

"I want the killer brought to justice, I really do."

"Then tell me and I'll do it for you!"

I saw the pain in this woman's eyes, in Elhnora's eyes. She held something in that look which hungered for release. Tears ran down her cheeks, but then I saw her face tighten. "I will tell you," she said.

"My lady, is the Owl upsetting you?"

I almost screamed with frustration. One of the men-at-arms forced his way between us. He had a high forehead and a pointed chin that reminded me of a kite with hair. His small eyes looked similar to those of an angry pig. The other soldier had a face like a collapsed lung and was probably the ugliest man I had ever met.

Lady Vornhelm burst into tears and turned away. Everybody at the market stopped and stared.

"Now boys, I was only asking a few questions." I took a few steps backward.

Both of the men-at-arms became aware of the spectators and decided somehow their honour was at stake. "You're coming with us," Pig Eyes said, drawing his sword.

I wasn't going to run with naked steel at my back, so before the weapon was clear of the scabbard I punched the man on his pointed chin. He fell with a grunt and hit the cobblestones.

His ugly companion tried to hit me with a roundhouse swing which I ducked under. Then I stepped and jumped in one movement, kicking him under the chin and sending his teeth through his tongue. He fell backwards and I ran.

Shaking my fist as I weaved between the stalls, I had forgotten how much punching a man in the temple hurt. My unarmed combat instructor had always told me to use my feet or to hit the softer parts of the head.

Yelling came from behind me and cursed the fact I had left all of my purchases at the market. Later, I stopped at a stall in the merchant's district and bought everything again except for the coco beans. At least

I found some tea. I supposed I had given Lord Vornhelm another reason to kill me, but the encounter with his wife was intriguing. She had been about to tell me who she thought had killed her daughter. If I could get her alone again I'd have the answer. I didn't know how I could make this happen – the men-at-arms who accompanied her on any future shopping trips would be more vigilant and I wouldn't be able to get near her.

As I thought about Lady Vornhelm, I remembered her eyes and the incredible pain behind them. She was another victim of these crimes, like I was, just as Petar was. Raging inside against the careless men who played with the lives of my friends, I couldn't perceive much difference between Grandfather, Sundeep, or Lord Vornhelm. Now, however I believed I knew who killed the noble girls, and that thought calmed me. I just didn't know why they were murdered. First I needed to complete my shopping and return to the shop.

Rackhime was pleased with the items I bought and, for once, accepted them with good grace. He cut some of the bread and shared the cheese with me before asking about the blood on my knuckles. I explained my encounter and he chuckled.

"I thought you would tell me what a fool I was," I said.

"I get tired of doing that. I was just imagining the chaos you created. It would have been a sight."

I smiled too, remembering the knocked-over stalls and the escaping chickens, the people yelling and the man-at-arms with the bleeding tongue screaming like a captured piglet.

"Well, one thing's for certain," Rackhime said.

"What's that?"

"Lord Vornhelm won't be letting his wife out for a while."

I nodded and sadly agreed.

The meeting with the Dance Master would take place at eleven bells and I was to meet his representative on the Long Pier. I knew this jetty was where the largest of the ships that travelled from the far west tied up. It was likely to be deserted so late at night.

Tickles waited for me with the short-haired woman by some barrels and crates.

"Kedra will scout ahead," the dwarf said. "I'll have to blindfold you and lead as before."

I nodded and allowed Tickles to take my weapons. The Cold Blade, sat under my robes as well as my assortment of daggers, but I'd left the hand-held crossbow behind, deciding to bring it would have been overkill.

"This blade as good as they say?" Kedra asked.

"There are only twelve of them for a reason," I said. "I'm still discovering its powers and I've had it for two years."

The woman stared at the blade for some time before looking away down the street. "I better do my job," she mumbled to Tickles, before disappearing into the gloom.

The dwarf slipped the thick material over my eyes before tightening it and tying it off. "No peeking." He took me by the wrist and led.

"I'm not the one who is the threat to your boss."

Tickles pulled me along at an increased rate. Stumbling, I nearly fell over hidden objects more than once. I thought of asking him to slow down but decided not to give him the pleasure of knowing his actions annoyed me.

Again, we clambered through tunnels and turned in different directions. I could hear the noise of Docklands behind me. It was another mild night, and rained lightly. The area was busy. I had a better idea of where we were than last time, but doubted I'd be able to retrace my steps. Tickles took my blindfold off in a narrow alley just outside a solid wooden door.

I could make out a number of figures in the shadows. Catching the glint of steel, I saw crossbows of various types resting against walls or cradled in hands.

Sundeep stepped away from the door. I jumped in surprised when he shook me by the hand. "I heard what you did, and even though it has inconvenienced an ally it was well done."

"I know you are associated with a certain lord, but from that statement I gather you are not close?" I said.

Sundeep shrugged. "The enemy of my enemy and all that, but no, I have as little to do with him as possible."

"I wanted you to help with identifying the owner of some initials. These letters could be part of a name or they might stand for something else."

I spotted movement in the dark on the eves near the end of the alley. "Do you have men on the roof?" I asked.

Sundeep's eyes widened and I pushed him toward the door.

"Bust it open, Tickles," the Dance Master yelled.

The dwarf moved slowly, but jumped at the door when the first crossbow bolt skipped off the brickwork near his head. I heard the grunts as steel slammed into bodies, then the screams of wounded. One of Sundeep's guards fired at a figure on the roof but the shot went wide. Men ran down the alley from both directions, firing as they came.

I pulled Sundeep to the ground and watched as Tickles hit the door with the back of his axe. The wood splintered and burst apart but a bolt took the dwarf in the shoulder before he could jump inside. He tumbled into the welcoming darkness. I sprang after him, hauling Sundeep with me.

The small room held only some folded tables and chairs but there was a door on the far side. I heard noises as the tenants of the upper floors woke and became aware something was happening.

Tickles climbed to his feet behind me and pulled the Cold Blade from under his cloak, along with some of my daggers, then tossed them to me. "Get out of here, boss. I'll hold the doorway."

Sundeep seemed to hesitate before moving toward the passageway. "Thank you, old friend," he called over his shoulder.

We dashed down the corridor, pushing frightened people back into their rooms as we went. I stopped Sundeep at the front door, not wanting to burst out onto the street into the midst of another group of Grandfather's thugs.

Listening, I opened the entry a crack. I saw three men peering down the alley to where the battle raged. Tickles bellowed like an angry bull while someone screamed and screamed.

"We will have to remove those three before we can go anywhere," I said.

Sundeep nodded and pulled a short sword from under his robe. I held the Cold Blade in my left hand, a throwing dagger in my right. We sprang from the door together and ran toward the men clustered at the end of the alley. One had a crossbow and the other two had blades.

I threw as I moved – my dagger hit the individual with the crossbow in the small of his back. He clutched at the wound while his companions spun around. The taller of the men swung overhand with his long sword. I caught it on the Cold Blade. I stepped into him and smashed my head into his face. He screamed and fell. Blood streamed from his nose as he hacked at me semi-blinded. My opponent had no skill and drew his arm wide to give power to the blow instead of chopping from the wrist. I flicked my blade across his throat and he stumbled into the wall, slumping sideways.

Behind me, the other thug choked Sundeep, lifting him off the ground. This man had a barrel of a body and his muscles strained as he squeezed. Both men had somehow lost their weapons in the early stages of combat and now used bare hands. Sundeep's face turned blue. He kicked his feet. The Cold Blade slid through the man's chain-mail vest and into his kidney before exiting at the base of his chest. He let go of Sundeep and slipped off my sword.

The Dance Master rubbed his throat and glanced down the alley to where Tickles still held the doorway.

"We can't leave him there," I said.

Sundeep nodded. The rain started to lash us and the road ran with water. I stepped into the alley. "We're down here, you idiots," I yelled down the street.

"What are you doing?" Sundeep croaked.

"Trust me," I whispered.

Three men broke away from the door and ran toward us waving maces and axes. I glanced at the roof for any snipers, they seemed to have gone. Putting the tip of my sword into the water, I imagined a cold frosty morning with the trees outlined in white. The wet road froze before me with a crack.

One of the running men slipped and fell, crashing into the wall before landing on his back. Another skidded toward me with arms flailing as he tried to gain balance. I stepped into him and stabbed his chest before he could steady himself and then pushed him off my sword. The third man stopped, turned, and staggered away.

Sundeep picked up one of the crossbows his men had left propped against the wall earlier and shot the running figure in the back.

Tickles finished the man at the door with a sweep of his axe and then came out into the alley. He still had the bolt in his shoulder but ignored it. "Thanks for not leavin' me," he said.

Sundeep shrugged. There was the hint of a smile on his face. The man who had fallen whimpered and the dwarf kicked him hard in the chest. A rib snapped and he moaned. All of the other wounded seemed to have stopped moving.

"We don't have time for that, Tickles," I said. "We need to get out of here."

"Wait," the Dance Master hissed. "I want some answers." He pulled a dagger from his belt and put his foot on the man's hand.

"Ash, don't let 'em hurt me."

I recognised the voice and a face came to me. "Trask, is that you?"

"Yeah, I was just doin' me job. I didn't know you was goin' to be here."

"A bit late for that now," the Dance Master said. "Please hold him, Tickles."

The dwarf took a firm grip on Trask's arm.

"Don't let 'em hurt me."

I knew Trask from Docklands and my visits to Grandfather's mansion. He was one of the few who had joked with me and showed me friendship. I remembered his freckled face and hooked nose as he laughed at my comments. Of course, he had just tried to kill me; though it wasn't personal it dampened my enthusiasm for helping him. "Tell us what you know and we will let you go," I said.

"I know nothin'. We was sent to kill everyone in this alley. We were told it would end the war and there would be a bonus in gold. I knew that meant the Dance Master would be here, but I didn't realise you would be."

"Well, that makes me feel much better," Sundeep said. "Now, if you just tell me who told you we would be here?"

"I don't know, I swear."

"Wrong answer."

The finger came off with a quick slice of the dagger and Trask screamed.

"That noise will bring the Watch, boss," Tickles said.

"You are right, of course, so speak quickly or I'll take off your manhood and throw it to the dogs."

"It was some woman, that's all I heard," Trask said.

The Dance Master nodded and stood. "Tickles, where is Kedra?"

"She was supposed to be scouting ahead."

"Well, she will have some explaining to do, if we ever see her again."

"She did seem a little too interested in my sword," I muttered. "She must have imagined taking it from Tickles' corpse."

"Will you let me go now?" Trask croaked.

The Dance Master nodded to Tickles and the axe swept down, cutting off the man's head at the shoulders.

I grimaced and looked away. "Was that necessary?"

"I was doing you a favour. If your old friend here had reported you were with me, how long do you think Grandfather would let you live?"

He had a point, but the execution had come too easily. It was a timely reminder of who Sundeep was.

We left the alley full of bodies and jogged toward Fish Street. The rain fell in sheets and I imagined the rivers of blood that ran from the victims of the assassination attempt before it flowed into the grate to the sewer.

Twelve men died. It would be a busy night for Captain Waldheigheim and I thought it would be unwise to explain my part in the carnage. Again, I had helped save a crime lord from death. This one seemed to have a streak of loyalty toward his followers – he could have refused to aid Tickles but hadn't hesitated when I made the suggestion to help. He wasn't a coward, unlike Grandfather.

In the end, I never asked Sundeep about the letters on Elhnora's thigh. We separated at Red Square – I headed toward Rackhime's shop and Tickles went to get treatment on the crossbow bolt sticking out of his shoulder. I didn't hear the dwarf complain about his wound and I marvelled at his fortitude.

I thought of what would happen to Kedra if the Dance Master caught her. I pondered on the way loyalty can sometimes be bought and sold. Maybe everybody had a price and I tried to think what mine might be.

The weather turned again. Rain the colour of ink poured from skies and the streets ran like mountain streams. It wasn't cold, but you didn't want to stay outside for very long. Occasionally thunder crashed and lightning split the clouds. I stayed in the stables at Petar's house and brooded.

Golden's arm hung in its sling. It healed slowly but soon he and Kat would take to the road and head east. Before then, though, I was supposed to attend the marriage of the woman I loved to a man old enough to be her father. I had pushed her in Petar's direction, yet part of me believed if she couldn't be with me then she shouldn't be with anyone. Killing rats in the hay with my crossbow and talking to the horses didn't help my melancholy.

All I saw were eyes. I visualised the lifeless blue orbs of Elhnora morphing into those of her mother – eyes full of puzzlement becoming those of intense pain and mourning. Then I would imagine Trix's bright eyes smiling at me across a bar or laughing at my stupidity. I didn't go to see Golden or Tearwyn, nor did I return to the bookshop to write. Instead, I tried to think of a way to make everything all right.

The only person who knew where I was sleeping was Miranda. She would leave bread, milk, and cheese on the bottom step of the ladder to the hayloft and then go without saying anything. Sometimes I would see her glance in my direction and shake her head.

Eventually Golden found me. I supposed Miranda told him where I was. His arm was out of the sling but he moved it carefully, and I could see it still caused him some pain.

"What are you doing?" he asked me.

"I don't really know anymore. Getting ready to bring the final killer to justice perhaps?"

"I thought you would be happy after you killed Trix's murderer. Instead, you're worse."

"It's not over yet, there's still one to go. Ther's also the question of why the girls were killed."

"I suppose it isn't finished for you. Ash doesn't believe in leaving a task half-done."

"I'm here," I snapped. "Don't start talking like Petar. That crazy old man is the other part of my problem."

Golden shook his head. "No, he's not. What happened with Miranda is entirely of your own making."

That shut me up. He was right.

"When I first brought you to Hope, Ash, you spent your time neck-deep in your own self-pity, hunched over a drink, spitting venom at half the bar, but by the gods you could fight. I dragged you into the wilderness and slowly you emerged as a sensitive and smart male who thought too much, but you always stood by me. Now, I give you a choice. End this downward plunge or Kat and I will take you east."

Looking at him, I felt the corner of my lips rise and could see him doing it, too. The thought of Golden carrying me from Hope in a sack, almost brought a smile back to my face. I couldn't leave, not yet. There was still unfinished business on the Peaks that shaded this city and I wasn't going anywhere until I could imagine myself facing Lady

Vornhelm and saying, "I did it. I brought your daughter's killer to justice. She can rest now." I had to visit the Vornhelm mansion one last time.

Then I would make sure her father was made to account for his crimes. Perhaps, after that, I could rest.

21

THE DEVIL ON THE PEAKS

The rain stopped but the air remained oppressive and heavy. I booked myself into another inn, the Foaming Mug, marvelling at the originality of the name. I found that my association with Lord Alder was now opening doors for me and I no longer had to pay more for a room than most patrons. Having a bath, I then ate a decent meal, and cleaned my clothes and equipment.

Tonight, I was going to go over the wall to find Lady Vornhelm and find out why her daughter had been killed. I went to Rackhime's shop soon after lunch to get some more silver – I wanted to recharge the ring Golden had given me and I needed more money to pay the magician. Only Kat was at the shop. She was toasting bread on the open flames. She spread honey on it. Offering me a slice, she sat down and pointed at a chair. I took a seat and ate.

"So, are you coming with us, or is Golden going to carry you?"

I swallowed and looked away. "I can't come. He was right. I have to finish this. I have a plan and I'm no longer brooding."

"Well, that sounds promising. I've been thinking about those letters in the tattoo and believe I've recalled the memory they triggered. When I was hidden in a closet in the Vornhelm manor, I heard the Lady of the house call for Akardy. I didn't know who she was talking about until Lord Vornhelm answered."

I dropped my toast. "Do you mean to tell me that Elhnora had tattooed her own father's name on her inner thigh?"

"It certainly seems that way."

"But why would she do that?"

Kat raised an eyebrow and picked up my toast.

"It's dirty now. I might as well throw it in the fire," she said.

It all fell into place like the spokes on a lock. I just had to confirm my theory.

Walking to Docklands early in the afternoon, I found Cassie at the Mermaid.

She smiled when she saw me, crossed over the floor and kissed me on the cheek. "I haven't seen you for a while, stranger. Has Stella frightened you away?"

"No, I was busy digging myself a deep, dark hole, but now I've decided to climb out."

Cassie stepped back and frowned. "Glad to hear it, but if you were feeling that way you should have come to your friends. You have a number of them, you know."

Nodding, I squeezed her hands. "I need you to tell our friend I'm not striking against him and my actions might indirectly help his cause."

"What are you planning?" Cassie said.

"A final reckoning, I hope, but I can't tell you more as it would put you in a compromising position."

"I'm used to them."

"I suppose you are, but I hope in a few days' time we will be able to celebrate an end to these murders."

"Do you know who killed the noble girls?"

I didn't answer, but I kissed Cassie again and walked out into the gathering dusk. I knew but I wasn't sure why.

This was going to be a difficult undertaking. I had to enter the mansion of Lord Vornhelm in the early hours of the morning and then find his wife by herself to ask my questions. Then I had to slip away unseen. I remembered Golden had mentioned the Lord didn't share a room with his lady. This was something Sophia had told him while being tickled. The memory of his investigations made me smile briefly.

I needed to find Lady Vornhelm's room and wake her. Arming myself with all of my weapons, I then dressed in leather armour. The ring Golden had given me was charged and would give me another means of defending myself, but I wanted to avoid confrontation. I was sure Lord Vornhelm would have strengthened his security, as both Kat and then I had slipped into his grounds with little difficulty. There would be dogs and guards, but I hoped the rain would help. It came down steadily and made it dark enough to trouble even my eyes. There was no one about on the walk to the Vornhelm residence due to the weather and the late hour.

Climbing the wall into the compound at the back corner near the line of rowan trees, I had to throw a thick hide of heavy material over the top of the broken glass that lined the crest. Creeping along to the long shed where the wood was stored, I hid the leather sheet among the cut timber. It remained dry here. I watched for a while, noting which windows were lit and the circuit of the sentries. Men-at-arms now circled the yard more often than on my last visit. One of them led a dog.

As they came past, I backed into the woodshed. The rain masked my scent and made the sentries less vigilant. I heard a guard mutter about the weather and even the hound appeared miserable.

Scanning the rear of the tall mansion, I looked for a point of entry. The backdoor would be locked and I didn't have the skills to open it. If Kat had been with me, she could have performed that task, but I had deliberately chosen to do this by myself. I hadn't asked the elf how she got inside, or even told my friends what I was up to. I knew they would have insisted on coming with me.

The arrow-slit ground-floor windows were too narrow to enter through and the upper ones were barred. I had the option of climbing to the roof and trying to find a way in from there, but I would be vulnerable as I climbed the walls. Then, I spotted the entrance to the wood cellar. I waited until the sentries passed a second time and sprinted to twin doors near the wall. As I did, the rain redoubled its intensity. The entry to the wood cellar was locked, but it was possible to slip my sword between the double doors and lift the offending plank off. It dropped onto the floor of the cellar with a thud I hoped nobody heard.

Once inside, I clambered down a pile of cut timber and closed the doors to the outside.

A set of stairs led to another door at the other side of the small room. I tried the handle and pushed. It was barred as well, but again, there was a space between the timber and the wall, though it was narrow. My sword wouldn't fit, but a flat-bladed throwing knife would. Remembering the thump as the last plank had fallen, I realised I couldn't take the chance of it being heard. Slowly and carefully I eased my cloak under the door. The crack was a little less than the length of my thumb, so it took some time to push the material through.

Finally, I was ready. It required three tries to lift the plank clear with the shorter dagger. Luckily, the beam wasn't heavy. It fell to the ground with a muffled thud and I gently eased the door open.

The smell of baking bread wafted along the passage. I was near the kitchen. I crept up a long corridor toward a light source at the end. The hallway hit an intersection. I chose to go right. All I found was a storage room filled with cheese, dried fruits, and salted pork, so it seemed left was my only option if I wanted to continue.

When I retraced my steps, I noticed stairs at the end of the corridor, but an open area led to the kitchen before I could get to them. The heat drifted down the passage and I could hear someone humming.

I dropped onto my belly and slid forward. Pulling a small mirror from my back pack, I held it just around the corner, angling it to see a man working at a long table kneading dough. His bald head glistened with the effort and he hummed as he worked. Another individual with an ample stomach carried a large iron pot to the fire, where he placed it in the coals with a number of other pots. These staff must be baking the bread for the Vornhelm's household. I'd have to cross the open space to the stairwell unseen, or they'd raise the alarm.

Having no enchanted item that would put them to sleep, I decided against confrontation – it didn't feel right to kill a couple of cooks. Watching with the mirror, I thought on how to move through that area quickly and quietly. Both men seemed engrossed in their tasks, so I took a deep breath and walked across.

It probably only took me a heartbeat. I expected a yell to come from behind me, but I crossed into the shadow of the passageway and made it to the entrance. The door swung easily and I was in the main building.

The wide corridor at the bottom of the grand staircase disappeared in shadow. Voices came from a room near the front doors and a light source emanated from near the smaller rear entrance.

A man came from the back room and walked toward my location, his boots heavy on the wooden floorboards. When he passed my hiding spot, I noted he wore a chain vest and carried a long sword at his hip. He called out. A guard stuck his head from the front room and answered, apparently about the intensity of the rain.

There were obviously sentries at both ends of the mansion, but I had no way of knowing how many without going closer. It wasn't worth the risk. There were no barracks at the noble residences so men-at-arms had to find their own accommodation before coming to do their duty – I knew the number of soldiers would be limited. The sentries patrolling outside and these men in the house would be all those available to Lord Vornhelm at short notice, though I thought there might be a few in the stables. I waited until the man-at-arms had returned before creeping toward the central staircase.

Realising the sound of rain would only cover any soft noises I made, I tested every floorboard before putting my full weight on it, avoiding those areas I heard squeak as the man-at-arms passed. The carpeted stairs allowed me to move a little faster. I listened for any movement from above or below – a small possibility loomed that there would be guards on the first level. Making my way up the grand staircase to a wide landing, I stopped and listened. A platform ran around the edge of this floor, leaving a large central open area. Ahead of me two smaller staircases went to the next level. Five doorways lined the passage with light coming from under one – I remembered it as the room where I interviewed Lord Vornhelm. He was probably in there now, working, and the bedrooms would be up on the highest floor.

I swiftly made it to the fourth step of the smaller staircase before the door to Lord Vornhelm's study opened. A large man with a scar on his chin stepped out and murmured something back into the room before making his way downstairs. I froze and crouched low as he passed the stairway entrance. He had come from a well-lit area and I was in the shadows. Letting out a long breath, I heard the man's footfall on the grand staircase.

The second floor consisted of a corridor that ran the length of the building, near the rear wall to the two towers that jutted above the roof. Another passage met the one I was in at the halfway point and went toward the front of the house. Four doors on this corridor indicated four rooms. I slowly opened the latch to the first one and peered inside. It was dark, but my eyes allowed me to see a large bed, a couple of high-backed chairs, a chest and a small table. The room held little warmth and the bed had not been used. This might be the guest area.

Carefully closing the door, I went down the corridor to the next. This one felt cosy and warm. A large chimney ran up the rear wall, the bricks giving off a soft heat. The furniture appeared the same as the last room, except the chest was larger and the table covered with embroidery. A figure lay under the blankets in the middle of the bed – as I moved closer I could see it was a woman sleeping on her front, with hair covering her face. I crept across to the bed and reached out to lift some strands of off her cheek so I would know who it was.

As my fingers brushed the skin, the figure stirred and rolled over.

"Daddy is that you? I fell asleep waiting." She pulled back the blankets to reveal a young woman's naked body.

I recoiled and walked quickly toward the door.

"Daddy, why are you going?" the girl asked.

I heard a shutter clank and realised a light source was by the bed. The hooded lantern lit up the room like a sunrise. She screamed.

The run to the stairway only took a breath, but already someone stood there. The large man with the scar charged at me, taking the steps two at a time. I launched myself feet first. Slamming into him, I rode him backward and then hit with an elbow to the face when we finally came to rest. Jumping up, I ran to the top of the grand staircase. Two men came at me from a side door, both dressed only in shirts and trousers but carrying weapons. A hand axe spun through the air. I just swayed out of the way. The weapon hit the wall at the other end of the landing. I triggered my ring.

A bubble of energy sprang from my fist and surged into both men, knocking them from their feet. Lord Vornhelm stood silhouetted by the light streaming from his study. He yelled for assistance. More guards came from another entrance on this level, while others sprang up the stairs.

My only chance was to get to the back door and kick it open. I'd have to run for my rope at the corner of the compound and hope nobody had a bow. I charged the men coming towards me, shooting one in the shoulder with my hand-held crossbow and another in the thigh. Both fell, yelling and cursing. I ran past them, but three more guards blocked the bottom of the stairs. My Cold Blade swept through the defence of the first sentry before he knew what was happening. I attacked the other men-at-arms, desperately pushing them away with a flurry of strokes toward the bottom steps. Feet pounded down the stairs behind me. I leapt over the banister, falling the height of a man to the ground. Turning, I sprinted toward the rear entrance but a foot shot out from the side passage, tripping me and sending me sprawling to the floorboards. I had started to roll over when I saw the fat cook from the bakery loom above me. My sword had skidded from my hands. I fumbled for a dagger as I tried to scramble upright. The heavy skillet descended. I think I heard a clang and then darkness reigned.

My head hurt and the ringing in my ears slowly became a buzzing. Cold water crashed over me. I jerked back to consciousness. My arms hung shackled to a beam that ran along a low roof, my feet were bound with thick rope, and my leather jacket and shirt had been removed. Seeing large barrels lining the wall, I smelled wine and cheese. Groaning, I realised where I was.

"So, you recognise this room, do you, Owl?" a deep voice said. "I thought you would. After all, it is where you killed three of my guards."

Lord Vornhelm stood before me in a silk shirt, wearing long striped pants, and high boots. Behind him, two men-at-arms held torches that sputtered in the moist air. Nearby the man with the scar watched while, pushing a damp cloth onto his jaw.

"I didn't kill them," I muttered.

I saw the blow coming but could do nothing to avoid it. When Lord Vornhelm struck me with the back of his hand, the impact split my lip and sent blood pouring from my nose.

"Liar. It doesn't matter if it was you or the pretty boy Golden."

I didn't see the signal but the fists of the Scarred Man caught me in the stomach and the jaw. He only hit me three times, but I was left gasping for air and spitting out blood.

"You have invaded my house and frightened my daughter. You accosted my wife and have undermined my efforts at becoming a member of the Notable Elders. I would kill you slowly right now, except it wouldn't be enough – I need you as bait to bring your companions here. Then I will destroy them in front of you before finishing the task. When you are all dead, maybe I'll be left alone."

I knew Golden would eventually work out where I was and then he would come and so would Kat. Tearwyn and others might help in any attempt to rescue me, but it would be a trap and they would die. I couldn't let that happen.

"I'll kill you and bury you out the back in my garden and maybe they'd come," Lord Vornhelm said. "But your friends are Hunters who probably have magical or mundane means to check if you are still alive. So, for now, you live."

"But later you plan on slicing me up like you did to your own daughter?" I croaked.

This time he punched me in the face. My tooth cut his hand. He sucked on his knuckle and looked at me. "She planned on betraying me. After all we had been, my daughter planned to tell Alder about the poison I was slipping into Lord Ern's food. She was soiled and dirty and beyond redemption."

"So why kill the other girls?"

Lord Vornhelm chuckled. "I thought it best to cover my tracks. By holding her prisoner for a few days until we killed the first whore it threw the fools of the Watch off. Killing Jalinta was just a bonus. She was part of my daughter's downward spiral."

"I thought that would have started the first time you crawled into her bed."

Someone grabbed my hand. "I know what you're trying to do, Owl. You think to provoke me until I kill you. Well, Jalinta played that card first and, much to my annoyance, it worked. It felt good to hack that harlot apart with a sword, but it meant the moment was over too fast."

My little finger was forced backward until the tendons popped. I screamed until Lord Vornhelm let go.

"You need to understand, Owl, my daughter needed to be punished and it had to fit the crime. My wife talked to you at the market so I beat her. My child sought to betray me and destroy my plans, so she had to suffer a traitor's fate."

I gulped in huge breaths as I struggled with the waves of pain. My finger throbbed and jaw ached. Blood still ran from my nose in a steady stream.

"But you tortured her," I gasped.

He grabbed my other hand.

"No, no," I begged.

Again, the twisting, tearing sensation rippled through me as he forced my little finger backwards. I thrashed in my shackles until the Scarred Man stepped forward and punched me in the stomach again. The air went out of me and I lay bent in my restraints.

"You need to understand, Owl – the punishment must fit the crime."

I woke in the dark some time later. The front of my chest and face was covered in blood. One eye had swollen but I could still see out of it. My torso burned and I had to keep my breathing shallow or the pain overwhelmed me. The pounding I had taken either broke or bruised some ribs. The little fingers on each hand throbbed with a burning sensation that travelled up my arms and into my spine.

Easing my feet on to the ground, I was thankful I hadn't been suspended in the air with my shoulders having to take the full weight of my body. I tried to slip my hands from the metal shackles, but they were well fitted. The ropes that held my legs together were tied by someone who knew knots. I was thirsty and needed to relieve myself. I didn't think it was likely there would be much relief in either of those areas. I was weak from my injuries and couldn't think coherently.

Looking around I tried to find a means to escape but soon gave up.

My suspicions about Lord Vornhelm had been confirmed. Nevertheless, there was nothing I could do about them at the moment. He had killed his daughter because she was going to betray him.

Elhnora's motivation was now obvious. She and her father had been lovers when she was younger, but as she'd grown older he tired of her and moved on to her sister. At first, she'd become wild, probably trying to find a way of paying Lord Vornhelm back for the abuse and subsequent rejection. The tattoo and the love affair with Jalinta had been part of her rebellion before she discovered her father's plot to kill a lord. So, she planned to betray him to a man she believed had enough honour and power to put a stop to the scheme and bring her father to justice.

Trix and Fendria were only murdered so that Lord Vornhelm could cover his tracks. The Man of Shadows was the paid assassin who didn't want to kill them, so their deaths had been quick and they weren't sliced up the same way as the noblewomen. They were a distasteful job and nothing more – random, and bad luck. The man who killed them was now dead, but the one who was responsible still walked. I promised myself I wouldn't die until he lay bleeding in front of me.

Golden was no fool. When he discovered where I was he'd be very careful. Still, it troubled me that Lord Vornhelm used me as the bait in a trap. There was nothing I could do now except regain my strength and wait for an opportunity.

A guard gave me a cup of water and washed my body waste away before Lord Vornhelm climbed down into the cellar, dressed in a cape and travelling clothes. He was not accompanied by the Scarred Man this time, and in his hand rested a cutthroat razor. Sweat broke out over my body.

He saw the direction of my gaze and smiled. "This is much like the implement I used on my daughter. She kept asking why, and I do admit her constant questioning made me angry. A woman should never ask a man questions. They are there to serve. In the same way the lesser races are." He drew the blade across my chest in one swift motion, cutting to the depth of a fingernail. The skin split and the sting hit.

Lord Vornhelm did this five times in quick succession, then stood back panting. "I will stop now. I don't won't you to bleed to death, but that doesn't mean you shouldn't be punished."

The tall man nodded to a guard who grabbed me by the hair. The other reached into a bucket and threw salt onto my chest. My eyes watered as the stinging fire rippled under my skin.

"Make sure you push it into the wounds. I want him to really feel it."

The guard glanced at Lord Vornhelm and then rubbed the salt in. I caught a brief glimpse of the man's look of distaste before I screamed. I blacked out, only to be slapped back into consciousness. I twisted and squirmed in my shackles until my wrists bled. Finally, I collapsed.

My body ached all over and my chest itched as though it crawled with ants. I wanted to scratch, but on this occasion it was a blessing my hands were shackled.

I didn't know how long I'd been hanging there. My neck throbbed and my feet hurt, but at least the swelling on my face felt as though it had gone down.

A guard came in several minutes later and threw another bucket of water over me. I opened my mouth to catch some of the liquid. He walked forward and trickled some wine onto my lips from a skin. I recognised him as the sentry who'd to rub the salt into my cuts. He was struggling to grow a wispy beard and looked only recently out of his teen years.

He reached into a sack on his back and pulled out some food. "I ain't supposed to give you more than the wine."

He fed me coarse black bread smeared with a honey, a piece at a time. It was the most delicious-tasting food I'd ever eaten.

"How long have I been here?"

"Three days. Your little visit sure put the house in an uproar. His Lordship went berserk and punched out the master-at-arms for letting you get in so far, then had him flogged before throwing him out on the street. I thought it all a bit harsh, you bein' a Dark Elf with your powers and all."

"Why do you work for him? He's a monster."

"I was lucky to get this job. My uncle gave me a sword and shield and I got a little trainin' with the city guards, but I've no armour. His lordship runs a tight ship, but if you follow orders and stick to the rules, you is usually all right."

"He killed his daughter!"

"His lordship had his reasons and they're nothing to do with me."

"Has he set a trap out there for my friends?"

The young guard went silent and stuffed the rest of the bread into my mouth. When I finished eating, he cleaned up the crumbs and gave me a final gulp of the wine before making his way out of the cellar, leaving me with the rats and the spiders.

22

DEATH

The bread and wine gave me some strength. I hauled myself upward on my chains until I could hang on the beams by my hands. The wounds on my chest opened and bled, and my little fingers screamed in pain. I tried to move myself along the beam so I could pull the chains free, but there was no opening. Eventually, I slipped the ropes off my feet, but that was as far as I could get.

I was just wondering what to do next when the trapdoor opened.

Three men came into the cellar, followed by Lord Vornhelm. He stood taller than all of them except the Scarred Man. The young guard who'd fed me held a torch.

"I see you've slipped some of your bonds," Lord Vornhelm said. "Don't you understand there's no way to get your arms free without chopping off a hand?"

I glared at him and hoped he'd come close enough for me to wrap my legs around his neck. Instead, the Scarred Man approached with a dagger in his hand. I waited for the chance to attack but he circled behind me and, though I twisted to follow him, the chains running over the low beam restricted my ability to manoeuvre.

He jumped forward and wrapped his arms around my chest,

plunging the dagger into my forearm. I screamed and tried to bite him but the other guards rushed in and pinned me.

"I've been giving some thought to the next part of your punishment and have decided you don't need all your body parts to be alive." He took the dagger from the Scarred Man and cut my little finger off with a quick flick of his wrist. I moaned deep and loud as the pain shot through me. My body shook. I thought I'd pass out.

Lord Vornhelm hit me with a casual back-hand before stepping away. "I want you to stay conscious, Owl. You need to experience the sensations wracking your body, and of course there's the news I'm sure you'd like to hear. I believe your rescue attempt is underway. Your friends are trying a new approach, but I have discovered their little game. For now, I'll leave you with your thoughts."

The finger throbbed, even though it was no longer there; and my jaw ached from the blow, but that was of small concern. My main worry was my friends walking into a trap.

The young guard brought me bread again that evening, as well as wine.

"I won't be able to sneak any food to you tomorrow. I'm off duty, but I heard some good news. His lordship has decided to send some stew for you to eat in the mornin'. It'll be leftovers but that's better than nothing, right?"

"What's your name?"

The young guard hesitated. "Don't suppose it hurts for you to know. I'm called Gavin Redhands. My dad and his dad were butchers see, but I want to be a soldier and fight in the wars to the East."

"The only battles I've heard of, Gavin, are against my people at the moment, and Hope isn't involved in them."

"Not yet. All the guards know if his lordship has his way, then the city will send an army to help the Southern Dukes. Then I'll get my chance to win fame."

"There's not a lot of glory in what you're doing at the moment, though, is there?"

Gavin poured some wine into my mouth before stepping away.

"You shouldn't 'ave scared his girl. She's special to him."

"That's because they're lovers."

"I heard that nasty rumour, but I don't believe it. Anyway, his wife would never let him do such a thing."

"He beats her. Haven't you seen the bruises?"

The young guard went quiet; obviously he had.

"They're going to kill me and my friends, Gavin."

He walked away but stopped at the ladder. "You shouldn't have come here, Owl, and your mates should mind their business. If you get in his lordship's way, you end up dead. It's what all the guards say and I've no reason not to believe 'em."

I don't know how long I slept for but when I woke up the Scarred Man stood before me. He had unshackled one of my hands and chained my feet together. A wooden board sat on the ground within reach, holding a congealed lump of fat and something quivering that appeared as though it were meat.

The Scarred Man gestured at the food. "Eat."

Even though it looked disgusting, the smell stimulated my stomach. I had to keep my strength up, so I pulled the board toward me and started to push the food into my mouth. The meat was fatty and chewy but tasted delicious.

The Scarred Man watched me intently; I became suspicious. Then I bit into something hard. I pulled a small piece of meat from gristle and noticed it had a fingernail. Then I realised my captors had fed me my own finger. Almost vomiting, I stared at the brown shrivelled appendage with its cracked nail. I saw the twisted smile on the face of the Scarred Man and heard the guards laugh. Picking up the board, I hurled it at my tormentor. It hit him on the chest, splattering the gravy across his shirt and chin.

The smile faded and the big man stepped toward me. I lashed out with my free hand but he blocked the blow and thundered a punch into my stomach. I couldn't avoid him. Doubling over with pain, I moaned.

"You'll pay for that, Owl," he growled.

He took a torch from one of the men-at-arms and thrust it at my chest. The flesh singed. I screamed. He stood back – the smile had returned.

"You know when the boss killed his daughter, she didn't scream. Oh how she whimpered, and her tears fell like rain. 'Why daddy, why,' she said, over and over. The old man screamed that she was a traitor and must die a traitor's death. I loved the stuck-up snot brought low by her own father. The bitch didn't see it coming, but I knew his rage had been building for a long time."

He thrust the torch onto my skin once more and my pain rang loud and pure.

"I just gotta keep you alive, that's all, Owl. I can hurt you all I want in the meantime."

"Not without my orders," a deep voice said. Lord Vornhelm appeared from the shadows. He must have slipped down the ladder while I'd been screaming. "You were to feed him and then leave, Turam, not punish him."

"Lord, he threw his food at us, so I was making him pay."

"Only because you fed me my own flesh," I groaned.

Lord Vornhelm's eyes narrowed. "He is bait, Turam, and, he is mine, do you understand?"

The big man looked at the ground and nodded.

"I didn't hear your reply," Lord Vornhelm whispered.

"I will obey."

"And put some honey on those burns. I don't want the Owl to die from an infection."

The thin lord gave everyone in the room a look before ascending the stairs. When he'd gone, the Scarred Man roared with frustration and slapped me across the face twice before storming off. The blows left my ears ringing and I barely felt the men-at-arms grab my arm and re-chain it to the beam above.

Later, I woke as someone smeared a sweet-smelling substance on my chest. The soothing sensation dulled the pain radiating from my skin.

"Do not think this a mercy, Owl." Lord Vornhelm stood with his hands behind his back as he watched Gavin spread the honey. "I will not have any of my men, even the most valued, violate the chain of command."

"Is that what your daughter did?"

Lord Vornhelm stroked his chin and seemed to ponder the question. "In a way, yes, but what she did in the end was much more serious. She was going to betray her own family. In the army, traitors are flayed, therefore she had to undergo a similar punishment."

"And the other girls, what was their crime?"

"Jalinta's sins were apparent to everyone, and I would have drowned her, as is the penalty for those who bewitch others. Circumstances dictated I kill her in a manner which fitted with the previous deaths."

"And my friend Trix – what did she do?"

Lord Vornhelm blinked a few times, as though he didn't understand the question. "She was nobody and her death was of no account. She died to serve my purpose."

There it was. If we were not from the nobility, then we were cattle to serve his purpose. Just like his soldiers who'd died at the breach into the Hobgoblin fortress. Even if you were a member of his family you weren't safe, unless you obeyed Lord Vornhelm's commands without question.

"Anyway, I'm here to give you some news. You see, the honey that my man-at-arms is rubbing onto your skin is truly ironic. You are now literally my honey trap and it seems the bears are getting closer."

"My friends are experienced Hunters and adventurers. They will not be taken easily."

"I know, and that is why the trap is to be sprung with deadly force. I will kill them in front of you and then I can complete your punishment, and I'll be safe from further interference."

I was left alone and tried to break free again, but I was too weak and my bonds secure. The honey on my chest slowly hardened. I felt it seeping into my skin and repairing the damage. The sticky liquid was just under my chin and I was able to lick it. It didn't do a lot to control my hunger, but it was better than nothing.

Gavin helped me drink some watered wine that evening, but he couldn't slip me any food as there was an older guard with him. I hung there by my chains and hoped Golden would be careful. Part of me wanted him to stay away, but I also longed for rescue. I didn't think I was could escape without outside assistance, and I knew I grew weaker by the day.

The cold water brought me around fast. I could smell lilac and rosewater and I thought Trix was with me.

"Sorry, Ash, I had to wake you. We don't have much time. I have to free you and get you to the wall before the guards return."

A slim figure stood before me. Curly hair framed by torch light came into focus. Cassie stood before me in the cellar.

"What are you doing here?" I croaked.

"I took employment with Lord Vornhelm a few days ago as a housemaid. I've been trying to find a means of getting close to you. Golden and the others are on the other side of the wall, waiting for my signal."

"Get out, Cassie, it's a trap."

"I was careful. They can't watch you every waking hour."

"No, fair maiden, that's why we watched you instead." Lord Vornhelm dropped from the open trapdoor, followed by the Scarred Man and two older guards. I groaned and felt Cassie press her back into me.

"You've done enough. Let me take him," she said.

"Fair maiden, I applaud your bravery. Even as your fate approaches, you think of someone else. This Owl seems to be held in high esteem by a number of the unwashed. Unfortunately, you are part of my plan to punish him."

"You don't have to do this. She's a minor player and not worth your time."

Cassie turned and looked at me, her eyes wide. It was then she understood the danger.

Lord Vornhelm spread his hands. "And yet, she is here. I will make it quick, relatively speaking."

I didn't like the sound of that. The tall lord clicked his fingers, the guards ran forward and seized Cassie. She struggled, but one of them punched her in the mouth and she slumped. Then the Scarred Man produced a rope and tied it around her neck.

"In the past, the penalty for being caught in a noble's residence was hanging. It was later changed to a term of imprisonment, but I have always pined for the old ways," said Lord Vornhelm.

The Scarred Man threw the rope over a low beam. He then slowly pulled. Soon Cassie lifted in the air, swinging as she kicked. She dangled at least an arm's length from the ground.

"Please don't do this. I'll do anything if you spare her."

Lord Vornhelm turned and tilted his head sideways as he looked at me. "Do you know, you're the first one who has begged."

Cassie turned blue. Her feet kicked the air. She clawed at the rope and tried to lift herself up, but her hands slipped. Still, she struggled fiercely.

"I do love a fighter," the Scarred Man said.

I closed my eyes but could hear the gurgling and the kicking. Slowly the noise faded, and then I looked at my dead friend. Cassie swung back and forth, much as Trix had done. I felt like I was falling into a pit. Only pain remained – not of the flesh, I would have welcomed that, but of the mind. I wailed and blubbered. Urine poured down my legs. I lost all control and thrashed until a fist stopped me.

"That's better," Lord Vornhelm said as the Scarred Man stepped away from me. "I could hardly hear myself think. Now cut this trash down and hang her body from the tree just outside the front gate. If the Watch object, tell them they are my orders. Maybe the sight of one of their own swinging from the branches might provoke the Owl's friends into some hasty action. Increase the watches and place extra guards in the towers. I don't want anyone to become complacent."

My mind retreated to somewhere else. I rode a shaggy pony bareback on the high plateau of my people. The wind streamed through my long hair. The air chilled me, but this is where I belonged. My brother, my younger sister Shade, and I raced through the winter grass along well-worn tracks toward our family encampment, over fast-flowing streams and through woodlands of spruce and pine.

I was determined to overtake Shade. She weighed the least of us and usually won, but today her horse tired. Shade looked back, saw me gaining and tried to force her pony to increase its speed. A fallen tree blocked the path ahead, and instead of diverting around the obstacle my sister forced the exhausted pony to jump.

They didn't make it.

I heard the crash and watched both Shade and the animal disappear from site in the bush on the other side on the massive trunk.

Dismounting, I ran to the tree and clambered over it, calling her name. Her pony was back on its feet, but couldn't put any weight on its left front leg. I looked for Shade in the bush and then heard a sound behind me. The branch caught me on the ear, knocking me from my feet. My sister's laughter washed over me.

"Sorry brother, I need your pony if I'm going to win."

By the time I got up, Shade had vaulted onto my mount. She turned it around harshly, sawing the reins in its mouth. They galloped away over the sloping field.

My brother galloped by and left me with a lame pony and blazing anger. Shade loved to win and didn't care the cost. I cursed her and led the animal back through the woods and onto the high plain.

The Family camp lay ahead by a willow-fringed stream. Mother got water from a beaver dam that blocked the meandering waterway while my father spoke to my siblings. The flags on the felt-lined tents flapped in the cold wind and soon I stood before the entrance to the largest tent.

Inside, it was dull after the brightness of the sky. My father sat and restitched the lining on his old jacket while Shade sharpened a skinning knife. "Nothing goes to waste in the mountains," he said. His hand moved the needle through the leather before savagely pulling it tight. "You are responsible for the disposal of your pony. It is lame and can never run again. Its meat shall feed the dogs and its skin will cover our bodies."

"I wasn't riding—"

"Your sister told me what happened. Now see to your responsibilities."

I glared at Shade. She rewarded me with a dazzling smile. She handed the sharpened blade to me as I walked from the tent. The pony stood tethered to a willow tree. It looked at me with big blue eyes and tried to pull clear of its restraints. Then it was dead and its blood pumped into the air, covering my face and chest. I could feel its warmth and smell a rich metallic odour.

The head of the pony turned toward me. "Why are you doing this?" it said.

I stepped away and looked at the blood on my hands.

"I did nothing to deserve death."

Before me stood Trix, her body in shreds as she hung from the branches of the tree. I screamed.

"I wanted to save you," another voice said.

I peeped between my fingers and Cassie hung beside Trix, her face blue.

"It's not my fault. I didn't kill any of you. I loved you all and want to be with you."

I came back to the cellar and moaned. Inside something broke. I couldn't live anymore. The pain was too intense. I had to end it. Zenta's death in the mountains years ago in the Devil's Cave, and now the murders of Trix and Cassie tore at me. Using the chains around my wrists, I tried to wrap it around my own neck but it was too short. Hammering my head against the manacle on my wrist only opened a shallow cut on my forehead which bled freely. I wanted to die. I might have begged Lord Vornhelm to kill me if he'd been present.

Passing out again, I dreamt of a dark forest surrounded by creatures that wanted me dead. Feeling no fear, I screamed a challenge before drawing my short sword. Then there was a presence and I turned to find Golden standing next to me.

"We would all die for you, as you would for us," he said as he drew the frost-covered Cold Blade from its scabbard.

Swirling beings composed of shadow and teeth attacked from all parts of the clearing but we drove them back. Kat appeared with Tearwyn, and we made a circle to defend each other's backs. Spike growled from my side and the monsters retreated into the forest.

"This is not about you, Ash," a voice said.

I turned. Elhnora appeared at the edge of the woods. Her blue eyes shone with an inner light and her smile lit the clearing. She wore loose leather armour and carried a scimitar. The scent of lilacs danced around her. "It never was about you. It's about setting something right."

"But everyone keeps dying," I wailed.

"We all die eventually. It is the marks we leave on the parchment after we are gone which matter. What will your story be, Ash?"

I came to again and eased my weight onto my feet. My shoulders ached. I felt dizzy, but my mind was clear. Crying, I remembered Elhnora's words. Wishing I had known her in real life, at least I now knew what must be done if a chance presented itself.

There would be a way to honour the young noblewoman, and to do that I would have to survive.

23

REDEMPTION

The wafting smoke made its way into the cellar. I could hear yelling and a faint crackling. Had the storeroom above me had caught fire? I'd burn to death. Shouting and screaming brought no one. The smell didn't get any stronger but the noise of steel striking metal became louder. There was combat in the compound above me – that could only mean Golden was attacking. I groaned, thinking of how outnumbered he'd be.

The trapdoor to the cellar crashed open and a large shape dropped down in front of me. The Scarred Man had come to finish. But, no. I recognized the stubble on the head and chin as Tearwyn. In three strides he crossed the room and smashed the chains with his axe. I fell to the ground and groaned as muscles that had been stretched into unnatural positions for days screamed in protest.

"What have they done to you, Ash?"

I lay on the floor, unable to move. The big man didn't say anything; he just tossed me over his shoulder like a sack of wheat and carried me up the stepladder.

Kat appeared at the top, in a room lit by dancing flames. Her hair was tied back and she held a crossbow in her left hand.

"He's in a bad way," Tearwyn said.

The elf peered into my eyes and poured the contents of a vial down my throat. It was the foulest tasting substance I'd ever drunk and I almost threw up. Kat held my lips closed and tilted my head backward. "You're going to need your wits about you for a while, so swallow. This is essence of black mushroom. It'll give you a little pick-me-up."

Within a few heartbeats, my muscles relaxed and my heart raced. Then I felt a tingling sensation behind my eyes. Everything fell into focus and I stood unsteadily on my feet.

"You look a mess. You better leave any combat to us," Kat said.

"There can't be enough of you to defeat Lord Vornhelm's men-at-arms. He must have at least twenty warriors in the compound."

"We are not alone," the elf said.

I stepped out onto the large cobbled courtyard in front of the main building. Flames licked from the windows. The entrance gates lay on the ground twisted and buckled near them, four men-at-arms covered in blood.

Some fighting waged on the wide steps at the front of the house. Then, a small number of Lord Vornhelm's guards charged from the burning building. Crossbow bolts cut half of them down before they crashed into a group of lightly armed men and women. A tall figure with blond hair stood at their centre flanked by a large wolf. Golden and Spike tore into the soldiers as the other warriors fell away. A slight man in a dark cape yelled at the retreating men and women. They turned and slashed at the flanks of the guardsmen. Before long, they had all fallen, except for one individual hacking at those who surrounded him with a shiny sword.

"Take him alive!" the man in the cape yelled.

As I watched, the hood fell away and I glimpsed curly hair and dark eyes.

"What is Sundeep doing here?" I asked.

"The Dance Master? You better ask him yourself," Kat said.

I limped slowly over toward him while watching his thieves

surround the tall warrior at the top of the steps. One of them slipped up behind him and laid him low with a blow from a wooden club.

Sundeep turned and gazed at me. His eyes were distant and cold. "Your friend Golden was right – you're alive."

"You don't seem too thrilled at the news," I said.

"I didn't join with your friends to rescue you, Ash. I'm here for revenge."

"I thought you and Lord Vornhelm were allies, of a sort."

"We were until he killed my sister and left her hanging in the street like a piece of meat. The moment he strung her up, he turned me into his most deadly enemy."

"Cassie was your sister?"

"Same mother, different fathers, but she was the closest thing I've ever had to family. And now, because of trying to rescue you, she's dead."

"I didn't kill her, and I would have done anything to take her place."

"And that is why you will live, though I never want to see you again."

I nodded and stared at the burning house. Hearing something collapse, I imagined the central staircase blazing.

"We cannot stay here. The roadblocks I set for the Watch and the Guards of the Citadel cannot hold for long."

"The Council of Notable Elders will come down hard on you for this," I said.

"That is why I plan to vacate the field. I figure they'll attack all crime figures in the town, including Grandfather. I'll let him try and defend his patch while I retire somewhere a little quieter for a while."

Three men-at-arms were brought before Sundeep. One of them was Gavin, and he looked at me imploringly. His left arm hung by his side, covered in blood and his surcoat had been ripped. "Owl, I treated you good, tell them."

I nodded and turned to Sundeep. "The kid is all right, he's not part of this."

"I can afford no witnesses. We need to leave a confused picture when we go. I have even brought some surcoats from the Snowfelds' household to point the finger in their direction. Any confusion will buy me time to escape Hope."

He gestured at his warriors and they quickly cut the throat of the men-at-arms. Gavin looked at me wide-eyed as the blade opened his neck. He had dreamed of glory on the battlefield but died at the hands of a thief. It reminded me that Sundeep had little mercy. He was a killer, just like Grandfather.

Golden shoved his way through the group of warriors and wrapped me in a bear hug. I groaned but leaned into his shoulder. Spike pushed his nose into my flank and I scratched him behind the ears. "I never thought I'd see you again," I choked out.

"I wasn't going to give up until I had got you out or until I was certain you were dead."

"How did you know I was alive?"

Golden smiled and his different-coloured eyes sparkled. "The Cold Blade told me. They're linked to each other. They allow their owners to see others who carry Cold Blades, if we know how to use the power. Yours was left in the room above you, so it maintained its connection to you. Kat picked it up and will give it to you later."

"Remarkable," I said.

Lord Vornhelm cursed and struggled as he stood before us with his hands tied. His eyes blazed above a nose covered in blood. Sundeep's thieves prodded him with their blades as he walked.

He looked at the Dance Master and his lip curled. "I should have known better than to trust a cur from the slums. The Ancient Men have never had any honour," he hissed.

"That is where you are wrong. I avenge my family. You see, when you hung my sister from the trees outside your mansion, you declared war on me."

"That little harlot! I didn't know she was from your family."

"It doesn't matter now. The act is done and my vengeance is almost complete."

Sundeep nodded to his men and they dragged forward the body of a young woman wrapped in a red curtain. Three crossbow bolts stuck from her flesh, one of them just under her chin.

"You killed my daughter! You're worse than an animal."

"Your daughter or your lover? My friend Kat tells me you found the distinction confusing. Her death was unintentional. She got caught in crossfire, though I would have had to dispose of her anyway."

"My friends will hunt you down and kill all of you and–"

Sundeep didn't let him finish the sentence. He hammered his dagger into the tall man's stomach and twisted it. Lord Vornhelm moaned and slumped to the ground.

"Tie him up and then hang him like he did to my sister."

The thieves hurried to obey, dragging the bleeding lord over to a tree. They hauled him into the air with a rope and then one of the warriors hung from his legs until he stopped struggling.

"We need to go and quickly," the Dance Master said. "The knights from the Citadel will be here before long and then there will be a battle we cannot win."

The thieves withdrew, flitting through the shadows thrown by the burning house to the broken gates and then out into the park and surrounding streets, carrying their casualties with them.

The Dance Master turned and stared at me. "Cassie died for you, so make sure it was worth it. My debt to you is clear. I hope I never cross your path again, in this world or the next."

And then he was gone.

Swaying a little on my feet, I looked at the burning house. I couldn't believe I was walking away from the Vornhelm mansion. Then I noticed movement in one of the upper windows. Looking more carefully, I saw a woman in grey standing, outlined by the glow of the flames. Lady Vornhelm was alive and trapped.

Staggering forward, I called her name. She glanced down at me and then out across the city. I imagined the tears on her cheeks and lines of pain carved into her face.

"Come on, Ash, we have to go," Golden said gently.

"I can't leave her."

"What, that woman is part of the horror that is the Vornhelms."

I felt his hand on my shoulder and turned savagely. "That is where you are wrong. Lady Vornhelm is a victim in this, just like Elhnora."

"We don't have time, Ash," Kat said. "If we stay, the Watch will take us."

"Give me a rope," I said.

"You have to be joking!" Golden exclaimed. "You could hardly fight a kitten right now. Climbing three floors is out of the question."

"Then you do it," I told him.

His eyes widened. He held my shoulders in his hands and stared at me. "You really need this, don't you?"

"I have to believe something can be saved of Elhnora."

He nodded and picked up the rope. It took three swings before the grapple held and then I watched as my friend climbed the wall. I saw him wince and realised his shoulder still troubled him.

"I should have made the climb," Tearwyn said from beside me.

"Take Spike and go," Kat said. "There's no point us all getting caught and we might need someone on the outside to help once they throw what's left of our little group in the dungeons."

Tearwyn nodded and disappeared.

Flames licked between the slate tiles of the roof and smoke poured from the front door.

Golden climbed through the window on the third floor and returned with Lady Vornhelm over his shoulder. He carried her over to me as if she was a child and placed her before me. Her face was covered in soot, her grey dress ripped and stained. She fell to her knees and wailed and beat the ground with her fists.

"Great, we have rescued a crazy woman," Kat said.

I walked over and lifted Lady Vornhelm to her feet. Then I held her by the chin and stared into her blue eyes.

"Why didn't you let me die?"

"I see her in you, but I don't know if you have her strength," I said.

Lady Vornhelm's brow furrowed.

"Your daughter possessed an inner fire that caused her to take a stand against the most terrifying figure in her life. Did she get that strength from you?"

The woman dropped her gaze and her hair hung in front of her face. "A long time ago I used to stand up to him, but the beatings and humiliations defeated me."

"You have a son who has been fostered to another family for his knightly training," I said. "He will need guidance when he returns so the Vornhelms can rise again."

"This family needs to be wiped from the earth."

"No, one individual is responsible for the deeds done here. It was not your daughter's fault or yours that this has all come to pass. I know Elhnora would have wanted you to live."

"You never met her."

"That is true, but somehow I feel connected to her."

The sound of hooves clattering on stone broke my concentration and I stepped back from the noblewoman as heavily armoured knights burst into the courtyard. They surrounded the four of us in a ring of steel and horseflesh.

Eventually, a large knight in shining mail dismounted and pointed his mace at me. "Drop your weapons or my men will strike you down."

Golden moved to unharness his Cold Blade and Kat dropped her crossbow when Lady Vornhelm stepped forward. "Knight Commander, these warriors are not the ones who attacked my household. Indeed, it is they who rescued me and helped drive the enemy away."

"Lady Vornhelm, I am sorry we did not get here sooner – the road was held against us and we had to force a passage. Are you certain these warriors assisted you?"

"Very sure. One of them climbed to my window and carried me from my burning house while the others fought."

"Do you know who attacked your compound, good lady?"

"Unfortunately, it was dark."

The Knight Commander turned and raised an eyebrow at us. "You look a bit beaten around, Owl. Did you lose half your clothes in the battle?"

I shrugged. "It was a tough fight, Sir Knight."

"And you just happened to be in the area and decided to lend a hand?"

"We saw the flames and came to investigate," Kat said.

"I saw them come to my rescue, Knight Commander. You surely do not doubt my word?" Lady Vornhelm questioned.

The man shook his head. "Of course not, my lady." He gestured to Kat's and Golden's weapons. "You may rearm and go."

The knights dispersed and set up a perimeter while some threw buckets of water onto the fire. Soon, they were joined by the Watch. I expected to see Captain Waldheigheim, but heard from the chatter of his men he had been lightly wounded at the roadblock and was still being treated.

Lady Vornhelm stepped up to me and kissed me on the cheek. "My family thanks you," she whispered.

The Knight Commander gave me a quizzical glance before shepherding Lady Vornhelm over to one of his men. Orders issued to take her to the house of Sir Gorsehime and his wife, distant relatives of the Vornhelm family. She soon disappeared in a carriage.

Kat and Golden carried me to Petar's house, where the old man and Miranda waited. Miranda paled at my condition. Petar clucked his tongue and told me to get into bed in the front room. The drug the elf had given me started to wear off and my head swam with exhaustion. The five scars crossed my chest and the burn marks on my stomach hadn't healed, though the honey had helped. My wrists were raw from rubbing on the manacles and I tottered from malnourishment. I also missed my little finger.

"The Dark Elf needs chicken broth to build his strength and more honey applied to his burns," Petar said. "Then he must rest. After that, we will clean him, yes, yes."

I dropped into an exhausted sleep and woke with Miranda standing over me. Her eyes were red and she clenched her hands together.

"I thought you were dead," she whispered.

"Didn't Golden tell you otherwise?"

"Yes, but I have little faith in magic."

"Well, I'm alive, though for a while there I wished I wasn't."

"They tortured you?"

"It was what they did to Cassie that drove me over the edge. Her death was to punish me."

Miranda walked over to me and kissed me slowly. She cradled my head in her hands and stroked my hair. "That wasn't your fault. None of it has ever been your fault."

I kissed her again, wanting to devour her, and she let me before pushing me away with a smile. "I'm actually here to feed you," she said.

Noticing the aroma of the chicken soup, I sat up. It tickled my nose and stimulated my appetite. I let her nurse me, enjoying the sensation of the warm broth running down my throat and settling in the pit of my stomach.

"I want you, Miranda," I said.

"I know," she sighed.

"But you're still marrying Petar?"

"Yes," she whispered.

"Where does that leave us?"

"More confused than ever." A smile touched her lips as though some part of the situation struck her as funny. "Ash, I'm always going to be here for you. I just don't know what form our relationship will take."

I slumped back and rubbed my forehead. Then she leaned over the bed and kissed me again. "Sleep now, and I'll return with more food."

Later I woke with Kat and Golden sitting next to me. Spike curled up in front of the fire, his head on his paws.

"You look a little better, though you still smell," Golden said.

"I haven't had a bath yet. Petar decided rest and food were more important."

"So, do you think it will be Miranda who washes you or the old man?"

I ignored the question and stretched my legs and arms and felt a surge of pain. Pushing the ache away I thought of food. "I'm hungry."

"There's bread baking in the kitchen. It will be ready soon," Kat said.

I nodded. "Where is Tearwyn?"

"He's down at Rackhime's and told us he's going to wander down to Docklands and see what's happening," Golden stated. "The Watch have been searching the area as well as Grandfather's businesses. They also stormed into his mansion and confiscated any parchment or books they could find."

"What about the Dance Master? Is he gone?"

"There is no sign of him, though his old haunts on Red Square have all been ransacked. Oh, and the Knights of the Citadel surrounded and then searched the Snowfelds' mansion this morning."

"They must have found the surcoats left by Sundeep," I said.

"There was a curfew after dark on the first day we got you out and there's been another proclaimed for tonight. It seems the Council of Notable Elders is most unhappy one of their own was found hanging from a tree with his stomach cut open."

"It won't be long before they put the attack together with Cassie's death and start to make links to Sundeep. He has disappeared, after all, and a number of people would have seen his sister hanging from the tree out the front of the Vornhelm residence. I know the captain doesn't believe in coincidences."

"Nobody knew they were related," Golden said.

"But they do now and the rumours will spread."

"They can be suspicious, but they won't be able to prove anything," Kat said.

"That doesn't matter to the Council. If they think Sundeep was involved, then they will try to find him and kill him."

"That won't be easy," Golden said. "From what I saw of the man he has many resources and tracking him down will be difficult."

"Speaking of people who are in hiding, I think it's important we look for the Scarred Man," Kat said.

"Did he escape the attack on the Vornhelm manor?"

"He wasn't there on the night," Golden said. "That's also another reason Tearwyn isn't here. He is asking the working girls to keep an eye out for him and to let us know if they see him."

Miranda bustled into the room carrying some sponges and soap. "Okay, time for your bath. I have put up with the smell for long enough. The bread is cooling and will be ready to eat when we are done."

Golden raised an eyebrow at me and grinned. "Oh, I don't know, it might take longer than you think."

Miranda narrowed her eyes and glared at my friend.

"Come on, you idiot," Kat said. "Let's go watch the knights annoying Lady Snowfeld. That should be an entertaining way to spend the afternoon."

I could hear Golden chuckling as he disappeared out the door.

"Does he think I'm going to jump in with you? The water will be only fit for the sewers by the time we're finished."

I could see Miranda was annoyed by Golden's innuendo but there was also a sparkle in her eye. As it turned out, it was such a relaxing experience I fell asleep.

24

A WEDDING

Groups of men whitewashed the walls of the Watch building while thatchers repaired one of the stable roofs during its renovation.

Walking up the front steps of the investigators' building, I felt on edge. I hadn't seen Captain Waldheigheim since my rescue, but he sent messages insisting on an audience.

Though I put him off until now by pleading illness, it did take me longer than expected to recover from my ordeal. There remained the mental scars, and I didn't know if they would ever heal. Most nights I woke at least once after reliving Cassie's death or finding myself witnessing the murder of Trix or Elhnora. Though when I dreamed of Elhnora, she always tried to comfort me or thank me for what I had done. When I talked to Miranda, she said her grandfather would say the young woman's spirit watched over me.

Golden put my slow recovery down to Miranda's nursing of my battered body. He accused me of drawing out my convalescence in order to partake of as many baths as possible. He was partially correct. Even though she never washed me again, we spent as much time as possible in each other's company. We often kissed and held each other, but we never went any further. Petar seemed to accept our closeness and left us alone.

The nearing wedding took Miranda away from me and I found myself alone. I used the time to continue learning to read the human language and study the ancient maps in Petar's study.

Golden and Kat left for the east with Tearwyn and Spike to adventure and hunt in the ogre lands. I missed my tall friend and often found myself wondering where he would be on the maps I spread on the study floor.

The upcoming nuptials were a thorn I tried to ignore as I didn't know what they would mean for Miranda. After the ceremony, the married couple were to travel to Sir Petar's small country estates. They would be gone until early summer.

It now approached the middle of spring and the trees of the city sprouted bright-green foliage. The red swallows had flown up from the south and congregated in great flocks, hunting midges and other insects above the river. I would soon be alone except for Rackhime, but the idea of working in his shop as I did through previous summers no longer interested me.

I found Captain Waldheigheim sitting behind a table in his small office. Parchments and sheets of paper sat in neat piles in front of him. He studied one of them before glancing up at me. I looked for any sign of the wound he'd received when leading members of the Watch to Lord Vornhelm's manor, but he seemed to have recovered.

Gesturing at a chair, he continued to stare for a little longer at the parchment before rolling it up and dropping it in a pile on the floor. "That was yet another request from the Council of Notable Elders to destroy all of the city's crime guilds. Don't they believe I've been trying to do that my entire career? They scream for the elimination of these organisations while half the members of the nobility either work with them or at the very least do business with them."

He looked older and his single eyebrow seemed to have more than a touch of grey in it.

"You need a break from all this," I said.

"You're probably correct, but what can I do? If I leave now, my position will be filled with a member of the nobility and the Watch will receive an incompetent as their leader."

"Not all of the nobility are stupid."

The captain snorted. He laced his fingers together and stared at me. "I think you've been avoiding me, Ashley. You don't look unwell."

"I would point out that you are not a physician, Captain, but that aside, I suppose you could say I wasn't looking forward to this meeting."

"Would that have something to do with your presence at Lord Vornhelm's manor on the night his lordship was killed?"

I stared away through the small window that sat high up on the other side of the room. Outside a sea hawk glided in circles, waiting for a chance to swoop.

"Lady Vornhelm has vouched for you and your friends. Indeed, she praises your actions most highly and has even pledged a debt of gratitude to you."

I didn't know that. My eyes widened.

"Her support has kept you safe from investigation, yet I was curious and spent some time with the Commander of the Knights who rode in to the Vornhelm manor that night. He told me you were only half-dressed and it looked as though a warhorse danced on your body. I asked if you were wounded in the assault and he said no. He also said you had honey on your chest."

I still didn't answer.

"Strange, how you would get honey on a wound you had just received."

I turned and looked him in the eyes.

He met my stare with an unflinching gaze of his own. "Just tell me what happened, Ashley, for the sake of my curiosity. If you believe there's an area where I might want to charge somebody, leave it out."

I sighed and ran four fingers through my long hair. "All those the city might want to punish are either dead or have fled."

Then I told him everything – well, almost everything. My story was that Golden and Kat arriving at the mansion after the assault had taken place, but that was the only thing I changed. I didn't want the captain to feel the need to arrest Golden for taking part in the attack on a noble estate.

"So, the only loose end is the Scarred Man?"

I admired the way the captain's mind always focused in on a single important detail. "We can't find him. The girls haven't seen him around Docklands, and we have no contacts in the slums in the South of Hope."

"He could disappear into that shantytown to the south of the Peaks and we'd never find him, unless somebody told us where he was. Leave that one with me. I don't like unfinished business."

"I'd be grateful if you found him. He's the only one involved in the murder of the girls who is free."

"Lord Vornhelm sounds as though he was at the centre of this, and his death rough justice. I know I would never get the opportunity to touch the man though. It looks as if he overreached when he killed your friend Cassie."

"I don't like to remember it, but her death saved my life."

"It can be strange how life twists and turns, though nothing actually surprises me anymore."

I suddenly felt drained and wanted to forget everything. Dragging scarred hands across sunken eyes I rubbed my face.

When I looked at the captain again, I saw his expression soften. "You went through hell to solve this case. I can see it in your face and hear it in your voice. There is little anyone can do to ease your pain, but I will say this – if you were one of my investigators, I'd be recommending you for a promotion. You should be proud of your efforts."

My eyes grew moist. Captain Waldheigheim was not one to give praise lightly. "That means a lot to me. Thank you."

The captain shrugged. "I'd ask you to work with me in an official capacity, but that of course is not within my power." He glanced down at his desk and shuffled the scrolls stacked there. I took that as my signal to leave.

The sky appeared light blue, and the wind came from the south as Miranda made her way down the steps at the front of Sir Petar's manor toward the open-sided tent. She looked stunning in a light-blue dress with its sweeping cape.

Sir Petar waited for her in a crumpled outfit of black and red silk that would have looked more at home on one of the clerics for the Dead God. He pulled nervously at his collar and shuffled from foot to foot as she approached. Behind her, Teel and Aneeta swung small incense containers and called the blessing of the day to the Gods so that they smiled on the occasion.

There was only a small group present, even though a large number of invitations were sent. Of the nobility, only Lord Alder appeared, alone. Lady Vornhelm would have come, but she had left to travel upriver to collect her son. Lord Alder, who now kept in close contact with her, later told me she decided to take sole charge of her son's education. The rest of the nobles ignored the invitations. Matron Snowfeld hadn't responded, but I heard she was ill and travelling south to a health spring.

The working women from Docklands came in numbers. Many bought new clothes and spent most of the morning preparing for the occasion. After all, it wasn't often one of their own married into the nobility.

All of them looked beautiful, but none of them shone like Miranda. It was her day and she floated before Aneeta and Teel. I understood her happiness, but couldn't share it.

We had spoken the night before about our friendship. Miranda vowed never to let it fade. I asked her if we would ever be more and she put her finger on my lips and said time would tell. Then she kissed me and left. After today, she would be away for a season and I'd need to wait until she returned before finding out what the future would bring the two of us.

Someone squeezed my hand. I turned to find Stella smiling at me.

She passed me a drink and stood back and looked me up and down. "All recovered, I see. A little skinnier than you used to be and missing a few bits and pieces here and there, but mostly intact."

I returned the smile. Stella always knew how to get me to relax. Her ability to create sexual tension as she did so, continually amazed me. She certainly looked incredible. Her dress showed more skin than most of the other women, while still managing to look elegant.

Stella noticed my appraisal of her outfit and stepped closer. "Do you like my new dress?"

"Very much."

"You know the best thing about it?"

"I dread to ask."

"It comes off easily."

I laughed loudly and a few people looked in my direction. Stella slipped her arm through mine and guided us to an area where we could view the ceremony.

The cleric of Tilion who was to seal the marriage before the Gods, was a young man who'd recently received his medallion. He looked nervous and sweated heavily, wiping his brow repeatedly with a small cloth. I heard Petar found it difficult to convince a cleric to run the ceremony. He discovered the young man down on the edge of the ports, where he probably married sailors and shopkeepers. The young man's robes were plain and frayed and he had probably never been up on the Peaks before today.

Miranda glided forward and only faltered briefly when she noticed Stella and me together. I felt guilty, before deciding that such emotions were ridiculous considering the circumstances.

The cleric rushed through the words of the ceremony, almost stumbling over them in his haste. He then put Miranda's hand into Petar's and the couple exchanged circlets of silver. Petar placed his on Miranda's head but she dropped hers, causing the audience to laugh before she picked it up and put it on her new husband's bald head. Then everyone applauded.

The group headed over to an open area where a wooden stage was set up. Two individuals with lutes played softly while a third player beat on a drum. Long tables piled with food and drink sat nearby and people helped themselves while the married couple spoke to the various guests.

A number of the women from Docklands gravitated toward Lord Alder, to the point where I thought they might overwhelm him.

"We better go and rescue him," I said to Stella.

"Do you think he wants saving?"

"I'm not sure, but I'll check."

By the time I got to him a number of the girls had drifted away, and some were even dancing. Teel and Aneeta, though, didn't moved away and were engaging Lord Alder with their view of the attributes of the different Gods. As we approached I saw his eyes run up and down Stella. She must have seen it too, because she pushed her chest out. I could never accuse her of being shy.

"I just wanted to see if these ladies were treating you well, your Lordship."

"Call me Alder. On such a beautiful day and in the company of these amazing women, how can I fall back on ceremony?"

Both Aneeta and Teel beamed and I wondered if Lord Alder knew what he was getting himself into.

"Is it true, Lord Alder, that Ash nearly ran you through with a sword in a duel?" Stella asked.

I groaned with embarrassment, but Alder seemed unconcerned.

"That is correct. We disagreed over some minor matter and your friend taught me the meaning of true swordsmanship and mercy."

"You are being far too kind," I said.

Alder smiled. "Yes, I probably am, but you did change my life, Ash, and that I won't forget."

There was a brief silence before Teel and Aneeta led Lord Alder onto the dance floor. The music became livelier and the drummer sang tunes that were well known at Dockside.

"Lord Alder is probably going to have the time of his life tonight," Stella said.

"The question is, who is he going to choose?" I said.

"My guess is that he won't have to."

"I didn't think Teel and Aneeta did anything but solo appointments."

Stella laughed. "They fool everyone into believing they are straight-down-the-line working girls, but I know in the right circumstances they're just as wild as I am."

"Well, I wish him well, and who knows, maybe there'll be another wedding."

"Sure, I can just see the most eligible bachelor in Hope walking down toward the high cleric with a commoner on each arm."

I agreed it was highly unlikely, though Lord Alder did look like he was enjoying himself.

More wine passed my lips and I relaxed. Stella dragged me onto the dance floor. I drank the right amount to lower my inhibitions and yet retain my coordination.

"You're good at this," Stella said in my ear. "That's a good sign."

"A good sign for what?"

"For later." She danced a little closer.

"I'll need to build up my strength then. I think I need to eat."

I found myself at the long table eating chicken and drinking ale when Lord Alder approached me. "I want to say, I haven't had so much fun in a long time."

"Teel and Aneeta are entertaining women and very sweet, and they're both good friends of mine."

"Are you warning me off?"

"On the contrary, I think you should enjoy their company, but I suppose I'm saying you should still respect them."

Lord Alder nodded. "I will, though I want to ask one of them to accompany me to my private residence tonight and I don't want to hurt the other one's feelings. I actually came over here to ask your advice."

"I was told if you play your cards right, you'll find you won't need to make that decision. Both of them will probably go with you. At least that is what Stella thinks."

Lord Alder's eyebrows shot up.

"Come on, you've been to Docklands. You know what goes on down there," I said.

"Yes, but that's for money and I've only gone there to observe the dancers."

"Then prepare yourself for an experience you will be unlikely to forget."

Lord Alder took a hurried mouthful of wine and glanced over at the two women who danced together. Their hair had come free; they wore no shoes, and had loosened their clothing. As they stamped their feet in time with the music, Aneeta's long dark hair swirled around her shoulders and Teel's freckled cheeks became flushed.

Alder glanced at them and then swallowed the rest of his wine in one gulp. The women spotted him and gestured for him to join them. He looked at me with wide eyes.

I pushed him in their direction with a grin. "Go."

"Thank you, my friend."

I shook my head as he disappeared into the swirling bodies on the dance floor. He had called me his friend; one of the most important nobles in town, whom I had sliced up with a sword, now liked me.

A black carriage suddenly pulled up. Two men in leather armour sat on the roof, and another man carrying a crossbow sat next to the driver. Behind the carriage rode another pair of heavily armed warriors. The door opened and a man in long robes trimmed in gold stepped down. I wondered what a magician was doing here when another individual became visible. Grandfather arrived at the wedding and he brought a pet mage with him.

The entourage fanned out around him as he made his way toward the married couple. He addressed Miranda. She turned pale.

Petar puffed up and yelled at Grandfather and a couple of the guards moved toward him. Grandfather said something else and the old man took a step backward.

I walked over as casually as I could, wishing Golden was with me. "I don't believe you were invited," I said.

The group surrounding him turned in my direction. I saw hands near weapons and felt the thrum of power as the magician started to concentrate.

"Call your dog's off. There will be no combat here"–I took a breath–"today."

Grandfather signalled his men and they relaxed. "I'm sure my lack of an invitation was just an oversight. I was just here to remind Miranda to be at work tomorrow. I haven't seen her for a while and I wanted to let her know that she still had a commitment to me."

"But I never agreed to anything or signed anything," Miranda said. Her fists were clenched and her eyes full of tears.

"A message was delivered on the risks you took if you decided to try and enforce your code of compliance on Miranda," I said.

"It was, but the signal I received informed me I would be left alone by the Watch if my contract with Miranda was not enforced. Then after a certain noble's residence was burnt to the ground, I find my mansion raided and most of my goods confiscated. Many of my old friends on the Peaks suddenly abandoned me and the Watch Patrol the Docklands in large groups which frighten off my customers. So, I reasoned that there is no deal."

"What's he talking about, Ash?" Miranda said.

"Even though there isn't any contract in the sense that you signed anything, Grandfather believes all of the women who work for him are his until he releases them."

"That's right – people are mine until I say. They don't just walk away. I let my employees leave when they negotiate an agreement that compensates me for their loss."

"But you get new girls all the time," Miranda said.

"He thinks he owns you," I said.

"I will have him arrested! Miranda is my wife and will not work for such a man," Petar said.

"If this old man talks again, kill him," Grandfather told his men.

Miranda gasped and I stepped forward. The music had stopped.

"What is the meaning of this intrusion?" Lord Alder stepped away from Aneeta and Teel.

"My lord, I didn't know you were here," Grandfather said.

"Is there a reason you're threatening the bride and groom?"

"I have a contract with the wife and I'm just trying to work out an end to her arrangement"

"There is no contract," Miranda growled.

"I understand what's happening. What would it take for you to leave the young lady alone?"

"Six thousand silver should cover it," Grandfather said.

I whistled and Lord Alder shook his head. "That is extortion."

"Times have been tough lately, and I would point out my business has been under siege and Ash is connected to my problems. He was seen at the mansion of the late Lord Vornhelm and the death of his noble Lordship is what led to my current difficulties. He needs to pay."

"I don't have six thousand silver."

"Come, Ash, I know you hide enough coin from your time as an adventurer to make you independently wealthy," Grandfather said.

In the back of my mind I wondered why I would want to pay for the woman I loved to marry someone else, but I also knew I didn't want her forced back into working for Grandfather. She desired to marry Sir Petar and didn't want to dance for men anymore, and I couldn't blame her for that. If she was forced back to Docklands Grandfather would make her life hell.

"What if I pay half?" Lord Alder asked.

"I can pay some too," Petar said.

Grandfather stroked his chin and looked around at the assembled guests. "I suppose that is acceptable."

"I will deliver a document for your signature with the silver by the end of the tenth day," Lord Alder said.

Grandfather nodded and then pointed at the other girls standing near the dance floor. "I'm feeling generous – you can take tomorrow off and I will see you all back at work the day after that."

I wasn't impressed. Docklands was almost deserted at the moment due to the large number of men from the Watch patrolling the area. Grandfather just wanted to remind the women he controlled them.

He climbed back into his carriage, and it disappeared in a cloud of dust.

"There goes one slimy individual," Alder said.

"One day I'll kill him," I said.

Alder put his hand on my shoulder. "But that day isn't today. We need to forget him and remember that this is a party."

I observed my noble friend as he spoke in soothing tones to Petar and Miranda. The tension drained from their faces and Miranda smiled.

Shaking my head, I walked toward the wine jug. I had just agreed to pay at least a thousand silver pieces so Miranda could marry Petar. That called for a drink.

25

ALONE

Light filtered through the frosty window into my room above Rackhime's shop. Stella lay curled against my side. As I stirred, I remembered the night of wild passion we shared. My mouth felt dry and a throbbing grew behind my eyes.

I went outside, emptied my bladder, and returned upstairs with tea, bread and honey. Stella stretched slowly and growled before beckoning me. I placed the food and drink on a small table near the bed and slid under the blankets with her. She reached for me. The tea got cold but neither of us cared.

"That was certainly worth waiting for," Stella said.

I passed her some bread with honey.

"You really let go last night – I don't think I'll be able to walk home."

"It seemed a fitting way to celebrate someone else's wedding."

She laughed. "Yes, Miranda doesn't know what she's missing."

Suddenly, guilt about the night I spent with Stella ebbed around my heart. I thought, in some strange way, I'd been unfaithful.

"I'm glad I can put to rest some of the rumours about your people.

The tale of Dark Elves' appendages being built like quills is well and truly dead. I was impressed."

Was I just a trophy to be mounted on Stella's wall? Now I knew how some of the women in Golden's life must feel. "Is that what this was? Just another story for you to entertain your clients with?"

Stella stopped eating and moved away from me. She pulled the blankets up to cover her chest. "Last night was something I've always wanted to happen, Ash. You don't seem to understand that most of the girls who work at Docklands are attracted to you in some way. You're extremely handsome and very caring. The woman sense that. I sensed that. Am I proud I was the one who got you into bed first? Yes, I can't deny that. That's part of who I am. Would I like to keep this going? Yes, again. But I'm smart enough to know it wouldn't be good for either of us. You're too intense and I'm unreliable. My friends tell me I'm commitment-shy. And, of course, there's the issue of Miranda. Everybody knows you're still in love with her."

"That doesn't seem relevant anymore. She's not even in Hope and won't be for some time."

"Miranda will return, and until she does, you'll pine for her."

"She's married now."

"So what? Half my clients are married, and besides, her relationship with Petar isn't based on any physical attraction. You might find you have a place in her life when she returns."

That got me thinking, wondering if Miranda and I could become lovers. I shook my head and grinned. Here I was, lying in bed naked with one of the most alluring women in Docklands, and I entertained thoughts of a love affair with a woman who wasn't even in the city.

"You know, Ash, your grin lights up your face."

I smiled at Stella and chased away negative thoughts. "When you cross a room, Stella, the quality of the air changes. You make it feel the way it does just before a storm."

The blankets fell away and Stella reached for the honey. "Let me show you another use for the nectar of the bees. One you won't forget in a hurry."

She was right. I never looked at that sweet nectar the same again.

After I walked Stella to her rooms, I made my way down to the river. It had swollen with the spring rains and the current washed the filth from the city out to sea.

Standing there, I felt a creeping sense of loneliness. My friends were gone and I missed them. There was still Rackhime. The summers I had spent with him copying manuscripts and scrolls had been some of the happiest in my life. But now, it didn't seem enough. I looked back on that time as being one of cosy slumber. In the future I wanted to wake up and live.

I tried to examine the deaths of Cassie, Trina, and Trix.

My Dark Elf lover Zenta's passing was the most complicated – it was linked to the exile from my people and the protecting of her reputation. I could see now that Trix's death was not my fault. She had been in the wrong place and Lord Vornhelm's assassin snatched her so he could confuse the Watch with her death.

Cassie's murder haunted me – I had watched her die. She'd come to save me and in a way she had. Golden and Kat pointed out to me that she'd spied for Sundeep for years and understood her calling was dangerous. What she hadn't known was I was the bait in a trap.

I visited the broken windmill where we'd found Trix and I did something I hadn't done in a long time – I prayed and whispered words to the Gods of the Dead and to those of Comfort and Rebirth. Trix deserved a quick trip through the underworld and I hoped to see her again in a different form in the future.

The air stirred and white mist flowed in through a shattered window. I thought I was dreaming or maybe the gods had heard my plea. A form coalesced in front of me and I stood back. Two blue eyes stared at me from the middle of a gentle face.

"I will never let you be alone," Elhnora whispered.

Falling to my knees, I started to cry. All of the pain, from the deaths of my friends to my own torment, rushed from me and I rocked slowly. Cool hands stroked me and I was enveloped in a presence that moved with me.

"Hush now, my champion, hush."

We stayed like that for some time until my tears stopped falling and my face dried.

"You saved me, Ash, I will never forget that," Elhnora said.

"But you're dead."

"Am I? Sometimes it doesn't feel that way, but I suppose you are correct."

"Can you come back?"

"No, and I can't cross over very often, but I will always watch over you until the day you join me."

Elhnora grew taller and seemed to fill the room. "One of my killers still walks the city. He has murder in his heart. Return to Rackhime's shop now."

And then she was gone.

I had no time to think about what had been said, or the fact I had just talked to a ghost. The Scarred Man was on the move and he may be at the bookstore. I ran.

The streets crowded as the day warmed, forcing me to weave around clattering carts and thread my way through market stalls and groups of pedestrians. Cursing, I slammed into a man carrying loaves of bread, bounced up and ran on without apology.

Fear stabbed at my chest, its spears lengthening as I sprinted. When I left earlier, Rackhime had been out delivering a finished book to a merchant on the slopes of the Peaks. He would be back by now.

I charged up Fish Street and past a patrol of the Watch that headed toward Docklands. For a brief instant I contemplated asking for their assistance but quickly dismissed the idea. They wouldn't listen to a Dark Elf, and by the time I convinced them to come with me the Scarred Man might have already attacked Rackhime and moved on.

Panting and exhausted, I reached the shop. I slowed and glanced around, trying to spot any sign of trouble. The door had been left ajar, but otherwise everything seemed quiet. Maybe I shouldn't listen to the warnings of dead people.

Slowly, I pushed the door open with my Cold Blade. The place had been torn apart; parchments lay on the floor and books burned in the fireplace. The couch had been tipped over and chairs were smashed by the stairs to my room. I crept inside, looking into the shadows for any sign of the Scarred Man.

Rackhime lay on his side staring at the fireplace. His unblinking eyes were glazed in death. I ran over to him and felt for the drum of his pulse in the vein on his neck. His skin was cold. I slowly closed his eyes and sighed. There was blood on the back of his head and his little fingers were missing. The Scarred Man was near.

The floorboards creaked. I stood, shifting to turn. A stunning blow crashed down on my neck. I pitched forward.

I woke a little later as cold water hit my face. Someone had tied me to the one unbroken chair in the room.

"Not again," I moaned.

"This won't be like last occasion, Owl. I don't have time for the games my previous employer liked to play and my motives are much simpler. You see, I need funds. I know you had to pay out a bucket-load of silver to Grandfather recently so your girlfriend could be happy. You still must have a lot of coin left. I want that money so I can set myself up in a new location. Hope's a little bit hot for me these days."

"You killed one of my closest friends. I'd rather die than give you a single piece of silver."

"I'm going to kill you anyway. It's just how much I have to hurt you before I do that's in question."

"Somebody could come in through the front door at any time."

"I've got the crossbow loaded and ready to go. Besides, only three or four people visit this place while it's open. I've been watching the shop for days – nobody comes here in the middle of the day."

He crossed to the fireplace and placed three daggers in the embers. They soon glowed and he picked one up moving toward me.

"Hello, Ashley, is this person bothering you?" Captain Waldheigheim stood near the rear door with a crossbow in his hand, pointed straight at the Scarred Man. "Sorry I took so long to get here, but it was difficult to climb over the back wall without a ladder. One of my boys had to give me a leg up."

My tormenter hurled the heated dagger then charged. The captain swayed aside and pulled the trigger. I heard the soft click and a yell. A thud resounded as the bolt from the crossbow hit the Scarred Man in the shoulder. He grunted in pain then crashed into the captain, throwing him to the floor. Meaty hands closed around the throat of the Head of Investigation and squeezed.

The front door burst open and three members of the Watch ran into the room pouncing on the Scarred Man. They dragged him over the floor, smashing their clubs into his chest and jaw. Bones snapped and teeth flew from his mouth.

"Stop!" Captain Waldheigheim massaged his neck. "I want him alive."

His men hit the Scarred Man one last time on the back of the head and he fell senseless to the floor.

"Throw him in a wagon and then chain him in a cell. I want to get a statement out of him before we hang him."

The three Watch members dragged the Scarred Man from the room while the captain untied me.

"I'm sorry we didn't get here earlier, Ashley. If we had, we might have been able to save the old man. The information the Scarred Man had been seen in the area came to me only recently. As soon as I heard, I came with a squad – I guessed he was after you."

Pulling myself clear of the ropes, I grabbed a length of calfskin from one of the shelves. I laid it over Rackhime's body before turning to the captain. "Thank you for saving my life."

"Just doing my job."

"What happens now?"

"I get a statement out of the Scarred Man, which I will archive. Hopefully I'll never need it – I don't want to blacken the reputation of the Vornhelm house, especially now that her ladyship has taken over. Then, we hang him. I'll make sure you can be there, if you want."

I shook my head. "Your word that he is dead is enough for me."

Captain Waldheigheim nodded at Rackhime's covered form. "Will you need help with the body?"

"I don't know. I'll have to give him to the river at some stage, but I can't even think about that right now."

The captain left and I sat with the body in the front of the shop. I got up and rescued some of the leather-bound books from the fireplace and smothered the smouldering pages with sand. Then, I opened one and started to copy it on to a new sheet of vellum.

The books had been on the founding days of Hope, and I knew Rackhime would not have wanted the knowledge lost. My quill flowed over the fine leather as I copied page after page. The smell of the ink filled my nose. I worked into the night by candlelight with only the company of Rackhime's body. Eventually I fell asleep across the workbench.

In the morning I woke stiff and sore. Captain Waldheigheim returned with three men and a cart. He looked at the burnt books and the ink bottle, then glanced at me.

"I've arranged everything and will let you know when we're going to give his body to the river. Did he have any family or anyone he would have liked to invite?"

"All his family are dead and most of his friends are out of town until the seasons turn. I'll ask a few people to come, as much for me as for him," I said.

The captain left as his men carried Rackhime's body from the shop that had been his life.

Climbing upstairs to my room, I then sat on my bed. The old man had been kind to me, allowing me first to rent the chamber from him and later encouraging me to copy parchments and then books. I often helping him finish large tomes or quantities of parchment. He'd frowned on some of my wild ways but had never judged my choice of friends. Now he was dead, his head caved in by a man who'd wanted to kill me. The tears came. I curled up on the blanket and wept until sleep took me.

"He has crossed over and doesn't blame you."

I looked up into those eyes of deep blue. They had gold flecks in them and lines of green that radiated out from the pupil.

"You tell me not to blame myself, but a lot of people have died around me lately."

Elhnora sat next to me. In the dream we were on the bench on Petar's front veranda.

"All of them made their own choices and were responsible for their own actions. Some of them were just unlucky. Even Cassie knew the risks she took when she decided to work for my father. The fact he was a rage-fuelled monster was not your fault."

"I feel so alone. Rackhime was a constant presence in my life."

"You must endure. I can help where I can. Don't forget you have new friends in Hope now. They will always welcome your company."

When I woke, darkness had taken hold, and though I felt calm, the guilt still filled me. I cleaned up the shop and continued to write until the door opened and a small bearded man stuck his head inside.

"Are you Ash, the Dark Elf?"

I thought the answer was probably self-evident, as there were few of my kind in Hope.

"I'm Rale Trurhem Lawer and scribe. I have some papers here for you. I had to read them myself first – that's what the parchment said to do if Rackhime died."

"Is this about the shop? If it is, I'll move as soon as I find somewhere else, though I would like to take the books with me."

"You don't have to go anywhere. Master Rackhime left the store and the building, including all of its contents, to you. Of course, you will need to pay a fee to the City every year for running a business and for the upkeep of the roads and the fortifications, but if you pay your taxes then you can stay here in perpetuity. Just make your mark on this copy and it's done."

In a daze, I signed, and the bearded man left. Rackhime had given me everything. I now had roots in Hope. It felt right. This building was my home, and I wasn't going to give it up.

The boat drifted out onto the waters of the Great River, pulled by the small sail and steered by the rudder tied in one position. It guided the craft into the faster currents.

Rackhime's body lay bound in oil-soaked parchment – that seemed appropriate. It rested on piles of kindling and logs that burned with bright-orange flames as the boat moved away from the shore.

The clerics groaned their lamentations before asking for their fee. I dropped ten pieces of silver into their palms.

Lord Alder stood arm-in-arm with Teel, watching the boat disappear. Captain Waldheigheim stood nearby with a few of his men.

Stella pressed into me, wrapped in a light cloak that protected her against the morning's chill.

I was grateful they all came. Watching until the boat started to sink, it became a speck marked by a pillar of smoke, way out on an expanse of green rushing water. And then it was gone.

The gathering at the shop ten minutes later was a subdued affair, with everyone speaking in hushed tones. Aneeta arrived with some of the other girls to say their commiserations. She then moved over to speak with Teel and Lord Alder, though I notice she kept some physical distance from them. It looked as if Teel and his Lordship had become a pair. I wondered where it would lead. I sighed. In the end did it really matter? Maybe they should both grab happiness while they could.

"That sounded glum," Stella said. She wore more clothes than I'd ever seen her in. I was sure Rackhime would have appreciated the respectful gesture.

"I was just wondering about Teel and Lord Alder."

"I'm glad they've found each other. I hope they can find a way to continue their relationship, despite his position. If he really wants to keep it going, though, he will. The nobility have their own set of rules, but they also know how to get around them."

I hoped she was right. At the very least, I knew Teel would be able to leave Grandfather's employment without too much difficulty. The old rogue would never challenge Lord Alder.

Stella leaned into my shoulder and her hair tickled my neck. It reminded me of the time she'd advised me out the front of Sir Petar's house. "I'm going to stay, Ash. You can just hold me if you want, but tonight I want to be here for you."

She was gentle and caring that night and soothed my battered soul. We never made love again after that day, but I always remembered the gesture.

Spring came to an end. I stood by the river and watched a slow-moving cog tack its way toward one of the berths at the port. The red swallows which would have followed such a vessel earlier in the season were no longer scooping up the insects the boat frightened away from the surface of the water. They'd moved north as the weather grew warmer.

On the far side of the river I could just see dust stirred up by large herds of cattle that gathered on the plains waiting to be brought by ferry to the markets of Hope. I turned away and looked back at the city, my city. The twin horns rose from either side of the mountain and cast their shadows across the northern flanks of the slope, almost reaching Docklands. The citadel was up there, carved into the dark rock of one of the Devil's Horns. I noticed the falcons nesting on the bare slope of the smaller peak circling over Hope, looking for pigeons to swoop on.

Darkness grew and I realised an order needed to be finish for a merchant house on the lower slopes. Seven parchments were to be copied into a large book before All Gods Day. I needed to go home.

I slowly walked back toward the shop, still uncertain about my future.

ABOUT THE AUTHOR

Kim Kerr is a primary school teacher in Melbourne Australia who has always enjoyed a great love of fantasy and historical ction. He lives with his wife and son in the hills on the city's fringe on a small plot of land with chickens, a few sheep, and his two dogs. His older daughter is o at university.

He has written since 1990 and Broken Star will be his first published novel.

Kim spent a number of years teaching in Outback Australia and trained teachers in Nepal where he also made four attempts to see a tiger in the wild, but without success.

His interests included surfing, fishing, and role playing games. He will keep chasing that elusive tiger until luck smiles on him.

PLEASE RATE THIS BOOK

For more information on this and other books by Science Fiction and Fantasy Publications, please go to:

https://scifantasypublications.com

Remember to let the author know how you liked his work. Review and/or rate this book on Goodreads and the retailer where you purchased it.

Thank you for taking the time to read this novel.